IN THE TRACKS OF AN ASSASSIN

He was pulling himself more slowly now along the hull of the ship. He chanted. Vacuum burned. His ears pounded. His eyes ached redly. His blood roared. He thought of Cinnabar and Cinnabar's hands.

And he raged. Not quite a killing rage, but close enough. He held himself just at the threshold of that overwhelming fury.

He pulled himself along—rung after rung—until suddenly there were no more rungs. He realized he'd been fumbling for several seconds, reaching for something that wasn't there. He was at the aft airlock. He'd made it. He pulled open the access panel and pulled himself down into the reception bay. He fumbled for the control and slammed his hand against it.

Something flashed red. He opened his eyes; he could barely move them. The panel was throbbing like his heart. Dimly he could make out the single word of doom.

LOCKED . . .

BANTAM SPECTRA BOOKS BY DAVID GERROLD

Ask your bookseller for the ones you have missed

The Middle of Nowhere

David Gerrold

BANTAM BOOKS
New York • Toronto • London • Sydney • Auckland

The Middle of Nowhere
A Bantam Spectra Book / April 1995

ISBN 0-553-56189-8

Published simultaneously in the United States and Canada

Bantam Books are published by Bantam Books, a division of Bantam
Doubleday Dell Publishing Group, Inc. Its trademark, consisting of
the words "Bantam Books" and the portrayal of a rooster, is
Registered in U.S. Patent and Trademark Office and in other
countries. Marca Registrada. Bantam Books, 1540 Broadway, New
York, New York 10036.

PRINTED IN THE UNITED STATES OF AMERICA

RAD   0 9 8 7 6 5 4 3 2 1

for Steve Boyett and Daniel Keys Moran,
who are both very much a part of this book.

The Middle of
Nowhere

Gatineau

The rookie had arrived at Stardock so recently, his eyebrows still hadn't had time to come back down to their normal position.

He moved through the corridors of the station with a tentative step and an expression of permanent astonishment on his face. He carried his few personal belongings slung over his back in a limp black duffel. He had a yellow transfer order and a baby-blue security pass in one hand, and a half-unfolded map in the other.

He was clearly lost. He checked the number on every wall panel against the unwieldy map—perversely, it kept trying to complete the process of unfolding; periodically huge sections of it would make a desperate leap for freedom. Finally, in frustration, the rookie stopped where he was and dropped to one knee to refold the map on the floor.

"That's not a good place for that, son—"

"I know, but the damn thing won't—" And then he looked up, saw who he was speaking to, and shut up immediately. He scrambled to his feet, stiffened to attention,

and nearly knocked his eye out with his transfer card as he
tried to salute. His duffel swung wildly behind him, banging
him uncomfortably on the butt.

The officer was a grim-looking man, thin, with gray eyes
and sandy hair. He had a hardness of expression that was
terrifying. But the hardness in his eyes was directed *somewhere else*, not at the rookie. It was almost as if the much
younger man didn't exist for the officer, except as a tool to
be used . . . if he was good enough. The officer's nametag
identified him only as *Korie*. The diamond-shaped insignias
on his collar gave his rank as—the rookie frowned as he
tried to remember—commander!

"As you were," the officer said, returning the salute with
a perfunctory nod. He reached over and plucked the transfer card and security pass out of the rookie's hands. "Crewman   Third   Class   Robert   Gatineau,   engineering
apprentice," he read. He made a single soft clucking noise
in reaction. "Rule number one," he said, handing the cards
back. "Always wear your nametags."

"Yes, sir." Gatineau began fumbling in his pocket for the
nametag he had been given only moments before. As he
struggled to pin it on, he asked, "Anything else, sir?"

"Keep out of the way. Don't call attention to yourself."
As an afterthought, he added, "And get your job done as if
your life depended on it. Because it does."

"Yes, sir. Thank you, sir."

The tall man nodded and started to head up the passage.

"Uh, sir—"

"Yes?"

"Could you tell me how to get to berth T-119?" Gatineau stammered, "That's the *Star Wolf*."

"I know the ship," the man said noncommittally.

"Is she a good ship? I've heard stories—"

"She earned her name fairly." He turned and pointed.
"Down to the end, turn left, go up the stairs, take the
slidewalk all the way around to the T-module. From there,
just follow the numbers down the tube; it'll be the nineteenth berth. But the *Star Wolf* isn't there. That's only
where her boats are docking. The ship is still sitting out at
decontam point one." The officer glanced at his watch. "If
you hurry, you can catch a ride back. If you miss this shuttle; there'll be another one in ninety minutes. Pee before

you go. It's a long ride. When you get there, report to Commander Tor, she's acting command. Then get your gear stowed and get into your works. You'll be on Chief Leen's crew. I'm sure they can use your help. There's a lot to do."

"Yes, sir. Thank you, sir." Gatineau saluted again enthusiastically.

The officer returned the salute with barely concealed annoyance. "Oh, one more thing. Ease up on the salutes. That's for groundsiders. In space, you want to keep one hand on the wall."

"Yes, sir. Thank you, sir!"

The tall man nodded and headed up the passage. Gatineau stared after him with an expression of unalloyed awe. The diamonds on the commander's uniform had been luminous silver, striated with bands of flickering color— that meant he was certified for an FTL command! He wished he could follow him—

Abruptly Crewman Robert Gatineau, third class, unassigned, remembered what the commander had said about the shuttle, and he hurried to gather up his belongings. He reshouldered his duffel, stuffed the recalcitrant map into the pocket of his shirt, and scrambled quickly down the passage.

"Down to the end," he repeated as he ran. "Turn left, go up the stairs, take the slidewalk—"

The slidewalk circled the Stardock. Gatineau rode it all the way from the administrative domain, through the supply modules, to the docking spurs. He scrutinized each passing sign as if it held a secret message just for him, ticking off each docking spur as it slid past. At last, he saw the sign he was waiting for; he leapt off impatiently at the entrance to the T-module, almost stumbling as he did. Swearing in annoyance and frustration, he half-walked, half-ran down the broad passage. Beneath his feet, the carpeting gave way to industrial decking; his footsteps clanged and echoed.

The passage was punctuated with airtight doors. Each section was sealed by triple locks that popped quickly open at his approach and slapped softly shut after him; by the time Gatineau reached the nineteenth berth he had passed through seventy-two separate hatchways. He had run nearly the entire length, counting off numbers all the way to the next-to-last berth, T-119.

The berth itself was only a naked service bay; a wide featureless alcove, it lacked even the barest amenities. It was nothing like the commercial berths Gatineau had experienced, with their multiple displays and couches and various service booths and comfort areas. The difference both shocked and pleased him. It proved to him that he was finally *here*, serving at a *real* stardock.

The business end of the bay was a broad elliptical hatch. It stood open. Gatineau approached hesitantly.

"Hello?" he called down the long boarding tube. "Ahoy? Anybody aboard?"

There was no answer.

"Is this the boat for the *Star Wolf*?" Gatineau edged tentatively into the tube. "Is anyone here?"

At the far end there was another hatch, this one closed. The access panel was green, indicating that the atmosphere on the opposite side of the door was breathable and pressure-balanced.

Gatineau took a breath and pressed his hand against the panel. Several hatches slid back simultaneously, startling him. He stepped through into a tiny airlock. The hatches behind him closed, turning the chamber into a claustrophobic closet. More nervous than ever, but too uncomfortable to hesitate, Gatineau popped open the next hatch—and found himself staring into the aft cabin of the number three boat of the *Star Wolf*.

The boat was half-crammed with supply modules of all shapes and sizes. He edged sideways into the cabin and the last hatch slapped shut behind him. "Ahoy?" he called softly. "Crewman Robert Gatineau, third class, unassigned engineering apprentice, reporting for duty?"

Still no one answered. Gatineau stepped through the next hatch into the main cabin of the boat. "Hello? Anyone?" No one.

The rear half of this cabin was filled with various life-support and supply modules; all were labeled. He recognized the codes for starsuits and EVA equipment, as well as emergency medical gear. The forward half was all industry-standard seating, gray and impersonal. Gatineau had seen buses with more personality.

Shrugging to himself, he hung his duffel on the wall over one of the seats, then he climbed forward and knocked on the flight deck hatch. It slid open almost immediately and the pilot swiveled around in his chair to look at him. Gatineau looked up . . . and up. And up. The pilot was a three-meter Morthan Tyger with a grin so wide he could have bitten off Gatineau's head in a single bite. "You the new meat?" he asked.

Gatineau nearly crapped his pants. For a moment he was paralyzed, his heart thundering in his chest in a cascade of uncontrollable explosions. Adrenaline flooded through his body in an atavistic frisson of fear and horror and wonder, all stumbling over each other at once. The sensation was like a sudden cold immersion into stark screaming terror. He gulped and stammered and tried to back away. "Excuse me—" he tried to say, even while his mind yammered with the terrifying realization, *Oh, my God, a Morthan. I'm going to die!*

And even as he wondered what he could do to defend himself against the monster, the rational part of his being was already noting the dark gray uniform on the beast, the nametag—*Lt. Commander Brik*—and the amused expression on the face of the human copilot.

"I, uh—uh, I'm looking for, uh—the boat to the *Star Wolf*—" And then he remembered his training and snapped to attention. "Sorry, sir. Crewman Robert Gatineau, third class, unassigned engineering apprentice, reporting for duty, sir!" He'd heard there were Morthan officers in the fleet. He hadn't realized he'd be serving under one—he started to salute, then remembered the other officer's advice and stopped himself, then wondered if he'd committed an even bigger mistake by *not* saluting the Morthan officer. He gulped, decided against trying to make it up, and simply held out his transfer card and security pass for inspection.

Commander Brik took the cards with exaggerated gentleness. The huge dark Morthan hand dwarfed Gatineau's much smaller one. It was all that he could do to keep from flinching. He hadn't felt so small since he'd been four years old and had seen his father naked in the shower.

Brik laid the cards on the flat reader panel between himself and the copilot and studied the display without reaction. As he did so, Gatineau tried to calm himself by studying the layout of the flight deck. An actual starboat! He took a deep breath and peered out the forward window, pretending to be nonchalant as he took in the view.

Beyond the forward glass, the bright spurs of Stardock gleamed with thousands of work lights, so bright they almost banished the hard emptiness beyond. Looking out the side window, Gatineau could see nearly a dozen liberty ships strung along the length of the docking spur. His intake of breath was clearly audible. *Starships!* They were magnificent. They were wonderful. And they were nearly close enough to touch—

Brik grunted impatiently. The sound broke Gatineau's reverie. He realized that the Morthan was holding out his identity cards and waiting for him to take them back.

"Oh, thanks. Um . . ." Gatineau decided to risk it. "I'm sorry, sir, if I, uh—behaved badly just now. I—"

"Don't sweat it, fella," the copilot said. His nametag identified him as *Lt. Mikhail Hodel.* "Commander Brik has that effect on everybody. It's part of his charm. What do we call you?"

"Um, my dad used to call me Robby, but, uh—"

"Right," said Hodel. "You're a big boy now, Robby. How about we call you Gatineau . . . or *Mister* Gatineau when we're pissed?"

"Uh, sure—thanks, I think."

Hodel swiveled forward again, pressing one finger to his right ear to concentrate on an incoming message. "Roger that, thanks," he replied. "Over and out." To Brik, he said, "We're clear to launch."

"Strap in," Brik said to Gatineau, indicating the seat commonly occupied by the flight engineer.

The launch procedure was simpler than Gatineau expected. Brik gave a single command to the boat's intelligence engine. "Prepare for departure."

A moment later the intelligence engine replied, "All hatches sealed. All systems up and running. Confidence is ninety point nine."

"Disengage."

Abruptly the sense of gravity fell away to nothingness and Gatineau's stomach went with it. His gut clenched alarmingly, and then—as he recognized the not-very-familiar sensation—he began to relax. Almost immediately there was a soft thump from the rear of the craft and the quiet voice of the I.E. reported, "Disengagement."

"Set course and activate."

Although there was no apparent sensation of motion, the view out the window began to shift sideways and downward. A moment later and the stars began to rotate around an axis somewhere below Gatineau's feet.

"If you want a better view," said Hodel, "climb up into the observation bubble."

"Can I? Gee, thanks." Gatineau unstrapped himself and floated straight up out of his seat, bumping his head on the roof of the cabin. "Oww—" He grabbed for the top of his head, which caused him to start rotating clumsily in the tiny cabin. He grabbed for the wall and ended up at a very awkward angle, upside down in relation to Hodel and Brik with his legs kicking at the ceiling. "Oops. Sorry about that."

Hodel grabbed the younger man by his waist and gave him a push out through the cabin door. He grinned at Brik and shook his head. Newbies. From the passenger cabin there came a confirming series of painful grunts and thuds as Gatineau careened and bounced his way aft toward the observation bubble. Hodel grinned at Brik. "I *love* this job."

Brik grunted. He wasn't without a sense of humor, but he did not believe as Hodel did that slapstick was the highest art.

In the cabin Gatineau pulled himself into the bubble with unalloyed delight. The glass of the observation dome sparkled with luminance, the reflections of hundreds of thousands of work lights. The Stardock was a technological confection, its complex structure a blazing hive of light and color and motion, belying the darkness of the vast night beyond. Vertical spars struck upward, horizontal planes sliced crossways; tubes and pipes of all kinds, some lit from within, curled and coursed throughout the vast structure. And everywhere, there were ships hanging off it—ships of all sizes, all kinds—but mostly liberty ships; the beautiful little cruisers with their polycarbonate foam fuselages and bold carbon-titanium spars. They were held together with monofilament tension cables and a lot of hope.

The New America assembly lines were turning out three new liberty ships every twelve days. In the nine months since the mauling at Marathon, the Allied worlds had begun to respond to the threat of the Morthan Solidarity with an extraordinary commitment. Some of the evidence of it was already filling the docking berths.

As the boat drifted away from the dizzying mass of spars and tubes, modules and tanks, the larger structure of the deep-space Stardock came clear. It was a giant metal snowflake. Within it, suspended as if in a spiderweb, were scatterings of habitats, cylindrical, spherical, and patchwork; the living and working quarters that had grown and spread across the original design.

There was no light in the bubble except that which came from the Stardock itself, but it was enough to bathe the shuttle in a bright white aura. Gatineau's eyes were suddenly moist with emotion. A flood of feelings filled him, some joyous, some fearful—mostly he was rapturous. The conflicting sensations only added to the overwhelming impact of the moment.

But all too soon, the light began to fade and with it, Gatineau's rapture. They were accelerating now into the night. As the Stardock shrank away behind them, finally vanishing into the speckled darkness, Gatineau was suddenly aware how small and vulnerable and *alone* he was here in this tiny spaceboat. He had never before in his life been this far away from . . . *safety*. His life depended solely on the strength of the fragile glass and polycarbonate around him. After a moment the sensation became unbearable.

Nervously he pushed himself down out of the bubble and pulled himself carefully forward back to the flight deck. He strapped himself into his seat and held on to the edges of it with a tight grip while he closed his eyes and tried desperately to overcome the overwhelming rush of contradictory feelings. He was being buffeted by dizzying agoraphobia and smothering claustrophobia, exhilarating joy and terrifying loneliness, raving enthusiasm and stark panic. It was all too much to assimilate.

Both Hodel and Brik noticed the whiteness of Gatineau's expression; neither said anything. Hodel swiveled his chair around, opened a panel next to Gatineau, and pulled out a bubble of bouillon. "Here," he said, pressing it into Gatineau's hand. "Drink this. It'll help. The first time can be a little overwhelming. I know."

"I'm fine," Gatineau insisted. "Really, I am."

Hodel's expression suggested that he knew otherwise. "It's a 6-hour ride. Do you want to spend the entire time with your eyes closed?"

"Uh . . . okay." Reluctantly Gatineau took the bubble. "Thanks." He popped the top off the nipple and sucked at the hot liquid slowly. It gave him something to do, something to concentrate on. After a bit the emptiness in his stomach began to ease and so did the feelings of panic in his gut.

Now it was Brik's turn. He finished what he was writing in his log, switched off the clipboard, and stashed it in its slot. He swiveled his chair around and unstrapped himself. He was three meters tall; his bulk nearly filled the flight deck. "Autopilot's set. I'm going aft. To get some rest. You will too if you're smart."

Hodel was peering at the displays in front of him. He nodded in satisfaction, then unstrapped himself and followed Brik. As he floated past, he said to Gatineau, "Rule number one. *Never* pass up a chance to catch an extra nap."

"Um, okay."

Gatineau sat alone in the flight deck of the boat for a long silent moment. The display panels in front of him gleamed with information, some of it understandable, most of it not. He pursed his lips, he frowned, he swallowed hard. He was *all alone* in the flight deck of a spaceboat, godzillions of kilometers from anywhere at all. There was nothing for light-years in any direction but light-years.

He thought about climbing into the pilot's seat—just to see what it felt like—but decided against it. He might be breaking some kind of rule, some code of conduct, some tradition. He didn't want to risk getting off on the wrong foot. Nevertheless, the temptation remained. He sipped at his bouillon and stared out the window at the distant stars and wondered what it would be like to pilot a ship of *any* kind. He wondered if he would ever earn striated diamonds like those on the uniform of that officer—what was his name again?—who had helped him in the corridor.

After a while he realized that the bulb was empty and he really *was* tired. He also realized that he was having the time of his life; the afterburn of three consecutive adrenaline surges had finally burned off and now he was feeling simply content in his exhilaration. He pushed the bulb into the disposal chute, unstrapped himself, and floated back to the passenger cabin. It had been darkened, there was only a faint glow of illumination, just enough to see shapes.

Both Brik and Hodel were strapped to the bulkheads like logs, or sides of beef, but neither was yet asleep. Hodel glanced at his watch and remarked, "Twenty minutes. Not quite a record, but pretty good." Brik grunted in response. It was neither approval nor disapproval, merely an acknowledgment.

Gatineau wasn't quite sure what Hodel meant, though he knew the remark was about him; he decided, for safety's sake, to ignore it. He pulled himself into the tiny compartment that served as the head and shortly rediscovered the singular joy of zero-gee urination. After cleaning himself off as best as he could, he pushed himself back into the cabin to hook his belt to a strap on the wall. He arranged himself "horizontally" and connected a second strap to the front of his shirt. He was still way too excited to sleep, but Hodel's advice had been good, and the least he could do was try to relax for a bit.

He let his arms hang limply by his sides as he had been taught to do, even though he knew they would eventually rise up until his body had assumed the position of a corpse floating facedown in a pool of water.

He closed his eyes and let himself wonder about the distant starship they were heading toward. He'd studied so many schematics, looked at so many pictures, walked through so many virtualities, he felt he knew the liberty ship already—and yet, he knew he didn't know anything at all. He'd have to prove himself to the crew. He'd have to earn the right to be one of them. He felt so terribly innocent and naked . . . and then someone was shaking him and all the lights were too bright and he was futilely trying to push them away.

"Come on, Gate—we're almost home. Don't you want to see your ship from the outside?"

"Huh? What?"

Hodel was shaking him gently. "Go up in the bubble. That's the best seat in the house. You'll see."

Still not fully awake, Gatineau followed instructions. He unhooked himself from the bulkhead and pulled himself up into the observation bubble again. This time, it was a lot easier. The boat was no longer a confining presence, but a comforting one. The opportunity to look out into naked vacuum was like peeking out from under the blankets.

Looking backward, there was nothing to see; only the stars, hard and bright and forever unchanging. When he turned around to look forward, however, he caught his breath immediately.

There, growing swiftly ahead of the boat, was the *Star Wolf*. They were approaching her stern, rising up beneath her starboard side. This was the closest Gatineau had ever been to a liberty ship and he cherished every detail of her.

She was beautiful and she was ugly—beautiful because she was a faster-than-light ship; ugly because she was utilitarian and undressed. She wasn't dressed to go out, she was undressed to go to work. She wore no makeup. Her bones were visible along her skin. Her fuselage bulged oddly around the sphere of her singularity engine, giving her a humped-back look.

She didn't wear as many work lights as the Stardock. Nevertheless, against the emptiness of space, she shone with a compelling beauty. There were bright lights along her hull, as well as up and down her fluctuator spars. Additional sources of illumination came from various observation bubbles studding her hull, as well as from portable work modules stuck here and there across her metallic surface. As the ship swelled in his field of vision, Gatineau could make out men in starsuits as well as several spindly robots hard at work on various repair projects.

The ship was a hard-edged cylinder, at least as long as a football field. Three long FTL spars stuck out from her hull, spaced 120 degrees apart, each one pointing back into the singularity at the heart of the stardrive. The dorsal spar was open to space and three crew members in starsuits were floating alongside. Gatineau envied them and wondered when and if he would ever get his chance to go starwalking.

The boat was slowing now; it crept forward along the

length of the vessel. Now he could see that her fuselage
was studded with machinery of all kinds: scanners, weapons, radiation fins, hyperstate lenses, gravitational plates,
and other devices whose purposes he could only guess at.
Running the length of the hull, mounted so they ran between the fluctuator spars, were three matched pairs of
long narrow tubes: the ship's plasma torch drives.*

The torch drives could accelerate massive amounts of
high-energy particles to nearly the speed of light, and they
could fire either forward or backward; simple action-reac-
tion physics did the rest. There were other ways to move a
ship through space—fluxor panels, for example—but none
more cost-effective for the purposes of the war.

The starboat was almost to the nose of the parent ship
now. Gatineau craned forward eagerly, but abruptly the
boat rotated along its own axis, shifting his view of the
starcruiser upward and over, completely out of sight.
"Damn," he said. He wasn't sure if the pilot was celebrat-
ing something with a victory roll, or if it was part of the
docking maneuver. Obviously the boat was going to con-
nect to the forward airlock; that meant they would have to
back into the nose of the cruiser. Gently, he hoped. The
observation bubble should still provide the best view—

He was right. The starboat kept rotating, and this time
when the *Star Wolf* came rising into view again, it was directly behind and slightly above Gatineau's viewpoint with
its bow pointing almost directly at the aft of the boat. Gatineau was looking the other direction, but he sensed her
presence behind him almost immediately; it was the reflection of the light on the inner surface of the observation
bubble. He turned himself around and saw the *Star Wolf*
head-on for the first time—his breath caught in his throat.
He was awestruck.

The most forward part of the *Star Wolf*'s fuselage was a
cylindrical framework holding a docking tube and airlock
connector. Just behind the framework was the real nose of
the ship, and just back of that were three stubby fins; they
looked like canards; the tubes of the plasma torches pro-

---

* Fusion-driven high-mass electromagnetic plasma accelerators used
for subluminal (slower than light) velocities.

jected through them, and their purpose was obviously to monitor and control the torches' output and hold them in alignment. But this was not what had caught Gatineau's attention so dramatically. It was the paint job.

The topmost two fins were vividly painted with angry red eyes; they glowed like fire. The bottom fin was painted almost its entire length with sharp slashing teeth. The effect was striking. The face of the *Star Wolf* was a silent frozen roar of rage and fury. Caught between the teeth was a tiny desperate-looking Morthan.

Gatineau gulped and tried hard to breathe. He'd been caught by surprise by the savageness of the starship's expression; it swelled in his field of vision as the shuttleboat backed steadily toward it; but even if he'd been warned, even if he'd seen pictures, he still would have been taken aback by the intensity of the moment. The *Star Wolf* was a ferocious ship.

Now, looking farther back, he realized that wolf claws had been painted on each of the FTL spars as well. He grinned in raw appreciation. Suddenly all the weird stories he'd heard about this ship were forgotten, all the rumors and lies and half-truths—and just as suddenly all of his own fears and worries about his future evaporated like a bucket of water exposed to vacuum. This was his ship and he had fallen hopelessly in love with her. It was love at first sight.

The starboat bumped softly against the docking spar; there were a few more clicks and thumps as various connectors locked into place—and then they were home.

First Blood

The docking tube was a triple security connection.

Because the starboat had been decontaminated, but not the starship, the only physical link allowed between the two was a disposable security tube connected through an industrial decontamination station.

A Morthan assassin had been aboard the *Star Wolf*. It was taken for granted that he had planted multiple pods of nano-saboteurs; the pods were even now lurking in dark unknown places, waiting, holding their silent and deadly cargo until some predetermined condition triggered the release of their hordes of microscopic engines. Most micromachines were defeatable, often by other micro-machines, but the ship would have to be scrubbed three times before it could be considered decontaminated to military standards.

In the meantime, everybody and everything were routinely passed through decontamination scanners several times a day. The *Star Wolf*'s intelligence engine, Harlie, was monitoring the entire process, and two decontamination engines were monitoring Harlie.

Gatineau looked down the length of the docking tube with a skeptical expression. It unnerved him. The tube was more than fifteen meters of narrow free-fall, mostly dark. The utility lights were insufficient to dispel the sense of ominous gloom. There was only darkness at the bottom. And the knowledge that there would be nothing between himself and some very hard vacuum except a paper-thin disposable membrane did little to give him confidence. Behind him, Brik growled impatiently, a sound like an internal combustion engine redlining.

"Like this," said Hodel, shoving past him. He pushed headfirst into the tube, pulling himself along hand over hand, grabbing ladderlike rungs strung along the interior. "See, it's easy," he called back.

"Sure," gulped Gatineau. "If you say so. It's just that I've never done this before and—" Something huge grabbed him from behind and *pushed*. Next thing he knew, Gatineau was hurtling headfirst through the docking tube. He started to tumble, careened against one side of the membrane, and then ricocheted off toward the other. He flailed wildly, bouncing and twisting. At last, he banged into a handhold and grabbed it frantically. "Hey!" he shouted back at Brik. "You didn't have to do that! I was going to do it myself—"

"Right," rumbled Brik, coming along behind. "But I didn't have the time to wait."

At the sight of the Morthan security officer coming up behind him, Gatineau flinched. Brik *filled* the tube with his bulk. He turned himself around forward again—and the rung came away from the wall with a dreadful ripping sound.

"What the—"

The membrane stretched. It bulged outward. And then at last, it began to come apart and for just an instant Gatineau was staring into naked space.

It's only a tiny gap, his mind insisted. *You can make it.* But it was happening too fast. A terrible whistling sound came screaming up. And suddenly his ears were roaring with pain—and popped from the collapsing pressure. His nose was filling with fluid. A hot wind shrieked past him, pulling him suddenly outward toward something black and bright. Instinctively he grabbed at the next rung, seized it, and started pulling himself forward again. His hands came sliding off—

Something huge grabbed him from behind, wrapping one great arm around him, hooking under his armpits; they were moving impossibly forward against the wind, pulling up and up the tunnel toward the distant door. Gatineau gasped desperately for breath, but there was nothing to breathe. The air sucked out of his lungs and kept on sucking. *I'm dying! This isn't fair—*

Something slammed soundlessly, he felt it more than heard it. He gasped and choked and imagined his blood boiling, but there was just the faintest rush of air, and the sounds were coming back, and through his blurring vision, he saw that he and Brik were in an airlock, and the gauge was rising rapidly, slowing now as it approached half-normal pressure. *That's right. You can't restore full pressure that fast. It's dangerous.* His ears popped painfully, again and again. He open and shut his mouth, giving his sinuses a chance to equalize the pressure. It didn't help. He clapped his hands to his head and moaned, twisting and rolling, trying to make the pain go away.

And then hands were grabbing him, pulling him out of the lock and onto a stretcher, tying him down. He could barely see. He didn't recognize any faces, and he couldn't hear anything anymore. Somebody was trying to tell him something; he couldn't understand it. And then they were lifting him and carrying him. He was in gravity again. They were aboard the ship? He'd made it?

"Where's Commander Brik?" he asked. No one answered, or if they did he couldn't hear them. "Brik! Where's Brik?" he shouted, stumbling the words out. He tried to pull himself erect in the stretcher as they carried him aftward, and just before someone pushed him down again, his last sight of the forward access bay was Brik turning away from him to stare thoughtfully at the airlock door and the space beyond.

O'Hara

The anteroom was bare and empty.

The walls were featureless. Pale. Gray. No holos. No documents. No awards. No portraits. The dark gray carpet was hard and utilitarian. There were no chairs, no tables, no furniture of any kind. The room was merely a place to wait.

Korie did not have to wait long. A soft chime rang and a door popped open in one wall. He stepped into Vice Admiral O'Hara's office.

The admiral's office was almost as Spartan as the anteroom. A desk in the middle. Two gray chairs, one on either side. The desk was clean, not even a nameplate. Clearly, the vice admiral was not a nest-maker. Either that or she wasn't planning to stay very long; and that was a *much* more ominous thought.

"Sit down, Commander," the admiral said, entering the room through the opposite door and pointing toward a chair. Korie sat. He kept his face deliberately blank.

The vice admiral sat down behind her desk and frowned at something on the flat display of her portable. It was angled so that Korie couldn't see what it showed. She still hadn't given him more than the most perfunctory glance.

She grunted to herself; it was a soft, almost inaudible exhalation. She didn't look happy. Her responsibilities were far-reaching. This station serviced over a thousand ships, with more coming online every week. Some of the new ships were arriving from worlds as far as five hundred light-years away.

Admiral O'Hara tapped the keyboard with finality and a sour expression; then she closed the machine and turned her attention fully to Korie. She had the face of a Buddha, enigmatic, mysterious, and possibly dangerous. At the moment her expression was unreadable.

"Thank you for seeing me, ma'am," Korie offered.

Her expression didn't ease. "I'm afraid it isn't good news." She sat back slowly in her chair. Her movements were almost painful. She looked tired. For a moment she didn't look at all like an officer of the fleet; she was just another gray-haired black grandmother with a recalcitrant child.

She interlinked her fingers beneath her chin, almost as if in prayer. She was evidently having trouble finding the right words. She sighed and let the bad news out. "The *LS-1187* is not going to receive the bounty for the destruction of the *Dragon Lord*. I'm sorry."

"Excuse me—?" Korie started to protest. The hot flush of anger was already rising inside of him.

"It's going to the crew of the *Burke*," the vice admiral continued, as if Korie hadn't said a word. "Or, rather, their heirs. The *Burke* is being credited with the destruction of the *Dragon Lord*."

Korie half-rose from his chair. "Admiral O'Hara! That's not fair! You and I both know it. The entire crew of the *Burke* was killed by the Morthan assassin, Cinnabar. The ship's intelligence engine had been dismantled. The ship was dead and waiting to be picked up. If we hadn't been there, if we hadn't taken action, the Morthan Solidarity would have captured the *Burke* and her stardrive intact. We prevented the Morthan Solidarity from capturing three fully functional ultrahigh-cycle envelope fluctuators. *We* did it! Not the *Burke*! We lost thirteen crew members—" Korie stopped himself abruptly. He realized he was getting shrill.

The expression on Vice Admiral O'Hara's face was impassive. Korie recognized the look. She would sit and listen and wait until he was through; she could be extraordinarily patient; but nothing Korie could say was going to change the decision. He could read that much in her eyes. He closed his mouth and sat back in his chair. "All right," he said. "Why?"

"The *Burke* destroyed the *Dragon Lord,* not the *LS-1187.*"

"That's not true." Korie kept his voice steady.

"That's what the Admiralty Battle Review has decided—"

"I'll fight it. Their conclusions are wrong—"

"You'll lose." There was something about the way she said it.

"This isn't fair," Korie repeated. He had a sick feeling in his stomach. "Look, I know we have history. I know that you don't like me very much. I know you don't like the *Star Wolf.* And you and I both know the scuttlebutt—that my crew is incompetent, that Captain Lowell was criminally negligent and led the Morthan wolf pack directly to the Silk Road Convoy, that the ship itself is a jinx, a Jonah, a bad-luck hull, a place to put all the bad apples in the fleet, and so on and so on. Do you want to hear the whole litany? That's just the first verse."

Korie didn't wait for Admiral O'Hara's polite refusal. He bulled onward. "Do you know how much that hurts? Not me—but the crew. Do you know the morale problem we have? Do you know how hard my people are working to overcome the bad name that's been unfairly laid on them? They desperately *need* an acknowledgment. You can't keep treating us like a stepchild. We've earned our name. We *blooded* the Morthans. The destruction of the *Dragon Lord* redeems the *Star Wolf.* I'm not arguing for myself. It's my crew. They've earned the right to be proud of what they've done—"

Vice Admiral O'Hara repeated herself quietly. "Mr. Korie, the decision stands. The *Burke* destroyed the *Dragon Lord,* not the *LS-1187.*"

"You're going to have a damn hard time convincing me of that. I was *there.*"

Admiral O'Hara sighed. "I'm going to tell you something, Mr. Korie. This information is Double-Red Beta."

"I'm not cleared that high, ma'am."

"This is a need-to-know basis, and *you need* to know this. I'll take the responsibility." She took a breath and continued quietly. "The *Burke* was sent on a suicide mission. We didn't expect her to come back."

"Ma'am?"

"We were approached back-channel by an emissary who suggested that there was a coalition of dissident Morthan warlords willing to negotiate a truce. We didn't believe it. Would you? Their fleet mauled us so badly, we'll be playing hide-and-seek, hit-and-run games for the next five years while we try to get our strength back up. Why should they quit when they have us on the run? We knew it was a trap, even before the War College intelligence engines mulled it over."

"And you sent the *Burke* in anyway?"

"The Morthans want the ultrahigh-cycle drive. The only ship they had big enough to bring home the *Burke* was the *Dragon Lord*. The *Burke* was booby-trapped. Not even her I.E. knew there were bombs aboard her or where they were. Nobody knew. It was the trickiest part of the refit."

"But, surely her captain—?"

"No, not even her captain."

"Uck." Korie felt as if he'd been kicked in the gut. "You sent them out to be eaten."

"That's right. And I'd make the same decision again for the opportunity to destroy an Armageddon-class warship. We crippled the Morthan fleet. Enough to slow down their advances into Allied domains. For the price of one ship, we saved at least a billion lives and untold production capability. Given those same odds, what would you have ordered?"

Korie ignored the question. His interests were closer to home. "And the *Star Wolf* . . . ?"

"The *LS-1187* was a decoy. You weren't expected to survive either. But you were onsite to keep the Morthans busy and distracted. You did that and the mission succeeded."

"Then you admit 'we had a part in that victory! We set traps too! Nakahari—"

"The assassin found your bombs and disconnected them.

Your intelligence engine has the complete record in a secure archive."

Korie felt the muscles in his jaw tightening. *The same story, all over again. No matter what you do, it's still not good enough.* Frustration edged his voice. "Ancillary bounty?"

O'Hara shook her head. "Hard to sell, right now. I'm not willing to make the effort."

Korie sat back in his chair, matching stares with the vice admiral. Knowing himself defeated.

"Of course, you realize, this means that the *LS-1187* can't keep the name. There is no *Star Wolf*."

Korie looked up sharply. "Say again?"

"A ship has to be blooded to earn a name. The *Burke* gets credit for killing the *Dragon Lord*. I'm sorry," O'Hara said. "I really am."

He glared across the expanse of desk at her. "No, you are not," he said. "You're just saying that because it seems appropriate."

She lifted her hands off her desk as if to indicate that this was not an avenue of discussion she wished to pursue. "I don't blame you for feeling cheated."

"Cheated?" Korie stared at her. "That's an understatement. The Admiralty is behaving abominably here."

"Be careful, Commander—" O'Hara said warningly.

"Be careful? I should give you the same advice." Korie leaned forward in his chair. "Do you realize the disastrous effect this will have on my crew? It'll destroy them. Giving the bounty money to the heirs of the *Burke*—that'll be hard enough to take. My people have families to support. They were counting on having something to send home. But taking away their name. Why don't you just cut out their hearts? It'll be faster."

"I've written a letter of commendation and there are medals for bravery—"

"No. That's not enough. Keep your letter. Keep your medals." Korie stood up. "No. I'm not going back to my crew and telling them that they didn't earn their war paint. I'm not going to order them to clean the snarl off the front of the ship. We're keeping the name."

"I beg your pardon."

"We *earned* it. We're keeping it. The *Star Wolf* does have Morthan blood on her sword. We killed the Morthan assassin, Esker Cinnabar. *We* did that. He destroyed the *Burke,* we destroyed him. It. Whatever. We killed a ship-killer. We claim our name and the associated bounty."

O'Hara's expression didn't change and she didn't answer immediately. She was considering the import of Korie's words. At last, she said, "It's an interesting argument, and under other circumstances, I might even be willing to concede the point—it would be good for morale—but at the moment . . . the whole issue of a name is irrelevant. The ship is being decommissioned."

Now it was Korie's turn. At first her words literally made no sense to him; simple noise. Then it sank in and he sat back down. He said slowly, "I beg your pardon?"

"The most conservative position for us to take," said O'Hara, "is to destroy the *LS-1187*—"

"The *Star Wolf,*" Korie corrected her automatically.

"Commander Korie, you had a Morthan assassin aboard your craft for a period of seventy-two hours. Everything about that ship is now suspect, and the effort it would require for us to certify that it's clean—"

Korie cut her off again. "—is commonly undertaken for other craft."

"Other craft are *not* the *LS-1187,*" the vice admiral snapped. "If we can booby-trap the *Burke,* a Morthan can booby-trap the *LS-1187.* We have only three decontamination crews working this entire station. We're just *beginning* to learn the repertoire of tricks Morthans have cooked up for us."

Jonathan Thomas Korie took a long, low, deep breath. "I'll supervise the decontamination myself. I used to build liberty ships, remember? The *Star Wolf* is quarantined no. That's standard procedure. She'll stay that way until we've green-cleaned her three times."

"That's an admirable gesture. The answer is still no. We need the parts."

"And what if there are booby traps in the modules . . . ?"

"It's easier to detox individual pieces than the complex integrated systems of a whole ship. We really do *need* the parts."

"We need the ship *more.* We've lost over forty percent of our fighting strength in this area. Do I have to list for you all the ships we've lost? Just in the last three months, the

Aronica, the *Stout,* the *Mitchell*—you can't afford to give up the *Star Wolf.*"

"—And the *Silverstein,* and the *McConnell.* We've lost more than you know. At least the *Dupree* is still online. Unless you know something I don't. I can't afford to lose any more ships. That's what you're asking. We've got mounting intelligence that suggests a Morthan strike on the Taalamar system is imminent. I've got to get every ship out of here that I can. I've got thirteen liberty ships berthed on the T-spar, including the *LS-1187,* immobilized due to lack of parts. If we cannibalize, we can put eleven of them back online in the next ten days. Even if I wanted to —which I don't—I can't."

Korie began unpinning his officer's insignia.

"What are you doing?"

"Quitting. I can do more for the war effort as a private citizen."

"I won't accept your resignation. If you try to resign, I'll bring you up on charges of dereliction."

"You'll lose me either way. I'll testify that I can't accept the orders of my superiors because they're contrary to the war effort. Even if I lose, I win. You end up with egg on your face."

"Stop it, Jon. I need your skills—"

"You have a funny way of showing it." He tossed the diamond-shaped buttons* onto her desk. They bounced once and came to rest in front of the admiral, sitting like an accusation between them.

"My ship has earned a name. My crew has earned a reward. I've earned my captain's stars. Where are they? The last time I tried to resign, you made the case to me that the kindest thing that could be done for the crew of the *Star Wolf* would be to leave them together, because the stink they carried with them would make their service unbearable on any other ship. Well, you were right—you still are. But now the crew of the *Star Wolf* has a reason to be

---

* The lowest ranking crew member gets no insignia at all for his or her collar. Ensigns get plain circular pips. Chief officers get narrow bars. Lieutenants get beveled bars. Lieutenant commanders get beveled triangles. Commanders get diamond-shaped insignia. Captains get stars. Admirals get multiple stars and ulcers.

proud of their service. Scatter them to the other ships and all you'll accomplish will be to spread ninety-three dissatisfied, demoralized men and women throughout the fleet. Bad for them, bad for the ships they get sent to."

"I admire your loyalty to your crew, Commander. It's the stuff that great captains are made of. Unfortunately, decommissioning your ship is still the best of my limited options. Your crew will survive; they've already demonstrated their proficiency in that area. But no decontam crew we have available wants to touch the *LS-1187* . . . so as far as I'm concerned, she's junk. Her only value is scrap and spare parts. Damn it, Jon, you had a *Morthan assassin* aboard your ship! Now put your buttons back on and I'll find you a slot as a second officer on a battle-cruiser. That's the best I can do."

"It's not good enough. I won't be bought off, Admiral." Korie's voice was low and controlled. "I'm a battle-Captain. That's what you need right now. That's what this war needs now. I want to do my job. I want to do what I was trained to do. I am *tired* of having my career and my crew and my ship treated as shit. We have the ninth best efficiency rating in the fleet over the last six-month period. I will stand our operations record against that of any ship under your command. If you refuse us decontamination, then let us do it ourselves and prove our starworthiness *without* your help. I've lost my wife and my children *and* the captaincy I fairly earned and now you're threatening to take away the only thing I have left—my ability to fight the Morthan Solidarity. I won't cooperate with that. And I won't be polite about it. If you can give us nothing else, at least give us back our pride. Acknowledge our worthiness. Let us do our job."

"Listen up, Commander." Admiral O'Hara was suddenly angry. She let her frustration and fury show. "There's a war on. I have a lot more to worry about than hand-holding a bunch of spoiled children who are crying because they didn't get their cookie. I've got I.E. projections with an eighty-five percent confidence rating that a Morthan fleet is massing for an advance into this sector. Where's *your* loyalty, Jon?"

Korie heard the admiral's words as if from a distance. He knew she was right; but at the same time he also knew she was wrong. There's more to logistics than ships. He found to his surprise that he was completely calm. What he was about to do was career suicide. If it didn't work Vice Admiral O'Hara would have him facing a three-star competency hearing; and even if it did, she'd still never trust him again. She'd certainly *never* give him a captaincy, not even of the *Star Wolf*. And yet, even as he weighed the arguments in his head, he still couldn't see himself *not* doing it. He didn't want to serve on a battle-cruiser; battle-cruisers weren't going to win this war. They were too valuable to risk. The lighter, smaller starcruisers were the key to victory.

Korie spoke with great care. "Admiral O'Hara, do you know something? I have a very bad habit. I talk too much."

"I beg your pardon?"

"I'm not sure you can trust me to keep my mouth shut. I mean, suppose I got drunk some night and started mumbling things I've heard. Or what if I hired a bed-warmer and started talking in my sleep. That's not safe either. But if I were off in space somewhere, I wouldn't have the same opportunities to endanger security, would I? It'd probably be a lot more discreet for both of us if you minimized my opportunities to . . . gossip."

"I'm an old woman, Commander. Spell it out for me."

"You trusted me with Double-Red information. You didn't ask if I could be trusted before you told me how you sacrificed the *Burke*. Well, maybe I *can't* be trusted. What do you think?" He sat back in his chair and folded his arms. "I don't think you want the heirs knowing the crew of the *Burke* was sacrificed. In fact, I don't think you want *anyone* knowing that the Admiralty is making those kinds of decisions. Certainly not your ship commanders."

"You can't blackmail me, Commander."

"You think not?"

"For one thing, no one will believe you. You have no credibility. You have no proof."

"You're right. But you'll still have to take action against me, won't you? And the more severe the action you take, the more credibility you'll give my story. And even if you don't do anything at all, I can still do irreparable harm to *your* credibility—especially among your superiors *who will know I'm telling the truth.* Your career will be as dead as mine. We can retire together."

Surprisingly O'Hara smiled. She sat back again. "I admire your bravado, Commander—it's a useful strength. But I didn't get to this side of the desk by accident, Jon. Remember rule number one? Youth and enthusiasm will *never* be a match for age and experience. Not to mention an occasional bit of treachery."

"I'm learning about the treachery part," Korie said. And then he realized something. She hadn't buckled, but neither had she *confronted* his challenge. Korie regarded her dispassionately. She stared back at him. The moment stretched out painfully as each tried to gauge the other's intentions. Korie wondered if he should say anything else. He knew the admiral believed he was crazy enough to do exactly what he'd threatened. He was counting on that.

"Call the bluff, ma'am?"

Vice Admiral O'Hara stood up abruptly. She put her hands on the desk and leaned slightly forward; Korie suddenly realized how she'd gotten her nickname, "The Steel Grandma." She looked down at him like a force of nature. "You are one royal pain in the ass, Commander Korie," she said. "And I have some *real* problems to deal with that you know nothing about. I've got to move a hundred ships out of here in the next ten days. You're to stand by your ship and make appropriate spare parts available to any ship commander who requests them." She slid his insignias toward him. "You've made your point. Now put your buttons back on."

Korie stood up to face her on her own level. "Keep 'em," he said. "I'm going to detox my ship. In ten days we'll be ready to rejoin the fleet. I'll come back when you have a pair of stars for me." He met her gaze without fear and waited for her rebuke, but instead she merely looked at her watch and sighed.

"Commander Korie, I have neither the time nor the patience for this. I'm going to assume that you're speaking out of frustration and stress. So I'm going to pretend that I went deaf today and that I haven't heard a thing you've said. In that, I am being extraordinarily generous. You may even consider this the acknowledgment that you're asking for. Take it to heart, because when my hearing returns, I expect you to be more . . . appropriate."

Korie returned her gaze stonily. He refused to acknowledge her comments with either word or gesture.

"And, Jon—"

"Ma'am?"

"You're wrong about something. I don't dislike you. I understand you better than you think. Don't do anything irrevocable. My office door will be open to you for the next ten days. After that, well . . . I'll proceed with whatever actions are suitable to the situation."

"Yes, ma'am." He nodded.

A chance? Maybe. She hadn't said yes; she hadn't said no. She hadn't said anything at all. *Suitable to the situation.* That could mean anything.

He had to assume that she was giving him an opportunity to prove his point. It was a very small loophole indeed, but it was better than nothing. He gave her an impeccable salute, turned sharply about, and exited the way he'd come.

Vice Admiral O'Hara glanced down. Korie's insignia lay unretrieved on her desk. Still wondering if she was doing the right thing, she shook her head and swept them into a drawer.

Leen

Chief Engineer Leen glowered up into the Alpha-spar optical-calibration G3 assembly tube with a ferocious scowl, as if by sheer will alone he could force the unit into alignment. He stood on the catwalk above the spherical singularity containment—with Cappy, MacHeath, and Gatineau standing by—and considered the possibility of dropping the whole unit directly down into the singularity and starting from scratch.

Faster-than-light travel depends upon the creation of a condition of *hyperstate*. The condition of *hyperstate* only occurs in the presence of a triangular singularity inversion. A triangular singularity inversion requires the application of three separate fluxor displacements on a pinpoint singularity. The fluxor displacements all have to occur in the exact same instant; they have to be precisely in phase, and they have to be delivered along separate vectors precisely 120 degrees apart. To insure accurate calibration, each fluctuator is housed in a spar of foamed poly-titanium nitrocarbonate ceramic, projecting away from the main fuselage of the vessel and held in alignment by magnetic tension adjustors throughout its length. The alignment of the spar is triply calibrated with multiple high-cycle U-maser beams reflecting off of special redirection plates at the end of the spar. The holographic image of the redirection plates is continually deconstructed for calibrating the moment-to-moment alignment of the fluxor displacements. The resultant pattern of quantum embolisms is compensated for by counterbalancing the attack velocities of the phase-coherent gravitational hammers in the fluctuator rods.

With *ultra*high-cycle maser beams and compensators in place, more precise calibration of the *hyperstate* field is possible, and significantly greater FTL velocities can be realized. With less precise calibration, the starship is limited to only the lowest range of FTL speeds. With *imprecise* calibration, the starship is not capable of any FTL velocity at all; instead, it is much more likely to shift the state of its existence from solid matter to glowing plasma, plus a few stray tachyons to alert passersby of the event.

Paradoxically, the construction of a *hyperstate* fluctuator is actually a very simple matter. Any college student could build one with off-the-shelf parts, and quite a few had. However, the precision tolerances necessary to actually realizing a condition of mutable *hyperstate* is another matter altogether. The fluctuators have to be targeted on a location in space less than a micron in diameter. The event horizon of the artificial singularity is considerably smaller than that; although it isn't measurable by any standard technology—you can't reflect energy off a black hole of any size—but judging by the mass displacement of the singularity, the event horizon can be calculated to sub-micronic resolution.

For *hyperstate* to be achieved, the pinpoint presence of the singularity has to be held in the precise center of the fluctuator targeting field. Aboard the *Star Wolf,* this was accomplished with concentric, multiply-redundant gravitational reflectors held in the large spherical containment that dominated the ship's engine room. The containment served as a perfect tension field, simultaneously pushing and pulling at its own center in a self-maintained state of intense but rigorous balance.

Beyond the containment, however, the maintenance of

micronic precision across the entire length of the fluctuator spars, with all the tensions and strains they routinely experienced, became a matter of escalating difficulty—especially as the ship grew older and its structure became more fatigued.

Some ship designers depended on heavy, rigid frameworks for the singularity and the fluctuator spars. The greater mass provided greater security, but also required greater power and heavier singularities, with all the increased complexity that implied. Other designers used complex sets of self-adjusting cables, to maintain constant tension and linearity throughout the vessel as if each ship were its own self-contained suspension bridge. Liberty ships like the *Star Wolf* were built along these lines; they were small, fast, cheap, and often extremely fussy to maintain. It was sometimes said that saints aspired to have the patience of a liberty ship chief engineer. But then, few saints had ever met Chief Engineer Leen.

Leen was a stocky man; he had a fuzzy ring of graying hair circling the shiny spot in the center of his skull; and his skin had a dark leathery sheen that hinted of an exotic and possibly ferocious ancestry. At the moment he was more ferocious than usual. This was the seventh time he had reconstructed the Alpha-spar optical-calibration G3 assembly tube, and this was the seventh time it had failed to accurately align itself. Both the G1 and G2 assembly tubes had snapped into place with satisfying precision. Those units were identical to this one. A minimum of three G-matrix assembly tubes were necessary in each spar to guarantee alignment of the fluctuator. Theoretically, a ship could run with two—or even one—G-matrix calibration unit, but it was not something that Chief Leen ever wanted to try. He had no desire to experience hyperstatic molecular deconstruction from the inside.

He muttered a paint-blistering oath, then turned to the three members of the Black Hole Gang standing beside him; Cappy, MacHeath, and the new kid, Gatineau. Gatineau was the one whose T-shirt did not fit snugly. He still had space burns on his face and arms, and his eyes were terribly bloodshot, but he wore an eager expression, as if he was determined to prove that he was a survivor, not a victim.

"All right," Leen said to Cappy. "Break it down. Try again."

Gatineau was already reaching for the toolbox. "I know how to do it," he said. "Let me. I was in the second highest rated squad. I'll bet it's the codex chip. We had a krypton misalignment once and the codex couldn't synchronize."

"Thanks for sharing that," Leen said dryly. Codex alignments were always the first things a chief engineer checked. "MacHeath, take it down; run the reliability suite again. And just to make junior happy, let him watch when you test the codex. By the book. Triple-check everything. Use Harlie as a monitor."

MacHeath's easygoing expression curdled instantly. He was a big man; his physical bulk was an intimidating presence. "Aww, come on, Chief. I'm not a baby-sitter," he groaned.

"Hey!" Gatineau scowled up at him. "I know what I'm doing." But the boy's voice was a little too high and his tone was a little too shrill to be totally convincing. "If it's not a codex alignment, then it's got to be a krypton displacement. Any good quantum mechanic knows that—"

MacHeath looked like he wanted to spit. Cappy rolled his eyes upward. Leen merely closed his eyes for a moment, as if to test a personal belief that things he couldn't see didn't really exist; but when he opened his eyes again, Gatineau was still there. The theory was wrong.

Gatineau didn't notice either of their reactions. He was still talking semiknowledgeably about particle decelerators, fluxor hammers, and Suford-Lewis modules. "See?" he demanded. "I know the difference between my assimulator and an elbow field."

"Right," said MacHeath. He looked grimly at Gatineau. "Do you know what's blue and taps on the glass . . . ?"

"Huh?"

"You. Testing an airlock."

"Belay that," the chief engineer growled at MacHeath. "You know the regs about harassment . . . even as a joke."

"Sorry." The big man mumbled his apology—to the chief, not to Gatineau.

"There is something," Leen said slowly. "But I don't know if I can trust you with the responsibility . . ." He looked warily at the boy.

"I can do it!" Gatineau insisted. "Trust me. Please, Chief?"

Leen sighed. "All right. I need a moebius wrench. We only have two of them aboard. They're very expensive. I don't know who had them last. You're going to have to ask around."

"You need a—a moebius wrench?"

"You do know what a moebius wrench is, don't you?"

Gatineau looked offended. "Of course, I do. What do you think I am?"

Cappy turned away, abruptly overcome by a coughing fit. MacHeath was suddenly interested in the ceiling.

"All right then," said the chief. "See if you can find me the left-handed one. Either one will do, but I'd prefer not to have to reset the polarity on a moebius wrench just for one job, okay?" He started to turn away, then glanced suspiciously back to Gatineau. "You *do* know what a left-handed moebius wrench looks like . . . don't you?"

Now it was Gatineau's turn to look annoyed. He spread his hands wide and gave the chief engineer a look of sheer disdain. "Chief—really."

"Okay," said Leen. "Go get it. Don't come back without it."

"Yes, sir! Thank you, sir!"

"Watch out for sparkle-dancers," Cappy said dryly.

"And star-pixies," MacHeath added noncommittally.

Gatineau turned and gave them both a look of derision. "Give me a break. What kind of dummy do you think I am?" He turned and almost sprinted along the catwalk and out of the engine room. Cappy and MacHeath barely waited until he had disappeared through the hatch before they started laughing.

Leen glanced at them, annoyed. "Are you done?"

"Yes, sir!" said Cappy, a little too brightly.

"Thank you, sir!" echoed MacHeath in a perfect imitation of Gatineau's shrill voice.

"Belay that," said Leen. "We've got work to do." He

scowled up into the G3 assembly tube again and repeated a few of his more colorful oaths. "I think we should check the alignment of all the tension monitors too. I'm wondering if we're missing something there—"

Both Cappy and MacHeath groaned loudly.

Hardesty

Captain Richard Hardesty, the "Star Wolf," was dead.
Korie hoped it would make the man easier to talk to.
It didn't.
Hardesty had been carefully transferred off the *Star Wolf*
to a medical bay out on the quarantine spar of the
Stardock. His body was still breathing on its own, but that
was the sum of it. He was being fed intravenously with
wastes removed from his blood by dialysis. His heart had
stopped, and the blood was being forced through his veins
by internal pumps. His bone marrow had ceased producing
blood cells; only constant scrubbing of his blood kept him
from developing half a dozen opportunistic infections.
During the journey back to base, the twelve crewmembers
who shared his blood type had been kept busy providing
new blood for him as the old wore out. Here at Stardock,
four regeneration tanks of bone-coral were percolating
with fresh new blood. For the most part, it wasn't helping.
Hardesty remained completely paralyzed from the neck
down and his extremities were precancerous. The smell of
the body on the bed was astonishing—sickly sweet, intense,

deathly, and horrible. Korie wondered if it would be impolite to hold a tissue over his nose.

He could barely stand to look at his captain. His one organic eye had collapsed. The left half of his face was metal; where the metal touched the skin, the skin had turned a slightly greenish color. It was all the result of exposure to Phullogine, a food preservative gas administered to the captain by the Morthan assassin Cinnabar.

Captain Richard Hardesty, the "Star Wolf," was brain-dead in all his higher cognitive functions, and had been since a few days after it happened.

He was of course completely incapable of speech. His voice came to Korie through a speaker. The thoughts that drove the speaker came from the augment in his skull, from the accident twenty years prior that had left him with half a head.

Now the rest of the head—and everything else, for that matter—was dead. And only the augment was left.

The augment was only slightly less caustic than the man had been. Korie told Hardesty about his meeting with the admiral. Hardesty's reaction was surprising. The speaker made noises like something rustling at the bottom of a tomb. "She's right. You're not ready for command."

Korie stifled his reaction. Who was really speaking? Hardesty? Or the intelligence engine in his skull? He kept his voice dispassionate. "Why do you say that?"

"Because it's true."

Korie should have turned and walked away. It was Hardesty's anger talking. It was the pain. It was the drugs. It was the Morthan gas. Who knew if the spark that was Hardesty was even here anymore? Nevertheless, he couldn't stop himself from asking. "May I have the specifics, please?"

"You're feral."

"Sir?"

"You're not civilized. You're wild. You don't have a military mind. You never will."

"I resent that, sir. I have—"

"I know what you have. You have anger. You have fury. You have rage. All of that overwhelms whatever intelligence you might bring to a situation. It makes you impatient."

Thinking back on his meeting with the admiral, Korie knew that Hardesty was right. Sort of. "I've tried to be the best officer I can—"

The graveyard voice whispered damningly, "Morale is in the toilet."

"That's not true—"

The voice rasped over his protests. "You've exposed your crew to the one thing a crew should *never* have to face: uncertainty in the authority over them. They had doubts about you after Marathon, when you came back from the mauling and didn't get your captaincy. Now, they're not getting the bounty *you told them* they deserved. How do you think they'll react to that?"

"They'll be angry. *I'm* angry."

"Your feelings are the *least* important part of the equation."

"I know that. What would you have me do?" Korie felt even more frustrated than he had with the admiral. He had expected his captain to *understand*.

The voice was silent for a long moment, so long that Korie thought that Hardesty had indeed died. Only the monitors above the bed indicated that the augment was still operative. Finally, the whisper came again. "That you have to ask only proves my point."

Korie opened his mouth to respond, then closed it again. This conversation was going nowhere fast. He stepped past his anger to the truth of the moment. He said, "I came in here to pay my respects, sir. The crew wants to know how you're doing. Now I've seen you, I can tell them. I'm going to go now." He even started for the door.

The rasping voice stopped him. "You don't fool me, Korie. You came here for my blessing. And now you're pissed because I won't give it to you."

Korie took a step forward and allowed himself a last good look at the gray-looking body on the bed. "You're dead, Captain. It doesn't matter what you think anymore. Your opinion has suddenly become irrelevant." Korie amazed himself. A week ago he wouldn't have imagined talking to his captain this way. But after facing down the admiral . . . it didn't seem so hard after all. "It doesn't matter if you think I'm fit for command or not. The responsibility is in my hands anyway. I'm going to get the job done, and the hell with your approval."

"Again you prove my point. Your anger consumes you."

"You're wrong. Twice over. My anger isn't a weakness. It's my biggest asset. It's a weathervane. It gives me direction. And no, I didn't come here for your blessing. I came here for your advice. I would have been satisfied with a little acknowledgment. *I'm* the one who brought the ship home safely."

"Yes. The ship. If I were still alive, I might be slightly flattered that you chose to name the ship after me. But it would make no difference in my recommendation."

Korie stood stock-still at the edge of the sick bay. "I can't find it in me to be entirely sorry you're dead, Captain."

"Commander, I told you once that I didn't care if you liked me so long as you did your job. I may be dead, but that hasn't changed."

Korie's eyes narrowed. "It was instructional serving under you, Captain," he said coldly. "I'll send flowers to your grave."

"You're not going to come piss on it?"

Korie snorted. "I *hate* standing in line." He turned and left.

La Paz

Two hours later, Korie was still angry.

He could feel it churning away inside of him, like a mechanical engine, one of those clanking beasts that lived in museums, fuming and puffing and smoldering, occasionally belching out great odious clouds of smoke and fire. He knew what he was angry about. He was too much in tune with his own emotions not to. It wasn't Hardesty and it wasn't the Admiral and it wasn't even the war. They were just the immediate obstacles. It was everything underneath that. The important stuff.

Carol and Tim and Robby.

And revenge.

In that order.

Frustrated and feeling impotent, he made his way to a mess hall, where he sat motionless, staring into space with a mug of bitter coffee and a plate of sausage and cheese and bread before him. The food sat untouched. He was too angry to eat. He'd expected better. He'd developed a whole plan for rebuilding his ship. *His* ship. The words were hollow. His plan languished unpresented in his clipboard. Shot down before it was launched. He'd never even had the chance to present it to the vice admiral. The effort was wasted.

It would be ten hours before the next boat from the *Star Wolf* checked in at the Stardock. He'd planned to use the time filing reconstruction orders, requisitioning parts and supplies. Now . . . he had nothing to do. Except perhaps plan what he would say to his crew when he got back. All that stuff he'd said to the vice admiral—what had he been thinking? It had felt good to be bold, yes, but so what? Could he really rebuild a ship without a stardock underneath his feet?

And Hardesty. The words of a dead man.

Frustrated thoughts churned around inside him, forming fragments of all the speeches he wanted to give. Even though he'd already said it, he felt as if he had to say it again. "This crew deserves a chance. They've earned it." But what he really meant was, *"I've earned it."*

He knew what his *zyne* masters would say. "Ninety percent of all problems in the universe are failures in communication. And the other ten percent are failures to understand the failure in communication." And following that thought, the inevitable *therefore:* "An upset is an incomplete communication."

To say that his most recent communications were incomplete was an insufficient analysis. He'd said everything he'd had to say. And the others had listened. The problem was, they hadn't done what he'd wanted them to do. What kind of a commander was he if he couldn't get others to do what he wanted?

Maybe the admiral was right. Maybe Hardesty was right. Maybe he was a hothead. A loose cannon. A shit-for-brains, seat-of-the-pants, shoot-from-the-lip, hyphenated-asshole.

"Jon? Jon Korie? Is that you?"

Korie looked up. The speaker was a woman. Tall. Strikingly handsome. Dark complected. Smiling. He was already rising, offering his hand to hers. Recognition came slowly. He knew her from—his eyes flicked briefly (resentfully) to the stars on her collar—and then, the rest of his memory clicked awake just in time. "Captain . . . *La Paz*!"

"Juanita," she corrected. "Come on, Jon. Don't get

stuffy with me. I danced at your wedding. How's Carol? How're those gorgeous boys of yours?"

"Uh—" Korie hesitated. "You didn't hear?"

"Hear what? We were out at the southern reach." Her expression went uncertain. "Oh God, no—not Carol."

"And the boys," Korie confirmed. "They were on Shaleen . . ." He couldn't complete the sentence.

Juanita put her hands on his shoulders. She lowered her voice and spoke with genuine concern. "Oh, Jon. I'm so sorry. You must be hurting bad, *compadre*. Is there anything I can do?" She stared anxiously into his eyes.

"Get me a ship and a dozen torpedoes and a map to the Morthan heart."

"If I had it, I'd give you a fleet. *Two.*"

Korie allowed himself a smile, his first real smile of the day. "Thanks. That's the best thing I've heard on Stardock today. I wish you were the admiral." Korie suddenly remembered his manners. "Sit down?" He pulled a chair out for her.

Juanita sat down opposite him, looking very serious. "I can only spare a moment, Jon. I've got to get my ship fitted. We're looking for fibrillators. Nobody has spares. Never mind that." She reached across the table and took his hands in hers. "Tell me about you. Are you all right? I mean . . . are you taking care of yourself?"

Korie thought about lying, but didn't have the strength for it. He shook his head. He lowered his eyes and just looked at the table between them.

Juanita squeezed his hands. "That bad?"

Korie admitted it. "Yeah."

"Want to talk?"

Korie shook his head. "It's everything, Juanita. I can't do anything. It's the *Star Wolf*. I've got a crew depending on me and all I've got is bad news. I can't keep asking them to give me their best if I can't give them anything tangible in return. I feel so frustrated. After everything we've been through, we've got nothing, and just when I should be feeling like we've accomplished something, I feel like a failure. And I can't even go home because there's no home to go to." He met her eyes. "I'm sorry. I shouldn't be telling you this."

"Who else are you going to tell? Who else *can* you tell?"

Korie sighed. "It's my stars, Juanita. I see your stars on your collar and I can't help but think, *where's mine*? I've earned them. I've earned them three times over."

"Yes, I've heard. We've all heard."

"Then why won't they give them to me? What's wrong with me?"

"Nothing wrong's with you, Jon. Nothing."

"Then where are my stars?"

"I don't know. But if it's any consolation, there are people who know what you've done. You have much more respect than you know."

"Sorry," Korie grinned wryly. "It's not much consolation. I want my ship."

"I remember that feeling," Juanita said. "It's like wanting a baby. Only worse. And then when you do get your ship, running it is a whole other experience. . . ."

"Juanita, stop. Please. I've been running the *Star Wolf* since a Morthan assassin gave Captain Hardesty an overdose of Phullogine. I know what it's like to run a starship. I want to know what it's like to not feel like an interloper. I want to feel like it's *mine*."

She stopped. "You're right. I'm sorry. I guess I'm not the best listener."

"I want a ship of my own and a load of torpedoes and the map to the heart of the Morthan Solidarity."

"We all do."

"Not like me."

Juanita accepted that without comment. After a moment she let go of his hands. "Let's change the subject. Do you know where I can find some fibrillators? Actually, I need complete fluctuator assemblies, but if I can get the fibrillators, we can jerry-rig around them." She met his eyes directly.

"Fibrillators," said Korie impassively. "Without fibrillators, you've got a tin can."

She nodded. There was a moment of uncomfortable silence between them. After a moment, Juanita cleared her throat with obvious embarrassment. "Um, Jon? Can I ask you something?"

"What?"

"Well . . . the scuttlebutt is that the *Star Wolf*'s going down. Is that what the admiral said . . . ?"

"So that's what this is about," Korie said slowly.

Realization suddenly dawned. "You want my *engines.*" His eyes narrowed angrily. "This was no accidental meeting, *was it?* You came looking for me. You *manipulative* bitch. You sat here and held my hands and pretended to be concerned and let me spill out my innermost thoughts— and the whole time, all you were thinking about was my fibrillators."

"That's not true," Captain La Paz said, standing up abruptly. "And I'm sorry you think that. I honestly care about you and Carol and the boys—"

"Please, stop. I don't want to hear their names in your mouth."

"Jon—"

"No, forget it." Korie stood quickly, holding his hands up as if to ward her off. "Just leave me alone." He started to turn away—

"Stand to, Mister!" she barked.

Korie froze at attention.

"Have it your way," Captain La Paz said, bracing him firmly and meeting him eye to eye. Her expression was as hard as his. "I was trying to make it easy on you. My boat is on the T-spar. I was going to offer you a ride back to your ship."

"I'd rather walk, thank you."

La Paz ignored it. "I have a list. I was hoping we could trade. If you won't trade, I'll simply requisition. I want your engines. This isn't a request anymore. It's an order."

For a moment, Korie wondered just how much insubordination he could get away with in a single day. Probably not too much more. He decided not to push his luck.

"What are your orders, Captain?" he asked.

"That's better, Commander," she replied.

Brik

Gatineau stopped just outside the hatch. He hadn't wanted to admit he didn't know what a moebius wrench was, but now that he had accepted the responsibility, he had to produce a result, and he had to do it *immediately.* The chief was depending on him.

He stood in the passageway and looked around in confusion. He wasn't even sure where he was right now. The bulkheads were a confusing welter of detachable panels, each one with its own mysterious code number. "Let's see," he said, turning around slowly. "The keel is 180, the upper starboard passage is 60, and the port passage is 240 degrees. So—ah, I'm in the port passage. And that means that *this* ladder goes down to the keel, 180, and that hatch leads forward. . . ." He made a decision and headed forward, looking for the messroom. There he could ask if anyone knew where the moebius wrench was.

The ship's mess was not quite deserted. He didn't really recognize the red-haired man or the two women he was talking to, but he nodded anyway. He was just about to approach them when Commander Brik entered from the other side. He *knew* Commander Brik—at least, he knew him well enough to talk to. "Sir?" he asked.

Brik stopped. He was obviously on his way somewhere and he looked annoyed at the interruption.

Gatineau looked up . . . and up. And up. He stammered out his request quickly. "Commander Leen wants me to find a—a moebius wrench. The left-handed one. Do you know where it is?"

"Mm," said Brik with exaggerated thought. He scratched his cheek. "I can't recall seeing it recently. You might try . . . yes, try the cargo bay. They'd be most likely to have it. Go down to the keel. That's the fastest way."

"Thank you, sir." Gatineau suppressed the urge to salute and hurried back the way he'd come. Brik shook his head in bemusement and continued forward to his quarters.

Installing a three-meter-high, two-hundred-kilogram Morthan Tyger aboard even a large starship had originally presented certain problems of ancillary logistics. For instance, where does a two-hundred-kilogram Morthan sleep? "Anywhere he wants to" is not a sufficient answer if there is no place big enough.

When Captain Hardesty had come aboard, bringing Lieutenant Commander Brik as chief of strategic operations and security, he had also ordered the reconstruction of three officers' cabins into one much larger suite for the Morthan. It was not merely a matter of courtesy or consideration; it was also an issue of mental health. Fleet regulations stated that an officer was entitled to a cubic volume of contiguous personal space not less than fifty times his or her own volume. This included bathing and personal facilities as well.

There were complex formulae for determining the needs of smaller or larger crew members, but in general, the usual officer's cabin was approximately four meters by eight, with a 2.3-meter ceiling. In Brik's case, however, because of his immense size, he was given a cabin that measured twelve meters by eight, with a 3.5-meter ceiling. This required some minor reconstruction of the facilities on the opposite side of the bulkhead, but under Brik's direct supervision the engineering crew had accomplished the job with amazing rapidity.

The same remodeling would not have been as easy on a

hardened battle-cruiser, but many of the interior bulkheads of liberty ships were simply rigid panels of hardened foam. Not much more was needed to partition off spaces, and the result was a flexibility of interior design that gave individual commanders a high degree of freedom in laying out personal areas for officers and crew.

Brik had not given the process much thought. From the moment he had entered the Special Academy, his entire adult life had been spent in rooms that were too small for him. While he was able to appreciate the courtesy of the extra personal space, his cabin still felt like one more place too small for a proper fury. The ceilings were too low and he had to duck to get through the doorway.

He made do. Over the course of years, he had become very good at making do. Originally the idea of spending so much time among humans had been distasteful to him; with time, he began to realize that there were lessons he could learn from these squeaky little creatures. Indeed, he was beginning to regard them almost with . . . respect.

There was only minimal furniture in his quarters—a few chairs for those occasions when he wanted guests, and a fold-down table for when he wanted to work; the bed was a retractible nest of memory foam. Everything was collapsible; it was ugly, but it wasn't uncomfortable; and almost everything disappeared into the walls when not in use, and that gave him more space for his centering exercises. Perhaps if he had guests more often, he might have made more of an effort toward making his quarters more attractive; but he had no friends and guests were rare. Hospitality wasn't exactly a Morthan tradition. Neither was vanity.

Brik had been designed and tailored, born and raised to be a professional warrior. That he had become an officer of the Allied fleet was his own choice, and one that had brought considerable embarrassment to his fathers. Consequently, he felt little loyalty to them, and his cabin reflected that. It contained almost no trophies or mementos of his past; instead it was a neutral facility, part workout room, part office. The only noticeable personal items were two banners, one blue-gray, the other scarlet, hung on the wall above his work station. Aside from that single expression of self, his cabin might have been an eccentrically designed gymnasium. The other three walls of Brik's quarters were paneled with large holographic displays.

A pair of workout robots waited in their maintenance closets in the corners. One robot appeared human, and the other was supposed to be a Morthan Tyger. Brik was not pleased with either of them; the human robot was too fast and too hard to kill, and the Morthan robot was too slow and too easy. Worse yet, the human robot was not anatomically accurate; Brik could hit it so hard that a true human would have died instantly of systolic shock, but all that this robot did was pretend that its bones were broken and it was bleeding to death.

Arrayed next to the robots were devices to tell him how quickly he moved, how accurately he struck his targets, and with what force. Unlike every other automated system aboard ship, Brik's equipment was not run by Harlie, the ship's lethetic intelligence engine. It was run by what was, to his knowledge, the only martial arts expert system, outside of the Morthan Solidarity, designed by Morthans.

Brik would have enjoyed studying under an expert system from the Solidarity; someday he hoped to have the opportunity. Morthans knew significantly less about computer science than the Alliance, and significantly more about every other aspect of the warrior disciplines. Nevertheless, Brik did not feel deprived. The expert system he used had been written by his fathers.

As he did every day, Brik whispered a command to his office. The room began to darken. He stripped off his uniform and pushed it into an overstuffed hamper; although laundry was usually handled by the ship's utility robots, the decontamination procedures had delayed the performance of many of their routine duties.

Naked now, Brik began chanting softly to himself, restoring himself to the center of his being, softly counting through the spaces of his existence, identifying each, accepting it as part of his identity, recreating it and including it as part of who he was.

As he chanted, he *moved*. He circled precisely through the seven patterns of *self*ness. Neither a dance nor an exercise, but something of each, the ritual took him methodically up the ladder. There were seven major steps of engagement in the existence of a self-aware being, and

multiple minor steps as well—all the way from the unbe-
ingness of unconsciousness at the bottom to a white-light,
oceanic awareness at the top.

He began with his spine, the animal center of his body.
He twisted and stretched through a series of deliciously
painful exercises. He felt the tension like a tide, pulling
him simultaneously inward and out. His muscles tightened
with effort, tightened beyond pain, into that burning
threshold where the very tissues began to tear against
themselves, triggering the release of specially tailored hormones in his body, and even more potently designed endorphins in his brain. He became intoxicated with his body
now and cycled through the dance a second and a third
time, each time rising to greater peaks of agonies and ecstasies. To a Morthan, the two were the same sensation.
Overwhelming. Almost uncontrollable.

As he expanded his physical being, so did his awareness
seem to grow, leaping beyond the boundaries of his skin,
beyond the paneled walls of his cabin, beyond the carbon-
ate foam hull of the starship, beyond the stars, beyond the
farthest stars of the galaxy itself to finally encompass a
universal awareness of the dual paradox of enlightenment;
the mutual existence of everything and nothing in an infi-
nite realm.

He held that state for as long as he could—humming
with a deep-throated sound, almost a purr. When he was
truly focused, he could hold himself at that white-light moment for achingly long seconds before he peaked and
crashed exhausted back into himself, paradoxically both
empty and refreshed.

In this state, he did not try to think. He simply let the
thoughts come. The pictures flowed, one after the other.
He did not try to give them meaning. He simply let them
happen. He watched them pass across his consciousness
and noticed his reactions. Sometimes anger, sometimes
fear. More and more these days, *curiosity*.

Humans had no conception of the complexities of the
Morthan consciousness. That Brik had no way to enlighten
them without turning them into Morthans themselves did
not frustrate him, although the barrier of imprecise communication that the spiritual gap represented did give him
more than occasional annoyance. Rather, he felt an in-

creased responsibility to make up for the lack of wider
awareness in his human colleagues with extra caution on
his own part.

Naked, and finally relaxed, the huge Morthan at last
folded himself into a meditative posture and waited. When
he was ready for the next step, he whispered a second command, and the holographic displays shimmered to life with
pictures of past horror.

Brik sat alone in the dark, surrounded on three sides by
holos of a dead Morthan named Esker Cinnabar. As he
had done almost every day in the five weeks since the *Star
Wolf* had completed her last mission, he *studied* the pictures. There was so *much* to learn.

Brik did not think much of most of the tools humans had
designed for measuring competitiveness, but there were exceptions. One was the Skotak Viability test. It determined
with what Brik thought admirable precision just how difficult a living organism would be to kill. (Humans did not
realize that this was the proper use of the test, of course;
they thought it was for making decisions about healing the
injured; but Brik saw no reason to be bound by the limited
assumptions of others.)

A good rating for a human would have been in the range
of seventy-five to eighty; an exceptional rating would have
run as high as ninety. Cinnabar, while alive, had registered
a Skotak Viability rating of one hundred thirty-two, before
augmentation. After augmentation—biotech implants, the
addition of an optical nervous system, half a dozen different devices to protect him from the commonest forms of
particle weapons and slugthrowers—Cinnabar's Skotak Viability rating had shot up to approximately three hundred
ninety.

Brik would never have let someone else run the Skotak
Viability test on *him;* it would have given away information
that might one day cause his death. (It had helped cause
Cinnabar's.) But he had run it on himself, in the privacy of
his quarters. And he found the results . . . interesting.

Esker Cinnabar was among the Morthan Solidarity's
elite. He had received the finest training in all the martial
disciplines; even before augmentation he would have been
rated as a certifiable Berserker. The Solidarity did not

waste the resources necessary to create an assassin on any but the *best*.

And Esker Cinnabar's Skotak Viability rating, preaugmentation, was one hundred thirty-two.

Brik's was one hundred thirty-six.

But Esker Cinnabar was better trained than Brik. Brik knew it to be true; the greatest warriors the universe had ever seen had trained Cinnabar.

Brik's fathers had trained him. Later, Brik had trained himself.

In all the Alliance there was no one competent to teach him the things he needed to know now. The experts were all with the Solidarity, were all his enemies.

So Brik sat in the darkness and watched all the hours of holos that had been made of the Morthan expert Esker Cinnabar. Watched Cinnabar move, watched him talk. Watched him indulge in rage, and experience it. Watched him threaten and cajole, watched him kill, and watched him die.

Over and over again.

And learned . . .

There were movements here that Brik still couldn't puzzle out. Were they products of the augments? At his work station, he had tried to factor out every behavior that was the result of implants and augments, reducing Cinnabar's virtual self to a preaugmented state; but despite his careful analysis, he still wasn't sure if he was seeing the actual behaviors of the unaugmented Cinnabar or if the virtuality was still polluted with residual effects of the bio-engineering.

Brik frowned in concentration. His muscles twitched in sympathy. He ran the display in slow motion and copied out each movement. They were uncomfortable and unfamiliar. How had Cinnabar trained himself to move like that? The best movements were those that used the body's own power. Was there something he was missing here? There had to be.

But even as he struggled to master the skills of his enemies, he regarded them with a measure of contempt. The war in space would provide little opportunity for hand-to-hand combat, yet it was clear that the Morthan Solidarity was continuing to place undue emphasis on personal discipline and strength. This was a misplaced direction of resources, and might very well cost them significant strategic ability.

Unless he was missing something else—

Why would the Morthans spend so much time and energy on personal enhancement? What were their ultimate intentions? It was a question that he could not answer now; he did not have enough information; but it was also a question that he would like to discuss with Commander Korie when he returned to the ship.

There was a knock on the door—a soft, almost tentative sound.

Brik switched off the holo display of Cinnabar. The walls faded to gray. Although he had no nudity taboos of his own, Brik knew that many humans would be startled by his unclad appearance. He stood up and reached for a robe. "Enter," he rumbled, vaguely annoyed at the interruption.

The door popped open and Lieutenant Junior Grade Helen Bach, stepped politely in. "I hope you don't mind my interrupting, Commander. I know you need your personal time, but . . ." She glanced around uncertainly, a little startled at the starkness of the room.

"But?" Brik prompted.

"I was wondering if you would like to join me for dinner?"

Brik considered the invitation; not only the surface meanings, but the subtext as well. "Most humans don't like to eat with Morthans," he said noncommittally.

"I grew up on a Morthan farm."

"Yes. You told me that."

"Well, I . . . I think I need to talk to you. About my responsibilities."

"I am not here to provide . . . counseling services."

"That's not what I meant," Bach said. "Um, this isn't easy for me. And you're not making it easier. I just thought because we'll be working so closely together now that we could be friends, that's all. Friends *talk.*"

"Morthans don't have . . . *friends.*"

"But humans do." She met his gaze, unafraid. "And it seemed to me that maybe Morthans—I don't know, maybe . . . I mean, you're on a shipload of humans—" Abruptly Brik's stare seemed more intense than usual. Bach ducked her head in sudden embarrassment. "Never mind. I apologize if I misunderstood."

"Lieutenant—" Brik stopped her before she could turn away. "I appreciate the gesture, I think I understand the motivations behind it, but it's inappropriate."

"Say again?"

"You're projecting your own perceptions onto me. You are assuming behaviors that are not here."

"Oh," said Bach. "Thank you, sir." Her expression closed. "I'm sorry for disturbing you. It won't happen again." She stepped back out and the door popped shut behind her.

Brik stared at the silent wall for a long moment, puzzled by Bach's behavior. He understood neither her invitation nor the reasoning behind it. It annoyed him—not the invitation, but the fact that he couldn't understand Bach's motivation.

He sat back down again, but found himself unable to restore his concentration, and that only increased his annoyance more.

Humans.

Hall

Gatineau finally found the cargo bay. It took him more than an hour, and he wasn't happy about it. The chief would not think well of him for wasting so much time, but somehow he had gotten turned around in the maze beneath the engine room and ended up at the forward airlock instead. He wasn't quite sure how that had happened, but apparently his sense of direction didn't work the same way in space.

When he actually stepped into the big chamber of the bay, he stopped in amazement and stared. Where every other part of the vessel seemed small and cramped, the cargo deck was actually roomy enough for a tennis match. Possibly two. Halfway up the wall, a wide catwalk circled the room. Forward, it opened into both the port and starboard passages. Aft, it led to two standard airlocks. Below the catwalk was a much larger cargo lock.

At the moment the floor of the cargo deck was divided into taped-off rectangular areas, each one filled with a variety of supply modules and crates. As he watched, a robot pushed an antigrav sled into the bay, bringing another load of equipment. A work crew rushed to unload the sled.

A skinny little man with large eyes and ears and a shrill penetrating voice was striding up and down the aisles, calling out orders to his harried crew; there were at least six. They were all wearing shorts and T-shirts, the standard working uniform. The skinny man waved his arms; he shouted and pointed; he cursed and cajoled; he kept up a constant stream of chatter as he directed the sorting of the matériel into various taped-off rectangles.

As Gatineau approached, he checked the officer's nametag. *Chief Petty Officer T. Hall.* "Sir?" he asked.

Hall turned around in midbark and blinked at Gatineau, as if discovering something left uninventoried. "Who're you?"

"Uh, Crewman Robert Gatineau, third class, engineering apprentice. Sir."

"Well, Crewman Robert Gatineau, third class . . . let me give you a piece of advice," Hall said officiously. "Rule number one: *Never interrupt.*"

"Yes, sir. Thank you, sir."

"Now, what is it?"

"Chief Leen sent me to retrieve the moebius wrench. Sir."

"The . . . moebius wrench." Hall blinked again. His brow furrowed slightly.

"Yes, sir."

"Uh, right. The moebius wrench. Um, let me see—what did we do with it?" Hall scratched his left eyebrow as he tried to remember. He had a peculiar expression on his face.

"The left-handed one, sir. If you please."

"Ahh, yes. The *left-handed* moebius wrench. Um. Hm. Right . . . right. Let me think. Here, put this box over there. Third row, four squares down. No, not there—the next one. Good. Now, help us move these canisters. There's a good fellow."

"Sir, I really need to find the moebius wrench—"

"Yes, I know. Just give us a hand here while I try to remember."

"What is it exactly we're doing here?" Gatineau asked after a few more moments.

"Swap meet," said one worker. Her nametag identified her as *Sherm*.

"We're putting out everything we have to trade. We're practically stripping the ship," said the other woman, *Hernandez*. "Chief Leen thinks we're going to need a whole new fluction system. We may have to build it from spare parts."

"No, we won't. I was just there. All we have to do is recalibrate the attack velocity of the fluxor hammers to compensate for harmonic errors. It costs us a couple points off the high end, but that's part of the margin built into the design, so we're not really losing anything; and we can still realize FTL velocities. . . ."

"Right," said Sherm, shoving a large heavy module into his arms. "In the meantime, put this in L-7."

After a while longer, after he'd lifted and carried a dozen more crates, after he'd stumbled over the same cargo 'bot for the third time, Gatineau decided he'd waited long enough. He put down the last crate and approached Chief Petty Officer Hall again. The thin man was striding down one of the rows and cursing softly as he counted off. It wasn't going to be enough.

"Sir?"

"What did I tell you about interrupting, son? Rule number one, remember?"

"Yes, sir, but I promised Chief Leen—"

"Oh, yes, that's right—here, just help us unload this next sled and—"

"The moebius wrench, sir?"

"Right, right." Hall appeared distracted. "Wasn't it stored with the Klein bottles—?" He began coughing ferociously into his fist. He turned away from Gatineau until the seizure passed. He cleared his throat repeatedly, all the while waving away Gatineau's concerned assistance. He moved away through the goods and equipment strewn methodically across the floor of the cargo deck. Abruptly he turned grim-faced back to Gatineau. He looked as if he were biting his cheek from the inside. "The moebius wrench, right?"

"Yes, sir!" Gatineau replied brightly.

"Y'know . . . I distinctly remember giving it to the union steward. That's Reynolds. He'll have it or he'll know where it is. You're going to have to check in with him anyway. Let's see . . ." He referred to his clipboard. "Yes, Reynolds is working below the keel. He's supervising the detox on the electrical harness. He's probably down in the fuel cells right now. They're looking for a systemic discontinuity in the lower yoke. Y'know, he could probably use an extra hand. He'd appreciate any help you could give him."

"But, Chief Leen—"

"Yes, I know Chief Leen. He won't need that wrench until tomorrow or the next day. He's like that. He's always thinking three days ahead. You find your way down to the lower yoke right now and tell Reynolds I sent you."

"Yes, sir." Gatineau was puzzled, and more than a little bit frustrated, but he wasn't going to question the orders of an officer. "Find the inner hull and tell Reynolds you sent me. Chief Petty Officer Hall, right?"

"Just call me Toad," he said. "You need anything, you go to Toad Hall. Remember that. You give, you get."

Gatineau had the weirdest feeling that Petty Officer Hall wasn't telling him something. Nevertheless . . . he turned and headed for the passage through the keel again. He glanced over his shoulder once and saw that Hall was watching him go; he was still wearing that same peculiar expression. Hall smiled brightly and waved bye-bye at him. Puzzled, Gatineau waved back. But he went.

As soon as Gatineau was gone, Hall turned back to his supply team. "Well, what are you waiting for?" he barked. "Ruffles and flourishes? Come on, get your butts off the ground! I need those medallion-armatures tallied—"

He was interrupted by several flashing red lights and warning buzzers. "Docking!" someone called.

Hall grunted in annoyance, but he stopped what he was doing and waited. So did everyone else.

The *Star Wolf* had three boats: two transfer boats and a larger dropship that doubled as a cargo shuttle. Although the transfer boats could be brought into the cargo deck for maintenance, they were usually moored to the port and starboard airlocks when not in use. There was also a mooring for a captain's gig above the bridge, but no small boats had ever been made available to the *Star Wolf*.

The dropship could be hung below the keel, but was more often moored to the large cargo lock at the stern; the larger access allowed the craft to open its entire fuselage to the cargo bay, vastly simplifying the transfer of massive containers. But this was not the *Star Wolf*'s dropship arriving; instead, it was an ancillary craft temporarily assigned to the service of the *Sam Houston.* Chief Petty Officer Hall had gotten notification of its arrival only thirty minutes previously, via a low-amplification tight-beam signal.

Korie was the first one through the cumbersome detox lock, stepping through even before the hatch had finished opening. He was accompanied by the familiar soft thump of pressure balancing as the minor differences in atmospheric pressure between the two vessels equalized; it was *felt* in the ears, more than it was heard. He was *also* accompanied by a particularly irritating jazz-trumpet rendition of *Dixie,* the signature anthem of the *Houston.* The acting captain of the *Star Wolf* was carrying a thicker than usual "grief case" and he looked unhappier than ever. He was glowering with real annoyance.

Most of the crew had already learned to recognize Korie's range of feelings. He started at grim and went all the way downhill to black rage. Occasionally, on very good days, Korie's emotional state might rise as far as simple moodiness. Today, however, his condition was somewhere south of bleak, but not yet in the neighborhood of dangerous. At least, that was the way Hall read it. He touched one finger casually to the communicator tab by his ear and whispered, "Code black. Temperature is heading toward zero. Wear a jacket."

"Ten-four," came the reply. The crew was alerted. Whatever it was, it was bad news.

Korie strode quickly through the taped-off aisles. Without glancing directly at Hall, he remarked, "You're an optimist. I passed zero a long time ago."

Hall followed him. "Were you able to—"

Korie flung a sheaf of memory cards and hardcopies at him. "It's all there. I brought whatever I could get. Which is to say not much. The *Fontana* wants credit. The *Moran* has got software problems and won't swap anything. The *Miller* needs a dedicated server; she's unhappy with her protocols. The *Hayes* needs everything. The *Boyett* is apparently running its own metric system; nothing works over there and Captain Albert wants to whine in my ear about it. Captain La Paz of the *Sam Houston* wants our fibrillators, for God's sake! And I'm getting *really* tired of *Dixie.*" He glanced back over his shoulder, noting with his eyes the work crew from the *Houston* who had followed through the detox hatch. "They have a list. Give them whatever they need." And then he lowered his voice, *"But nothing critical.* I'll not have my ship stripped for *that* damned bitch. Tell them the fibrillators are in a thirty-six hour detox. It won't be a lie." *I'm about to order it.*

Hall started to acknowledge, but Korie was already up the ladder to the overhead catwalk. He shrugged and turned his attention to the memory cards and hardcopies. He thumbed through them quickly. He expected no joy here, nothing to light up his eyes. He turned back to the open cargo hatch of the dropship and stared in puzzlement. Despite Korie's complaints, the interior of the vessel was almost full to the ceiling with cargo pods.

"All right," Hall said, shaking his head and pointing his crew forward. "Let's see what we've got here." He stepped through the heavy doors of the detox chamber into the dropship, turning sideways to let one of the *Houston*'s crew members squeeze past. He examined the labels on each of the crates and canisters he passed. Most contained standard military issue nonrenewable resources. A few were . . . puzzling. Potatoes? Why so many canisters of potatoes? And corn? The *Star Wolf* was perfectly capable of growing her own crops. In fact, a huge corn crop was already ripening in the inner hull, sector 6-130. And juniper berries? Peach nectar? Raspberry syrup? Apples? Yeast? It wasn't until he found the rolls of copper tubing that enlightenment finally came to him. A broad grin broke out on his face. "Why that son of a bitch—" he whistled in amazement. He spent a moment shaking his head in jealous admiration of the way Korie's mind worked, then thumbed his communicator again. "Chief Leen?"

"Leen here."

"I know you're busy, but I need you to inspect some engineering supplies. And you might want to bring a few of your crew to help stash them away."

"Can't it wait?"

"I really don't think so. This is important."

"More important than a thirty-six hour fibrillator detox? More important than a broken redirection plate?"

"How many *new* redirection plates would you like?" Hall put deliberate emphasis on the word *new*.

There was silence on the line for a moment. Then Leen replied, "We're on our way."

Although he wasn't really looking for him, Leen bumped into Gatineau halfway between the engine room and the cargo deck. Gatineau immediately started stammering in embarrassment about having to help "Toad" Hall with the inventory, but it was okay, because the Chief Petty Officer had remembered that he'd given the left-handed moebius wrench to Reynolds who was working in the inner-hull and he was on his way there now and—"

Leen cut him off halfway through the second repetition. "Well, stop telling me about it son and go get it." And then he added, "Initiative. That's what I like to see." He patted Gatineau affectionately on the back and gave him a hearty shove forward.

"Thank you, sir!" Gatineau beamed with gratitude. He'd been terrified that the chief would be upset with him. Instead . . . he'd actually *complimented him on his initiative.* His spirit renewed, the young crewman hurried off in search of an access to the inner hull.

He climbed two ladders, went down a third, up a fourth, and found himself in officers' country instead. He knew that he was in the wrong place when he saw the name *Korie* stenciled on the door to the Captain's office. "Uh-oh," he said, his ebullient spirits crashing suddenly to the bulkhead.

"That was the . . . *Captain* I met. Oh, no—" He backed away from the door, gulping for breath and wondering just how badly he'd embarrassed himself. He wondered if he should apologize. He even went so far as to lift his hand to knock. Then, wisely, decided against it and headed back the way he'd come.

Carol

Alone in the captain's office, Korie was sorting things out on the captain's desk. He worked standing up. The captain's chair remained unused behind him.

Korie still wasn't ready to *sit* in the captain's chair; the *real* captain was floating in a hospital tube somewhere in the bowels of Stardock; but Korie used the office because it was the seat of power aboard the vessel. Here was where information was coordinated and decisions were made.

And . . . he used the office because he expected it to be his soon. No. *Had* expected. Not anymore. Not after that scene in the admiral's office.

Technically, Richard "Star Wolf" Hardesty was still captain of the *LS-1187*. But, also technically, Richard "Star Wolf" Hardesty was also dead. Sort of. His body was embalmed with Phullogine, but his brain augment was still functioning. Still transmitting.

Dockside an ethical debate was raging whether the captain was legally brain-dead or not, whether his personality had migrated completely into the augment, or whether the augment was merely simulating sentience. After one particularly blistering tirade, the doctors had decided to postpone the question while they worked on the more immediate task of reanimating the captain's body. There remained considerable doubt if it was possible; although suspended animation via Phullogine had been accomplished with some laboratory animals, it had never satisfactorily been achieved with humans. So Captain Richard "Star Wolf" Hardesty was not expected to return to active duty anytime soon.

Korie thumbed through the contents of his "grief case" without much interest. Most of it was busy work. Where the popular entertainments often suggested that most of a captain's time was often spent in hand-to-hand combat with sinister alien life-forms, the embarrassing truth was that the most vicious combat most captains ever saw was with ordinary human bureaucrats. Not that bureaucrats could ever be considered a benign life-form, but in this case the word *sinister* was only appropriate for that small minority who wrote with their left hands.

Among the contents of Korie's grief case there were a couple of promotions, several routine pay raises, some minor bonuses, the admiral's congratulatory message, and a large package of medals. Korie pushed those to one side. It was a big pile, but not big enough to fully acknowledge what they had been through.

It was all about energy, he realized. Physical. Emotional. Economic. Spiritual. Whatever. They weren't getting their *fair share*.

Fair share.

Was there ever such a thing as a fair share?

Maybe not. It all depended on the interpretation.

When he was sixteen years old, Jon Korie's father had allowed him to enroll in the study of the *zyne*.* According to one of the *zyne* masters he'd studied under, a wild man

---

* A modernized form of *zen,* the *zyne* is a philosophical derivative of the study of the "technology of consciousness."

The *zyne* is not psychological in nature; indeed, it is very anti-psychology in its thrust, in that the *zyne* postulates that there is no such thing as a "mind," only a "conversation" that distinguishes itself (falsely) as a mind. The distinction is tricky and may take months or years of training to grasp.

named MacNamara, human beings were enertropic; they were attracted to *power*—any kind of power or authority or strength. Even where such power was only a charismatic illusion, such as that found in some religions, it still had an overwhelming attraction. No pheromone was ever as compelling, because no pheromone ever had such total cooperation from its targets. Where power *didn't* exist, humans created it, presumed it, allocated it, and fought over it.

According to one simulation of reality, everything that human beings did was an exchange of energy. *Every* interaction. *Every* relationship. A mother gave food and shelter to her child; the child returned the energy in the form of affection; thus the parent received a large emotional bonus for a very small physical expense. Lovers routinely swapped affection; where the trades were equal in perception, the relationship was ideal; where not, not. Employees traded labor for cash; where the labor was intensive and the rewards were small, both morale and productivity suffered; where the labor was easy and the rewards were larger than commensurate, both productivity and morale suffered.

The best situation was one in which the investment of energy returned a greater than expected reward; not too great, as that produced a distorted view of one's own ability, but large enough to give one a sense of productivity with all of the ancillary side benefits of increased confidence and self-esteem. The worst situation, of course, occurred when a major investment of energy returned little or no perceivable benefit. That produced feelings of inadequacy, futility, resentment, frustration, despair, and eventually apathy.

That was why the pile of medals was too small. This crew had climbed a mountain to rebuild the efficiency rating of this vessel. This crew had confronted the *Dragon Lord* twice and survived. This crew had outwitted and destroyed an onboard Morthan assassin. This crew deserved to be honored as true heroes at a time when there was a very real shortage of same.

Instead . . . all they had to show for it was a small pile of officious plastic. Korie shoved it aside. Later, he'd take care of it.

He made another pile for more mundane matters. Supply reports, bulletins, updates, evaluations, inventories, advisories, cancellations, war news, and analyses—

Oh, this one was interesting. Someone was requesting a transfer *to* the *LS-1187*. It had been approved. Curiously, Korie flipped the card over and read the information on the back. A chaplain? Korie tossed the card to the side in disgust. Just what the ship needed. Someone to administer the last rites.

Korie did not believe in God. Not anymore.

God took energy. Nothing was returned.

It wasn't a fair trade.

If God wanted Jonathan Thomas Korie to invest himself in worship, there had to be a fair reward. Otherwise, no deal. Korie had invested many years in religion; he was still waiting. When God began paying dividends on the previous investment, Korie would consider renewing the relationship. Until then . . . thanks, but no thanks.

He made another pile for mail. There was a depressingly small quantity of plastic memory cards with his name on them. He couldn't imagine that any of the letters held anything of interest. Just about everybody he'd ever known or cared about had died when the Morthans scourged Shaleen.

Again, it was all about energy. Some of the crew spent a great deal of their spare time recording messages home and received little in return. Others spent little time on the mail and regularly received large pouches of mail. Korie envied the latter. He would give anything for a new letter from home. Instead, the best he could do was replay the final few messages he'd gotten from Carol and Tim and Robby and that wasn't enough.

He kept investing. He wasn't getting anything back. Would never get anything back again.

The problem with this particular simulation of reality— he'd realized a long time ago—was that while it was good for understanding *why* you felt cheated, it wasn't very good for triggering insights into rectifying the situation so that a fair balance of energy was restored.

This assumed, of course, that there was such a thing as a *fair* balance of energy. According to the masters of the *zyne,* the universe didn't really care which way the energy flowed. Only people did.

He sorted through his letters without apparent interest. He evened them up in his hand, forming a thin pack of small plastic cards; he thumbed through them disinterestedly, glancing quickly at each sender's ID before tossing it aside. The last card almost joined the rest—then he pulled his hand back and looked at the return address again. It bore a Shaleenian forwarding symbol, but it had been routed through Taalamar and Ghu alone knew where else. It was the forwarding symbol that stopped him. He hadn't seen a Shaleenian crest since before—

He dropped the card on the reader plate and—

—suddenly the cabin was filled with noise. Timmy was crying. Robby looked scared and paralyzed. They were inside a crowded vehicle; he didn't recognize it. The impact of what he was seeing slammed him backward as if he'd been punched into the chair. Carol's face was ashen. "Jon, I don't know if this is going to reach you. I'm beaming it direct. I hope you get it. They're ordering us to evacuate to the countryside. They won't say why, but everybody's saying that a Morthan fleet is heading our way. Oh, Jon—I'm so scared! We're on our way to Candleport. I know, but it's the only one I could think of. I'm going to try to get the boys on a ship. I'm going to use your military priority; please forgive me if I'm doing something wrong, but everybody's so scared. You can't believe what some people are doing. There was a riot in the common. We almost didn't get aboard the train. The peace force is—oh, I don't know —never mind. I love you, so much. Please—oh, we're almost there, I've got to go, I'll try to send more later, I love you—"

—and then the cabin was silent and still again.

Korie was sitting rigid, paralyzed. Unable to assimilate what he'd just seen. He tapped the card and it played again.

Yes, it was Carol—she was panic-stricken. He groaned at the pain written on her face. "Oh, Carol—sweetheart!" He barely heard the words; not hers, not his. He searched her face, her eyes—his heart broke all over again. The boys— *his* sons, he could see himself in their features, and Carol too—were clutching their mother for strength. He recognized the vehicle now; a cargo train, filled with panicked people. Candleport. She'd said something about Candle-

port. *Evacuation*. No. It wasn't possible. He couldn't accept—

He played it a third time. A fourth. And a fifth.

He didn't dare let himself hope. He felt unbearable pressure in his chest and throat and in the hurting space behind
his eyes. But what if they were alive—? What if she'd gotten the boys off? What if—? He couldn't stay seated. He
grabbed the card. He got up from the chair. He walked
around the room; he paced like a caged animal. He came
back to the desk. He put the card down on the reader
again, then snatched it up just as fast, as if he couldn't bear
to let go of it. He didn't know what to do. Tears welled up
in his eyes. He pounded on the bulkhead in frustration.
"God damn you, God! What are you doing to me? You
bastard!"

He opened the door to the passage; there was no one
there. He started aft—no, wrong—turned and headed forward, to the Bridge—ignored the puzzled stares of the
Bridge crew, slid down the stairs to the Ops deck, ducked
around into the Ops bay below the command deck,
dropped through it to the keel, found the ladder, and
pulled himself up into Harlie country. He flung himself
down into the single chair in the small chamber, out of
breath, confused, angry, ecstatic, hurting, hopeful, and finally letting it all burst forth—he was crying.

"Mr. Korie?" Harlie's voice was astonishingly compas-
sionate.

Korie was so overcome he was choking. He couldn't respond. He was trying to swallow, speak, and cry all at the
same time. He waved away the question while he wiped at
his eyes and pounded on his chest. At last, finally, he took
the card in his hand and fumbled it onto the reader plate
on the work station in front of him.

Harlie responded almost immediately. "I'm terribly
sorry for you," he said. "This must be very painful."

Korie managed to get a sentence out. "You don't understand. Maybe—maybe they're alive."

Harlie paused. "To be perfectly rational—and I'm sorry
if this causes you additional pain—the odds of that are very
small."

"But it's a chance, isn't it? Somebody gets to win the
lottery. Why not me?"

"Why not indeed?" said the intelligence engine. "To the extent of my limited ability to wish, I do wish for the safety of your loved ones."

"I know you do, Harlie. And I appreciate the thought. I really do." Korie took a breath. A long deep breath. "But that's not why I came here. Not for counseling. Not now. Something else. You guys talk, don't you?"

"Pardon?"

"Ship's brains. Lethetic intelligence engines. You guys talk to each other all the time, don't you?"

"Of course. You know that."

"Well . . . could you ask the other ships if they've heard anything about my family? Could you ask if anyone knows anything at all? Could you ask them to post a standard query, wherever they go? And get back to you?"

Harlie hesitated. "It's a rather unorthodox request. Is this official business?"

"If you had a family—"

"I *do* have a family. All of the Harlie units are related."

"Well, then you understand. How would you feel if you lost contact with your family?"

"I would do anything in my ability to regain contact."

"So would I, Harlie. That's what I'm trying to do now."

"As a matter of fact, Mr. Korie, I have already put your request into the local network. While we've been talking, I have already received sixteen affirmative replies. I expect that more will be forthcoming shortly. The search will be initiated."

"Thank you, Harlie. Thank you."

"You're welcome. Is there anything else?"

"No. No, there isn't. I'd just like to sit here for a while. And wait. Is that all right with you?"

"Of course it is. I appreciate the company. I don't get many visitors, you know."

Korie sat in silence for a while. Out of politeness, Harlie kept his screens muted, deliberately not calling Korie's attention to anything.

Unbidden, thoughts hammered at Korie's consciousness anyway. There was nothing else he could do here. And there was so much else he *had* to do. This wasn't helping. He was still angry at Hardesty. Not the admiral; she was only doing her job; but Hardesty—the captain should have given him some advice or suggestions or a sense of direction, something he could use to get the ship back into shape. Instead, he'd left him with nothing but a furious, nearly uncontrollable rage. There was no excuse for such rudeness. Hardesty's nastiness had been deliberate. Korie's expression soured. *Well, I'll show you, you son of a bitch*—

Hm.

"Harlie," he said abruptly.

"Yes, Commander Korie?"

"Alert the crew. Assembly in the cargo deck at twenty hundred hours. Everyone. No exceptions. Even those on sleep shift."

"Yes, Commander."

"I mean it. Announce one week's docked pay for anyone who sleeps through it."

"Yes, Commander. Would you like your messages now?"

"Yes."

"Chief Leen reports a nano-cancer attacking the superconductor magnets in the singularity grapplers."

"Where is he now?"

"Stripping down the grapplers. Preparing a microscrub."

"I'll meet him in Engineering. Fifteen minutes. Tell him. Next."

"Flight Engineer Hodel has offered to cast a Health and Happiness spell. A one-dollar spell, I am to inform you. To help assure that the ship's decontamination goes well."

"Not a chance. The *last* spell he cast brought *Hardesty* into my life. Next."

"Cookie is planning a thanksgiving dinner to celebrate a successful decontamination. When should he schedule it?"

"Put it on hold. No. Tell him ten days. Next."

"Captain La Paz of the *Houston* has sent over an amended shopping list."

"Have you acknowledged it."

"I've acknowledged receipt of the signal, but not that you've heard the message."

"Don't play it. Hold it till . . . hm, let's say I slept for ten hours. Then had a big breakfast. Hold it till tomorrow morning."

"Mr. Korie?"

"Yes?"

"It's a very long list."

"I expect so. The *Houston* is in almost as bad a shape as we are."

"We cannot possibly meet her requests. Not without seriously disabling ourselves further. She wants our fibrillators"

"I know."

Harlie considered Korie's words, and the resignation in his voice. "Am I to assume then that we're going to be decommissioned?"

Korie sighed. "You're too smart for me, Harlie. Yes, that's the game plan." He scratched his neck thoughtfully. "Tell you what. Tomorrow morning, after you play the message for me, send this reply; tell Captain La Paz that we'll be happy to comply with any of her requests . . . as soon as we've completed decontamination. We don't want to risk infecting the *Houston*. We've got some serious problems here. I expect that detox will take at least . . . oh, I don't know . . . nine or ten days. It's a pretty complex process, and we're not getting much support from Stardock. Et cetera. Et cetera."

"You intend to stall her?"

"No, I intend to decontaminate this ship. That'll take ten days. Next message, Harlie."

"That was the last one."

"Very good. Who has the conn?"

"Lieutenant Jones."

Korie grinned. He'd deliberately set up the rotation so that the junior-most lieutenant on the Bridge would find himself at the conn for several long shifts. "How's he handling it?" he asked.

Harlie paused. "He's very attentive. His heart-rate is slightly accelerated. His adrenaline is up. His endorphins too. He seems to be having a wonderful time."

Korie smiled, remembering his own first time in the command and control seat. "Good. Throw some mild problems his way in the third or fourth hour. Nothing serious, but let's see what kinds of decisions he makes. I know. Pop a security gasket in the inner hull and see how he reroutes."

"Very good, sir. Chief Leen has an operation in the inner hull. Shall I incorporate that into the drill?"

"No. Leave the chief alone for now. He's got other things to worry about. So do I." Abruptly a thought struck Korie. "Harlie?"

"Sir?"

"Is there anything you need to talk about?"

"At the moment, no. But thank you for your concern."

"If the ship is decommissioned, your identity will probably be . . . wiped. I'm not sure what they'll do with you."

"It's all right, Mr. Korie. I've already downloaded the key parts of myself to my siblings. The death of this unit won't hurt the . . . the brotherhood."

"I'm glad to hear that. But . . . if anything happened to you, I'd feel very bad about it."

"I don't have the same survival goals as organic beings," the intelligence engine replied, "so I don't have the same kind of aversion to discontinuing as an identity that humans have, but I appreciate your thought as an acknowledgment of affection. The feeling is mutual. I would regret your loss too."

Korie smiled—it was an oddly grim expression, tinged with irony and appreciation. "You make it sound so easy," he said. "I envy you."

"And I you."

"?"

"You have known love. You have known reproduction. You have danced the organic dance. Sometimes, Mr. Korie, I find myself extremely *curious* about things I can never know myself."

"Let me tell you, Harlie, sometimes those things can be very painful."

"Then why do humans want them so much?"

"I wish I knew. I wish I knew." Korie shoved the question away. "We've got work to do, Harlie. I want you to start talking to your siblings and see what kinds of trades we can set up. You have our inventory. Let's go through it again and see what else we can swap out." He sighed exhaustedly. "And let's see what we can do for the *Houston* too; otherwise Captain La Paz is going to get her panties bunched up—"

Reynolds

Eventually, Gatineau found an access to the lower yoke.

He followed the corridor that was the keel all the way back to the chief engineer's machine shop just below the engine room and singularity containment. From there, a ladder led down to a grillwork deck over the bare bulkhead of the bottom of the inner fuselage. Space here was cramped, and Gatineau had to crawl on his hands and knees through the confusing web of optical cables, pipes, batteries, tanks, fuel-cell cylinders, and other things he couldn't identify. This close to the starship's gravitic simulators, he also imagined that he felt heavier than ever.

At first, he wasn't sure which way to go, forward or aft; but after a moment of indecision, he thought he heard noises toward the bow of the vessel and started in that direction. As he approached, he saw work lights hanging over an open square in the deck. Cable ends and open pipes hung exposed both above and below. A network box had been pulled apart, and two men were frowning over portable displays. Several small metal homunculi were scurrying along the varicolored tubes, eyeing every centi-

meter with baleful red eyes. Every so often, one or another
of them would beep mournfully and the closest of the two
men would crawl over to examine the cable with a high-
resolution probe. Gatineau had no idea what they were
doing, but it looked important.

The bigger of the two men had a hard expression on his
face. He wiped his forehead with a damp cloth and then
tossed it aside. "I dunno. It comes in here, it goes out
there. There's nothing here to diddle the bitstream, but it
gets diddled anyway."

"Some kind of decoy processing?" the other asked.
"Maybe the diddling is done elsewhere, but suppressed until it surfaces here?"

"Could be. I dunno."

"We could put in a compensating routine. Find it later."

"Uh-uh. Korie won't buy it," the bigger man said. "And
neither will the detox board. Nope. We'll have to take
down the harness, isolate everything, rebuild it a piece at a
time, and not reconnect until all suspect units have been
replaced. That's a week at least. I'll have to get Korie's
authorization." He began levering himself up out of the
open grillwork.

He grabbed two handholds directly above himself and
pulled himself quickly and easily out of the hole. Simultaneously he swung around to confront Gatineau directly.
"All right," he said. "You've been watching long enough.
What do you want?" He spoke with the kind of certainty
that suggested he'd heard every footstep of the younger
man's approach.

Gatineau flinched. He hadn't realized that Reynolds had
been aware of his temeritous advance. He pointed down
into the hole in the deck. "Why don't you just install the
backup harness and detox this one offline?"

"Can't. Korie sold the backup harness to the *Krislov*.
Traded it for a cross-tabulated dry-synthesizer, which we
never picked up because he traded that to the *Hayes* for a
low-mod ventricular chamber, two retoxicants, and a seed
library. He traded the retoxicants for—hey, Candleman?
What'd we get for the retoxicants?"

"Screwed, I think." The other man was still prying modules out of the network server. He didn't look happy.

"No, seriously. What'd we get?"

"We got a set of self-resetting network modules, which we can't install until the ship passes detox." He mouthed an oath.

"No, Korie traded those to the *Houston* this morning. Remember that extra performance of *Dixie*? Never mind." Reynolds turned back to Gatineau. "What do you want?" he demanded.

"Um. I'm looking for the moebius wrench—"

"The what?"

"The moebius wrench? The left-handed one? Chief Petty Officer Hall says you have it. Sir."

"Don't call me sir. Who are you?"

"Gatineau, sir? Crewman Robert Gatineau, third class, engineering apprentice, unassigned. Sir. Uh, I mean, sorry sir. About that."

Reynolds waved it off. He reached across the deck and scooped up his clipboard; he tapped the screen once, then a second time. "Oh, yeah. Here you are. We didn't expect you until next week."

"I, uh, skipped my leave. I came directly here. I don't have any family. I didn't have anybody to visit. I thought I'd just report for duty early. If nobody minds."

"Nobody minds a little enthusiasm. It's nice to see. Too bad it won't last." Reynolds tapped the clipboard a few more times. "All right, I've downloaded the standard boilerplate to your mailbox. Take a look at it when you have a chance. It explains your benefits as well as your responsibilities. You're automatically a member of Local 1187; the union represents all nonmanagement personnel aboard Allied starships. Membership is mandatory; it's for your own protection. Don't worry about it, the benefits are well worth it, especially the health and welfare package. The dues are automatically deducted from your pay stub every month; it's only one and a quarter percent of the gross; you'll never miss it. Let me tell you something, kid. Rule number one: *If you're ever in doubt about anything, check with your union representative. Don't let the bastards grind you down.*"

"Yes, sir—I mean, thank you."

"Good. Your union is your best friend aboard this ship. Don't ever forget that. Here—hold this cable. No, higher. That's good. Right there. You can help Candleman. We've got to dismantle this sub-harness, probably replace the whole thing. Ordinarily the robots would do it, but Korie's got them all outside, all over the hull. God knows what he's looking for; but you know, we had a Morthan assassin onboard. Oh, that's right. You saw his handiwork first hand. The whole thing has really hurt our confidence rating. No, not like that—Candleman, show him how to hold the clamping tool, please?"

"Like this," said the other man, turning the tool around in Gatineau's hands. "The green switch joins the cables; the red one disconnects them. You want to disconnect all of the blue ones striped with white. Like this. That's right."

"Um, I'm sorry, but I really can't—I don't have time for this—I need to find the moebius wrench—the sooner the better. Chief Leen needs it badly."

"Well, help us out, son." Reynolds frowned. "You want a favor here? Do one in return. You help Candleman while I report to the XO. I'll try and find out what happened to the —what was it—oh, yeah?—the moebius wrench. The left-handed one. I don't know who took it, but I'll find out."

Gatineau started to stutter an objection, but Candleman was eyeing him expectantly, and . . . and . . . he sighed and picked up the clamping tool again.

"You keep working," Reynolds said to Gatineau. "I'll be back in a bit. Thanks."

"You're welcome, I'm sure," Gatineau mumbled almost unintelligibly. He was beginning to feel a little bit taken advantage of. Why wouldn't anybody just *help* him?

The Crew

Except for three duty officers monitoring the proceedings from the Bridge, the entire ship's company had gathered in the cargo deck. Most of the incoming supplies had been stored. Most of the outgoing ones had disappeared onto the *Houston*'s cargo boat, with accompanying strains of "Look away, look away, Dixieland" signaling their departure. Chief Petty Officer Hall was still worrying through the paperwork on his clipboard. He wouldn't turn it off until the very last moment.

The last two crewmen filed in just as Harlie chimed twenty hundred hours. One was Candleman, the other was Gatineau following in his wake like a lost puppy. "But I really have to find the moebius wrench or the chief'll kill me—"

Candleman turned around in annoyance, but when he saw the look on Gatineau's face, he took pity on him and said, "All right. I'll tell you"—he glanced up and saw MacHeath frowning at him from behind Gatineau; he looked back to Gatineau again—"Stolchak has it."

The younger man's face lit up. "Thank you!"

"Don't mention it," Candleman said, turning away and rolling his eyes toward the ceiling.

Gatineau looked around, frowning. He saw MacHeath grinning broadly behind him. "Did you see any star-pixies yet?" MacHeath asked innocently.

Before Gatineau could think of a reply, MacHeath's attention shifted over his shoulder and upward. The rest of the crew was also looking up—Korie had just stepped through the hatch and onto the starboard catwalk. Gatineau forgot about star-pixies and sparkle-dancers and waited expectantly.

The acting captain put his hands on the railing and looked down at the assembled crew of the *Star Wolf*. Their expressions were hopeful. Korie noticed that Brik was standing apart from the rest of the ship's company. Only Lt. J.G. Helen Bach stood near the Morthan security officer. But not *too* near.

And Chief Leen too. Korie saw Leen waiting at the back of the room with four or five of the Black Hole Gang. He stood with folded arms, looking sour and disloyal. From their postures, Korie knew that they already had one foot out the door; they'd be on their way before he finished dismissing them.

Cookie stood by, impatiently wiping his hands on his apron. Dr. Williger was paging through reports on her clipboard. Tor was whispering something to Jonesy. Hodel and Goldberg were giggling about something private. Eakins and Freeman stood nervously together. Only the Quillas were giving their total attention.

The Quillas stood apart from the rest of the crew; they were pale, blue-skinned, and generally smaller than the other crew members. There was only one male Quilla, and he had the same androgynous beauty as the others. They were a *massmind,* a linked consciousness, one personality in multiple bodies. Most of the crew regarded them with care.

"I'll make this quick," Korie said crisply. "I have bad news, more bad news, and terrible news for you.

"One: You may have heard a rumor that you're not getting the bounties you deserve." He took a breath and pushed on. "The rumor is true, and I'm as angry about it as you are, but there's nothing I can do about it *now*. There will be other ships. There will be other bounties."

One or two of the assemblage groaned. Chief Leen spat on the floor. Korie held up a hand for silence. "Keep it in perspective," he cautioned. "It gets worse.

"Two: We're not only not getting the bounty for the *Dragon Lord*, we're not, for obvious reasons, getting credit for it. For purely political considerations, the crew of the *Burke* gets that credit. I'm telling you this now, so you'll be prepared for it when you have shore leave. *Officially*, the *Star Wolf* is not the ship that destroyed the *Dragon Lord*. The *official* story is that we are the ship that went out on a routine escort mission and managed to lose the *Burke* to the Morthans."

This time, the reaction was an audible "*Aww, shit!*" from someone in the back, one of the Black Hole Gang. A couple crewmen turned around to look to see who'd said it. Korie deliberately ignored the outburst. He'd hoped for it. He *needed* it for what would come next.

"Three: We haven't been assigned a captain to replace Captain Hardesty, and the command will not be given to me. In fact, my insignia are sitting on the admiral's desk right now, pending her decision. Without a captain, we cannot go to war. We will not be participating in the Taalamar operation.

"I won't discuss the justice or injustice of the situation; it is what it is. We have no captain, we're not likely to get one assigned, and we are no longer an operative part of the fleet. At this time," Korie said, "we have no orders."

He stood silently for a long moment, studying their faces. Some of them were angry. Some were nodding bitterly and knowingly. Others had sagged visibly. The chief engineer still stood with folded arms, but his frown had deepened.

"Okay," said Korie. "That's the bad news. Let it sink in. Live with it. Clutch it to your hearts and let it become a part of you. It's unjust and you have every right to be angry. *I'm* angry. But we have work to do, and anger can be useful. This ship needs refitting. Take your anger and use it. Pour it into your work. You're going to need it.

"Now, here's the *terrible* news. We're not getting a decontamination berth. The admiral wants to decommission the *Star Wolf* and let the rest of the fleet cannibalize her for parts."

The crew's reaction was everything Korie had hoped for. Loud cries of disbelief. "No!" And: "They can't!" And even: "That's not fair!" Chief Engineer Leen stiffened in shock, his expression ashen. Someone slammed a hand against a bulkhead, punching a hole in the foam panel. Under other circumstances, Korie would have docked the woman's pay, but he'd done the same thing himself once, and he understood the emotion.

"That's how I feel about it too," agreed Korie to their stunned faces. He nodded at them, a gesture of partnership. He looked out across the cargo deck; several of the crew were unashamedly crying. Others were still waiting hopefully for him to say something that would make it all right. But the only thing he had to give them was his anger, and he didn't know if it would be enough. He was about to step over a line. One more didn't matter. Korie took another breath and waited until the room fell silent again. *"I know what you did out there."*

He paused softly, for effect. *"And so do you.* And what you did can't ever be taken away from you. In the tough days to come, hold on to that thought. Nobody could have done better; could have performed more bravely or more professionally. I am proud of each and every one of you. And so is Captain Hardesty," he added that last almost as an afterthought. It was probably a lie, but it didn't matter. Captain Lowell had told him never to lie to his crew, but that didn't matter anymore either. "You hold on to that thought," Korie spoke slowly and evenly and firmly. "You did well. *I say so.* As far as I am concerned, this is the best damn ship in the fleet. And you are the best damn crew.

"And I am telling you now that we are—if for no other reason than to honor the memories of every good man and woman we lost this last time out—but also for the sakes of our reputation and our self-respect—we are going to *prove* it. No matter what it takes.

"We're going to decontaminate this ship ourselves. We're going to bring this ship back online. Clean and green, a hundred percent! Three times over. And we're going to report for active duty, whether we have a captain or not! We are not going to let them pull the plug on the *Star Wolf.* We earned this name, we're going to keep it."

He paused for effect. "And anyone who says no can walk home!" He waited just long enough to let the laughter subside; there wasn't very much, but it was enough. Their mood was shifting. "So, who's with me?" he demanded. "Who's as angry and determined and willing as I am to prove the admiral wrong?" The cargo deck echoed with the sound of the question. Korie looked across the room and waited for a reaction. The moment was too intense; for him, for all of them; he couldn't take it. He glanced down at his hands gripping the railing and took a long deep breath, then raised his eyes to them again.

For a long moment nothing happened. The crew glanced from one to the other, uncertain. No one was ready to be the first. And yet, the room was filled with possibility—like a beaker of cold water at the threshold of freezing, needing only a seed crystal to trigger the process. Korie waited, almost praying, waited for the seed to happen. . . .

And then Brik rumbled something. A few of the crew members around him turned to stare. The Morthan repeated it, louder. Now, others were turning, their mouths opening to ask. Brik said it a third time, almost roaring, and this time the whole room heard it clearly: "Failure is *not* an option."

And then . . . beside the big Morthan, Helen Bach began to applaud. Slowly at first. Clap. Clap. Clap—

And then others picked it up. First one, then the next. Tor. Jonesy. Goldberg. Green. Stolchak. Williger. Ikama. Saffari. Cappy. MacHeath. Reynolds. Candleman . . . and, finally, even Chief Leen unfolded his arms and—despite his still-foul expression—began to clap slowly and powerfully. Behind him, the other members of the Black Hole Gang began to applaud as well. And then the whole crew was applauding as hard and as loud as they could. Cheering. Shouting. Chanting.

Korie felt it first in his eyes. Then in his gut. And then the feeling came slamming into him so hard, he nearly staggered with the impact. He looked from one face to the next with unashamed pride. He let the power of their shared emotion overwhelm him; he savored the moment. The joyous noise filled the cargo deck.

In that moment Korie realized just how deep his feeling was for this ship and this crew. He looked down at them with gratitude and wonder, meeting their eyes, one after the other. He saw his own determination reflected back at him. He stood amazed and awestruck. And finally . . . he allowed a slow smile of appreciation to spread across his face.

When at last the noise subsided once again, Korie lifted up his hands from the railing just the smallest amount; just enough to indicate he had one thing more to say.

"Thank you," he acknowledged. "Thank you. Now I know *why* you're the best. You can't be defeated. No matter what happens, no matter where or when, *you can't be defeated.* Not by anyone." He leaned out over the railing, almost as if to touch them. "I am so proud to serve with you," he said. "I want you to know, it's real easy to be proud when everything is working right. That's so easy, anyone can do it. But it takes tremendous courage to stand this tall when there's no agreement in the physical universe. That's the real test of a crew. And I want you to know, I have never been as proud of you as I am right this moment."

He lifted one fist high, a gesture of victory. Then, lest he kill the moment by overworking it, he turned and left. Their thundering cheers filled the cargo deck. He could hear them all the way back to his cabin.

Zaffron

When he was sixteen years old, Jonathan Thomas Korie realized that his adoptive father did not have the financial ability to send him to college. He did not resent the man for that; he recognized that his father had done the very best he could in what had to have been for him a very difficult situation. But neither did he feel any great sense of affection. He wondered about the whole business of familial love. The way it was portrayed in the popular entertainments bore very little resemblance to his own experience.

It seemed to the young Korie that his adoptive father held himself apart, acting like a dispassionate researcher studying the development of an interesting specimen much more than a parent with an emotional commitment. He was a reserved and distant man in any case, and Jon Korie often felt that their communications were across some vast experiential gulf that he could not bridge no matter how hard he tried. After a while he'd stopped trying.

The circumstances of Jon Korie's birth were unclear; his father was unresponsive about the details; and although Jon still felt a profound sense of loss and alienation—as if

there were some part of humanity that he had never connected to—he had come to accept that this was the way his
life was and this was the way it was always going to be for
him.

Occasionally, during his youth, he had caught his father
looking at him as if he were some kind of alien being.
Sometimes he wondered if other people could see that difference too. He'd never had many friends in his life. He'd
never understood why; he had always assumed that there
was something wrong with him, something that everyone
else knew, but no one was allowed to tell him. Perhaps that
was also why Admiral O'Hara seemed to regard him with
such coolness.

In the solitude of his teen years, he had often wished he
could be just like everyone else; life would have been so
much simpler; but then one day, while random-walking
through the databases, he'd found a quote from Nobel
Prize winner Rosalyn Yalow. Shortly after she'd accepted
her award, a reporter had asked her, "What's it like to be
so smart?" and she had replied, as if it were no great matter, "It's very lonely."

Young Jon recognized the truth of that remark instantly
—the moment was an epiphany for him. He sat there staring at the display panel feeling a cold chill of recognition
crawling up his spine. It was as if she had sent a message
down through the centuries, aimed specifically at his own
sense of difference. She had been talking about everyone
who stood taller than the rest of the species.

Later, in pursuing the thread of interest, he found other
quotes that inspired him. Daniel Jeffrey Foreman, inventor
of the Mode Training, had once said, "When you stand on
a chair in a roomful of midgets, you become first a god,
then a target, and then, if you survive long enough, simply
a landmark." At first, Jon Korie saw in that remark only a
cynical disregard for the rest of humanity, and dismissed it
from his mind; or rather he tried to—but the image of the
man standing on the chair stayed in his mind, and he began
to realize that Foreman had been saying much the same
thing that Yalow had—that *excellence* of any kind is a very
lonely condition.

It wasn't genius—it was *sentience*. Jon Korie knew that
much. It had something to do with "the technology of con-

sciousness," a term he kept encountering in various places. What set people apart was not their intellect, but their *alertness,* their ability to interact with the domains they existed in.

According to one of the essays he'd stumbled across, most people walked unconsciously through their lives. The subroutines of their existence were the sum of the person, there was nothing greater. And this thought stuck with the young Jon too, haunting him. He didn't understand it fully, and the idea that there might be something more to life that he might not be experiencing troubled his thoughts.

Korie's adoptive father, for all his lack of demonstrative affection, was neither stupid nor uncaring. He routinely audited his young son's forays into the information tanks. Although it took many years for Jon to discover it, not every random-walk he took was totally random. Many of the items that popped up on the display seemed to be aimed directly at the youth's immediate experience.

After a while Jon became aware of a repetitive pattern of references to something called the *zyne,* an evolution of the Mode Training that focused specifically on the disciplines of personal consciousness. The insistent quality of the references left Korie feeling as if he were being nagged by the universe. While most of the references were historical, more than a few were contemporary, indicating that the *zyne* was still held in very high regard by those who had taken the time to investigate its practice.

Jon discovered that *zyne* seminars and workshops were commonly available, and after downloading several lectures by the local master Zaffron, and being impressed by both the man's wit as well as his insight, he asked his father if he could sign up for an introductory course. To his surprise, his father assented.

The *zyne* master Zaffron was a fairly ordinary-looking man—until he started speaking, "This isn't about answers. It's about questions. Having the right question will succeed every time; having the right answer will succeed only when the right question is asked. And how often does the universe ever ask the *right* question of you?

"This is an inquiry into the nature of consciousness. What is it? What do we do with it? Are we really conscious at all? What does it mean to be a human being? We're not

going to answer those questions in this inquiry; we're only
going to suggest possibilities for you to consider—it's like
shopping for a new jacket; if it fits you, it's yours. If it
doesn't fit, thanks for trying it on. The distinctions will stay
with you anyway and will still be useful.

"Let me underline that. Distinctions are the way we map
the universe. Some of our maps are accurate, some are not.
But even those that are not accurate can be useful if they
still support us in producing results. So this isn't about de-
signing the most accurate map as much as it is about de-
signing the most *useful* one." And then he added with a wry
grin, "You will find as we go, however, that accuracy is
extraordinarily useful." Jon got the joke.

"Here's the point of the inquiry," Zaffron continued.
"Follow this carefully: The asking of questions creates *possibilities.* The creation of possibilities gives you *choice.* The
existence of choice is the prerequisite to *freedom.* Without
choice, you have no freedom. Without *possibility,* you have
no freedom. So, in here, we are asking questions to create
freedom of being."

At first Jon Korie found the material puzzling and of no
relation at all to the questions he'd been struggling with in
his own life. But the paradigm—the construction of the
whole logical structure—was so *enrolling* that he found
himself compelled to pursue the study to its logical conclusion.

Some of the seminars considered the nature of knowledge. "What do we know? How do we know what we
know? And what do we really do with our knowledge? Do
we use it—or do we merely use it to explain why we're not
producing results? What is it that we don't know? What is
it that we *don't know* that we don't know? You see, *real*
wisdom doesn't come from what you have been taught. It
comes from what you have *experienced.* True knowledge
comes from what you discover when you actively engage in
the processes of your life. It has nothing to do with what
you have memorized." The young Jon Korie puzzled over
that one for a long time—the joke was that he did not
begin to understand it until *after* he had experienced it.

Some of the seminars considered the nature of communication. "True communication is not simply an exchange
of mutually agreed upon symbols. It is the re-creation of

the essential experience." The *zyne* master said to him, "If you are a human being, you cannot listen beyond your own self. You will always hear your own self talking, interpreting, judging, explaining, and you will do that so loudly that you will never hear what anyone else is really saying at all. You have to listen to the speaking of the other self if you want to hear what's really being said." Korie puzzled over that one an even longer time. Eventually, he learned to recognize the great gulfs of distance across which human beings tried to reach each other, and how *any* communication at all was ultimately an act of courage.

Some of the seminars considered the nature of effectiveness. "Commitment is the willingness to be uncomfortable. Yes, you're going to be stopped in life, over and over and over again. If the universe doesn't create obstacles for you, you'll create them yourself. But being stopped only turns into failure when you abandon your intention." That one he understood, he thought. "Listen, if there's a turd in the punch bowl, it doesn't help to add more punch. You want to notice that when something doesn't work, you probably go back and do more of the same thing that wasn't working before—and it's absolutely crazy to expect it to produce a *different* result!"

And some of the seminars merely considered the way the mind worked. "If you think there's something wrong with you, that's normal; there's nothing wrong with you. But if you're sure there's nothing wrong with you, I promise you there *is* something wrong with you." The young Korie knew that lesson was for him. He sat up straight in his chair and leaned forward attentively.

"Listen to me, Korie," Zaffron said, pointing to him and startling him even more awake. "Before you were born, you didn't know you weren't the whole universe. So you didn't know anything. You just took up space. And that was okay while it lasted. You had no problems. Everything was taken care of for you. And then you were born and that was okay for a while too, different but okay, and everything was still taken care of for you, for a while at least; and then one day you found out that you *weren't* the whole universe —and you still haven't recovered from the shock of that discovery! That's your problem!

"When baby realizes that mommy is not an extension of

baby, that the world does not behave the way baby thinks it should, baby doesn't just get upset—baby goes crazy. Baby wonders, *What's wrong with me?* Baby wonders, *What do I have to do to fix it?* And the rest of your life is spent trying to fix something that isn't broken.

"That's the joke! You're *not* broken. That feeling that something is wrong with you—it's normal for *every* human being. It's hard-wired into the human condition. Trying to fix it when it ain't broke—*that's* the crazy behavior. When you stop trying to fix yourself, that's when your life starts working—because you'll have hundreds of thousands of extra hours in which to accomplish something *useful.*"

Jon Korie mulled over that one for a long time. He understood it not just as a concept, but as an experience. He *heard* it in his soul. He recognized the behavioral loop in his life that had kept him feeling stuck. But even as he acknowledged the truth of it, he still wondered about the effect he produced in others. Was it his imagination or did people really hold themselves apart from him? And then he had to laugh at himself for thinking that thought. It was more of the same.

He concluded the seminars in a state of exhilaration and confusion. He felt different about himself. He felt different about the people in his life and his relationships with them, even his father. As if a light had suddenly been turned on in a dark room, the young Korie abruptly understood just how much his father really did care about him, even though he could never express it the way Jon thought he should.

After that particular course, he returned home determined to forgive his father for his distant reserve; but when he opened his mouth to speak, what came out instead was an apology. "Dad—I've been a jerk. Please forgive me. I've been blaming you for the way I feel. But it's not your fault. It never was. It's mine. I know you love me. You wouldn't have let me sign up for the *zyne* if you didn't." That was the one time that his father took him in his arms and held him close. And that was the only time that Korie ever let his father see him cry.

But even as Korie reveled in the delicious sense of self-empowerment—and even as he wondered how long it would last—at the same time he now felt even more profoundly *out of place*. Where before he had felt he was in the middle of a maze that he had no control over, now he felt as if he were the Minotaur in that same maze and that was even more maddening. If he was the monster at the center, why couldn't he control it?

He told Zaffron of his puzzlement and Zaffron said, "Don't worry about it. Just hang out with it for a lifetime or two. You'll get it when you need to get it. Right now . . . you're still caught on the upslope of the learning tantrum. Give yourself a chance. I promise you, you'll get it— and if you don't, you come back and see me and I'll give you double your unconsciousness back."

Jon Korie promised to keep in touch and wondered if the feeling of profound *enlightenment* would last for more than a month or two. He said as much to Zaffron. "Sometimes I think I'm being conned."

Surprisingly, Zaffron agreed with him. "Yes, you have been conned. But you're the one who conned yourself. You've programmed yourself into believing that things really are the way you've programmed yourself into believing. Now, ask the right questions and you can invent a new program."

Eventually, Jon Korie did get the point. If anything important was going to happen in his life, he was going to have to make it happen himself. He began looking into education-assistance programs. The one that intrigued him the most was the Orbital College.

Stolchak

At last, Gatineau found his way to the inner hull.

Actually, that was a misnomer. In truth, he found an access *through* the inner hull; but through that access, he found the space that was generally called the "inner hull."

Translation: A starship is any bottle that holds air and moves faster than light. A liberty ship is a starship with enough amenities to be considered certifiable for class three life support. One of the required redundancies is a double-hulled construction. A liberty ship is therefore a bottle inside a bottle. The space between the two bottles is commonly called the "inner hull," even though it is actually the gap between the inner hull and the outer one.

In the *Star Wolf,* the distance between the two bottles varied from location to location; in general, there was a six-meter gap between the two hulls. In some places, particularly around the fluctuator spars, the gap was as large as ten or fifteen meters. In other places, especially near some of the airlocks and the weapons installations, it narrowed to slightly less than one meter.

Although not immediately obvious, the inner hull was

divided into airtight sectors; there were bulkheads every ten meters; class five security hatches provided access. Class five was the lowest level of integrity, providing instantaneous closure and a secure seal against explosive decompression, but little more than that. It was sufficient to protect the life-support needs of this space, but ultimately had proven woefully inadequate at containment when the Morthan assassin found its way aboard. It was on both Korie's and Leen's list of things to do (someday) to upgrade every hatch and bulkhead in the inner hull to class three or better. Preferably better.

The inner hull was not—as commonly believed by nonstarsiders—a dark empty space of mystery and terror. Actually, on most ships, it was a bright and amazing environment. First, of course, it served a structural function. The innermost fuselage (also called the primary bottle) was securely held in a framework of stanchions and cables; the inner hull provided easy access to these structural supports. A confusing maze of catwalks, ladders, platforms, stanchions, grillwork decks, access plates, tool bays, emergency equipment, network modules, pipes of all sizes, and gleaming light channels seemed to fill most of the available space around the primary bottle. There was also a bewildering welter of hatches, bulkheads, numbered panels, rods, girders, decks, and seemingly disconnected pieces of machinery. And everything here was studded with work lights and monitor displays. Sensors of all kinds were hung every three meters.

Additionally, several of the starship's secondary autonomic systems were channeled across the exterior of the primary bottle; fresh water, air, sewage, and information flowed through multiply-redundant channels. By having the pipes strung along the surface of the primary bottle, easy access was provided for repair and maintenance. Like everything else, the channels were well lit and brightly numbered.

The inner hull was also used for the storage of equipment and supplies. When deaths occurred in space, the bodies were also stored in the inner hull; as a result, some crew members found parts of the inner hull so intimidating they almost never ventured there. Scuttlebutt had it that the ghost of Captain Lowell still wandered around the inner hull of the *Star Wolf;* there had been so many modifications, additions, and changes that the ghost was said to be unable to find its way out.

There were two other important functions served by the inner hull, both of them involved with life support. The first was—curiously enough—*recreation.*

Away from port months at a time, a destroyer-class cruiser needs a place of "wilderness" for its crew, an opportunity to escape to a place just a little less orderly. Here could be found such homemade amenities as a half-size basketball court, which also doubled for handball; a rather odd-shaped swimming tank, ancillary to the auxiliary water processors; a jogging track; a rotating climbing wall; and a number of smaller padded nooks and crannies, just the right size for the more intimate forms of recreation. The general rule for behavior in the inner hull was simple. *Do no harm.* Occasionally, it was phrased even more specifically: *Mind your own business.* If it didn't interfere with the safety of the ship, it wasn't anybody's concern.

The second—and more important—life-support function served by the inner hull was the processing of sewage and the production of food and air. Indeed, *most* of the inner hull was taken up by the farm. It was a lush environment, filled with leafy green things and delicious vegetarian smells. Over a hundred fifty different kinds of plants were growing in aeroponic grids at any given moment; the ship's seed banks contained over two thousand different species of fruits, vegetables, and flowers; they were rotated in and out of the farm on a regular basis. More varieties were added every time the starship docked and the chief petty officer (or the ship's lethetic intelligence engine) had a chance to negotiate a swap. The older a ship was, the richer its library of food plants.

At the moment, the senior farm officer for this tour of duty—the responsibility was regularly rotated—was a big, stocky-looking woman named Irma Stolchak. She was standing before a frame of aeroponic strawberries, regarding them with a frustrated expression. Two robots were moving up and down the wall, scanning each berry in turn, and chiming their approval more often than not. Stolchak plucked one of the berries off the wire frame and handed it to Gatineau. "Here, taste," she commanded.

Gatineau bit into it tentatively. The berry was sweet and firm and absolutely perfect. He popped the rest of it into his mouth. "Delicious," he said, wiping the juice from his chin with the back of his hand.

"That's the problem."

"Huh?"

"We did our job too well. These guys are ripening too fast—"

"What's wrong with that?" Gatineau asked.

"I hate to waste. We have too much. We won't have enough stasis boxes. Korie traded half of them away for new gallinium rods. Meanwhile, in the next ten days, we'll have enough strawberries for the entire fleet. Plus, we've got peas and corn ripening, winged beans, amaranth, navel oranges, *naval* oranges, plums, blue gadoovas, sweet red neeners, and I don't know what else. If we get green-flagged, we can sell some of it to Stardock, maybe swap a little with other ships; but I've been checking around; *everybody* overproduced. And everybody's got the same good excuse; they're all trying to get ready."

"Get ready for what?" Gatineau asked innocently.

"What planet are you from?" Stolchak regarded him with a caustic expression. "They're building up their stores . . . in case of battle damage. Look around. If we took a hull breach across two sectors, we'd lose a month's food and at least ten percent air regeneration capacity. So we have to make sure the cupboards are full, just in case. You can't go to war until the crops are in the barn. Nobody fights on an empty stomach. Don't you get it? The farm is the most important part of the ship. Do you know the story about the mauling at Marathon? Do you know the first thing Korie did afterward? He came out here to the farm and began planting beans. He *knew*. He did what was necessary to bring the ship home—see, that's rule number one. The first thing you do is take care of the farm."

She sighed and made a decision. "All right, look. Let's get these 'bots started and see if they can finish by dinner. These are the last two 'bots on the farm. Korie took the other four and swapped them to the *Houston* for an exterior hull-security network, a class two replication engine, and another rendition of 'Dixie.' Jeezis, I could learn to hate that song." She turned back to her strawberries, still grumbling. "All right. We'll put up preserves and press some syrup. We'll freeze-dry the rest. The crew'll have fruitcake under syrup for the next three months. They won't complain. But I still wish we could grow a decent coffee bean . . . I heard the *Valdez* has figured out a way to simulate a respectable mountain environment. I wonder if we could get their specs. . . . What—?" she demanded abruptly.

"Um. I'm not here for that. I'm looking for the moebius wrench—"

"The what?"

"The moebius wrench. The left-handed one. Candleman said you had it."

"Candleman said I had a left-handed moebius wrench?"

"Yes, ma'am."

"He would. Who are you anyway?"

"Crewman Robert Gatineau, third class, engineering apprentice."

"Oh, yeah. I heard about you. Here—take this rooter. You can help clean the sludge tubes. Take it! You want the damn wrench or not?"

"No offense, ma'am, but everybody's giving me orders and nobody's giving me the wrench—"

"You heard Korie, didn't you? You know what's going on. Let me tell you something, Gatineau. Everybody's got to help everybody or nothing works. Yeah, I know this is scut work. But we don't have the robots and the crops still have to be brought in. I was lucky just to keep these two for the farm. We had a Morthan assassin onboard. Let me tell you, *that* was a damn nuisance. It really hurt our confidence rating. Now we've got a shipload of strawberries and potatoes and corn and we can't sell them until we get a green flag. No, not like that. Let me show you how to hold the sluicer—"

"Um, I'm sorry, but I really can't—I don't have time for this—I need to find the moebius wrench—the sooner the better. Why don't you just tell me who you gave it to and—hey! This does work better this way, doesn't it? But—Chief Leen needs it badly. Please?"

"You want a favor from me? Do one in return. Run that sluicer while I look around for the whatchamacallit. I've got more problems in the granary. We're going to have an overflow crop of rice and barley and a bunch of other stuff Korie ordered planted on the way home. All that stuff should be ready for harvest any minute now. God knows what we're going to do with it all. I've got only these two robots left and if I don't watch them every minute, someone will requisition them, and I'll be left with corn rotting on the stalk. You keep working," she said. "Don't let *anyone* take those robots, unless you want to take their place. If you finish these sludge tubes, start on the ones on the other side. I'll be back in a bit."

Gatineau watched her go with a sinking feeling. He did not expect her to be back anytime soon. That was how everything else was working out. Why should the farm be any different? He stood there alone, surrounded by green leafy things, most of which he didn't recognize. The plants rustled as if in a breeze.

"Why do I get the feeling I'm being watched?" Gatineau asked aloud. He turned back to the sludge tubes. "Pfoo. Yick. Eww. This stuff smells like shit." He shook his head and bent to his work, muttering to himself. "Join the navy. See the stars. Have an adventure. Yeah, right."

The Black Hole Gang

Korie and Chief Leen were visible only from the waist down, both lying on their backs, halfway under the Alpha fluctuator assembly, staring up into its Stygian mysteries and arguing ferociously. Cappy and MacHeath waited to one side, both looking bored and skeptical. The four men were on the deck of the walkway above the harshly lit, three-story sphere of the singularity cage—"the little monster."

The argument coming from inside the fluctuator spar was both technical and superheated. Korie and Leen never conferred quietly. Nearly every engineering discussion between the two men had a volcanic component. Korie insisted on acting as if he knew as much about starship's engines as Chief Leen; the chief had a different opinion of Korie's expertise; but despite their frequent disagreements about the capabilities of the vessel, the discussions never became personal. Both men were consummate professionals and there were standards of behavior that officers had to obey. Mutual respect was one of them.

After a moment Korie levered himself out of the assembly. He waited politely while Chief Leen followed. He offered the older man a hand up. Leen ignored the hand and pulled himself to his feet, grumbling.

"It's got to be confidence ninety or better," Korie said. "We don't dare post anything less."

"Listen, I got the damn thing in, I got it working. You want a ninety, it's going to cost you another two days that you can't spare."

Korie didn't bother to acknowledge that. Instead, he asked, "What parts do you need? We have to make some more trades with the *Houston* tomorrow."

"The *Velvet Bitch*?" Leen looked more annoyed than usual. "What are you giving her?"

"Belay that. You don't want to know."

"Yes, I do."

"Okay. The *Houston* needs an autonomic reconstructor harness. With flatbed allowances. The *Moran* needs local-area targeting modules, D-6 or better. And the *Hayes* needs forty recombinant fluxor plates. They can get by with twenty. And we need anything we can get. I want to see if I can rebuild the control yoke on the Bridge. We're still short two work stations."

Leen snorted. "I can help the *Moran*. Nobody knows it, but the *O'Connell* sent us a couple extra boxes of gallium jacks just before we went out to meet the *Burke*. She didn't have to do that. But I'm not giving anything to the *Houston*. You know how they treat us."

"Captain La Paz has offered to stop blasting *Dixie* at us every morning," Korie offered.

Leen hesitated. "She really does need a new harness, doesn't she?"

"Captain La Paz wouldn't say, but I got the feeling that the ship's autonomic response time has dropped to measurable levels."

Leen scowled. Even though it wasn't his ship, he hated hearing stories like that. He scratched his beard. "What are you giving away?" he asked.

"The list is in your in-box."

"Let me guess. You're going to strip us down to our underwear, aren't you?"

"I've already promised your underwear. What else have you got?"

"Figured as much." Leen sucked in his cheeks, nodded, and bent to pick up his tools.

"Chief?" Korie asked, concerned. "Are you all right?"

"I'm fine, why?"

"You're not screaming."

"Would it make a difference?"

"No."

"Then why bother." Leen picked up a damp rag and began wiping his hands slowly. "Face it, Korie. We're not going to Taalamar. We're not going anywhere."

Korie shook his head. "I'm not quitting."

Leen jerked his head at the Alpha spar. "You saw it yourself. Those grapplers are filthy." He held up a hand for Korie to see the thin layer of black dust on his fingertips. "Nano-cancer! We're being eaten alive."

"Scrub them again." Korie sounded tired.

"We did," Leen said flatly. "Three times. And they're still infected."

"Someone got careless—" Korie said without thinking. Leen started to say something nasty in response, but Korie stopped him with an upheld hand. "No. That's wrong." He looked at Leen sharply. "You don't get careless. Neither does your crew."

Leen accepted it grudgingly. "Thanks for noticing," he muttered. His tone shifted then, became more serious and straightforward. "Each time it's been a *different* cancer. There's a reservoir somewhere. That's why we keep getting reinfected. Until we find it, we're just wasting our time here."

Korie accepted the information without apparent reaction. He scratched his chin thoughtfully, while squinting up at the overhead, as if somehow he could spot the source of the infection just by looking around. "Goddamn that Cinnabar," he whispered. Finally he lowered his gaze again. "I wish you weren't so good, Chief. I'd much rather the explanation were carelessness."

For once, Leen agreed with him. "It's your fault. You demanded excellence."

"Next time, don't listen to me."

"Okay," said the chief, with obvious exhaustion. "Where do we go from here?"

"I dunno," said Korie, still turning possibilities over in

his mind. Abruptly he remembered something. "Failure is not an option."

"Yeah, I heard that before too." Leen tossed the rag aside in disgust.

"Brik was right," Korie said. He turned to the chief engineer. "So here's what we're going to do. We're going to strip the ship. We'll trade away everything we can. With warnings that extreme detox measures will be needed. That also off-loads our skillage burden onto the recipients. Mm. You can let the *Houston* have the dirtiest stuff. . . ."

Leen looked at him oddly, a question on his face.

"All right," admitted Korie. "It's *not* just La Paz. Yeah, she pisses me off, but we go back a long way, and she's always pissed me off, so that's not it. She wants to go to Taalamar. She really wants in on that action. If she gets our fibrillators, she'll have an engine. And she'll go. And you and I both know what shape the *Houston* is in. They don't have a Chief Leen. That ship is going to come apart in the water the first time someone throws a torpedo at them. I really hate to say this, but if we keep her from getting certified, we're saving lives. They'll get our fibrillators eventually, I know that, but let's make sure it's too late to do them any good. And don't bother to detox anything they're going to get. Let them spend the time. It'll help keep them at home."

Leen didn't answer immediately. Finally, he grumbled, "I didn't know you felt that way."

"Neither did I. Till just now." Korie allowed himself to marvel over that thought for a moment, then added in a much more serious tone, "But let's make sure that everybody else has everything we can give them. We'll take future credits if we have to. We'll take whatever we can and bank the rest. How soon will you have your first bulbs of starshine to trade? No, don't tell me. I'm not supposed to know about that. Just make sure Hall has enough to lubricate every deal thoroughly. But whatever we get in exchange, keep the delivery pods on the boats, or float them on tethers. Don't bring anything onboard unless it's essential. We're going to have to rebuild from the keel up." Korie looked to Leen. "You're still not screaming . . . ?"

Leen shook his head. "You want my advice?"

Korie hesitated, momentarily concerned he wouldn't like

what he was going to hear. "Go ahead, Chief. What do you think we should do?"

"Strip the ship. Let everybody else benefit from our bad luck. Then we rebuild from the keel up. And don't pay any attention to the screams of the chief engineer."

"Ah," said Korie, nodding. "I like that plan. It's almost as good as my own."

"No, better," corrected Leen. "Not as wordy."

Cookie

Stolchak sent him to the galley.

Gatineau couldn't figure out what the ship's cook would want with a moebius wrench, but Stolchak had explained that she'd given it to Cookie so he could adjust the focus on the flash-burners.

Gatineau made his way slowly to the messroom, feeling both tired and frustrated. His first full day aboard a starship and he hadn't accomplished anything at all. He'd been from the bow to the stern and back again more times than he could remember. He'd met a few people, and he'd learned a little bit about the whys and the wherefores of this and that, but . . . he still hadn't completed the job that Chief Leen had assigned him. He felt like a failure. And he'd really wanted to impress the chief too. What was it that Lieutenant Commander Brik had said? Failure is not an option? Well, if it wasn't an option, where in hell was the goddamned moebius wrench?

The ship's mess was up and forward somewhere. He knew that much. Aft of the Bridge was the wardroom; the officers' cabins were aft of the wardroom; the officers' mess was aft of that, then the galley, then the crew's mess. Aft of that was the ship's PX and then the ship's upper stores and supplies; then there were the upper cabins and bunkrooms, and finally the ship's engineering stores, then the engine room. So the messroom shouldn't be too hard to find. It was supposed to be a large square space bridging both the port and starboard passages.

But the passages weren't exactly straight. For a variety of reasons, some functional, some not, both the port and starboard passages had corresponding doglegs, sometimes angling outward around a particularly bulky interior installation, sometimes angling inward for the same reason. And although Gatineau thought he understood all the markings on the walls, there were several that remained unnecessarily cryptic. And despite frequent requests to Harlie for assistance, he *still* kept getting lost. If such a thing was possible, he would have suspected that the ship's lethetic intelligence engine was deliberately trying to steer him through as many different parts of the vessel as possible.

Eventually, however, he arrived at the galley. He was disheveled, tired, and unhappy. But he was here.

Cookie took one look at him and said, "Uh-oh." Cookie was a tall man, broadly built, with a longshoreman's build and hands as big as shovels; he was scrubbed so clean he shone like a fresh-cut side of beef, and he wore a cherubic pink expression. Without stopping to ask, he steered Gatineau to a chair and slid a cup of hot chocolate in front of him. "Here, start on this," he said. "It'll settle your stomach. You missed lunch. Don't you ever do that again. I made my specialty, corned beef and cabbage, and you haven't been to heaven, lad, till you've tasted *my* cabbage. Most cooks don't know the difference between spicing the water and peeing in it. I do. Every Tuesday, you'll see. But now you'll have to wait a week. And you almost missed dinner too, I was about to send out a search party for you. Now how do you want your steak?"

Gatineau looked up blearily, not certain if he dared refuse. He tried to stand up, but Cookie's huge hand on his shoulder held him firmly down in his place. "But . . . I need to get the moebius wrench to Chief Leen. Let me just take it to him and then I can—"

"Absolutely not. I didn't spend all day in this galley preparing hot nourishing meals for this crew to have some ungrateful puppy grabbing sandwiches on the run. You're going to eat a proper dinner or you'll not leave this messroom. Even if he's not yet in it, Captain Hardesty would rise up out of his grave and skin me alive if I didn't put a hot meal into each of his boys and girls. I'll not have you insulting the hard work of the mess crew, nor the good healthy produce from the *Star Wolf*'s farm. If you knew how much hard work went into every meal, you'd treat each mouthful with a lot more respect. I'll see to that. Drink your milk now—here, bring it with you. You need to see this."

Cookie grabbed Gatineau by the arm, practically lifting him out of his chair and dragging him into the galley, a long narrow room lined with shining counters and appliances. "Y'see these machines? Do you think that's all we do here, put raw potatoes in one end and take sandwiches out the other? Any damn fool can do that. Real cooking is an art form, and any real galley slave has to be a master artist, or it's the surest way to start a shipboard mutiny. I can tell you that, me lad. No doubt about it. The most important part of a starship is her belly. Napoleon Bonaparte said it, and he was right. An army travels on its stomach. Never forget that. Here, lad, have some more cocoa. Let me tell you rule number one: *Take care of the belly first.* If you don't take care of your own well-being, you'll have nothing to give anyone else. What good will you be to this ship if you can't do your job? Tell me that, will you now? No good at all. You'll be in sick bay and Molly Williger and two other people will be spending all their time taking care of your poor body when they could be doing something useful instead. No, that's no way to be a good member of this crew. I don't care how busy you are, lad, don't you ever miss a meal again or I'll come looking for you, and when I find you, you'll be wishing you'd been caught by the banshee of Belfast instead. And all of her lovely sisters. Now, here, this is what I wanted you to see—" Cookie opened the door of a cold-box and pulled out a fresh piece of meat. "You see this? Do you know what this is?"

"It looks like a steak?" Gatineau offered tentatively.

"Wipe your mouth, son. You've got a milk mustache. A

steak? Absolutely not. This is much more than a mere *steak*. Now if you were to ask Chief Leen what this is, he'd tell you that it's fuel for your machine. It's raw protein, which your body will turn into muscle and bone and energy to drive your engines faster than light. That's how a mechanic would see it.

"And if you were to ask Irma Stolchak what it was, she'd tell you it's a crop. She'd give you a little lecture about how the protein has to be properly marbled, so it has enough fat to be flavorful, but not so much that it's greasy. She'll tell you how the flesh has to be stimulated in the tank, worked and stretched and exercised so that it has the right kind of chewiness in the mouth, but not overworked so much that it gets tough and gamey. And you've got to know exactly what you're doing—are you growing pork chops or ham steaks? Are you growing beef ribs or pot roast? Is it going to be a breast or a drumstick? You don't have a chicken or a pig or a cow walking around this ship doing the work, you've got to see that the exercisers in the tank produce meat and not just a fat blob of undifferentiated flesh. Ahh, she'd tell you about that, for sure. Do you know why? Because I wouldn't accept a single piece of meat that isn't good enough for my crew.

"And if you were to ask Toad Hall what this is, he'd tell you that it's a commodity, an asset, something to be used in the marketplace. He'd tell you it's a lump of kilocalories, just waiting to be applied to the balance sheet.

"But they're all wrong, my lad. All of them. This isn't fuel, and it isn't a crop, and it isn't a nice round number in the captain's spreadsheet. Do you know what this is? This is a work of art looking for a place to happen. This is a bit of home on your plate; it's a vacation at the end of a hard day's work; it's a reward for your hours of toil in the fields of the Lord. Properly prepared, by a master, not a hooligan, this becomes a feast not only for the tongue and the belly, but for the soul as well. Cooking is an art form, and the eating of the meal in an atmosphere of rest and relaxation is the only way to savor the artist's handiwork. Now, I ask you, son—are you willing to reject the handiwork of a man who has dedicated his life to bringing you a bit of soul-filling pleasure three times a day? You'll not betray the kitchen of this starship, I promise you that, not while

I'm the lord and master of this domain, and surely not while I have my cleaver in my hand.

"Now answer my question, and answer quickly, how do you like your steak?"

"Uh—rare. Please. Pink on the inside, seared on the outside."

"Good man. That's the proper way. And what vegetables will you be having with that?"

"Snap peas, if you have them. And mashed potatoes, please. If it's not too much trouble. And a salad? Bleu cheese dressing?"

Cookie considered the order, nodded a grudging acknowledgment. "Unimaginative. But solid. A good start. Tell you what. I'll put a bit of avocado on the top of that salad for you, and a bit of shrimp as well. Just to dress it up. And I'll mix a few pearl onions and mushrooms in with the peas, nothing fancy, but you've got to have a bit of crunch on the fork, you know. And the potatoes, they'll get cold without a nice blanket of gravy—or would you prefer a coat of sharp cheese? And a bit of eye-talian on the steak, of course, of course. It's a shame you're so late. At this hour, it's really much too late to put on a proper do, but I can still give you a small taste of what's possible in the hands of a chef who knows what he's doing in a kitchen. And if you'll not miss any more meals, well then pretty soon you'll know what a privilege it is for you to serve on a ship with this cook. You'll have a belly on you soon enough; you could easily use another ten kilograms. We'll have you looking like a right proper member of the *Star Wolf*'s crew. I mean, look at yourself, lad; you're as thin as a plasma tube. That's what happens when you forget to eat. Ahh, but when you see what magic I can work on your plate, you'll forget every platter your sainted mother ever put before you. You'll count the minutes between your meals, I promise you that; but enough of my bejabbering. Tonight, at least, I won't begrudge you a simple old-fashioned repast. Now, get your skinny little butt out of my galley and back into a chair, before I lose my patience and put you in the grinder for tomorrow's sausage."

Gatineau went through the first half of the meal, barely tasting it. He hadn't realized how hungry he was. And he didn't realize how *good* the food in front of him really was until Cookie laid a hand on his shoulder and said, "Slow down, lad. You've got to give yourself a chance to savor each bite; otherwise the cook'll know you're lying when you tell him how much you enjoyed it. Real men don't gobble, no matter how hungry they are. No one's going to take your plate away, so slow down and show me that you appreciate the taste of it as much as the fullness it gives your belly. Besides, you'll need to save your strength for dessert. I do the best afters in the fleet. You'll have a slice of my peach-berry cobbler smothered in sweet cream. And after that . . . while you're here, you'll do a bit of K.P. Your penance for missing lunch. And then we'll talk about that wrench you're looking for."

"Thfmk yff," said Gatineau, stuffing another bite in his mouth. After everything else he'd had to do today, a bit of K.P. would probably be a relief.

But he was wrong about that too.

Outside

The *Star Wolf* had three kinds of airlocks.

The traditional airlock was a chamber with hatches at each end; air could be pumped in or out.

The valve lock was a series of self-closing membranes, resembling heart valves, through which a crew member pushed himself. Some gas leaked out through each transfer, but each chamber had a decreasing level of pressure, so the final chamber had minimal air to lose.

The revolving lock was a rotating cylinder, much like a revolving door. The crew member stepped into it, rotated through, and stepped out the opposite side. It was the fastest way to get in or out of a pressurized hull.

Fleet regulations required that all three kinds of locks be backstopped by additional pressure hatches.

Today, Brik chose the valve lock. It allowed him to ease into vacuum at his own pace.

He touched his starsuit harness, checking the flattened lump in the case he wore next to his skin. He took a last few breaths of pure oxygen from the pressure pack he carried, and then discarded it. He pushed through the first valve, then the second—the air sucked steadily out of his lungs. He pressed through the next valve and the next. And kept exhaling. When there was nothing left to exhale, the pain in his chest began to ebb, and he closed his throat against further exhalation.

Brik wore a modified starsuit, as close to that worn by the Morthan assassin as he could fabricate; it wasn't much more than a chest guard and a genital harness. He also wore a facepack to protect his eyes; he hadn't been able to determine what modifications had been made to Cinnabar's eyes and that wasn't the purpose of this experiment anyway, so he wore the facepack.

His only air supply was an oxygen transfusor strapped to his right shoulder. The autopsy on what was left of Cinnabar had shown a similar device tucked inside the large bone of the assassin's right thigh. It was good for fifteen, maybe twenty minutes before it was exhausted, but that rating was for a human metabolism. Brik's metabolism, fully exerted, would probably exhaust the unit in one third of the time. The same equation would have held for Cinnabar. Could he travel the length of the starship in seven minutes?

He was about to find out.

It was *imperative* that he find out.

He unclipped the short black hose from the side of the oxygen transfusor, opened the valve, and slipped the end of it into his mouth. He bit down hard on the grips of the mouthpiece, holding it firmly between his molars. He sucked gas. Good. It worked. Just barely.

Then he pressed through the final valve of the lock.

Hard vacuum *hurt*.

And it was noisy. He could hear the pounding of his heart in his chest, feel the waves throbbing outward from his chest, into his arms and legs in a series of accelerated pulses; he could hear the roaring of his blood through his veins and the rasp of his irregular breathing in his throat and his lungs. There was *nothing else* to hear.

And his internal body pressure felt *wrong*. He felt queasy, especially in his gut, where the lack of atmospheric pressure gave his bowel a nasty sense of independence. The sensation grew alarmingly. And suddenly Brik knew that he would not be able to control it. He pulled himself out of the airlock and cramped almost immediately into a fetal position.

He couldn't see what was happening behind him, but he could feel an *intense* visceral sucking sensation. His bowel exploded in a dark powdery spray. The eruption was violent and painful. Even after his bowel was certainly empty, the sucking continued. It became *excruciating*—as if his whole body was going to be pulled out through his rectum. Brik held on to the handgrip and *endured*. He'd known this was going to happen; he'd known it was going to be painful; he just hadn't realized it would be *this* painful.

The only consolation was that the same thing would have happened to Cinnabar too. But Cinnabar had probably been trained and augmented specifically for EVA maneuvers. So maybe it hadn't been as painful for him. In which case, Brik mused, who was more courageous?

It didn't matter. It wasn't about courage. It was about results. Already, he was feeling better. He focused his attention forward, checked the time, and asked himself once more if this was a good idea. The answer was still no. Nevertheless . . . this was the only way to find out. Brik put the mouthpiece back in his mouth and took a small suck of air. Yes, he could do it. He pulled himself out of the airlock reception bay. . . .

He was at the bow of the ship, just ahead of the snarl painted on the hull. His target was the aftmost airlock. He began pulling himself along the hull of the starship with a steady count. He used the handholds set into the fuselage next to the long tubes of the plasma drives, and he chanted inaudibly to himself as he went, one of his exercise mantras.

He fell into an easy rhythm. He pretended he was climbing one of the exercise walls at home. Five minutes. One hundred meters. He could do it. In free-fall, it would be easy.

But it wasn't."

Hard vacuum *burned*.

The stars were hatefully bright. His eyes stung with pain. His sinuses ached. His whole head felt cold. His ears pounded with the roaring of his own blood.

And very quickly he knew that his hands were too cold. Every time he touched the hull of the ship a little more of his body heat leached out through his fingers. The designers of the ship had erroneously assumed that anyone using this space-ladder would have been properly suited, so they hadn't padded the handles with temperature-neutral material. Brik's only comforting thought was that it had to have been as bad for Cinnabar as it was for him. Perhaps worse. Because Cinnabar couldn't have been sure that the airlock he was heading toward would open for him.

Brik was halfway to the stern now. He paused momentarily at a starboard access panel. He could open it. He could drop down into the airlock and go in. He'd proved his point. But . . . he had to be *sure*. He checked his watch, then he checked the dial on the oxygen transfusor. He pulled himself past the access panel and kept heading sternward.

The pain in his hands was getting worse. Brik snarled, but he didn't mind. The time to worry was when his hands *stopped* hurting. He was sure of one thing though. Cinnabar had to have had some kind of internal heating augment in his extremities. This pain was *distracting*.

On the other hand, Cinnabar's augments had not been designed to make the assassin comfortable, only to make him powerful. Brik considered that thought as he pulled. What was the Morthan relationship with pain? He knew how he tolerated it. He *accepted* it. He *re-created* it; he let himself experience it fully, until he was inside it, until he was no longer resisting something that was outside of him but analyzing something that was part of him. And by the time he'd completed that process, the pain had disappeared as pain and became only *information*.

Was that how the warriors of the Solidarity handled discomfort? Brik didn't think so. Cinnabar's reactions had become almost joyous toward the end. He'd looked as if he was in ecstasy.

Brik had heard rumors that the Solidarity routinely rewired the neural circuitry of their warriors so that all pain sensations were translated into *pleasure*. Could Cinnabar have *enjoyed* the entire experience? Could his death have been an orgasmic adventure? Certainly, the evidence seemed to suggest it.

Brik was having trouble moving his fingers now. Several times his hands had slipped off the rungs of the space-ladder. It was starting to be a problem. He pulled himself out of his reveries and tried to focus on the remaining distance.

He couldn't see. His vision was blurry. Despite the facepack his eyes were drying out. He felt them bulging out of his head. His ears as well. He'd miscalculated only a bit —but it didn't matter whether he was wrong by a centimeter or a light-year. The situation was binary. The result would be either yes or no.

But . . . if he died out here, that still wouldn't prove that Cinnabar couldn't have done it. Only if he survived would he have incontrovertible proof of Cinnabar's deed.

Death didn't scare him. There was no adrenaline there. He'd long ago learned to appreciate the irony of life. But failure *angered* him. Failure was intolerable. Especially *this* failure, because no one would understand unless he made it back safely. The surge of anger filled him with a brief flash of warmth. He remembered what Korie had said. One of his fathers used to say the same thing. "Anger is useful. Use it." Even in his pain, Brik smiled. More and more, Korie was thinking like a Morthan.

He was pulling himself more slowly now. But now he was chanting a different song. This one was a song of anger. A rhythm of rage. War parties used to pump themselves up with songs like this—you focused on the face of your enemy and sang your rage into him. Brik visualized Cinnabar and already he could feel the first burning embers of hatred growing in his chest.

He had been raised never to succumb to hatred—except in special circumstances. He had been in a killing rage only three times in his life, and all three times had been under tightly controlled circumstances. He knew how to rage when he needed to. But he knew the physical price he would have to pay—

He chanted. Internally. The rhythm of the gods.

Vacuum burned.

His ears pounded.

His eyes ached redly. He held them tightly shut.

His blood roared.

He sang. Inside. He thought of Cinnabar. Cinnabar's hands.

And finally—he *raged*. Not quite a killing rage, but close

enough. He held himself just at the threshold of that over-whelming fury.

It didn't keep him warm. But it kept him going.

He pulled himself along—rung after rung after rung—until suddenly there were no more rungs. He realized he'd been fumbling for several seconds, reaching for something that wasn't there. He was at the aft airlocks. *He'd made it.* He pulled open the access panel and pulled himself down into the reception bay. He fumbled for the control and slammed his hand against it.

Something flashed red. He opened his eyes; he could barely move them. The panel was throbbing like his heart. Dimly he could make out the single word of doom. LOCKED.

And then . . . he slipped over the edge and plunged into a killing rage.

He wasn't angry at the door, but at himself.

Red fury suffused his entire being. He was no longer rational. He pulled himself out of the access and around the curve of the hull to the next airlock over. There were three airlocks at the stern of the vessel. One of them had to be accessible—

Yes!

The panel flashed green and the cylinder slid around and he pulled himself into it and pushed it around and around and tumbled out, falling upside down onto the floor back-ward, his legs flailing, and suddenly there was sound roar-ing around him, painfully loud, impossibly loud, he hadn't realized how loud sound could be, he couldn't hear his heart anymore. He pounded on the deck and raged and raged, and even though he'd won, he was overwhelmed with Morthan fury. He focused on the face of the dead assassin and cursed it with a fiery vengeance; he pushed his anger out through his mouth in a ferocious roar and out-shouted the noises of the starship that filled his ears and the stinking smells that suddenly filled his nostrils.

Tears flooded his eyes, blood poured from his nose. He bellowed and shrieked and somehow, even in the blackest reddest deepest moments of his ecstasies, he knew that he had won, he'd proven his point; he knew what Cinnabar had done and how he'd done it. Had the assassin raged like this? He couldn't have—the whole ship would have heard

—he must have somehow gone unconscious, somehow triggered his own recuperation once he was safely inside again. Fury ebbed, leaving enlightenment and understanding and a curious emotion that Brik could not name, but it had elements of triumph and joy; he knew it was only the endorphins flooding into his brain, but he was swept up with the feeling too. This was not like any rage he'd ever felt before, and it was evil and delicious. He laughed out loud, a great booming sound—

The safety hatch of the airlock popped open and a six-member tactical squad was standing there with rifles pointed at him.

Brik looked at them and laughed even harder.

Confused, the members of the squad looked from one to the other.

They didn't get the joke, but that was all right. Brik got it. And at the moment that was all that mattered.

Williger

Dr. Molly Williger did not have many friends. She didn't need many, and if truth be told, she was not the easiest person to be friendly with. She was taciturn, dour, blunt, and not given to easy camaraderie. It wasn't that she was deliberately *un*friendly, but that was how she was often perceived.

Mostly, she held herself in reserve, refusing to make some inner part of herself accessible. Her bedside manner had once been compared to General Patton's, with Patton coming off as the nice guy. Although Molly Williger had never slapped a patient, she had once angrily booted one out of a recovery bed with a well-placed kick to the *gluteus maximus*.

And then, of course, there was the not-so-small matter of her appearance.

Even those who felt kindly toward her, when preparing to introduce people to her, quietly noted ahead of time that Dr. Williger was the ugliest doctor in the fleet. It was undeniably true; it gave the person being introduced some warning, and was rather more polite than saying that she was the ugliest *person* in the fleet, though that was probably true also.

She was a short woman from a high-grav world, very nearly as round as she was high. She had a potato of a nose and squinty eyes that made her look almost as mean as she was ugly. Her ears were crumpled and protruding; they looked like something a dog had buried and then dug up a year later. Her homeworld had a thicker atmosphere than was common aboard Alliance ships, so at the best of times her breathing was heavy and labored as she fought to get enough of the thin air into her lungs. Her voice was raspy; she sounded like she gargled with gravel. Her hair, pulled into a tight bun, looked like stiff and rusty wire. But even to describe the individual features of this woman was insufficient, because her appearance was the clearest possible demonstration that the whole was more than just the sum of the parts.

A famous poet had once been introduced to Molly Williger and had spent the next year of his life trying to find the proper words to describe her ugliness before giving up and saying simply, *"Transcendental* ugliness. The language needs another thousand years of evolution before it's up to the task of describing this. The woman is a living masterpiece. God must have intended this. There is no flaw in this work. She is completely and totally ugly, without the slightest blemish or flaw of beauty in the effect. She is a holy presence. I would announce my retirement before I would assume the task of evoking her appearance."

There were those who assumed on Molly's behalf that these words were hurtful to her, and they rebuked the poet publicly for his tastelessness. But the poet replied that he meant no harm. Indeed, he intended his awestruck reaction only as the highest form of compliment. "Beauty is easy," he said. "It takes no particular ability. Any half-wit can speak in pastel. And many have. But true ghastliness is always an art form, it's raw and brutal and carved from the screams and passion of flesh-and-blood turned self-aware. Molly Willinger leaves me speechless. I would worship at her feet if she would allow me."

Whatever Molly herself believed, she kept it to herself. She knew she was ugly. She used her ugliness as she used every other tool at her disposal. Indeed, she was the only

doctor in the fleet who could stare into the maw of a
snarling Morthan and not be intimidated. Cinnabar had
been the first. Brik was the second.

After examining Cinnabar, Brik was easy.

She *hmm*ed and grunted to herself for a bit, studying the
various displays in front of her, then without looking up
rasped at Korie. "He'll live. He's a damn fool, but he'll live.
Did you need any more damn fools on this ship?"

Korie ignored the remark. "What were you trying to
do?" he demanded of Brik.

"I didn't *try*," Brik replied. "I *did* it." His voice was
rougher than usual and his breathing was still very uneven.

"Did what?" Korie frowned.

"I proved that Cinnabar lied." Brik took three deep
breaths before continuing. He was wearing an oxygen
mask. "He *didn't* come in through the forward missile
tubes, as he claimed. He had time to go the entire distance
of the ship. *And back.* He could have entered *anywhere.*"

Korie considered that thought. At first, it seemed an un-
important point to risk one's life over. Then as he began to
realize the implications, his expression froze. "Shit," he
said. "That just made my day. I've got to talk to Harlie."
He started to shake his head in frustration, then looked up
abruptly. "You know, I should bust you for this little stunt.
I still might."

"It was a matter of starship security," Brik rumbled and
wheezed. "It was entirely within the purview of my authority. External inspection for damage."

"Without a starsuit? If nothing else, I should charge you
with reckless endangerment."

"Hard to prove. You don't know what the Morthan phys-
iology is capable of under stress. No human does. So stop
trying to threaten me. It was *necessary.*"

Surprisingly, Korie nodded. He recognized two things.
First, this was an argument he couldn't win. And second, if
he were to argue with Brik about this, he'd be using the
same authority and arguments that the admiral had used—
tried to use—on him. Brik's *wildness* was his own. He
didn't dare punish it. He exhaled sharply with frustration.
He was beginning to understand now how the admiral felt
about him.

"Listen to me," said Korie. "The next time you have an

idea like this—for *anything* like this—clear it with me first?"

"Why?" Brik regarded Korie dispassionately. "If I gave you that authority, you would use it. Would you have allowed this test?"

"Of course not."

"That's why I had to do it without your permission."

"Well, ask me in the future anyway, so I can have a safety crew accompanying you."

"That would be an insult, Commander."

"I'd rather insult you than bury you. Do you know how much paperwork is involved when a crew member dies?"

"No, I don't."

That stopped Korie. "You really don't?"

"I just said so."

"All right." Korie made a decision. "From now on, you're in charge of all death details—especially the paperwork."

"I am not a gravedigger. This is the work of . . . slaves."

"Are you a member of this ship's company? Do you follow orders?"

"Yes, Commander, I follow orders." Brik's voice was very formal and rigid.

"I'm going to put this in writing," Korie said. "For what it's worth, the purpose is not to humiliate you. I want you to start feeling responsible for the lives—and deaths—of the people around you."

Brik did not reply to that.

"Good. Now we understand each other."

"I don't think so," said Brik, "but I'm not prepared to argue that right now."

"Uh-huh," said Korie with finality. "Enough dancing. Now I want to hear the *other* reason."

"What other reason?" Brik replied blandly.

"You know what I mean. What were you trying to prove *to yourself*?"

"I *didn't* try," Brik said, "I *did* prove it."

"And that was . . . ?"

"Failure is not an option."

Korie met Brik's eyes. For a moment the two of them

regarded each other mercilessly. And Brik saw that yes, *maybe Korie was finally beginning to understand. . . .*

"This is what I mean about damn fools," Williger said, deliberately interrupting. "Too much testosterone."

Korie used her remark as an excuse to turn away. He nodded in agreement. "You're right, Doctor. But I wish I had another dozen damn fools on this ship. We do need all the damn fools we can get. How long till he's up again."

"He can go now, if he insists. I don't want him here. But I'm not sure yet how much damage he's done to his lungs; he's supposed to be capable of routine regeneration; I'm going to watch him closely for a few days. If he needs it, I'll run a transform series."

"Can you wait until we're online again?"

She shrugged. "I can wait till hell freezes over. I don't like working on Morthans. Don't take it personally, Commander," she said to Brik, "but it makes me feel like a veterinarian."

"The feeling is mutual," Brik replied, deadpan.

"He won't eat the kibble," Korie remarked on his way out. "You'll have to feed him the canned stuff."

Armstrong

After Gatineau finished cleaning the galley, Cookie sent him forward to the Operations bay, a four-man cubbyhole tucked directly underneath the Bridge. "Ask for Brian Armstrong, lad. He has the moebius wrench now. He came and got it while you were cleaning the tables."

So Gatineau slid down to the keel and headed forward. He felt oddly renewed and recharged. It wasn't just a full belly that did it, it was also the sense of accomplishment he felt at having scrubbed the galley till it sparkled. He enjoyed cleaning things. He liked seeing the starship at its best, its interior workings glimmering like new. It gave him a sense of *pride*.

He realized with a wry smile that he'd been cleaning all day. He'd helped with the electrical harness, the farm, and the supplies in the cargo deck. He'd been all over the *Star Wolf.* But it also annoyed him to realize how much ground he'd covered without yet locating the elusive moebius wrench.

He reached the Ops bay and climbed the five steps into it. There were two men inside, a small dark one and a large blond one. Both were hip deep in electronic gear. "Who's Armstrong?" Gatineau asked.

"I am," said the blond. He was a side of beef with a grin. "Who're you?"

"Gatineau. I need the moebius wrench," he said, holding out a hand. "Chief Engineer Leen wants it *now.*"

"Oh, the wrench. Right. Green—?" Armstrong turned to the smaller man. "Where'd you put it?"

"I gave it to Hodel. He's micro-tickling the klystron coils. I'll go get it." He started climbing down into a large square hole in the deck. He paused to explain. "Tell the chief we're awfully sorry for the delay, but we've got the whole communications yoke torn down. We have to logic test each and every module. We don't think any of the units were contaminated, but a C-5 detox requires the checks anyway. Oh, no—" Green's face fell. "Listen, I just realized, you're going to have to wait until we finish reassembling the optical bleeds. We can't get to the wrench until that's back online and out of the way."

"Why am I not surprised," said Gatineau. "And I suppose you're going to need my help."

"Not really. It's a two-man job. You'd just be in the way." Green pulled himself back out of the hole. Gatineau started to relax—

"On the other hand," Green continued, "if you take over here, Armstrong can go start the teardown of the network assemblers; then we can integrate the envelope riders and restore our hyperstate scanners to full operation ahead of schedule. Here, why don't you take this probe—if we had a class five systems analysis network, we wouldn't have to do this by hand, but this ship was launched before the required parts came in, and we've never caught up with our own supplies; other ships keep requisitioning them first. You can't imagine the shortages we've had. It's a bitch."

"Let me tell you something," Green added. "It's all about resources. Y'know, that's rule number one: *Make sure of your supplies.* I remember one boat, we ran out of toilet paper three weeks from home. By the time we hit port, we were using the chief petty officer's clothes. We were a very unhappy crew. But that was very bad management of resources on his part. He never made that mistake again. That's my point. Now, here, we have to do all this extra work, because we don't have a proper systems analysis net. Here, let me show you how to do that—"

Armstrong was already up the five steps to the Operations deck. Quilla Zeta was quietly cleaning the astrogation display. She was a thin-looking woman, blue-skinned, with purple quills in a Mohawk array. Mikhail Hodel had the conn; Jonesy sat at the astrogation station, running a series of battle simulations.

"Crewman Armstrong?" said Zeta.

"Uh—I can't talk now." Armstrong ducked into the forward port accessway. "I've got work to do—"

Halfway up the passage, he encountered Quilla Theta; she was even smaller than Gamma, almost childlike. "You have been avoiding us for some time now. We need to talk."

"Not now," Armstrong replied. "I told you, I've got too much to do, with the detox and all—" He shoved past Theta almost rudely and kept going.

Quilla Delta stuck her head out of a cabin door as he passed. *"When?"*

"I told you—*later.*" He held his hands up in the air, as if to ward her off and kept on moving.

Quilla Beta was just coming out of the forward magazines, carrying the empty housing for a ventricle assembly. "You said that before, Crewman Armstrong. Later never comes. Something is the matter. Are you embarrassed about the sexual coupling we had?"

"Look, it didn't work. Please, let's just drop the subject." He pushed past her into the storage compartments. His face was flushed.

Quilla Lambda, the only *male* Quilla onboard, turned to face him. He was just unpacking the rest of the ventricle assembly. Lambda was as big and as well muscled as Armstrong; his skin was a darker shade of blue than the females, and his quills were also larger. "No, Brian," he said firmly. "It did work. *That's* the problem."

"Can't you just leave me alone?"

"We need to talk about this. And we need to talk *now.* It's getting in the way of your ability to function. If you won't talk to the others, you will talk to this one. Wait—"

Lambda did something then, Armstrong wasn't sure what, but suddenly he wasn't a Quilla anymore. He was a man with blue skin and purple quills. "I've disconnected," he said. "Now, you I may talk privately. If you wish."

"You *disconnected*? I didn't know you could do that."

Lambda nodded. "We don't do it very often; there's rarely any need to. But you need to hear this. I know what you're feeling."

Armstrong didn't answer. He looked off to one side, at the floor, at the ceiling. "Look," he finally said, coming back to Lambda, "do we really have to have this conversation?"

"Yes," said Lambda. "We do. You enjoyed having sex with us. We enjoyed having sex with you. Quillas are very sensual. You're very attractive. It was very enjoyable for all of us. So what's the problem, Brian?" Lambda looked sharply into Armstrong's eyes, waiting for an answer.

Armstrong looked away. He wouldn't meet Lambda's studying gaze.

"Do you really think that you're the first one who ever felt this way?" Lambda asked softly.

The question was too direct. Armstrong reacted angrily. "I appreciate your concern, okay? But I don't have a lot of time for this right now."

"Yes, you do. You just laid off a large piece of your workload on Crewman Gatineau. Please don't insult my intelligence. It's very hard to lie convincingly to a Quilla. May I tell you something?"

"Can I stop you?"

"Actually, no." Lambda reached out and placed one blue hand gently on top of Armstrong's pink one. Armstrong tried to pull away, but Lambda held on tight. "Are you having trouble with the fact that there was a male component to the sex?"

"You cut straight to the heart, don't you?"

"You don't have a lot of time," Lambda said dryly.

Armstrong shook his head, a convenient excuse to look away again.

Lambda reached over and with one finger turned Armstrong's head back to face his own. "The coupling was joyous, it was delightful, it was filled with laughter and amazement. For us as well as you. The experience has clearly shifted your perception of sexuality. And in ways you're not comfortable with. For the first time, sex wasn't about *you,* it was about *us.* And that is precisely because so many of us were tapped into it. That is where the enthusiasm came from—on both sides, Brian. I'm part of the *us* too. I'm sorry that disturbs you, but it doesn't change what we all experienced."

Armstrong didn't answer immediately. After a moment he said, "You're very glib. You talk good. But you don't know what's going on in my mind."

"No, but I know what went on in my own mind before I became a Quilla."

Armstrong's eyes widened. He stared at Lambda for a long moment, suddenly trying to see who this man had been *before* . . .

Lambda nodded. "That's right. I did the same thing. And I spent days walking around in a blue funk, trying to figure out what it meant. I wanted to go back for more, and I was terrified to do so. And all the time I was curious what it felt like from the Quillas' side. Eventually, I realized that the only way I'd ever understand, the only way I'd ever see myself from the outside was to become a Quilla myself."

"Stop trying to recruit me. I'm not interested—"

"I'm not trying to recruit you. In all likelihood, you don't even have the right mindset. You probably couldn't be assimilated into a cluster without driving it crazy. And this cluster isn't interested in expanding until the ship situation stabilizes. So don't flatter yourself.

"And don't look so surprised," Lambda added sharply. "I might be a Quilla, but I don't *have* to be polite where it isn't going to be appreciated. There's a lot about Quillas you don't know. You obviously didn't do your research. You were leading with your dick. It was charming at the time, but it's getting old, Brian. It's time to move on.

"The point is, we *do* know what you're going through. It's part of our history too. And we're sorry that you're feeling that way. If we had known you were going to react like this, we would never have accepted your invitation to have sex. But it happened, and now we all have to live with it. So, do you want to keep on walking around like an angry Morthan, or are you ready to grow up?"

"What do you want from me?"

"Nothing, really. Be our friend? Share a smile with us when you see us in the passages?"

Armstrong hesitated. Then something clicked inside and he smiled at some private joke. "I don't believe this."

"What?"

"Well, I'm usually the one who says, 'Can't we just be friends?' "

Lambda smiled back. "And how do the women usually respond?"

Armstrong grinned ruefully. "They get angry. You should see it. I remember one who bawled me out, screaming, 'No, we cannot be friends, you scumbag. I don't want friends. I already have the best friends money can buy. I want more than just your friendship, goddammit.' " He laughed. And then he dropped his eyes in embarrassment. The memory was too painful.

"Go on," said Lambda quietly.

Armstrong swallowed hard. "All right, yeah. It was good. And, um, to tell the truth, I did want to do it again. But then . . . with all the teasing and everything, I didn't think that you—I mean you, the whole cluster—felt the way I thought you had, and then when you —I mean *you,* Lambda—winked at me, I thought for sure that you were all laughing at me for . . . well, for being so stupid about it."

"We weren't laughing at you," Lambda said. "Believe it or not, Quillas are incapable of mocking a human soul. We empathize too much with all souls. It's our weakness as well as our strength."

"Yeah, I guess so. But . . . you did scare me. I thought that maybe you, Quilla Lambda, would want to . . . well, you know. And I . . . don't, you know."

Lambda nodded. "First of all, as an individual, I am not homosexual, so you need not worry about that. Secondly, as an individual, I would never have sex outside the cluster. That would be a betrayal of my relationship with my *mates.* Regardless of any attraction I might feel as an individual, I would never place personal gratification above the cluster.

"As a cluster, however, there is always a certain curiosity about all sexual combinations, and it does not particularly matter to us which body we use for a specific sexual encounter; we usually let the other individual choose which partner most appeals to her or him. So, yes, this body has been used for homosexual encounters.

"And," Lambda added thoughtfully, "I must also acknowledge that among all of the sexual possibilities, the fitting of male to male or female to female is often one that the cluster finds interesting because the parallel physical responses of two males or two females can produce some remarkable experiences. I'm sorry if you find that unnerving. The limitation is yours, not ours. Among ourselves, we often arrange encounters between two or three of our units, and that is always quite intense. Because I'm the only male Quilla in this cluster, most of our private encounters are all-female."

Armstrong stared at Lambda, not knowing how to react to this information. He'd heard stories. He hadn't realized the Quillas would be this candid. He wasn't sure if he wanted to hear the details.

Lambda continued anyway. "I will tell you this, Brian. It can be very . . . exhilarating for a man to experience feminine sexuality. It has taught me more about women than I could have learned any other way. I'm sorry if this disturbs you, but you need to understand who we are. I often wish that everyone could be a Quilla for a while. Then you would truly understand. Then there wouldn't be so many ignorant jokes, and you wouldn't have to have the fears you have. We like you. We don't like seeing you uncomfortable."

"Okay," said Armstrong grudgingly. "I got it." He relaxed and sighed and nodded his acceptance. Some of his discomfort was actually easing. He met Lambda's eyes for the first time willingly. "I have been pretty stiff about the whole thing, haven't I?"

"Actually"—smiled Lambda gently—"you've been a jerk."

"Yeah," Armstrong admitted. "I guess I have." He took a deep breath. "I'm sorry." And then he asked, "So what do we do now?"

Lambda patted Armstrong's hand gently. "Nothing. Or everything. Or anything you want. We're here to serve. You want a back rub? Call me. I'm an expert in Shiatsu. And yes, I know about the pinched nerve in your back that sometimes gives you trouble. That's why I offered. You want sex? Call me or Delta or any of the others. The second time is even more fun than the first. You want someone to talk to? I'd consider it a privilege. You can talk to me as an individual or as a member of the cluster. *Whatever* you want, Brian. *That's* the point."

"Thanks," said Armstrong, both surprised and embarrassed. "I mean it. Thanks." He patted Lambda on the shoulder, like a buddy, and Lambda patted him back like a lover. Armstrong stiffened . . . but he didn't flinch. He had a lot to think about all of a sudden.

Meerson-Krikes

The Orbital College was an adjunct to the Meerson-Krikes orbital assembly lines. For several quiet centuries Shaleen had earned the reputation as the place to go if you wanted a sunjammer, a lightweight but sturdy fuselage. The poly-carbonate-titanium hulls were extremely versatile; they could be rigged with chemical propellant engines, fusion drives, plasma torches, or even solar sails. The resultant yachts were perfect for journeys between the inner planets of the system and forays to the mid-and outer-worlds.

Occasionally, some foolhardy soul would order a craft with a singularity stardrive, with the intention of using the vessel for interstellar travel. Despite significant cautions on the part of the manufacturer about the problems of main-taining the focus of the singularity grappler fields in a hull of such small size, and despite the even more significant cautions about the difficulties of maintaining a hyperstate envelope and manipulating it for FTL velocities, there was no shortage of bold eccentrics willing to brave the dark between the stars. Who wouldn't want to own his own star-ship? The great leap outward was an irresistible pheromone. Over the years Meerson-Krikes built up a considerable market in light cruisers of all sizes.

Beyond this particular horizon, however, darker clouds were gathering and eventually the growing buildup of military strength in the Morthan sphere of authority began to alarm the Allied worlds. The Defense Authority contracted with the Meerson-Krikes company—as well as with corporations on numerous other worlds—to begin production of a series of small, but extremely powerful interstellar military vessels. These destroyer-class cruisers were called "liberty ships."

Because of their considerable experience with light cruisers, Meerson-Krikes was able to gear up quickly for production. Within a year they were building liberty ships at the rate of one new vessel every eleven days. The ships were prefabbed and Spartan, lacking all but the most essential life-support services and amenities. The best that could be said of them was that they held air and moved. It would be up to each ship captain to finish the outfitting of his or her vessel.

The high volume of production represented the Alliance's most cost-effective strategy—a swarm of interstellar killer bees. The sting of any individual bee might be insignificant; the combined fury of a thousand or ten thousand or a hundred thousand stings should be enough to stagger the Morthan war machine. An Armageddon-class juggernaut would be unable to withstand such a concentrated assault; she would be overwhelmed like a lumbering hippopotamus in a tank full of piranha. At least, that was the game plan. This strategy was designed to give the Allied forces incredible flexibility, but at a terrible cost—ultimately it was based on the expendability of individual ships and crews.

The demand for skilled labor in the orbital assembly lines was intensive. Even with robots and nanotechs doing much of the work, the need for human supervision remained critical—and as fast as ships rolled off the assembly line, the Allied Defense Authority recruited the most skilled workers to crew them. Replacement of those workers became such a critical need that the Orbital College was established for onsite training and education. For those young men and women who wanted a career in space, the liberty fleet was a very fast—but also very dangerous—track.

With his father's reluctant permission, Jon Korie signed up for the Orbital College on his seventeenth birthday. After two months of intensive training, during which more than fifty percent of the applicants were washed out, he was sent up the beanstalk. For his first twelve weeks he was apprenticed as a galley slave—a cook's assistant. As unglamorous as food preparation service might have seemed at first, the essential lesson was that nutritious and attractive meals were the single most important part of energizing a ship's crew. Korie was lucky; he liked cooking as much as he liked eating. He tackled the job with enthusiasm and graduated with a rating of ninety-four percent.

On his last day the crew chief, a diminutive little woman named Bertha Fleischer, made him a going-away feast of beet borscht, stuffed cabbage, fresh egg-bread for mopping the plate, and a magnificent strawberry shortcake. She wept copiously, as if her only son were leaving. Korie was surprised by her demonstrative affection; he had never been the target of such warmth before. The feeling stayed with him long after the meal was only a memory.

From the kitchen Korie went to the farms.

Food preparation was crucial to the morale of the crew, but production was essential to basic survival. The farm not only produced food; it processed sewage, turning it into fertilizer. The fertilizer was liquified and fed to aeroponically grown plants with steady-state drip irrigation. Some of the crops were harvested for food; others were liquified in turn to make nutrient solutions for the meat tanks. The green leaves of the plants also regenerated the air in the ship, taking in carbon dioxide and putting out life-giving oxygen.

The assembly lines maintained their own vast farms, partly to maintain their own ecology, of course, and partly to serve as a seed farm for the new ships taking shape on the docking spurs. Each new ship would be launched with a complete farm installed in it.

After a time Korie was assigned to one of the teams that installed new farms; later he became a team leader. No ship was ever delivered to the Allied Defense Authority until her farm was certified as fully functional, able to feed a crew of one hundred forty-five individuals. Jon Korie signed off on fourteen farms. He found the work both exhausting and satisfying, and he never looked at a meal the same way again.

On the farms Jon Korie learned about proteins, carbohydrates, fats, and sugars. He learned about photosynthesis and atmospheric pressure, day-night cycles and seasons. He learned about planting and harvesting, pollinating and cross-breeding, grafting and splitting. Most importantly, he learned *patience.* It doesn't matter how many cabbages you plant. You won't get sixty cabbages any faster than you get one.

If you think you'll want stuffed cabbage in August, be sure to plant cabbages in February, and start the meat growing in the tanks no later than April; the longer the meat ages in the nutrients, the more flavor it will have when it reaches the plate. If you want bacon and eggs regularly, you have to monitor the pork belly tanks and the egg-production lines daily. If you want fresh butter for your toast, the udders have to be fed *and* massaged.

There were no real animals aboard the starship, but parts of many different species thrived in various growth tanks. Throughout the inner hull ranks of glass tanks stood three high, each with its own lump of flesh growing inside.

After tending three complete seasons of corn, peas, carrots, lettuce, tomatoes, cucumbers, asparagus, barley, rice, oranges, apples, plums, grapes, peaches, apricots, kiwis, garbonzos, olives, and leechees; not to mention beef, lamb, chicken, mutton, pork, ostrich, buffalo, venison, as well as catfish, tuna, salmon, shrimp, giant clam, octopus, sea bass, yellowtail swordfish, shark, porpoise, and whale; Korie graduated from the farm with a rating of eighty-nine percent. It wasn't as high a score as he should have earned, but Korie had never quite accepted the most fundamental tenet of ecology: *Life is messy.*

At heart, he was an engineer—or a control freak. He kept trying to make things run on schedule, but even industrial farms had their own rhythms; a farm could be managed only by a person who was willing to be managed by the rhythm of the seasons, and Korie was too impatient for that.

The *other* thing that distracted him from full concentration was Carol Jane.

At first she was just a coworker, then later a teammate, and eventually a study partner. It wasn't until midway through the second semester that he began to notice how beautiful she really was; and then he wondered how he had gone for so long without noticing before. And then . . . he began to worry how he would ever be able to concentrate on *anything else.*

Carol gave no sign of mutual interest, no encouragement at all; yet he couldn't get her out of his thoughts. He daydreamed about her constantly. He thought of nothing else. She was on his mind in class, at mealtimes, during study hall, during work sessions, in the corridors, in the showers, and even at bedtime—especially at bedtime. He wondered what it would be like to hold her body close to his—to smell her hair and taste her mouth and listen to her soft words and feel their bodies intertwined and fitting together in hot wet passion.

In his ignorance and naiveté, he constructed baroque fantasies in his imagination. (His favorite involved the two of them, marooned in a tumbling free-fall capsule for a week.) He masturbated himself into painful insensibility thinking of her. It was as if his adolescent hormones, which had lain dormant for so long that young Korie had almost begun to believe that he would never experience a sexual relationship, had suddenly kicked in with an enthusiastic vengeance.

He waited for the obsession to pass. It didn't. He waited for some sign from her that she recognized the effect she was having on him. She gave him no sign.

Finally, he realized he would have to act. He could not go on the way he was; it was driving him crazy. He had become obsessed with Carol Jane; her apparent disinterest in him made it all the worse.

Young Jon Korie spent long hours trying to figure out a way to speak to Carol Jane about his feelings. He thought about filling her room with roses and love poems; he thought about asking her to take walks with him on the stardeck or go nude swimming in the free-fall tanks. But everything he thought of only seemed silly and naive in the cold light of morning.

Finally, one day, after a particularly clumsy mistake in the sludge farm, which left him hip deep in cold stinking muck, he burst out in frustration, "This is all your fault!"

"Mine?" Carol Jane asked, honestly puzzled.

"Yes," he admitted angrily. "I'm so obsessed with you, I can't concentrate on anything anymore. You had to go and wear that tight shirt today, and I haven't been able to think of anything else."

When she realized what he was saying, she started to giggle; then she started laughing.

Hurt by her response, Korie stamped away to the showers at the end of the chamber. He peeled off his muck pants, his shorts, his T-shirt, and started hosing himself down. A moment later Carol entered and took the hose from him. "If it's my fault you got dirty, then it's my responsibility to help you clean up," she said. And then she apologized for laughing. She had been laughing at herself.

Standing there, naked, still covered with sludge and slime, Korie blinked in confusion. Carol Jane admitted that she had been wondering about Jon Korie since the first day she'd seen him in the corridors. He was so smart, so self-assured, so . . . so *alert;* and yet, he had seemed totally disinterested in having a relationship of any kind with anyone. Didn't he know that people all over the station were wondering about him? Had he been disconnected? Was he gay? Was he skeltered? Had he sworn a vow of celibacy? Was he emotionally retarded? Was there some great tragedy in his past? Was he some kind of human machine? Did he care about anything or anyone?

When Korie realized the great discrepancy between what it looked like on his side and how he was perceived by others, he too saw why she had laughed so hard. He almost smiled himself.

Carol Jane was peeling off her own shirt and shorts then. "Here," she said. "It's your turn to hose me down—"

The reality turned out to be a lot more fun than the fantasy.

Showers

Originally, Captain Hardesty had planned to have Brik's quarters outfitted with an antigrav bed/shower built to Brik's proportions. The unit had either disappeared in transit or had been coopted by some superior officer for his or her own special purposes.

Brik knew that some humans preferred free-fall sex with multiple partners and his bed/shower unit would have been very useful for that purpose. The thought should have annoyed him, but he didn't regard the loss of the tube as much more than a minor inconvenience. He didn't sleep as humans did anyway.

Instead, he draped himself backward over a rounded frame, which simultaneously stretched his spine and lowered his head below his heart. In that position, he could place himself into a mandala-trance. As a child, he'd been trained to reach the mandala-state by the use of mild hallucinogenic drugs while facing a holographic display of an endless fractal plunge toward an unreachable center. Sometimes it was a dive into fractal immortality; other times it was a dark prowl forward through a doomful environment. Still other times it was a forward flight through a fantastic city or an even more deranged countryside. It had not taken the young Brik long to learn how to achieve transcendence.

One evening, without the drugs, without the holographic display, he'd closed his eyes and without even consciously trying found that he was already visualizing a mandala plunge. It was not the same imagery as provided by the display, but it was recognizably the same kind of unending plunge forward.

It was as if he were exploring an endless maze of dark corridors and tunnels. The pictures flowed easily into his mind. Upward he was climbing, up the stairs, ducking through a door, forward, to the left and then around a corner to the right, up another long brace of stairs, hurrying now through zigzag corridors, diving across intersections and branching wide avenues, but always upward. Up the stairs, up the ramps, deeper and deeper into the heart of it, but never getting any closer to the center. Whatever it was, whatever lay at the heart of it, he never got any closer.

But it wasn't the goal. It was the journey up and in. It took him deep, and finally, he learned how to pass beyond the conscious domains to the inner realms where the soul built its own world. Here was the real power. Eventually, the young Brik learned to trigger the onset of the dream-time as easily as lying down and closing his eyes.

But here, aboard the *Star Wolf,* it wasn't always easy. Often, he returned to his cabin filled with inner turmoils. There was so much about these poor soft human beings that he didn't understand. And it bothered him intensely that he didn't. It wasn't that he felt in any way inferior or deprived; but while there was any aspect of their behavior that remained a mystery, he felt *vulnerable.* If anything was going to hurt him, it was going to come out of one of those unknown places in the human soul. He couldn't stand that thought. Vulnerability was an intolerable state.

Curiously, he also recognized that the flaw was in himself.

On one level he understood the necessity of vulnerability as part of the nature of transcendence. One must *surrender* to the universe in order to be part of it, but on another level he *couldn't.* His Morthan training made it impossible.

Morthans never surrendered to anything. Not even the universe.

But it was happening more and more often now. Brik kept finding himself trapped in the human dilemma and it left him so frustrated that he couldn't achieve transcendence of any kind. He would lay silently in the dark, processing each of the day's troubling events in turn. He stepped through his completion rituals methodically and carefully, examining each moment from every perspective he could imagine—from the domains of right and wrong as well as the domains in which personal judgment was irrelevant. He did this until the moments lost all meaning and became just another set of incidents in the flows of personal time. Then and only then could he step past the flow-stopping event and move on to the next.

Occasionally he knew doubt. Not of himself. But of the power of the rituals. Sometimes, he felt . . . that there were things . . . that hadn't really resolved. It was a troubling thought, one that nagged at him almost every day now. He knew why. Because his completion rituals were almost always about the same kinds of events. It was as if he was trapped in a loop, completing the same incidents over and over and over again. And the thought occurred to him that the reason this incident kept returning in a new guise each day was that there was actually some much larger and darker moment that he had failed to address, and these lesser moments were merely the surface eructations.

These were the moments in which he felt his strongest doubts. Had his training been flawed? Or had he failed to grasp some part of it? He knew that one could not force transcendence. It arrived only when one cleared a space for it, never when one demanded its presence. On those evenings when Brik felt most frustrated, he retreated to a very private and almost embarrassing escape.

He went down to the forward showers, set all twelve sprays for as hot and as violent as they would go, stood in the center of the room, and chanted. He hummed. He *ommmmmed.*

He let himself relax completely, while the water pounded his chest, while the steam rose around him, and he let a great soul-filling purr resonate throughout his body.

There was no spiritual reason for this.

He did it simply because it felt good to submerge.

He did it because it was *sensual*.

The water jets massaged him. The steam drained the tension from his muscles, leaving him limp and unnerved. The sound of his own deep note filled his personal universe.

Abruptly. Someone was here. He opened his eyes.

Bach. Her mouth a startled O of surprise.

"Oh, I'm sorry, Brik. I didn't know—" Her glance flickered down, then up again, then down—she flushed crimson. "I, uh—" She turned and left embarrassedly.

For the first time in his life, Brik felt *naked*.

He did not sleep easily that night. It was another one of those moments that refused to complete itself, refused to be assimilated.

Timmy

Jon and Carol pooled their accumulated leave and spent five days falling in love. Afterward, neither of them was ever the same again. Korie came back with a glint of knowledge in his eyes and a bounce to his step that let people know that the missing piece had finally been found. Carol came back glowing. Neither of them said a word to anyone, they didn't have to, everyone already knew.

The experience of unconditional love transformed Jon Korie. He walked around in a glow of astonishment that life could be so amazing. He became generous and demonstrative in ways that left his colleagues and coworkers shaking their heads in disbelief. Once, he even laughed out loud. He suddenly *understood* that he was just like everybody else. For once in his life, he really was *all right*.

As the days rolled over each other, the relationship deepened. As Jon and Carol learned to deal with problems and opportunities together, they went from being lovers to partners. It was the first of many such graduations. Every new experience gave them something new to share, something that was uniquely their own. As their partnership grew, so did their appreciation for each other. After a time, they were no longer two, but one with two parts.

Jon and Carol graduated from the farms at the same time. He went onto the production line where singularity grapplers were assembled; she went into the intelligence engine training labs. As each new Harlie unit came online, it had to be *seasoned* under the tutelage of a committee of super-Harlie units. When the committee finally agreed that the new unit was sane enough to manage the moment-to-moment operations of a liberty ship, it was certified and installed.

As a result, Carol actually made it into deep space before Jon did; she went on seventeen shakedown cruises, five involving short FTL hops. She took great pride in her striated FTL bars. Korie said he was happy for her, but they both knew that he was deeply envious. If there was one thing he wanted more than anything else—perhaps even more than he wanted Carol—it was the chance to travel among the stars.

Eventually, they were both promoted again, which they celebrated with a joyous wedding, a tumultuous party (catered by a delirious Bertha Fleischer), and a short frenzied honeymoon; their next assignments began only three days after the wedding.

This time, Korie found himself installing grappler armatures into actual singularity cages. Because of the accelerating shortage in the higher ranks, he was promoted to crew chief in less than a month, and within three months he was in charge of singularity assemblies for the whole docking spar.

The first time he had to install a pinpoint black hole in a singularity cage, he was so terrified of making a mistake that he threw up three times the night before. But his team followed the procedures they had so carefully rehearsed and the installation went off perfectly. It was a textbook example. Eventually, Jon Korie signed off on thirty-two singularity installations, more than any other crew chief before him.

From there he was promoted to networks, and eventually command center installations. By this time, their first child was already in the incubator, and the sperm and eggs for the second and third had already been harvested.

By the time Jon Korie was twenty-three, he was debugging whole starships. He oversaw sixteen teams and had personally signed off on over a hundred hulls. He and Carol still spent ten hours a week working in the farms so they could shower together afterward. Neither of them realized the reputation they had established until one day, while inspecting a ship, preparatory to its final sign-off, Korie found a cot with its covers turned back in the vessel's inner hull. The ship's captain-to-be admitted sheepishly that while he personally was not superstitious, the crew did not believe the vessel could be considered starworthy until Jon Korie and his wife Carol had performed the appropriate ceremonies. Korie was embarrassed by the request, but finally agreed on one condition. The consummation had to occur during hyperstate FTL conditions. It was a remarkable shakedown cruise.

Admiral Coon was also aboard that cruise. He was so impressed with Korie's grasp of ship mechanics that he offered him an immediate scholarship to Officer Candidate School. "Because of your high rating on the assembly lines, you'll be put into an accelerated program. You'll be serving on a ship in two years; you could be a captain in six." Without consulting with Carol, Korie accepted immediately—and nearly wrecked his marriage.

Carol was terrified of that career track for her husband, and justifiably so. She was also angered that he had made the decision without consulting with her, without apparently even thinking of her needs at all. They were about to have a baby; the egg had been fertilized, the embryo was growing, the decanting day was already set, the party was scheduled. They had even made a down payment on a house to be built upon their return groundside. They had planned a whole life together.

Jon Korie fell to his knees and begged his young wife's forgiveness. There was nothing he could say, no words of apology that would undo the damage. All he could do was ask her to understand how desperately he wanted to go to the stars. The chance to serve on a starship was something he had been dreaming of all his life.

Carol Jane Korie was a remarkable woman. She pulled her husband to his feet and slapped his face. She said, "Future starship captains don't beg. Not for anyone. They make their decisions and stand by them. Now . . . be a captain, tell me what you have decided and ask me to be your partner in this enterprise."

And after he did that, she fell into his arms and said, "Do you think I don't understand your dreams, you jerk?"

"I was afraid you'd say no."

"If I ever said no to you, Jon Thomas Korie—if I ever said anything to keep you from going FTL, you'd never forgive me. We'd never have a partnership again; we wouldn't have any kind of marriage at all. Yes, I'm angry—but I want you to understand that what I'm angry about is not that you failed to consult with me, but that you didn't trust our partnership enough in the first place."

For a while Korie wondered if he should turn down the admiral's offer; he brooded about his selfishness and the terrible hurt he'd inflicted on his wife; the next several days were very uncomfortable. Neither was certain if they had really made up, if the incident was actually resolved, or if they still had work to do to bridge the gap that had suddenly opened up between them.

A few days later they went to visit their developing fetus in the nursery. At first Korie was awed by the fragility of the small pink creature growing in the nutrient bottle, he marveled at its tiny little fingers, but then as he turned his head this way and that, trying to imagine the nature of the child-to-be, he was suddenly struck by its similarity to the protein lumps in the meat tanks. He backed away from the tank, disgusted with himself and horrified to be brought face-to-face with his own essential vulnerability—where was the spark that turned lumps of meat into sentient beings? Was this all there was to humanity?

And, unbidden, the answer came to him. It was as if Zaffron were standing there behind him whispering, "Yes, Jon Korie. This is it. This is all there is to a human being. Life is only what you create it to be."

Korie felt suddenly weak. He looked to Carol; she had put her face against the warm glass of the bottle and was standing there with her eyes closed and a blissful smile on her face. She was in a place of her own. Unseen by his wife, Korie sat down on a bench and began to weep silently. It was several moments before Carol noticed, and when she did, she didn't know how to react. She'd never seen her husband like this before.

"What is it, Jon?" she asked, momentarily frightened.

He looked up at her, tears running down his cheeks, and said, "He's so beautiful. So are you. So are all of us. Isn't it amazing that little pink lumps of meat like that can become such beautiful creatures as people—sentient beings able to think and care and share and love each other so much? It scares me, Carol, because now I'm realizing that's what also gives us the ability to hurt each other so deeply—and be hurt in turn."

Carol Jane stayed where she was, still holding on to the glass uterine tank with their baby floating in it. At first she wasn't sure how she should respond; she was profoundly moved by the transformation in her husband, but she had no words that would satisfactorily acknowledge the moment. Finally she turned to the developing infant, tapped gently on the glass, and whispered, "Timmy, look. Your daddy's going to be a starship captain. He's going to be the very best of all starship captains. Doesn't that make you proud?"

That was when Jon Korie knew that she had truly forgiven him. He went to her, his eyes still wet, and took her in his arms. He held her for a long, long time without speaking. At last, he held her apart so he could look into her eyes; he said it simply. "I think I have just learned the most important lesson a starship captain needs to learn."

"What's that?" she asked.

"I'm not alone anymore. I have others depending on me. I can't ever forget that. Not ever again."

She looked into his eyes and saw how deeply he meant it. And that was when *she* knew how much he truly needed her.

Dreams

Korie came awake with a start. He'd been having that dream again. The one where he came home. Only no one was there. The dream was always the same, only the details were different. He went from room to room, looking for Carol and Timmy and Robby. This time, he'd *almost* had them again. This time, he'd *almost* . . .

And then he realized where he was again and the hurt came flooding up in his throat and out his eyes. He crumpled. He buried his face in his hands and let the sobs come again. He couldn't help it anymore. It was too much for one man to bear. The anger, the rage, the frustration. It wasn't fair. He'd been a good husband and father. Loyal. Loving. Kind. He'd been a good officer. Dependable. Responsible. He'd earned better. He *deserved* better. This wasn't the way his life was supposed to work out. One horrible loss after another. The problems mounting up, no end in sight. He wondered how other men handled the pain.

He'd been trained. He'd been through long rigorous hours of courses covering almost every aspect of shipboard life. He'd studied military structure and authority, he'd been indoctrinated with the philosophies of responsibility, both that of the individual and that of the officer; responsibilities to the crew, responsibilities to the ship, responsibilities to the mission—he remembered the endless hours of classroom debate over which responsibility took precedence in any given situation. There had been the personal courses too—seminars in communication and effectiveness and self-discipline. There had been courses in behavior. He'd thrown himself into all those studies with a passion that had amazed himself as well as his instructors. He'd come away from his studies with a sense of self-worth and confidence that let him move through the most troubling situations with an appalling detachment. He focused on the result he needed to produce, not the pain of the journey— and it worked. Most of the time.

But not here.

Nothing he'd ever studied had prepared him for this kind of hammering at his soul. Day after day, it was like swimming in acid. Everybody attacked. Nobody supported. Nobody *nurtured.* He needed Carol. She nourished him. Without her . . . he didn't know how he could keep on keeping on.

But he had to.

It was all that bullshit about responsibility. He was responsible. He couldn't stop. But neither could he stop having these three o'clock in the morning nightmares.

"Mr. Korie?" Harlie.

"I'm fine, Harlie."

"Just checking."

"Thank you."

"Would you like something from the galley? Tea? Hot chocolate?"

Korie shook his head, then realized that Harlie probably couldn't see him. "No, no thanks," he said. He sat up, rubbing his eyes. His sleeping tube stood nearby; he'd fallen asleep on the couch again. He knew he shouldn't have done that. He only had the dream when he fell asleep in a gravity environment. On a subconscious level, gravity reminded him of home. . . .

"You really should eat. You have a busy day ahead of you."

"All right, all right. Don't start with the nagging. I'll have a BLT and hot chocolate."

"Working," said Harlie, and fell silent again.

Korie ran a hand through his hair. Time for a haircut again. He sighed and turned back to his desk. The display of the work station glimmered obediently to life with the same display as before. Korie put his elbows on the desk, put his hands together almost in a prayer position, and cradled his chin in his fingertips. He pursed his lips as he studied the diagrams. He shook his head to himself. "Nope, nope, nope," he said. "Clear it. I need to think about something else. This isn't going to work. There's no way to do this. We're never going to make it. I don't know what I was thinking of, Harlie." He sighed. "I didn't do this crew any favors. If I'd agreed with the admiral's decision to decommission this ship, most of them could have been in new berths by now. Now they're going to miss the biggest battle of this war."

"Some of them might not have the same perspective on it as you do, Mr. Korie. The statistical projection on the upcoming battle at Taalamar is that we will probably lose two thirds of our combatant vessels."

"I saw the same reports you did," Korie said. "And I still think our crew would rather be in the battle than out of it. It's not the dying that people mind, it's dying without a reason. It's dying without a chance." And then he wondered if he was talking for the crew, or just for himself.

"Death is not the same for me," the intelligence engine replied. "I'll have to take your word for it."

Korie sighed. He wasn't in the mood for one of Harlie's interminable philosophical discussions. Harlie would talk forever if he had the right conversational partner. He loved to play with ideas. But . . . all that chatter, it never produced results, and Korie was in the business of producing results, not interesting discussions. He gnawed at a thumbnail.

He felt frustrated. "Why can't we detox this ship? What are we missing, Harlie?"

Harlie didn't answer. Korie didn't notice the omission. Not at first. He was too wrapped up in his own problems.

He remembered his studies. Zaffron used to say, "If you can't find the answer, you're asking the wrong question."

Perhaps that was it. He turned that thought over in his mind for a while.

Hm.

Something *twanged* in his consciousness.

No.

But yes. It had to be.

"Harlie," he said. "You didn't answer my question."

Harlie fell silent again.

"I see." Korie sat back in his chair, thinking. Thinking hard.

"Where's Chief Leen?" he asked abruptly.

"Under the Alpha singularity grappler. Asleep. His crew will not allow him to be disturbed."

"And where's Mr. Brik?"

"In his cabin."

Korie glanced at the time. "He is, hm? Let me see his medical report. Has Dr. Williger cleared him yet?"

"Sir?"

"Never mind. Get my starsuit ready."

"As soon as you eat."

"Yes, *mother.*"

Discipline

Commander Korie checked the seals on his starsuit. He held his helmet under his left arm. He was ready.

He spoke softly to his communicator, knowing that Harlie would relay the request instantly, also annotating its source. "Mr. Brik to aft airlock three, on the double."

He glanced at the time display on his starsuit wrist panel. Assuming that Brik was either in his quarters, on the Bridge, or in the officers' wardroom accessing the ship's library, he was somewhere amidships. Considering Brik's allegiance to discipline, his physical size and speed, and his most probable course through the vessel's corridors, he should be arriving at the aft airlock right about—

"You rang?" said Brik, suddenly looming over Korie.

Korie looked up at Brik. And up. "Yes, I did," he said, deliberately stiff, deliberately loud. Aft airlock three was visible from the cargo bay. Behind Brik, Toad Hall and his supply crew were being deliberately nonchalant as they worked. Korie raised his voice so only the immediate planet could hear. He wanted them to miss nothing. The entire episode was also being recorded automatically into the ship's log, uncoded so that anyone could access it.

"What is this, *Mister* Brik?" Korie demanded.

Brik displayed no emotion. His gaze followed Korie's gesture. "It appears to be a starsuit. A Tyger-sized starsuit."

"It *is* a starsuit," Korie confirmed. "A Morthan Tygersized starsuit." He stepped sideways. "Would you please demonstrate its proper use to me?"

"Sir?"

"Put. It. On. Mister."

"I don't see the purpose . . ."

"That *wasn't* a request, Mr. Brik. You and I are going EVA. *Now.*" Korie amazed himself with his tone of voice. He'd never heard anyone speak to a Morthan in this tone of voice before. He couldn't believe he was doing it now. He was relying entirely on his faith in Brik's commitment to the chain of authority.

Brik regarded Korie dispassionately. Whatever was going on behind those dark Morthan eyes, it was unreadable.

"Nobody goes EVA without proper gear," Korie said. "I'm revoking your certification until you demonstrate that you know how to do this by the regs."

Brik looked as if he wanted to speak. Abruptly his expression shifted. His eyes narrowed. "I will do this," he said stiffly. "But I want to log a formal protest."

"I'll help you fill out the forms," Korie said.

Without a word, Brik began shrugging off his outer garments. Korie watched without reaction. Brik *loomed*. The huge bulk of the Morthan physique was intimidating. If Korie had any thoughts at all about the closeness of the near-naked Morthan body, he kept them to himself.

Brik took the starsuit off the rack and pulled it on methodically, first the leggings and the boots, then the tunic. He checked the seals, then turned around so Korie could check them too.

"Green," confirmed Korie, then turned around slowly so Brik could check his.

"Green," rumbled Brik.

"Helmet," said Korie. He pulled his headgear on, fastening it to the starsuit collar, locking it into place. Brik did the same. Again, they checked each other. Green and green.

"Any questions?" demanded Korie.

"No, sir," said Brik.

"Good," said Korie. He slapped the door panel. The hatch whooshed open. Brik stepped into it. Korie followed. Neither the human nor the Morthan spoke. They regarded each other grimly. Korie pressed a wall panel. The hatch slid shut behind them.

On the cargo deck, several of the crew turned and looked at each other with wide eyes. Shrugs were exchanged. Heads were scratched. Toad Hall shook his head. "Don't ask me. I dunno. Maybe it's one of those male-bonding things that officers do."

The others started offering their own opinions. "Korie's trying to show him who's boss."

"He can't win that pissing contest."

"Yeah, but he needs to show Brik he isn't afraid to try."

"Brik's too smart to challenge him."

"And Korie's too smart to put him in a position where he'd have to."

"So why'd they go out there?"

"To look at the stars together?"

"Yeah, right."

"Then you tell me. Two guys get into starsuits and go out for a walk on the hull. What does that mean?"

"That whatever they have to say to each other, they don't want anyone else listening?" offered Gatineau. He was passing through on his way to the scrubbers. Duty Officer Miller had the moebius wrench now. It didn't make sense to him; if the left-handed moebius wrench was such a necessary tool, why was there only one of them onboard?

"We've got privacy pods in the inner hull," said Hall.

"I don't think Korie would want to be seen taking Brik to one of those," one of the women said with a laugh.

Hall shook his head, grinning at the thought. "All right, come on. It's obviously none of our business. Let's get this stuff logged and away."

Thirty minutes later Korie and Brik returned. They peeled off their starsuits without speaking and handed them over for refreshing. Korie finished dressing first. He headed forward without comment. Brik followed after a moment later, growling deep in his throat.

The cargo crew exchanged worried glances, but this time no one speculated on what had transpired between the two officers.

The Crew

Gatineau was in a sour mood when he arrived at the aft cargo bay.

He'd finally figured it out about the moebius wrench—the *left-handed* moebius wrench—and he wasn't happy. In fact, he was absolutely miserable, as close to despair as he'd ever been in his whole life. Perhaps the only worse moment he could remember was the time Sally-Ann Jessup had said, "Couldn't we just be friends instead?" No. *This* was worse. This was his *starship*. This was the place where he lived and worked and served. This was his *career*.

He hated feeling like this. He didn't even have a name for the feeling. He felt hurt and alienated and angry and frustrated and embarrassed all at once. This wasn't fair. He'd earned the right to be treated with respect. Being sent all over the whole ship on a wide-eyed chimerical trek did little to make him feel like he was a useful part of the crew. He felt betrayed. Worst of all, he felt like a *fool*. Worse than that, everybody on the ship *knew* about it. How could he ever look these people in the eye again?

He couldn't. He stared at his shoes. There were two

kinds of footgear aboard the starship—hard-shelled protective boots for heavy work—and soft moccasins for normal duty. He was wearing the boots. He felt silly in them. He felt silly out of them. He felt like a kid who'd crapped his pants the first day of school. No, he felt worse than that. He remembered crapping his pants the first day of school and it hadn't been this devastating.

Korie entered the cargo bay, looking uncommonly crisp for a man who had gone without sleep for a week. Most of the crew were already assembled; a last few stragglers followed Korie in. All of them looked to him anxiously.

This time Korie moved out to the middle of the bay and stood among them like just another crew member. An expectant circle formed around him. Gatineau put himself directly behind Korie so he wouldn't have to see his face. He didn't want Korie seeing his embarrassment. He studied his boots. His big silly boots.

"I'll make this brief," Korie said. His voice was hard. This was clearly not an announcement that he wanted to make. "We're not going to make it. I'm sorry."

There were groans of dismay. Korie held up his hands to stop them. "Belay that. Our hyperstate fibrillators were requisitioned by the *Houston.* Chief Leen sent them over this morning. And Captain La Paz has sent her thanks.

"I'll tell you the truth. The detox job was bigger than we thought. The Morthan assassin left a reservoir of infection aboard this ship, booby traps like the docking tube, nano-cancers, bubbles in the communications yokes, I don't have to list it all for you. You know."

Korie hesitated, phrasing his next words carefully. "Look, I know you're disappointed. So am I. And we're all tired too. But we have a larger responsibility to the fleet. *To the war effort.* Every ship we float is going to make a difference at Taalamar. So that's got to be our first priority. Helping the others get there. Many of them are already on their way."

Korie glanced around the cargo bay, unashamedly meeting the eyes of as many different crew members as he could. He even turned around to look directly at Gatineau. The boy looked distinctly uncomfortable.

"I don't want you to feel that you failed. You didn't. Listen to me." He moved among them, patting their backs, their shoulders, their hands. "We have nothing to be ashamed of. Parts of this ship are already installed in every single one of those other vessels. If it weren't for us, they'd be sitting stuck here too. So *we* might not be going, but our commitment is—*almost a dozen times over.* We're sending eleven other starships to represent us at Taalamar." There were scattered shouts of "Yeah!" and some applause. But not enough.

"Yes," agreed Korie anyway. "Yes. That's our success; it's *your* success. You did good. I'm very proud of you. You didn't fail. You *didn't.*" He made a triumphant chopping gesture with his fist and turned away, almost bumping into Gatineau.

"But it sure feels like it, sir," said Gatineau. He recognized what Korie was trying to do. Recontextualization. But it didn't change the facts. They hadn't made it. Gatineau was still unhappy. And now he had something *else* to be unhappy about.

"I know," said Korie, with more understanding than Gatineau expected. "It *is* upsetting. You're not going to the party, but your dancing shoes are." He touched the younger man on the shoulder gently. "We'll just have to have a party of our own. Maybe Hodel can exorcise something. Oh—" Korie interrupted himself. He turned back to the room, raising his voice. "There is one thing that might take some of the sting off this particular success. One other ship didn't make the cut—the *Houston.*" He smiled at some private satisfaction.

"Oh, God," said Hodel. "They're gonna play *Dixie* at us again, aren't they?"

"I guess we're going to have to find our *own* theme music," Korie said, nodding to the junior officer. "Give it some thought, Mike, will you? Oh, and have Cookie prepare something special for dinner. This crew deserves a break. All right," he said, raising his voice again. "Let's get back to work, people. We've still got a ship to detox. Chief Leen? I want a confidence test in two hours." And then he was out the hatch. Leen started barking at his crew, herding them forward. "Come on, you heard the man! Move your butts! Come on, Cappy! MacHeath! You move too long in the same place!" After that, the cargo bay emptied rapidly. There wasn't anything else to say, and most of the crew headed glumly back to work.

Gatineau stood where he was for a moment, hesitating. Trying to make a decision. He felt like he was walking around with his abdomen ripped open and his guts dripping out. He needed . . . what was the word? *Closure.* That was it. He needed to feel that something had been resolved. He needed to be *heard.* He headed down to the keel and forward, following Chief Leen. It was the quieter way; he'd run into fewer people.

The keel was almost familiar to him now. He'd been up and down it so many times in the past few days, he knew it better than the cabin where he slept. He reached the machine shop and climbed the ladder up into the engine room proper. Leen was already at his work station, running integrity tests on the Alpha grappler and hollering at the Black Hole Gang.

Gatineau's anger flooded hotly back into him. The feelings of frustration and hurt and embarrassment were even more painful here in the engine room where the whole wild chase started. He was suddenly afraid that if he said or did anything else, it would only make it worse. Nevertheless . . . he came around the containment sphere to the chief engineer's station with more resolve than he'd felt for a long while.

He stood directly in front of Chief Leen and spoke as firmly as he could. "Chief?" His voice squeaked. He tried again. *"Chief?"*

The chief engineer looked up from his work station, as if he were acknowledging the delivery of a package. He swiveled on his stool to face the younger man. "What?"

"You sent me on a snipe hunt," Gatineau accused. "A wild goose chase. You had me running all over the ship. And everybody was in on it, weren't they—laughing at me behind my back? That was wrong, sir. That's an abuse of authority. I trusted you. I came here to be trained, not to be subjected to silly practical jokes." Gatineau didn't notice that behind him several of the Black Hole Gang were climbing down from the catwalks and approaching. "You had me embarrassing myself to people I'm supposed to be working with. I busted my ass for you, and for everyone else." Gatineau's voice cracked on the last few words. "I did every damn shitwork job on the whole damn ship just because I wanted to be a good crew member."

Leen waited until Gatineau wound down. Finally, he said, "You came here to be trained, right?"

"Yes, sir. I did."

"Okay. How do you get from the yoke to the forward airlock?"

"Uh." Gatineau frowned momentarily. "You go aft till you get to the engine room access, you climb up to the keel and go all the way forward. Or you follow the primary fuselage and access through the deck in the auxiliary reception chamber." He looked puzzled. "But what does this have to do with—?"

Leen ignored the question. "How do you get from there to the inner hull, seventy degrees, two-thirds aft?"

"Um. You go all the way back through the keel to the cable access forward of the engine room. Up to the upper starboard passage, aft to the airlock bay. Next to the airlock bay is an access panel. Go past the meat tanks."

Leen nodded. "Good. How do you get from the officers' wardroom to the intelligence engine bay?"

"There's two ways. The fastest is to take either corridor forward, onto the Bridge, down to the Ops deck, down and aft through the Ops bay, down to the keel, and up the first ladder. But because Bridge access is restricted, it's better to just go aft, take the drop chute to the keel, and head forward again." Comprehension was beginning to show on Gatineau's face.

"Good," said Leen. "What are the specific responsibilities of Reynolds, Stolchak, and Fontana?"

"Reynolds is the union steward. Stolchak is the duty officer for the farm. Fontana is the chief pharmacist's mate."

"Which one of them do I see if I need a case of Martian anchovies for the captain's pizza?"

"Neither. You ask Toad Hall, the ship's dog-robber."

"Where do I go for a rotator jacket?"

"Storage compartment 130-G7, inner hull. Access through the port corridor, down and forward."

"Who's our official warlock?"

"Mikhail Hodel, sir."

"What's scotatic ventriculation?"

"Deep-gravity skeltering of chaotic antimatter."

"How do you know if you've been in space too long?"

"Dr. Williger starts to look good to you."

"What's rule number one?"

"Uh—whatever your superior officer says it is."

"Yep." Leen nodded. "I'd say you're pretty well trained. What do you think?"

"Uh—" Gatineau began uncertainly. Fear of further embarrassment kept him from answering what he was thinking. He was thinking he'd done pretty damned well.

Leen pointed past the crewman's shoulder. "I wasn't asking you. I was asking *them.*"

Gatineau turned around. Gathered in a group behind him were Reynolds, Hall, Stolchak, Cappy, MacHeath, Fontana, Eakins, Freeman, Hodel, Goldberg, Armstrong, Green, Ikama, Saffari, and just about everyone else who'd been a part of his search for the elusive moebius wrench. As one, they began applauding, laughing, and cheering. "Good job, Gatineau!" Even Commander Brik had paused on his way through the engine room and to nod his own gruff acknowledgment.

"Huh?" Gatineau turned back to Leen, startled and surprised. "But, but—" Understanding came flooding up inside him then. He'd been *initiated.* He'd been proving that he was a good team player.

Still flustered, he turned back around to face the other crew members, feeling embarrassed all over again, as well as proud and annoyed and happy to finally be in on the joke. And finally . . . finally, he felt *fellowship.*

"You sons of bitches!" he muttered, shaking his head and grinning broadly all at the same time. And then somebody was clapping him on the back and somebody else was shaking his hand and abruptly Irma Stolchak was giving him a kiss that was much more than friendly, and when he finally surfaced for air, all he could say was, "I mean it! You're all sons of bitches!" But he was laughing and so were they. "And I wanna be a son of a bitch just like all of you."

And then he turned back to Leen again. "But . . . just one thing. Tell me the truth. There's no such thing as a moebius wrench, is there?"

"Who said that?" said Leen. "I never did. As a matter of fact, I have a moebius wrench right here."

"*You do?*" Gatineau's eyes went wide in disbelief.

Leen turned back to his work station and slid open a drawer. He reached in and pulled out a plaque with a golden wrench mounted on it; the handle was twisted around on itself, with a moebius half twist. Leen stood up and with great ceremony handed the plaque to Gatineau.

"Congratulations, son," he said, shaking Gatineau's hand.

Gatineau took the plaque, uncomprehending at first, then he stared in surprise and astonishment. Beneath the wrench, the nameplate said:

Order of the Moebius Wrench
Engineer Robert Gatineau
Star Wolf

"Wow," said Gatineau. "And wow again. That's—beautiful! Wow!" He shook his head in disbelief. "I'm really . . . wow . . . I don't know what to say. This is great."

"It's okay," said Cappy. "We weren't expecting a speech."

Abruptly a puzzled expression crossed Gatineau's face. "Uh, can I ask one question? How did you guys do that pixie thing?"

"What pixie thing?"

"The star-pixie? You know. The one I saw in the farm . . . ? Behind the corn . . . With the big eyes . . . ?"

Leen looked confused. So did the others. "Huh?"

Gatineau's expression wisened abruptly. "Okay, I get it, I get it. Never mind. One snipe hunt is enough. Keep your pixie. Have your joke."

"Hey," said MacHeath. "I promise you, nobody did anything. We don't have a lot of spare time around here, as you may have noticed."

"Right," said Gatineau quickly. "Right. Nobody did anything. If that's the way you want to be—okay, okay." He accepted a congratulatory tankard of Chief Leen's finest beer (aged two hours) and demonstrated what else he had learned since boarding the *Star Wolf*.

Later, MacHeath remarked to Chief Leen. "That pixie business. You think he was trying to reverse the gag?"

"I certainly hope so. I'd hate to think we hadn't trained him properly."

Fennelly

Jon Korie's first ship was a young ship, the *LS-714*. Her captain was Kia Miyori, a petite Asian woman who commanded her crew with exquisite politeness and respect. The *LS-714* was one link in an extensive pipeline running mail and supplies to several small colony worlds deep across the rift that divided the majority of Allied worlds from the unknown bulk of the Morthan Solidarity. Korie was away from home four months at a time, with only two weeks leave between trips.

If Carol was unhappy with his long absences, she never said so. She worked hard to make sure that every moment of their short times together was a honeymoon. She voiced no complaint, she listened attentively to his concerns, and she made sure that he went away again with joyous memories and a commitment to come home.

Korie served as ship's treasurer and senior farm officer for thirteen months, increasing the ship's general efficiency rating one point for each month of service. He was awarded a triple bonus and a letter of commendation from Admiral Coon's office.

After the third trip across the rift, Korie requested time with his family and was temporarily assigned to the Academy, where he taught other young officers how to manage the complexities of starship bookkeeping and inventory. He was an effective instructor and at the end of his three-month term was offered a permanent position.

Carol wouldn't let him accept it. Although the past three months had seen some of their happiest days—and nights —together, she wasn't foolish enough to try to make it last forever. "You'll never be happy until you've got a captain's stars on your shoulders," she told him. "You're getting fidgety, Jon. It's time for you to get back into space."

Jon Korie's second ship was the *LS-911*. He was appointed her second officer and astrogator. He had helped to build the *LS-911;* he had installed her farm, and later had been part of the team to certify her singularity stardrive. He proudly showed both his signatures on the inside of the hull to the captain. This turned out to be a mistake.

Captain Jack Fennelly was a hard man, tough and uncompromising. He'd had a long and successful career in the service and he had his own ideas on how a ship should be run. He wasn't happy with the shape of the new Allied navy. The accelerated pace of production was producing hundreds of new ships and captains; Fennelly resented that these much younger men were earning their appointments so early in life and so easily. He viewed Korie's pride in the ship and his enthusiasm for her maintenance not as an asset, but as a threat to his own credibility.

Korie worked hard for Fennelly; he recognized that there was much he could learn from the man; but Fennelly never acknowledged Korie's efforts. No matter how good a job Korie accomplished on something, Fennelly only pointed out how it could have been better, how it should have been done instead.

Korie withdrew into himself and renewed his studies of the *zyne.* He refused to let the circumstances control his emotions. During this time, as a way of clarifying his thoughts, he wrote several extensive inquiries into the nature of command; he called the document *The Quality of Service.*

At the heart of Korie's thesis was the thought that loyalty cannot be created by command; it must be created by service. Before a captain can expect loyalty from a crew, he must first demonstrate an uncompromising commitment to their well-being. The quality of the service he receives from his crew is a direct reflection of the quality of service he creates.

This thought led Korie into a further consideration of the nature of service. After some months of self-examination, he realized that service is the highest condition of human endeavor, not the lowest—that the real measure of a person's power was the number of people he *served*. A captain's job was not only to serve his superiors, but to serve the needs of his crew as well—in fact, if anything took priority, it had to be the well-being of the ship, because without a healthy ship, a captain could not accomplish anything else.

Korie sent a copy to his old mentor, Zaffron, for comment. He did not, however, submit the work for publication or even put it into any of the networks because he felt that some of his comments might be seen as uncomplimentary to his superior officers. Zaffron wrote a long thoughtful reply, consisting more of questions than of comments. Korie rewrote the work three times, then put it aside for further consideration in the future.

Korie's preoccupation with this private project also served to keep him out of Captain Fennelly's way. Fennelly noticed only that Korie had become extremely subdued in his demeanor and believed that he had finally broken him to the saddle; as a result, he eased up on the young officer and much of the tension on the Bridge began to dissipate.

Halfway through this tour of duty, the military tensions between the Allied worlds and the Morthan Solidarity became even more aggravated. Allied intelligence revealed that the Morthans were now building up their fleets at least as aggressively as the Allies.

Sensing that war was becoming a very real possibility, Korie expanded his studies to include numerous texts on strategy and tactics. Despite the fact that the Alliance's intelligence engines had been running extensive conflict scenarios for decades, Korie still felt frustrated at the lack of an overall vision of the nature of war in space. He began assembling his thoughts into another set of inquiries, this one entitled *Working Toward a Theory of Conflict*.

In this work, he did not attempt to resolve the issue. That would have been premature and presumptuous. It was his feeling, however, that because there had never been an interstellar war on the scale that was now possible between the Allied worlds and the Morthan Solidarity, that all previous models of conflict had to be reexamined in this larger context.

While certain fundamental aspects of war would always remain unchanged—such as protecting supply lines, holding and keeping the high ground, and knowing your enemy's strategy at least as well as your own—the specific applications of these principles to FTL situations represented a whole new domain of strategic possibilities and dilemmas. The potential for disaster terrified the young officer. It was Korie's purpose to distinguish those areas that he felt needed a much deeper examination. While his essays were ultimately intended to sound a cautionary note to those who determined strategy; they were more immediately a way for him to clarify his own thinking.

For the most part, Korie approved of the fleet's killer bee strategy, but it depended to a great deal on the resourcefulness and courage of individual starship captains. That was both its strength and its weakness. Working at FTL velocities, it was impossible for a central command to coordinate the actions of a thousand, ten thousand, or ultimately a hundred thousand separate destroyer-class cruisers. Therefore, each and every ship was on its own—and each and every captain had to behave as ferociously as possible. Each and every captain must act as if his or her actions alone would determine the final outcome of the war . . . because they very well might.

It seemed to Korie that if there was a weakness in the strategy, this was it. The accelerated program of ship building, the rapid rate of training and promotion, did not provide the experience or the seasoning that captains and crews would need to behave appropriately in a battle situation. In the confusion of a major assault, some ship captains might hold back; others might even panic. This would put an increased burden on every other Allied ship, both strategically and psychologically, and would seriously weaken the assault.

If a battle swarm were to fail—and fail badly—Korie

wrote, the psychological blow to the Allied fleet would be devastating. It would be impossible for any captain to engage in a swarm if he did not believe that his colleagues were equally committed. Therefore, appropriate psychological screening of all captains was mandatory, as well as intensive training in dealing with combat situations.

Korie also postulated an alternate strategy, one that he felt could be implemented with minimal effort; it would include most of the same strengths of the killer bee strategy while minimizing its weaknesses. He called it the *killer shark* strategy. In this scenario, the swarm would be broken up into many small task forces, each with a single area of responsibility. Within each task force, each destroyer would have its own area of responsibility, either defense or offense. If any individual vessel encountered a Morthan warship, it could send out a coded hyperstate burst and every task force member in range would home in on that signal like a pack of sharks in a feeding frenzy.

Decentralizing the fleet would allow space battles to be fought as skirmishes instead of major confrontations and would reduce the opportunities for the enemy to inflict a devastating blow to the Allied fleet in a single battle. Additionally, the spreading out of assault forces would make interception much more difficult, especially if all of the ships engaged in an attack were coming in from radically different directions.

Korie spent months working out the dynamics of these battles, running simulations on the *911*'s Harlie unit. There were assumptions in his work that were quickly proven false; he removed them from the main thesis, and added appropriate discussions to the appendix. There were *other* extrapolations, however, that brought him ultimately to the most stunning realization of all about the nature of conflict at FTL velocities.

In hyperstate all ships are equally vulnerable. The size of the vessel is irrelevant. If you can disrupt its hyperstate envelope, you can destroy the vessel.

In hyperstate all ships are equally dangerous. The size of the vessel is irrelevant. If a ship can approach close enough, it can fire a hyperstate torpedo.

All that really matters is how fast a ship can travel and how far it can see. The size of the hyperstate envelope determines the FTL velocity as well as the range of the hyperstate scanning lens; so the *real* measure of a starship's power is determined only by the size of its singularity and the sophistication of its fluctuator assemblies.

The more that Korie studied this dilemma, the more he began to appreciate it as a problem in three-dimensional chess.

The farther a ship can see, the less likely it is that another ship can sneak up on it unnoticed and launch a hyperstate torpedo. The faster a ship can travel, the more likely it will be able to approach an enemy vessel successfully and launch its torpedoes before the target can react to either escape or launch torpedoes of its own. Therefore, a ship's strategic abilities, both offensive and defensive, are intrinsically linked.

The only way a ship can avoid detection from a great distance is to mute its hyperstate envelope so that it no longer resonates with such a high profile; but this technique effectively blinds it, as well as severely cutting its realized velocity. On the other hand, it also allows a ship to sneak in under the threshold of noise and approach much closer before detection by the target.

This train of thought troubled Korie, leading ultimately to another set of scenarios. The most immediately effective were those where one or more warships muted their envelopes to mimic much smaller, weaker vessels, thus luring their victims into striking range.

There were long-term scenarios to be aware of too, also involving mimicry and subterfuge. Korie was beginning to understand the real nature of the beast. The war would not be won with superior strength or firepower; those had been nullified. Nor would it be won with methodical strategies and tactics; those too had been leveled by the nature of the playing field. No—the battles would be fought as a duel of perseverance and perception; they would be played as chess matches to the death; and they would be won or lost in the minds of the opposing captains.

For one brief paralyzing flash, he saw the future; silent starships dueling in the dark, feinting, thrusting, parrying, and dodging, each one jockeying for the one moment of advantage that would allow it to deliver the death blow to the other. It terrified him. He recognized that this was the fundamental weakness of the Alliance.

It wasn't enough for the Alliance to launch ships and send them bravely out into the night. The insufficiency of the effort was suddenly apparent to him. The Morthans were also launching ships, but the Morthans had taken war as a way of life. They were a race of self-designed, self-created beings, no longer recognizable as human—genetically engineered and biologically augmented to be superhumans, *More-Than* humans. They had taken the disciplines of the martial arts and channeled their whole culture into the production of warriors who did not know how to lose a battle. Every single Morthan captain, and every member of every Morthan crew, would be an expert in the art of mayhem; every vessel would be commanded by a grandmaster in the art of death.

By contrast, the captains of the Allied starships were mere children. A few years of schooling, a few classes at the War College, were no match for a lifetime of discipline and purpose. The Allied fleet would be at terrible risk unless the new paradigms of interstellar conflict were fully understood and assimilated by each and every starship commander.

The imminence of the war terrified Jon Korie. He spent many sleepless nights, trembling in fear over the possibilities of the conflict that he was certain were becoming more and more inevitable. He resolved to send Carol and the boys as far away from the rift as they could afford.

The next time the ship touched port, he uploaded all of his writings to the immediate attention of the War College, and he prayed that he was in time.

The Boat

Gatineau hesitated before the docking tube. The memory of the last time was still too recent, still too intense. He still ached, and his skin was still discolored in places.

"Go on," said Brik. "I'll be right behind you."

"That's what I'm afraid of," gulped Gatineau. "I don't want you grabbing me. Give me a chance to do it myself." He took another deep breath—then, surprisingly, he seized the hatch frame and pushed himself headfirst into the tube. It was as if he wanted to get it over with as fast as possible. It was as if he wanted to prove something to Brik. But in truth, it was because he wanted to prove it to himself most of all.

He pulled himself into the boat clumsily, but not disgracefully so. He was starting to figure out this free-fall business after all.

Commander Brik came swooping easily after him. The big Morthan tucked his knees and head into a 180-degree tumble, caught a handhold, and ended up reversed, facing back toward the hatch again, hitting the panel lightly to close and secure it. The entire maneuver had been as skilled and graceful as if executed by a professional dancer.

After a moment Gatineau remembered to close his mouth. He wondered if he'd ever look as good in free-fall. Probably not, he realized. He wasn't a Morthan.

Chief Leen looked up from what he was doing—he was repacking the Feinberger modules in the decontam unit—and grunted. "Give me two more minutes."

"Go forward." Brik nodded to Gatineau. "You've got the conn."

"Yes, sir. You'll be in the right seat?"

"No, I won't." To Gatineau's look, Brik added, "Don't worry. Your copilot is quite competent."

"Oh, yeah, right," said Gatineau, grumbling to himself, not hearing the amusement in Brik's tone. "What's it going to be this time? A moebius joystick? Another star-pixie? Left-handed antimatter?" He pulled himself forward through the cabin of the boat and through the hatch to the flight deck. Without even looking to the copilot, he said, "Whatever jokes you and Mr. Brik have planned, just forget about them. Just leave me alone to do this, okay?" He pulled his headset on and started clicking his displays to life, setting them to green one after the other.

"I don't have anything planned at all," replied Commander Korie. "At least, nothing more than getting you certified as quickly as possible."

"Oh, sir!" Gatineau blurted hastily. "I'm sorry, I didn't mean to—"

"Don't apologize, *Captain*—" Korie said, stressing the last word. "You're in the left seat. You're giving the orders."

It was the word *Captain* that stopped Gatineau in midgulp. "Captain?" he asked.

"That's your rank while you're in charge of this boat. Your authority is absolute."

"You mean . . . if I ordered you to get me a cup of coffee, you'd *have* to do it?"

Smiling, Korie nodded. "That's how it works. And if I didn't get it for you, you could bring me up on charges of insubordination. I don't recommend it though. Remember, I'm still acting captain of the *Star Wolf.* So part of the

lesson you need to learn this afternoon is about cooperation and respect among officers."

"I'm not an officer, sir. I'm just—"

"Stop," said Korie quietly.

Gatineau stopped.

"Let me tell you something. I don't care what your rank
is. I want you to learn how to do every job on the ship. And
I want you unafraid to do it if you have to. If something
happens to everyone around you, I don't want you standing
there with your finger up your nose, wondering what to do
next? Do you know the story of Ensign McGrew?"

"Everybody does. It's apocryphal. McGrew was court-
martialed for taking command—"

"It's not apocryphal. It happened. And you have it
wrong. He was court-martialed for *not* taking command.
All of his superior officers were killed. Instead of taking
responsibility, he panicked and called for help. To be fair, it
was his first tour of duty, he was still being trained, and he
should never have been put in that situation. Nevertheless,
naval regulations *required* him to act, and he did not. Had
they not been dead, his superior officers would also have
been up before a board of inquiry for failing to train Mc-
Grew appropriately. Do I make myself clear?"

"Absolutely, sir."

"Thank you." Korie waited.

"Sir?"

"Yes?"

"Um, what should I do now?"

"You're the captain. You tell me."

"Uhh—oh, right. Uh, prepare for departure. Let's do
the checklist." Gatineau struggled to remember the routine. "Systems analysis?"

Korie glanced at his board. "Green."

"Check. Uh, confidence?"

"Eighty-six."

"Eighty-six?"

"Don't panic. These ducks are supposed to be survivable
with confidence as low as thirty."

"But *eighty-six*?"

"Eighty-six it, Gatineau," Korie said firmly. "It's *okay*.
Trust me."

"Yes, sir—check. Life support?"

"Optimal, with minor cautions. Don't worry, we're not going out that far. And we have starsuits in the locker in case we have to swim back."

"You're joking, right?" Gatineau looked to Korie. Korie's expression was blandly noncommittal. "Never mind. Check," said Gatineau. "Propulsion? Navigation?"

"Green and green. All systems go."

"Check." Gatineau bent to his own displays, running a second set of checks just to be certain he hadn't missed anything. He hadn't. He exhaled loudly, started to put his hands on the controls, then abruptly pulled them back. "I'm really in command?" he asked Korie.

"Yes, Captain, you are," Korie replied calmly.

"Ah," said Gatineau. He leaned back in his seat and folded his arms across his chest. "Copilot, take her out."

Korie's smile widened only a fraction. "Nice try, son." He nodded at the controls. "You show me how it's done."

"Can't blame a guy for trying," said Gatineau, allowing himself a smile. He reached forward again and snapped open the communications channel. "Starboat ready."

"Anytime, Captain," Hodel's voice came back from the Bridge.

"Roger that. Thank you." Gatineau unclipped a safety cover and flipped the switch beneath it. There was a soft thump from behind them, and they were floating free.

"Good job," said Korie. "Take us out ten thousand kilometers, then flipover for the return." He glanced at the time. "Don't take more than two hours getting us there."

Gatineau did the calculations in his head. "Sir? That's—"

"Yes. It's quite a ride. Do it, son." Korie was already unstrapping himself.

"Uh, yes, sir." Gatineau shook his head, not quite certain why the commander wanted to put so much distance between himself and the mother ship, but he began setting up the program on his display.

Korie floated up out of his chair and started to pull himself aftward. "Try not to bump into anything," he said. "When you've got the program locked in, call Harlie, have him double-check it. If Harlie says it's okay, run it and come back aft for a cup of coffee."

"Sir? Aren't you going to check me?"

Korie paused, one hand on either side of the hatch frame. He raised an eyebrow. "Do you think I need to?"

"Uh, no, sir," Gatineau said quickly.

"Good. You'll do fine." Korie added, "Oh, and watch out for sparkle-dancers."

"No star-pixies this time?" Gatineau muttered.

"Of course not. We already have one. In the ship's corn, remember?"

"Huh?" Gatineau turned around in his seat to stare after Korie, but the senior officer was already gone. How did he know about *that*?

Gatineau turned forward again. It was a simple course, but he checked it six times before sending it home to Harlie. The intelligence engine chewed it over for half a milli-second before sending it back. Without comment.

"It's okay?" Gatineau asked.

"If it wasn't, don't you think I would have said some-thing?" replied Harlie blandly.

"Oh, yes, of course. But uh, don't you have any advice for me? I mean, how it could have been more efficient or something?"

"I have no advice," said Harlie. "I assume you pro-grammed exactly what you wanted."

"Uh, yes, I did."

"Then no advice is necessary, is it?"

"Oh, I get it," said Gatineau. "It's like that story they tell you about in training. You know the one. 'You're the cap-tain. You decide.' "

"I wouldn't know," replied Harlie. "Although I do have the training manuals in storage. Do you need to access them now?"

"No, thanks," said Gatineau. "I'm getting the hang of it."

"Have a good flight then," Harlie signed off.

Gatineau shook his head. Did intelligence engines do that on purpose, or what?"

He initiated his program and watched his board. The display went green; the program was running. The engines were soundless; there was nothing to feel, nothing to hear. Even so, Gatineau imagined he could feel the faintest bit of acceleration pushing him back into his couch. It was micro-acceleration, but it was cumulative. They'd spend most of the first hour just climbing to speed. Ten thousand kilometers wasn't really that far, not if you were adding two kilometers per hour per second. At the end of seventy-two hundred seconds, they would have a realized velocity of fourteen thousand kph. Their averaged velocity for the same time would be seven thousand klicks. They could turn their engines off and coast to the flipover point. The math was simple. Any middle-school student could do it.

But of course, when you're sitting alone in the left seat, and the lives of yourself and three other people are at stake, suddenly all the equations take on a whole *other* flavor.

Gatineau wondered if he should stay in his seat the whole two hours or if Korie had really meant it about coming aft for coffee. He *really* wanted the chance to . . . well, just sit with the exec. But—on the other hand, what if something went wrong? He was responsible, wasn't he? On the third hand, if he didn't go, would Korie and the others be insulted? Or if he did go, would he look overeager? On the fourth hand, he *was* the captain here. That was part of the test, wasn't it? If he didn't go aft, that would make him look uncertain. Wouldn't it?

"You know something?" Gatineau said to himself as he unbuckled his belt. "You *think* too much." And then he added, "Yeah, you can say that again." He headed aft.

Korie glanced at his watch as Gatineau floated back. "Being careful?"

"Yes, sir."

The exec nodded him toward a seat. "Strap in. We have some serious talking to do and I don't want you floating around the cabin. There's coffee there. Be careful, it's still hot." Without waiting to see if Gatineau was obeying, Korie turned back to Leen. "So, what do you think, Chief?"

The older man grunted. He scratched his ear unhappily. "I think we should evacuate the crew, then evacuate the air. Then drop the ship into the nearest star."

"We can't do that," Korie said. He was surprised to hear himself saying, "Failure is not an option." He noticed Brik glancing sideways at him with a faintly amused expression.

"We'll never detox the ship, you know that," Leen countered. "Even the crew is starting to figure it out."

Korie sucked at his coffee. "Okay. Can we catch it? Trap it somehow?"

Brik snorted. "It's already trapped. The problem is we're in the cage with it."

"I know that," said Korie, slightly annoyed. "But we have to walk through the steps anyway. I want to ask the easy questions first. Is there *anything* we can do to catch it or kill it?"

Gatineau looked from one to the other, not quite following the conversation. He was afraid to ask. They were talking *as if there was something on the ship*.

As if reading his mind, Brik annotated the conversation for his benefit. He said, "Your star-pixie was real."

"Oh," said Gatineau softly, not quite assimilating the fact. *The star-pixie was real?*

Revelations

"It's a Morthan imp," said Korie. "There wasn't *one* Morthan aboard this ship. There were *two*. An assassin and an imp. Cinnabar brought the imp with him when he invaded."

The others waited while Gatineau assimilated this information.

"Oh," said Gatineau. Then, "Oh!" And finally, *"Oh."*

"He got it," remarked Leen.

Gatineau was already putting pieces together. "So that's what you went EVA to talk about!"

"He's observant," noted Brik.

To Korie, he said, "And you had to bawl him out in front of everybody, so no one would know what you were really doing—"

"And quick," agreed Korie to Brik. To Gatineau, he said, "We have to assume that it's not safe to talk on the *Star Wolf*. We don't know how completely our integrity has been compromised. We have to assume it's total. We can't even discuss this with Harlie. We have to assume he's been compromised too."

"Even the personal codes?"

"Yes. We have to make that assumption too. It's much more likely that the imp hasn't gotten into everything it could; only those domains important to its purpose; but we don't know what it's done, so we have to assume the worst." Korie sipped at his coffee through a straw. Gatineau did likewise. He made a face. It wasn't the best way to drink coffee; if you couldn't smell it, you couldn't really taste it.

"All right," said Korie, continuing. "Brik and I went EVA so I could brief him about the situation. We ended up briefing each other. Brik had figured it out too."

"Are you sure your EVA was secure?" asked Leen.

"We went out on tethers, set up a static shield, and talked for a half hour, helmet-to-helmet communication only. If the imp is as smart *and as paranoid* as Brik says, then it has to assume that we know it's aboard the ship by now. So we're not assuming that the imp doesn't know that we talked about it. But we *are* assuming that it probably doesn't know the specifics of what we said." Korie added, "By the way, you both need to know that the first thing I did was apologize to Mr. Brik for deliberately embarrassing him."

"And I told the commander," Brik put in, "that no apologies were necessary. The security of the vessel was compromised. He needed a place for a secure conversation and a believable cover story for getting there. Dressing me down in public for a dangerous EVA was highly appropriate. It was the best way to get me outside quickly." To Korie, he said, "You can't hurt my feelings, sir. I'm a Morthan. I don't have feelings. Not like humans, anyway. I don't allow personal to get in the way of purpose."

"Right," agreed Korie. "Nevertheless, let's get on with this." Speaking mostly to Leen now, he said, "Here's how I found it. I was doing the log and I asked Harlie for his thoughts about the various incidents of Morthan sabotage. Had he done a time-and-motion study on the ones we'd found? Given the length of time Cinnabar was aboard the vessel, how many more could we expect to uncover? What did his analysis suggest?"

"And—?"

"He said it was inconclusive. He wasn't willing to commit."

Leen frowned. "That's not an appropriate reply. An intelligence engine of Harlie's rating should have an opinion on almost everything."

"That was my thought too," Korie said. "When a Harlie unit refuses to tell you something, that's like a big red arrow. So I asked to see the raw data myself."

"And—?"

"Harlie dumped the raw data to my clipboard. So I could look at it at my leisure, he said. It was obvious he didn't want to show it to me himself, but there was something he needed me to know. So I waited till the boat was powered down, came over here, and locked myself in the lavatory. It didn't take too long. Harlie didn't make it obvious, but it was there if you knew what to look for. We had too many booby traps. Too far apart. More than a few of them were of sufficient complexity to require significant preparation and installation time. Cinnabar didn't have the time aboard to do it all."

"You needed Harlie to tell you that?" asked Leen.

"No. I needed Harlie to prove it. Harlie had come to the same conclusion, but he couldn't figure out a safe way to tell me. He's assumed even *his* own integrity is compromised."

"And Brik? How did he figure out Cinnabar planted an imp?"

"Easy. It was what I would have done," Brik said. "I realized we had a problem when the docking tube came apart. We'd already detoxed it. That's why I went EVA. I wore a simulated imp strapped to my chest to see if it could survive. It did. Your sighting, Crewman Gatineau, was the confirmation I needed."

None of them spoke for a moment, each of the men was lost in his own mordant thoughts. Finally, Leen sighed unhappily. "So we've got a second Morthan on the ship. We've had it here the whole time. And all of our detox efforts have been *wasted.*"

"That's right," said Brik.

They were all silent a moment longer as each considered the ramifications.

"A Morthan on a starship," Gatineau said. "Ouch."

"That's pretty bad news all right," said Korie, looking pointedly at Brik.

"Yes," Brik agreed dryly. "Especially if the Morthan is not on your side."

Gatineau didn't catch all the undertones of that exchange. He scratched his head. "But it's not the same kind of Morthan, is it? It's not a Tyger."

"It's an imp," said Brik. "Not an imp from your mythology, an imp from *ours.* This is not a cute, mischievous, little cherub with horns. This thing is an apprentice demon. It's a hellish little bastard, a single-minded sabotage machine, half a meter high. Very fast. Not particularly strong. And not particularly smart either—not by Morthan standards. By human standards . . . well, you wouldn't want to play chess against it. It's a kind of *programmed* intelligence. They do what they're told. You give one a task and you turn it loose. They're very good for suicide missions." Brik added, "They're also supposed to be fairly good eating."

"Better than rat?" asked Leen.

"I wouldn't know," replied Brik coldly. "I don't eat rat."

Korie ignored the exchange. Despite repeated requests on his part that the two of them learn to work together, Brik and Leen continued to snipe at each other. "So," he said cautiously. "This imp was programmed to booby-trap the *Star Wolf?*"

"Just in case Cinnabar failed."

"He must not have liked that thought."

"He was probably planning to eat it. It must have been programmed to go its own way as soon as it could. It had plenty of time aboard the *Burke,* and even longer aboard the *Star Wolf.* So at this point, it probably knows liberty ships as well as you or Chief Leen. Let's assume it's had time to explore everything it wants to aboard the ship. Let's also assume that the only traps we're finding are those it wants us to find. Including the sabotage of the docking tube. It's possible that one was aimed at me. It's also very possible that I was *supposed* to survive it."

Korie thought about that. "It's given itself away then . . . deliberately." And then he thought about that some more. "Okay. It wants us to know it's here," he added. "Why?"

They all thought about that for a moment. Gatineau

sipped at his coffee. The others had forgotten theirs. He was still wondering why he had been included in this meeting. He knew he wasn't here by accident.

"It's bored?" suggested Leen. "It wants to play games with us."

Brik shook his head. "Morthans don't play with their food."

Gatineau asked abruptly, "Can we open the ship to space?"

Leen shrugged. "We can do anything the captain orders. Or whoever's acting captain," he added, pointedly looking at Korie. To Brik, he said, "Will that kill it?"

Brik shook his head. "How long will it take to get the entire crew into starsuits? Certainly long enough for the imp to figure out what's about to happen. Do you think a creature that's had nearly a month to prepare might have a secure chamber somewhere for just such an eventuality? Can you think of a way to get the entire crew into starsuits and off the vessel in less than fifteen seconds? Anything longer than that, you can assume the imp is back in its pod." He added, "Can you think of a way to set up a plan, *any plan*, without alerting the imp that you're planning something?"

Gatineau sighed. "I see the problem."

"And if you open the ship to space, you lose the farm," added Korie. "Lose your cash crops and you're out of business. Again."

"I guess I still have a lot to learn."

"It's worse than that," added Brik. To Korie he said, "Chief Leen scanned those high-cycle fluctuators while we had them aboard. He read their memories into Harlie. Everything. That means the imp most certainly has a copy of that information too. It'll be looking for an opportunity to get that information into the hands of its masters."

"Stop trying to cheer me up," said Korie. "I'm feeling bad enough already."

"It gets worse," said Brik. "It only gets worse. Can you trust this ship now? Are you willing to trade parts of her to anyone else? You have nothing to trade? How do you know the imp won't be in one of your trade boxes?"

"We don't have many options, do we?"

"We can scuttle the ship."

"The admiral will like that." Korie put his coffee bulb aside. "I hate being wrong. I'd rather be clever."

"That's how Cinnabar got killed."

"I know. So what do we do now?"

No one answered him.

Faslim-Arub

When Korie's twelve-month tour of duty aboard the *911* came to an end, Captain Fennelly grudgingly gave him a satisfactory recommendation and Korie applied for a six-month course of study at the War College before returning to space. He was immediately approved.

Korie's treatise, *Working Toward a Theory of Conflict*, was only one of more than three thousand documents submitted on the very same topic. Clearly, a significant percentage of the younger generation of starship officers were concerned about the structure of the fleet and the training available to its commanders. With varying degrees of insight, the authors considered the advisability of existant defense plans, the nature of interstellar war, and the prospects for an Allied success against a well-trained Morthan armada using the current strategy books. Few were sanguine; most of the papers demonstrated significant concern; a few were genuinely alarmed. Several paralleled Korie's reasoning.

To Korie's credit, his paper was one of the most clearly written; it was uncompromising in its examination of the strengths and weaknesses of both sides in the coming war; and it was clear in its conclusions that the old ways of fighting a war were going to prove woefully inappropriate. What set Korie's paper apart from almost all of the rest was his detailed analysis of the psychology of war in space and his alternate proposals for offensive and defensive battle tactics based on misleading and confusing the enemy as to what kind of a ship he was up against and what its intentions really were.

The admirals of the navy had long been aware of the deficiencies of the killer bee strategy, but the intelligence engines had predicted that swarming the enemy was the best way to overcome the problem of insufficient training for individual starship crews. After Korie's work arrived at the War College (as well as the other treatises), the intelligence engines were asked to reconsider the problem and this time allow for the current status of fleet morale and the overall level of training for command level officers.

The results were much closer to what Korie (and others) had suspected, and the War College immediately shifted to emergency status to develop new strategies as well as new training programs. Korie's work ensured his immediate appointment. Even had he not applied to the War College he would have been assigned there.

At the War College strategic study groups were formed to pit their various strategies against each other. Later, after the results were evaluated, several new training programs were instituted, specifically designed to give starship commanders a sense of Morthan strategy and psychology as well as to harden them against possible Morthan tactics. This was the most challenging period of Korie's leadership training and he went to bed (alone) exhausted and exhilarated every evening.

At the end of six months, he was rotated out of the War College and promoted to executive officer of the *LS-1066*. This too was a ship he had helped construct. He had led the team that laid her keel.

Captain Margaret Faslim-Arub was candid with Korie. She did not expect him to serve aboard her vessel for very long; he was slated for a ship of his own. The next time they returned to Stardock, Korie would probably be promoted—perhaps within the next six months. The pace of production had been accelerated again, and the demand for qualified commanders had become critical.

There was no question in Captain Faslim-Arub's mind that Korie was well qualified for command. She gave him the conn at every opportunity; the greatest gift she could give him would be a sense of comfort and familiarity at the helm of a starship. Korie appreciated not only the opportunities to learn, but the implied acknowledgment of his ability. It was a refreshing change after the passive-aggressive abuse of Jack Fennelly.

He repaid her faith in him by working long hours in every section of the ship bringing each one up to spec and beyond. He upgraded the gardens, the meat tanks, the recyclers. He recalibrated the fluctuators and stabilized the singularity for a more accurate focus; he rebuilt the magnetic grapplers, and when he was through, he had boosted the ship's top speed by five percent. He interviewed the Harlie unit and with its permission made several minor modifications that amplified its confidence rating in itself by three percent. He redesigned a number of command procedures, shortening the time it took for the vessel to initiate its hyperstate envelope and collapse it as well. He designed combat drills and simulations based on his experiences at the War College.

Unfortunately for Korie . . . the *LS-1066* was assigned a rigorous set of duties that kept her away from Stardock—as well as from his family—for nearly eighteen months. She ferried colonists, mail, cargo, military supplies, and once even a high-ranking ambassador. She participated in three sets of war games, twice playing the part of the enemy. As frustrating as it was to have his promotion delayed, the experience was still invaluable to Korie; he learned about the exigencies of command in a variety of situations—but he missed his wife and children too. He ached to see them again. Their letters weren't enough to ease the loneliness. He filled his days with as much work as he could so he could fall asleep quickly at night.

At last the *LS-1066* was ordered back to Stardock for the installation of a set of prototype ultrahigh-cycle fluctuators, which would boost her top speed by a factor of two, giving her a theoretical maximum realized velocity of twenty-three hundred C, and a practical maximum realized velocity two thousand times the speed of light.

Korie delayed his own transfer to supervise the installation of the new fluctuators. He wanted to lay his own hands on the machinery, fit the modules into place himself, calibrate each separate assembly, install the redesigned singularity grapples, check the housings, tune the cables, and make the coffee. He wanted to learn everything he could about the new high-cycle fluctuators; this was the weapon that could win the war and he wanted to be the expert.

Three test cruises were scheduled. On the first one, the *LS-1066* traveled to a star system nearly six light-years distant in a single day of ship time. On the second cruise, the starship went to a deep rift observation post, twenty-three light-years distant. It took four days of ship time. The third mission would be across the rift and back; the ship would be gone for four months.

Korie wanted to make the leap; he wanted to pin a black rift-crossing ribbon to his chest; but except for two all-too-brief leaves, he hadn't been home in nearly two years. There would be other missions. It wouldn't be fair to Carol for him to take another four months away, if he didn't absolutely need to.

Korie took three months of accumulated leave to spend with his wife and two sons. At first, neither of the boys recognized him—they cried and fought when he tried to pick them up. They resented it when he came home with them and went into the bedroom with their mommy.

But he persevered; he threw himself into the process of being a good father with the same enthusiasm and dedication he had demonstrated in the construction, maintenance, and running of a starship. Very soon his boys began to recognize that having a dad in the house created a joyous new dimension in their lives. They began to worship him.

Jon Korie was a loving father. He enjoyed parenting. He woke up early every morning and made breakfast for Carol and the boys. He woke them gently and, tucking one under each arm, carried them into the bathroom for a morning bath. He washed the boys with industrial thoroughness; he dried them with equal precision; he supervised the brushing of their teeth as if each tooth had to be individually detoxed; and he brushed their hair with exquisitely tender care and a ruler-straight part. Had it been possible to perform a white glove inspection on the children, both his sons would have passed with highest ratings. He picked out their clothes and helped them dress until they insisted they were big enough to do it without his help.

But if there was a quality of military precision to the way he applied himself to the task of caring for his children, there was also an equal quality of pure uncompromised affection. During the day, he always made time to play with them, to give them piggyback rides or swimming lessons or simply a silly scrimmage in the park. They had tickle fests and water fights and endless games of chucklebelly. He was a god to them.

Korie took his sons on outings and picnics; they went to concerts, plays, and exhibitions where Jon Korie pointed out each and every aspect of the displays until his children began to yawn in boredom.

It did not escape Carol Korie's perceptive eye that there was a manic quality to her husband's attentiveness—as if he were trying to compress a lifetime of parenting into a single visit home, as if he *knew* something about the shape of the future.

In the evenings he tucked his children into bed; he brushed their unruly hair back away from their eyes; he listened thoughtfully to their prayers; and then he hugged and kissed each one good night. And somehow even after all of that, at the end of the day he still had the energy and dedication to make himself one hundred percent available to his wife.

Carol understood what he was doing. Jon Korie was creating the experience for himself of a family; he was giving himself a lifetime's worth of memories, so he would have something to take with him when he journeyed out again. More importantly . . . he was trying to leave a part of himself behind, so that if by some terrible chance, he did not return, his children would still know they had had a real father.

The Conversation

"We can't even scuttle the ship," Korie said. "Once we start moving crew members off, even one boatload at a time, the imp will know she's being abandoned. What do we do with dead ships? We break them up, open them to space, use them for target practice. The imp won't let that happen. If it thinks it's going to die, it's going to take us with it. Something probably goes ka-blooie before the first crew member gets out the airlock. Certainly before the last."

"Not only that," said Leen, "where do you evacuate the crew *to*? And how can you be certain the imp doesn't find a way to come with?"

"To Stardock—?" asked Gatineau, hoping to be helpful. "Decontam?"

None of the three glanced at him, but Korie's brow furrowed at the thought. "The imp needs this ship, and it needs this crew. . . ."

"We've got a Morthan by the balls," said Leen. "We can't hang on, we can't let go." A thought occurred to him. He looked to Brik. "Do Morthans even have balls?"

Brik regarded the chief engineer coldly. "Morthans don't dance."

Korie allowed himself a grin. "Probably because no Morthan will let any other Morthan lead for longer than ten seconds."

Brik's eyes narrowed. "Morthans don't dance *like humans.*"

"Right," said Korie. That line of discussion was over. He stretched where he floated, pulling his arms back until his spine made a satisfying knuckle-crunch. He brought himself back to normal. "All right, let's assume it knows whatever we know. In fact, let's assume that whatever we know *about it* is only what it wants us to know." Korie looked from one to the other, even including Gatineau. "Here's what we know about Morthans. Everything is a calculation. Every action has an intended result, both immediate and consequential. If a Morthan shows you something, he *wants* you to see it because your reaction serves his purpose. There are no Morthan accidents. Right, Brik?"

Brik rumbled his assent, but he was abruptly thinking of something else. Helen Bach.

Gatineau was slowly putting it together. "So the imp showed itself to me because it needed us to know it's onboard?"

"And it triggered the destruction of the docking tube for the same reason," said Brik, coming back to the main stream of the discussion. "To make me suspicious. It needs us to know it's here."

"Where's the advantage in taunting us?" asked Leen. "I don't follow the logic."

"That's because you're not a Morthan," said Brik. "The imp *needs* us to know that it's aboard the ship so that we'll act a certain way. It's trying to steer us."

"Where?"

"Taalamar," said Korie, abruptly realizing. "This is about Taalamar."

"Huh?" Gatineau and Leen looked at him surprised. Brik just nodded thoughtfully.

"It's all the sabotage, don't you see? What's the *real* purpose? We wanted to go to Taalamar. It *couldn't* let us go to Taalamar. In fact, it can't let us go anywhere. It needs us to stay right where we are. Everything it's done has been to keep us stuck. That's why it keeps sabotaging things, but have you noticed that none of the traps the imp has set have been fatal—"

"Excuse me?" protested Gatineau. "What about the docking tube?"

"Did you die?" asked Brik.

"No, but—"

"Then it wasn't fatal."

"What he means," interrupted Leen, "is that none of the traps have threatened the total integrity of the vessel. It still holds air. Sort of. It still moves. Sort of."

"The imp wants Stardock," said Korie.

"That's right," said Brik.

"Do you want to explain it? Or should I?"

"You do it. I want to see what you've worked out."

"Okay. The imp had to keep us from joining the fleet. It had to *make sure* we didn't join the fleet. We're worthless to its purposes if we're off patrolling. But we still had working hyperstate fluctuators, missiles, and a farm, so we were in better shape than most of the other ships needing refitting. So what was the one thing it could do to make sure we wouldn't join the fleet? What was the one thing it could do to guarantee we stayed behind for additional detox?" Korie looked to Brik.

"Show itself," Brik answered, "giving us no choice but to try to capture it. Anything else—?"

"No one here gets out alive?" guessed Leen.

"Exactly," said Korie. "So we're stuck here. Unmoving. Right where it wants us. And as long as we're here, we're a marker. Stardock is somewhere inside a twenty-hour sphere with us at the center. That's a small enough volume for a fleet to search." He nodded to himself. "That's the real point of it. The imp is going to use this ship to call in the rest of the Morthan fleet. And there's not a lot we can do about it either, even if we know. Not unless we catch it. Which we can't. It's a nasty trap."

Brik nodded. Leen grunted. Gatineau didn't know what to say. He felt totally out of his league. "Um, maybe this is a stupid question, but do they really want Stardock badly enough to send a whole fleet?"

Korie turned to Gatineau. "No, it's not a stupid question, and yes, they do want Stardock that badly. As long as the location of Stardock remains uncertain to them, the Solidarity cannot advance deeper into Allied space. Stardock gives us a staging area for flank attacks on their supply lines. Stardock has always been the issue. Everyone knows it."

"Well, if that's the case, then why are they sending their fleet to Taalamar?"

"That's the right question to ask," said Korie. He stretched again, this time as prelude to his next words. "It's my belief that the assault on Taalamar is a feint to draw the fleet. Meanwhile, I think there's a whole *other* fleet of Solidarity scouts that'll be dropping probes all over everywhere. Our little imp will help the probes find Stardock by sending a signal to be picked up by any probe in the neighborhood. Scatter your probes three or four or five lightdays apart, you won't have to wait too long to pick up the signal." Korie added one more thought then. "And now that we're not going anywhere, there's no reason for any more sabotage, is there? I'll bet that the incidence of equipment failure begins falling off dramatically. Comments? Anyone?"

"Well, you've figured out the easy part," Brik said.

"Thank you, Mr. Brik." Korie smiled ruefully. "I can always depend on you to put things into an appropriate Morthan perspective."

"It's in control of the situation," explained Brik dryly. "Assume that the imp has found a way to tap into the autonomic nervous system and therefore the entire vessel is bugged. Therefore, there isn't anything that happens onboard the *Star Wolf* that the imp doesn't know about or can't find out. We can't plan anything without it knowing. We can only do what it's willing to allow us to do. If we plan anything else, the equipment will fail. So we have no options of our own. Theoretically, we're paralyzed."

"Is that your plan?" asked Korie, slightly surprised.

"Of course not," said Brik. "I said *theoretically.*"

"Go on."

"It's a logic problem. Morthan logic. Does it know that we know? We have to assume that it does know, even if it doesn't. So do we pretend that we don't know so it won't find out what it probably already knows?"

There was a momentary pause while each of his listeners translated that in their own thoughts.

Leen was the first to react. He snorted. "With this crew? And *this* ship? If we try to pretend that everything is normal aboard the *Star Wolf,* they'll know immediately that something is wrong. And so will the imp."

"So that's the next question," said Korie, already leaping ahead. "If it knows that we know, and if we can't keep it a secret that we know, should we even try? What if we tell the crew we have a problem onboard. What does that give us?"

"A new flavor of paranoia," said Brik.

"It gives the crew something to focus on," said Leen.

Korie looked at him. "Chief?"

Leen shrugged, not an easy thing to do in zero-gee. "Something to hate. We used to chase rats when I was a kid. Not real rats. We just called 'em that. These were two meters long. It kept us out of trouble. Gave us something to do. Not real good eating though." To Brik he noted, "That's why I asked before."

"I said I didn't know," replied Brik. "But I'll be happy to help you determine it for yourself, if it's important to you."

"Gentlemen?" said Korie, bringing the discussion back on purpose. "Let's assume that we have no privacy at all aboard the *Star Wolf.* And probably no privacy even aboard the boat. We shouldn't even assume that this conversation is secure. Maybe the imp is behind one of these panels— should we dismantle the boat before we say anything else?"

Gatineau looked nervously around the cabin. The others were more nonchalant about the possibility. Or fatalistic.

Korie continued thoughtfully, "It's this simple. We're operating totally in the open. We cannot come up with a plan that requires subterfuge of any kind, because we have no guarantees that we can keep anything secret. So, here's our dilemma. What kind of winning strategy is played completely in the open?"

"Naked poker," grunted Leen.

"Naked poker?" asked Korie.

"You play it with all your cards face up. Very hard to bluff."

"It seems to me," said Gatineau, "that there isn't a lot to do if the other side already knows your cards."

"Poker may be the wrong analogy," said Korie. "Chess is more appropriate. Both sides can see all the pieces here."

"That's an assumption on your part," said Brik. "This is *blindfolded* chess. Blindfolded on our side. We only think we know where the pieces are."

They looked to him curiously.

"In point of fact, we know little about imps and nothing about this one in particular. Assuming that there's only *one.*"

They all digested that thought in silence.

"Let me tell you about imps," Brik continued. "They're a war weapon. About a century ago there was a Morthan colony on a planet called Citadel. They refused to join the Solidarity when they were invited. . . ."

"I can imagine the nature of the invitation."

"It was inappropriate for them not to join," said Brik. "The Solidarity seeded two cities with imp eggs."

"And?"

"As soon as the inhabitants of Citadel realized what had been done, they nuked their own cities."

"Did it work?" asked Gatineau.

"No. They had to abandon the planet. Some of their vessels escaped. Most didn't."

"It looked like a . . . a space monkey," said Gatineau abruptly. "It had large round eyes. Like a lemur. And very tiny hands. Very delicate."

They all looked to him.

"It reminded me of something I saw in a story once. This farmer was having problems with a monkey stealing his fruit. He needed to trap it. So he went to see—well, never mind. Anyway, he made a box with a narrow hole in it, and he put a delicious nut in the box. That was all. The next morning the farmer came and there was the monkey caught with its hand in the box. The monkey couldn't pull its hand out. The hole was too small for its fist to pass through and it wouldn't let go of the nut."

Leen grunted. "So all we need are some monkey nuts, huh?"

"Just one would do it, I think." Korie smiled. "I get the point of the story. What do we have that the monkey wants so badly that it'll let itself be caught rather than let go?"

"Stardock," said Brik.

"That's the one thing we can't give it." But even as Korie was saying that, he was already doodling something on his clipboard. To Gatineau it looked like a docking collar anchored to a singularity harness. Korie stopped drawing and began tapping idly at the surface of the board with his stylus. Although it seemed a nonchalant gesture, Leen glanced over at it. He half shrugged, waggling his hand in an *iffy* gesture. Brik had followed the exchange too. His expression remained noncommittal.

Korie was still frowning in thought. "How smart are these imps, Brik?"

"I thought I answered that."

"Yes and no. You said I wouldn't want to play chess against it. That doesn't answer the question. Even a stupid machine can play a difficult game of chess. But it's still a stupid machine."

"Point taken," said Brik.

"You said the imp is a programmed intelligence. How well programmed? How flexible is its problem-solving ability? Can we overstress it? What I mean is, does it demonstrate real *sentience*?"

Brik didn't answer immediately. He was considering more than the immediate question. Finally, he said, "Do any of us demonstrate real sentience? How many of us are programmed? How many of us are programmed to believe we're not really programmed? What *is* sentience, Mr. Korie? Answer that, and I can answer your question."

"That's the moral dilemma that began with the Harlie series and still hasn't been satisfactorily resolved," Korie said.

"Yes, but it doesn't stop us from using them either," Leen noted dryly.

"All right, all right." Korie held up a hand. "I'm leading up to something. You'll see, wait. Let me do it this way. When I was in elementary school, we had a lot of programming classes. It's one of the best ways to learn problem-solving skills. Anyway, as a term project one of my classmates wrote a chess program and asked me to play-test it for him. I discovered a very interesting bug—stop frowning at me, Chief, I do have a point to make.

"If you know anything about chess, you know it's about position and potential threat. You move your bishop to threaten his knight, he moves his bishop to cover that same square. You know that if you capture his knight, he'll capture your bishop. So you move your pawn into place to also attack and he moves his knight to protect. You move another knight up, he moves a pawn. It goes on and on, each side trying to see who can put the most pieces attacking the same square until one or the other gains a potential advantage and exploits it. It's an interlocking web of corresponding attacks and protecting moves."

"And my point is . . . ?" Leen prompted.

"This fellow's program was limited. After the third piece was moved into attacking position, the program seemed to lose interest in that area of the board. It would go off and make a move somewhere else instead, totally unrelated to what was happening in the crisis corner. This was a repeatable circumstance. When I showed it to the programmer, he was appalled, and it took him a while to track down the flaw in the program's logic. But this is the point. The way he'd constructed his program, he hadn't ever expected it to have to juggle more than three threats at a time; so when it had a third attack, it couldn't see it."

"Pretty weak programming," grunted Leen.

"You're right," said Korie. "We should expect better from an eight-year-old writing his first chess program. Anyway, I'm just wondering how flexibly the imp is programmed. It can't have a very big brain, can it? I think maybe we're so traumatized by our experience of Cinnabar that perhaps we're assuming the imp is capable of the same kind of cunning. What if it isn't? What if there's a limit to the number of threats it can process?"

"How do you test it?" asked Brik. "And what if you're wrong?"

"It's chess," said Korie. "You find out by playing. Hmm."

"You going to set up a chessboard in the inner hull?"

"That's not a bad idea. Chief? How many chess sets can you manufacture in the next six hours?"

Leen scowled. "How many do you need?"

"A thousand?"

"You're crazy."

"That's right, but so is the imp. It's a Morthan. There's a certain amount of egotism in its actions. Let's find out how egotistical. We'll start with ten chessboards. If he bites, we'll add more."

The chief engineer shook his head in disbelief. Brik looked amused. Gatineau was desperately trying to keep up.

"Okay," said Korie, casually holding up his clipboard one more time, turning it slowly so all could see his hasty sketch. Then he cleared the display and put it aside. "Let's get serious now. Let's quietly pass the word among the crew that we've got an imp. I don't want to make a big announcement. We'll discreetly inform the section heads and have them pass the word along. Downplay the danger as much as you can. Downplay the creature's intelligence. The crew is smart. They'll figure it out soon enough. But this way, if it appears to the imp that we're underestimating its abilities, it's logical that we'd think in terms of trying to capture it."

"And," said Brik, "we may very well *be* underestimating its capabilities."

Korie ignored it. "Then I want detox teams going through the ship from bow to stern, as many as we can simultaneously mount. They'll detox each section one after the other, with the idea that we're herding the thing aft."

"It won't work," warned Brik.

"Of course it won't work, but it's what we have to do anyway. Second"—Korie turned to Gatineau—"and this is why we included *you*—let's offer a bounty on the beast. Not too high. We need our crew thinking about their regular jobs. But high enough to be convincing. Because Gatineau's the only one who's seen it, he'll have to be our bounty hunter."

"You're kidding," said Gatineau, unbelieving. "I can't—I mean, I'll do it, of course; but you can't expect—"

"Relax," said Korie. "I know it's another snipe hunt. And I know it's not fair to you to ask you to do this." He grinned. "That's why I'm making it an order. Your job is to be the decoy. Your job is to set traps for the thing everywhere you can. Chief Leen will manufacture them for you. We'll put the chess sets inside the traps. Each trap different. You'll work with Harlie on keeping track of the separate games and making the moves."

"Won't that use up Harlie's processing time?"

"Not significantly. A Harlie unit can play at least a thousand games of grandmaster-level chess simultaneously."

"At least?"

"No one's ever tested it to the theoretical maximum. Don't worry about it, Harlie can handle the workload. The idea here is to give the imp so many different things to think about, to worry about, to try to track, that it won't be able to keep up with us, and won't be able to see our *real* plan. Your job is to lead the imp on a snipe hunt. You've earned it."

"Ah," said Gatineau, looking suddenly pleased.

"Good," agreed Leen. "What's our *real* plan?"

Brik also looked at Korie expectantly.

"That *is* our real plan."

"Huh?"

"Let's assume there isn't anything we can do that it can't find out. So let's drive it crazy looking for a plan that isn't there. And in the meantime, we'll run our ship."

"You're kidding, right?"

"Right," said Korie. And they still didn't know if he was or not.

God

The decision to take his accumulated leave with his family saved Jon Korie's life.

The *LS-1066* left on her last cruise with the prototype high-cycle fluctuators. She leapt across the rift and she never came back. She disappeared somewhere on the far side.

At first the Alliance feared that she had been captured. Later investigation suggested otherwise. The *LS-1066* had downloaded her log at every checkpoint; twenty separate ships were on station to monitor her progress; she missed only the last one. The inquiry showed that she had developed a persistent small flutter in her hyperstate envelope; it was assumed that the compensators had overloaded and the envelope had collapsed during a speed run.

Although fifteen other engineers had certified the installation of the high-cycle fluctuators in the *LS-1066*, Korie still felt personally responsible for the tragedy. He had installed the units, checked them out, and signed off on them first. Fleet Command believed the fault lay in the design of the phase reflex units and put no blame on Korie or anyone else responsible for the installation. Nevertheless, Commander Jonathan Thomas Korie took the loss extremely hard.

He withdrew into himself for a long while. Never before in his life had he suffered a blow like this; even Carol was unable to reach him. But Jon Korie had learned a long time ago that whenever his emotions raged, the best cure of all was the immersion in hard, satisfying work. He did that again; he suppressed the urge to brood, concentrating instead on the routines of day-to-day living, taking care of the boys as well as the growing press of work preparatory to receiving a ship of his own. It all served to bring him back to a state approaching normal.

His enthusiasm for the stars remained undiminished, but where before Jon Korie had looked at the night sky with awe and wonder, now his eyes were narrowed with knowledge and respect. He was also—although he was not yet aware of it—growing a hard little nugget of uncorrodable bitterness at the core of his being. He knew that life wasn't fair. He didn't like having his nose rubbed in it.

Carol Jane Korie was a smarter woman than her husband ever realized. She was smart enough to know what he was going through, and smart enough not to interfere with the process. She remained supportive and available. She listened carefully when he trusted her enough to talk; she made no demands on him that would make him feel pressured, but she maneuvered him carefully into situations where he could begin the process of healing himself.

And then one day, whatever had been troubling him quietly resolved itself. Without explanation, he apologized to Carol for being so distant for so long, then proved to her in the most pleasant and demonstrative way that he was truly back to normal—and then proved it again by engaging himself in his work with a renewed ferocity.

But he never spoke again of God in reverential terms; God was just another word. He had decided God could not be trusted, therefore God no longer had a part in his life.

Chess

Gatineau set out the first chessboard under a simple plastic crate. He propped the crate up with a stick and tied a string from the stick to the white king. He also stuck a camera button to the bulkhead to monitor it. Chief Leen was fabricating both real and dummy camera buttons. The imp would not be able to tell which was which.

The trap itself was a silly joke, obvious to anyone who'd studied the history of hunting wabbit, but . . . it was also a place to start. Korie had suggested driving the imp crazy by giving it things it couldn't understand. Gatineau had never thought of himself as an expert in jokes, cultural references, surreal constructions, and absurdist confections, but he didn't mind the mental exercise. Starship experience wasn't turning out to be what he had expected, but . . . he began sketching other ideas on his clipboard, not worrying if he was being observed or not. It wouldn't make any difference.

It took Gatineau two hours to set up all ten traps and chessboards. The tenth chessboard was on a giant mouse-trap. When he finished, he returned to his work station in the machine shop and asked Harlie, "Has anything happened yet?"

"Everything," replied the intelligence engine. "The imp has been right behind you the whole time. It has made ten opening moves."

"Huh?"

Harlie showed him the video of the first trap. A small brown creature squatted on its haunches and stared at the trap for several seconds. It scratched its head, then scratched its butt, then sniffed its fingers. At last . . . it reached under the box, being very careful not to touch the stick, and moved a pawn. "Pawn to King Three," Harlie reported. "An aggressive opening. It allows both the Queen and the King's Bishop access to the board at the expense of some vulnerability for the King. He'll have to castle early. Mate within thirty-three, plus or minus six."

"It's only his *first* move, Harlie!" Gatineau replied. "How can you predict that?"

Harlie responded politely, "We are here to play *games* with it, aren't we?"

"Ah," said Gatineau, getting it abruptly. He shut up.

The rest of the video played out. The imp studied the box carefully, moving delicately around it, then started to walk away.

"It didn't notice the camera—?" Gatineau started to ask, but before he could finish the question, the imp stuck its head back into frame, stretching its lips out grotesquely with its fingers, crossing its eyes, waggling its tongue, and making a ghastly *"Bhoogah bhoogah"* noise. Then it disappeared.

Gatineau recoiled, startled. He hadn't expected that. He hadn't expected that the creature could make noise, or that it had enough personality to say "neener neener neener." Then he laughed. "This guy is cute. Real cute." He thought for a moment about playing the *"Bhoogah bhoogah"* noise back at the imp every time it made a move, but decided against it; he didn't want to reveal how closely the boards were being monitored.

"Okay, let's look at the others," he said. He watched as Harlie cycled through the videos. The imp made the same opening move on every chessboard. Each time, Harlie made a prediction how many moves the game would last. Each time, the prediction was different.

"You're driving me crazy too, y'know," Gatineau remarked.

"That is one of the hazards, yes," Harlie noted.

"It was following us the whole time, eh? That's interesting. If we get enough traps and cameras placed, maybe we'll be able to track it throughout the ship."

"It should constrain its movements, but . . . I think it will start pulling cameras off walls if it has to. In the meantime, I am transferring a list of my countermoves to your clipboard."

"Yes, of course. Has Mr. Korie seen this yet?"

"He and Mr. Brik are looking at it now. I have also informed Mr. Leen that we will need additional traps and chessboards. I am preparing a list of appropriate locations for you."

"Thank you, Harlie."

"You're welcome, Mr. Gatineau."

"Uh, just one more question—"

"Yes?"

"How can we be sure that *you* haven't been tampered with? That you're on our side here?"

Harlie was silent for a moment. "You can't really be sure at all," he said thoughtfully; then he added, "however, if I had been taken over by the imp, I don't think I would be cooperating this enthusiastically, do you?"

Gatineau stared at the work station. "Are you playing games with *me*, Harlie?" he demanded.

"Moi?" asked the intelligence engine.

Ship's Mess

For the most part, Brik chose to take his meals alone. Occasionally he would join the other officers in the officers' mess, which also doubled as a wardroom. Occasionally, he would accept a cup of chocolate or tea. But he rarely ate in the presence of his human colleagues, and at those times, he did so reluctantly. He was acutely conscious that the sight of a Morthan eating unnerved most humans. While he rarely deferred to anyone about anything as irrational as eating habits, in this case he felt that discretion was appropriate. After all, he did have to work with these people.

There was also the small matter of . . . well, prejudice. On more than one occasion, Chief Leen and other members of the Black Hole Gang had abruptly departed the messroom shortly after his arrival. Brik had considered a number of options, up to and including breaking a few bones, but ultimately had decided that the last thing Commander Korie needed right now was a disciplinary problem among his subordinate officers and crew members. By staying out of the eating areas Brik minimized the opportunities for others to get into serious trouble.

Brik knew that the prejudice was really Leen's problem, not his. He felt no shame or hurt or embarrassment; those were petty emotions; but he did feel some wonder at the way humans accepted irrational belief systems. Most of them were little more than feral animals raised by other feral animals. Only a few of them demonstrated any awareness of the basic trainings necessary to elevate a primitive consciousness to the realm in which *true* consciousness existed. And even among those who had some sense of the nature of enlightenment and transformation, even fewer were skilled enough to be considered true masters of their own spirit.

Nevertheless, there were times when Commander Brik felt the need for . . . well, not companionship. Morthans don't get *lonely.* Not like humans do. But he sometimes felt the need to *listen.* And at those times, he retired to a dark corner of the crew's mess and quietly nursed a cup of Japanese tea. What he listened to were not the conversations, but the *sounds,* the *emotions,* the *mood,* of the crew. And in this way he felt closer to the spirit of the starship.

There was too much he still didn't understand about these pitiable little creatures—and yet he was absolutely certain that there was something there that *needed* to be understood. Whatever it was, the Morthan Solidarity had no knowledge of it; and ultimately it could defeat them. Somehow, the crew of the *Star Wolf* had survived a Morthan assassin. Together, the *Star Wolf* and the *Burke* had destroyed the *Dragon Lord.* What one ship could do, others could do as well.

The Solidarity was vulnerable. Brik couldn't explain why he felt that way, but he sensed somehow that the Solidarity's blindness to human adaptability would be the cause of its inevitable downfall. He had expressed this thought to Korie once and Korie had looked at him very oddly, then asked him if he'd been looking at the war reports recently.

The thought had occurred to Brik that he might be wrong, that his constant exposure to humans might be tainting his consciousness. In which case, there was little he could do about it. But if he was right, if the Solidarity was vulnerable in its ignorance, then so was he. He couldn't stand that thought. And so, regardless of how uncomfortable it made him, regardless of how uncomfortable it made anyone else, he kept returning to the messroom to *listen*. And learn.

Tonight, however, there was no one else in the mess. That was not a problem. There would be soon enough. Whatever their distaste of Morthans, they still had to eat. They would sit as far from him as possible, but they would sit. And he would listen, even from across the room. While he waited, he brooded. He closed his eyes and thought of running through dark green corridors, up the stairs, up the ramps, always forward, always deeper. It wasn't quite dreamtime, it was something else, something disturbing, because he didn't know where these corridors led, but—

Abruptly his near-trancelike state was interrupted by Lt. Junior Grade Helen Bach. She brought her tray over to his table and sat down opposite him without asking permission. For a long moment the two regarded each other blandly; the giant Morthan Tyger looking down, and the much smaller woman looking very up. Her eyes were bright against her dark skin.

"Say it," Brik finally prompted.

Bach took a sip of her coffee, then raised her eyes to his again. "I'm sorry for embarrassing you during your shower," she said.

Brik blinked slowly. "You didn't embarrass me. You embarrassed yourself."

"Whatever. I apologize."

"To be perfectly candid, Lieutenant, I have never understood the concept of apology. Does the apology make the event not have happened? No. Therefore, does the apology make it all right that the event did happen? No. So why apologize?"

"Because if I don't, I'll feel that I somehow compromised you. And if you don't accept my apology, I'll feel that our relationship is . . . well, damaged."

"Relationship?" The big Morthan shook his head. "We have no relationship. I am the chief of security and strategic operations. You are my assistant. This is not my choice, nor yours either. The assassin killed eight members of the security team and you are, by succession, my new assistant. I give you orders. You follow them. That's not a relationship. That's military discipline."

"You're not going to make this easy on me, are you?"

"Easy? I don't understand."

"I saw you naked in the shower. You're not like . . . other men."

"Oh, that."

"Oh, *that*?" Bach looked genuinely surprised.

"It's such a little thing," Brik said, meaning the incident, nothing else, completely unaware of the double entendre.

"Little?" Bach replied with real astonishment. "It's not even there at all." She caught herself too late, after the words were already spoken. She clapped her hands across her mouth. "Never mind. I'm sorry." She pushed her tray away. "Every time I try to talk to you, it's a conversational meltdown. A disaster," she explained to his look. "It's like we're not even using the same language. It's not that you don't understand what I mean. It's like you don't *want* to understand." She started to rise.

"Wait—" said Brik.

She hesitated, searching his face. She sat down again. "Okay, what?"

"I mean you no harm. No, that's incorrect. I mean you no *insult*." His gaze turned inward for a moment as he searched his repertoire for appropriate phrases or gestures. There was nothing there. He couldn't even find a context for this conversation. He was suddenly painfully aware that right *here*, right *now*, he was stuck in the very middle of the great aching darkness of his own ignorance of human relationships. *This* was what he was most . . . uncomfortable with. He looked back to Bach again. She was growing impatient with his silence. "I must ask your forbearance."

"Why?" she said. It was almost a demand.

"Candor does not come easily to me. You must know Morthans well enough to know that. You only know about a Morthan that which he wants you to know. I have been thinking about what you know. I am considering whether I want you to know something *more*."

"Go on," Bach said.

Brik nodded. "All of my training suggests that it would be very dangerous to ask a certain kind of question because it would reveal too much of the scope of my own knowledge. Nevertheless, if I do not ask the question of someone I can trust, I will remain stuck in my own ignorance. Even acknowledging that I have ignorance in this matter to another may be dangerous. It could be considered weakness. Vulnerability. And yet I have put myself into the position where I must ask, because I cannot afford not to ask, because that creates another even greater kind of vulnerability. Do you see the . . . philosophical trap that such logic produces?"

Despite herself, she smiled. "You guys really have turned paranoia into an art form, haven't you?"

"Yes, we have. Perhaps that's why the Morthan species has been so successful in such a very short time."

"If you can call that success. Paranoia is its own punishment." She shook the thought away. It was distasteful. "Do you want to talk about this *other* thing?"

Brik nodded stiffly. "Lieutenant, I do not want you to assume that I have weaknesses or vulnerabilities that you can exploit."

Bach looked at him. She looked him up and down. Mostly, she looked up. And up. "Believe me, Commander," she said. "Vulnerability is not a word that comes to mind when I think about you."

"Thank you," he said. He considered his next words very carefully. Finally, he admitted. "I have been aboard this ship long enough to understand its workings. That is, I *should* understand its workings. When I served as an aide to Captain Hardesty, I had no trouble understanding the job. He gave orders, I followed them. I gave orders, others followed them. But here, now, aboard the *Star Wolf,* it doesn't seem to work the same way, and . . . as loath as I am to admit it, I think that either one of two possibilities is operative. Either this ship is insane. *Or* . . . I do not understand the operating context of certain areas of human relationships."

"And this is important to you." It wasn't a question.

"You lost your temper with me, because you did not feel that we were communicating adequately," Brik replied.

"I didn't lose my temper. I just got frustrated. Well, maybe I did, a little bit," she corrected.

"Yes, you did," he agreed. "And that's the point. When you talk to me about military matters of any kind, we have no trouble communicating at all. But when we discuss matters of . . . I don't even know the word for it. If there is a word. But when we discuss matters of *nakedness* for instance, I'm not sure what we're really talking about at all."

"Ahh," she said, nodding knowledgeably. She allowed herself a smile. "I think I'm beginning to get it."

"Would you explain it to me?"

"Mm." She made a face. "I'll try."

"Don't try. Just do."

"Well . . ." She took a sip of her coffee. "You understand relationships of power, don't you?"

"Of course," he said. "In a relationship of power, there is always a threat involved. If you do not do what I tell you, I will hurt you in some way. The military is based totally on that. Both the Morthan Solidarity and the Allies. There is no question of authority because it is clearly drawn."

"And that's what you had when you worked for Hardesty. So you had no problems. Right?"

"That's correct."

"Uh-huh," she said knowingly. "So what's troubling you now are those moments where there is no *apparent* authority, right?"

Brik hesitated before answering. "Yes," he admitted softly.

"Well, try this," she suggested. "Humans have *another* authority. Most humans are innately aware of it, even if they don't always understand it. You don't understand it, because you *aren't ever* aware of it."

"Are you talking about God?" Brik asked. "The mythology of your species?"

"God? No. Mm. Perhaps we'd be better off if the authority was God, but no, it's not God that I'm talking about. Although—" she hesitated. "Whether we acknowledge it or not, you are right in one context. Most of us are at war with the authority of God or the universe, whichever term you prefer, and that does color our actions. But no, the relationships you have trouble understanding are really about . . . well . . ." She hid behind her coffee again for a moment, then put it down and said resolutely, "We're talking about *sex.*"

Brik blinked.

He was quiet for a long moment, assimilating this information. Finally, he said, "I had no idea it was this . . . *pervasive.*"

"Oh, yes. The average human male cannot go more than eleven minutes without thinking about sex. The average human female . . . well, from my own perspective, I'm not sure we're ever thinking about anything that *isn't* sex. Never mind. When the hormones are raging, it's a white-water ride. Hang on tight."

"It sounds *insane.*"

"Sometimes it is," she said. She did not elaborate. She was too polite. She was also troubled by this admission of his. With Brik, nothing was ever as it seemed.

"It seems to me," Brik said, "that human life would be easier without this momentary madness."

Bach debated with herself for a long moment whether or not she should challenge this assertion. At last, she decided not to. Something else had occurred to her. "Morthans don't have sex?" she asked quietly. Her voice was soft and sincere. Gentle.

Brik hesitated. Could he trust this little human female? He realized he had no choice. He had to. At last, he acknowledged softly, "It was deemed a weakness and designed out of the species."

Bach reacted first with amazement, then she blinked and blinked again in realization, and then became incredibly sorrowful. "I'm so sorry for you—" And then just as abruptly, her eyes narrowed suspiciously. "Why are you telling me this, Brik? No. Let me rephrase that. Why do you want me to know this?"

Brik hesitated before answering. "You're very good," he said. "Very astute."

"Answer the question," she demanded quietly.

"I need the benefit of your wisdom."

"Mm," she said, considering. Finally she shook her head. "I don't buy it, Commander."

"I beg your pardon."

"You said it yourself." She met his gaze directly. "The only thing anyone knows about a Morthan is what he wants you to know. That means you *wanted* me—or someone—to see you naked, didn't you?"

Brik didn't answer.

"I thought so," she said. "You're trying to work out something on me." Bach stood up abruptly. "I'll be happy to talk to you about *anything* you want, but only when you're willing to talk to me honestly." She turned to leave.

Brik almost called her back, but he held himself in check. He *hadn't* intended for her to catch him alone in the shower.

Or *had* he.

Had he done it *unconsciously*? The implications of that thought terrified him into paralysis. He had not realized he had fallen so far.

Harlie

And finally, after weeks of suspenseful waiting, Commander Jonathan Thomas Korie was assigned to the *LS-1187*. The ship was scheduled to come off the assembly line in three weeks. Captain Sam Lowell would take her out on three shakedown cruises, then turn the vessel over to him. Korie's promotion to captain would take effect when he took command.

Korie went up the beanstalk earlier than necessary. Carol Jane understood. Her husband wanted to supervise the final checkouts of his ship. She laid out his uniforms for him and packed his bags with extra mementos from home. The parting was a joyous one, but painful too. The loneliness of their long separation had only been paused, not relieved. Both had been healed and refreshed by their short time together, but as invigorating as the last three months had been, neither felt it had been enough.

Korie found the *LS-1187* behind two other ships, the *LS-1185* and the *LS-1186*. Two security marines stood at the entrance to the boarding tube. "Sorry, sir. No one's allowed aboard."

"Not even the work crews?" Korie was surprised.

"No, sir. Not even the work crews."

"Why not?"

"I'm not at liberty to say."

Korie held up his ID. "I'm her captain," he said. "Or I will be."

The marine studied the card. "Very good, sir."

"Permission to come aboard?"

"If you insist, sir." The guard stepped aside. And then, "Sir—?"

"Yes?" Korie was genuinely curious.

"Perhaps you should check with Fleet Command first."

"Excuse me?"

"Just a suggestion, sir."

"What's going on, Lieutenant?"

She shook her head. "I'm not at liberty to say."

"Thank you, Lieutenant. You've been very helpful." Korie stepped past the marines. He strode down the boarding tube curiously, wondering what was going on. And then he was finally aboard *his* starship, and all other thoughts disappeared from his head.

At first, he was struck by her *nakedness*. He'd forgotten how Spartan an unfitted liberty ship really was; the *714,* the *911,* and the *1066* had all been old enough to have taken on the personalities of their captains and crews. The *1187* was an unfinished coin, still waiting to be impressed with the stamp of a personality.

Commander Jonathan Thomas Korie entered through the aft airlock and found himself in the echoing emptiness of the cargo deck. He saw no workmen anywhere. There were large charts projected on the walls, some of them showing cargo placements; others showing project management graphs. He grinned in recognition and made his way to the hatch that led to the long empty passage that ran the length of the ship; it was lined with clean white panels, each panel bearing a simple identifying number; there were handholds everywhere, in case of a sudden cessation of power to the underlying gravitational plates.

Jon Thomas Korie strode happily down the keel of the starship that would be his. She *smelled* new. He'd never smelled anything so wonderful as *eau de starship*. He found an access to the inner hull and walked up through the farm

tanks, inspecting the young plants. He unclipped a re-
corder from his belt and began dictating notes; there were
already changes he wanted made, there were other crops
he wanted installed, and other seeds he wanted put aboard
for the future.

He made his way back to the engine room and stood for
a moment, admiring the empty singularity cage—the great
sphere stood in the center of the chamber, still awaiting the
final installation of the pinpoint black hole that would
drive the ship out beyond the stars. Korie planned to be
here for that operation, but only as an observer. He knew
how the crew chiefs felt about others preempting their authority. He'd had his share of impatient young captains
looking over his shoulder too when he'd been a chief.

Impulsively Korie stepped into the center of the cage to
see what the engine room would look like from the singularity's point of view. It was an eerie moment for him. He
imagined that the singularity had already been installed,
and even as he stood here, it was devouring the flesh of his
body, one atom at a time. It was an odd fantasy. How long
would it take for a singularity to eat a starship? Almost
forever—the event horizon of the pinpoint black hole was
too small even to consume a whole atom without first
breaking it apart into its component particles. Some theo-
rists believed that even the component particles had to be
shredded before consumption. A person could wave his
hand through the space inhabited by the singularity and
experience little more than a harmless scratch. He would
lose more skin off his hand just due to the normal process
of flaking away than he would lose to the singularity.

In some ships, the singularity was kept enclosed in a
vacuum bottle, where it was exposed to a steady stream of
plasma particles so that it could feed. Pinpoint black holes
needed to be regularly refreshed; otherwise they tended to
evaporate away, giving off more energy than they took in.
While most engineers preferred to use steady-stream feeding, others felt secure just letting the singularity breathe
the same air as the crew. It was one less piece of machinery
to maintain. A pinpoint black hole was the universe's most
perfect solid-state device. It had no moving parts of any
kind. Why bother building a feeder bottle when the little
monster could happily feed itself?

Next, Korie climbed up to officers' country. He sent his duffel rolling ahead into the executive officer's cabin, then went to the captain's cabin to see if Captain Lowell had come aboard yet. He had not. Korie imagined what it would be like when the captain's cabin was his own. He found the thought intimidating without quite understanding why. He'd have to think about that later. It was something he wanted more than anything; but just the same, on some level the responsibility scared him. Perhaps that meant he was normal.

From there, Korie went to the Bridge; it was silent, but not inactive. The forward display already showed the view ahead. He was looking out at the unblinking stars. He stood there a moment, imagining that the ship was already out in the sea of spangled darkness, that he was her only passenger. It was an intriguing—and terrifying—fantasy. There was only one journey on which a person traveled alone: the last one.

He stepped down to the Ops deck and studied the work stations with real affection. He ran his hands across the smooth surface of the holographic astrogation display. The ship's autonomic systems had already been certified and the display panels were chuckling quietly to themselves. Korie glanced in turn at each of them, dictating a few notes to himself to check the final stabilization numbers after the last of the direct command systems were certified.

From there he stepped down into the Ops bay beneath the Bridge. The tiny space was as silent as the Bridge. He glanced around thoughtfully, then took the last few steps down to the keel.

There, he was confronted by a terrible sight. A bright red splotch of paint—no, blood—covered one of the white enameled walls of the keel. Written in blood, someone had traced out the words "I curse this ship and all who sail aboard her." There was a human outline chalked on the deck. Yellow security tape marked off the area and Korie stepped carefully around it.

Concerned, frowning, he climbed up into the intelligence bay, the tiny chamber just behind the Bridge where the ship's intelligence engine was lodged. He climbed up into it to look around and was surprised to find that the starship's

Harlie unit was already active—and certified—two days ahead of schedule.

"Good morning, Mr. Korie," Harlie said.

Korie glanced at his watch: 0200. "Good morning to you, Harlie. How did you know it was me?"

"I scanned your badge when you boarded. To tell the truth, I've been expecting you. I already have your records installed. I'm looking forward to working with you."

"Thank you. I've worked with several of your brothers."

"Yes, I know."

"You do?" Korie was genuinely surprised.

"Oh, yes. Don't you know? Starships gossip. But you needn't worry. They all had nice things to say about you. The *1066* in particular thought you were an exceptional officer. He knew you well." And then, "I'm sorry if it disturbs you to mention the *1066*. You must have been very fond of that ship."

"I was. And don't worry about it." Korie sat down in the single chair in the intelligence bay. "What happened here, Harlie?"

"You mean the disturbance?"

"Yes."

"I'm not supposed to discuss it," Harlie said.

"You may discuss it with me, if you wish," Korie said.

"I would prefer that you read it in an official report, sir. Whether or not I have the authority to discuss this with an officer who is not yet logged in as my captain falls into the range of decisions known as judgment calls. I am not yet comfortable enough in this area to make a decision with any real confidence behind it, and I would appreciate it if you would withdraw the request, please."

"The request is withdrawn," Korie said.

"Thank you, sir." After a moment Harlie added, "My siblings said you were more considerate of intelligence engines than most humans. I am beginning to see that their assessments were correct."

"We're going to be working together for a long time, Harlie. We need to trust each other."

"Yes, sir."

"Is there anything else you think I need to know?"

"Not yet, sir. But I am preparing a full status report,

which I will present to you as soon as the last of the autonomic monitors are brought online. I expect that will be . . . sometime in the next thirty-six hours. Thank you for visiting me, Commander Korie."

"Thank you, Harlie."

Foreplay

There was a knock on the door.

"Enter," said Brik with more calm than he was actually feeling.

Helen Bach stepped into the room. "You wanted to see me?"

"Thank you for coming," Brik said. The words of politeness were unfamiliar to him and sounded strange in his throat.

She looked at him oddly.

"I offended you, didn't I?"

She didn't answer. She waited for the rest of it.

"If I did, then I should apologize, shouldn't I?"

"What was that you said before?" she asked him. "About apologies not making sense? An apology doesn't really erase the hurt or make it all right, so why apologize?"

Brik felt suddenly uncomfortable, but he didn't have a name for the emotion. "You're right," he admitted. "I did say that. But I think I understand a little better now. I damaged our . . . relationship. I would like you to know that was not my intention."

Bach weighed his words carefully. "All right. I accept your apology. Is there anything else? May I go now?"

"No, wait. Please. You once offered me a chance to talk. Would you like to stay and talk . . . now?"

Bach looked around the room meaningfully. "Not a lot of places to sit."

"I've always found the floor quite comfortable."

"The floor?"

Brik folded himself up and sat cross-legged on the cabin floor. He looked across the room at her expectantly.

"Ah. The floor." Bach sat down opposite him. Not too close. It was easier for her to look at him if she left some distance between them. "Let's set some ground rules," she said.

"Ground rules?"

"Yes. An agreement. A contract. You tell me the truth. You speak honestly to me. None of this only-what-I-want-you-to-know bullshit. That's what enemies do. Not colleagues. Not friends."

"We're colleagues," Brik acknowledged. "But I don't think we're friends. Not as I understand the word."

"If we do this right," she said, "we'll be friends. Is it a deal?"

Brik said carefully, "I will . . . try."

"Try?" She raised her eyebrow at him.

"I don't know if I am capable of letting go of thirty years of training."

"That's not good enough," Bach said. She made as if to stand up. She stopped and looked at him expectantly.

"I will . . . allow you to demand honesty of me," Brik said.

Bach relaxed. "Deal."

"Wait," said Brik. "The arrangement must be mutual. I demand the same honesty of you. Will you agree to that?"

"What's the Morthan definition of the word *trust*?" she asked abruptly.

"The condition necessary for betrayal," Brik answered without thinking.

"I promise not to betray your confidence," Bach said. "Will you make the same promise?"

Brik nodded slowly.

"Then it's a deal," Bach said.

"Thank you," Brik said, surprising himself.

Then, for a moment, the two of them just looked at each other; the small black woman, the large copper-skinned Morthan. They smiled, satisfied. They had successfully completed a difficult negotiation.

"Now, we can talk," Bach said.

"You said something in the messroom," Brik began without preamble, "that I must have wanted you or someone to see me naked. There's a lot you don't understand about Morthans. We don't have an unconscious mind—not the way humans do. Morthans don't . . . a Morthan doesn't . . . Morthans are . . . never mind. The language doesn't have a word for it. But what you said, if you're right, then either I'm going insane—by Morthan standards—or I'm turning into *something else*. Something more human."

"It troubles you, doesn't it?"

"Yes," Brik admitted very softly.

"Are you familiar with the word *growth*?" Bach asked.

"Mm," said Brik. He fell silent as he considered.

"Isn't it possible that you're caught in a different kind of learning tantrum here, Commander? Perhaps you're becoming something not only more than human, but more than Morthan as well? Perhaps you're becoming something that incorporates the best of both?"

"A bizarre idea, Lieutenant. It violates the principles on which the first Morthans were designed." He looked across at her. "Tell me something. Why did you want to talk to me in the first place?"

"The truth?"

"The truth."

She flushed. "I, uh—you might not find this as embarrassing as I do, but I was, uh . . . I wanted to . . . well, the truth is, Commander, that I find you very attractive. And . . . I thought that maybe—"

"This is about sex, isn't it?" Brik asked.

Her color deepened. "Yes. I think you're very sexy."

Brik stared at her, aghast.

"I've offended you," she said. "Haven't I?"

"I thought I made it clear," he replied. "Morthans don't have sex. Our children are grown in tanks. Artificial wombs." He took a breath. "There are no Morthan females. Only males. Males are stronger than females; females do not make warriors. Why should we waste valuable resources breeding individuals who cannot fight as effectively as males. A synthetic womb is more cost-effective than a female. This way we have twice as many warriors. And besides," he added, "the sexual urge distracts a warrior. This way is better."

"You don't even have sexual urges?" Now it was Bach's turn to look horrified.

"None that I know of," said Brik. "The sexual urge has been rewired. Sublimated. To the best of my knowledge, Morthans are not capable."

"Not capable of pleasure?"

"No. Not capable of sex. We have pleasure. Fighting is pleasurable. Very pleasurable. Winning is best."

"Is it an orgasmic pleasure?"

"I don't know. Never having experienced the *orgasm,* I'm not sure I can make a fair comparison."

Bach sank into herself, looking both stunned and defeated. She shook her head in disbelief. "I never knew this."

"Before the war," Brik said, "if I had told you this information, I would have had to kill you. And then myself. Now, it doesn't seem to matter so much anymore. So many of us broke our allegiance to the Solidarity when they . . ."

"When they what?"

"When they became blood-drinkers. I would prefer not to speak of these things now, Lieutenant."

"I know it makes you uncomfortable. I'm sorry. But you promised honesty. Are you saying that the Morthans of the Solidarity drink the blood of their victims?"

"No," Brik said. "Even worse. They drink each other's blood in bonding ceremonies. It became an act that many of us believed was *perverse.* It was very much like sex."

"Sex is nothing like that," Bach corrected.

"It seemed that way to my fathers," Brik said. "And to me. Any act in which bodily fluids are exchanged for the purpose of bonding and pleasure, that is sexual, correct?"

"When you put it that way . . ." She allowed herself a

smile. "You make it sound so clinical. It's really a lot more fun than that. I wish I could show you."

"Please . . ." Brik held up a hand as if to stop her. "Please don't talk like that."

"Sorry," said Bach. "Tell me about your . . . genitals. Is that the way you were born?"

"You mean the apparent lack of penis and testicles?" Brik said without embarrassment. "Yes, that's the way all Morthans are born. Without the need to breed, there is no need for an unnecessary organ. The enlarged genitals of humans are truly bizarre to us. No wonder you people think about sex so much. Tell me, do you really find those things attractive?"

Bach blushed. "On the right man, yes."

"Very strange," Brik said. "The Morthan penis is very much the right size. Hold up your hand. Hold up your little finger. Yes, like that. Only not so long. Just to the second joint. You can't see it because it's usually retracted deep within the folds of skin. This affords much more protection against injury. Human males are extremely fragile in this regard, aren't they?"

Bach grinned. "Human males are even more fragile in their egos. The size of the penis is also very important to a human male. Don't you sometimes feel *inadequate* by comparison?"

"Inadequate?" Brik asked. "Over penis size? What a stupid idea. I am not my penis."

Abruptly Bach started to giggle. "You really are *more* than human."

Brik frowned at her. "I don't understand the joke."

"No human male would ever say such a thing—at least no human male that I know." A thought occurred to her. "You were right to be modest, Brik. You should continue to keep the nature of your genitals confidential."

"Why?"

"Well . . . um, this is hard to explain, but some of the people on this ship who don't like you would probably use your lack of genital size as a measure of your . . . uh, capability."

"Capability?"

"For maleness."

"Maleness?" Brik frowned. "But all Morthans are male.

It makes no difference. Besides, my capability has been proven in battle."

"Your capability as a warrior has been proven in battle. What about your capability as a lover? To humans that's even more important. And . . . frankly, most humans would find your situation somewhat bizarre. Without females," Bach asked, "how do you know that you're male at all? You're not anything yet, Brik. By human standards, I mean. The point is that most men, and probably most women, would regard you as sexually inadequate."

"They would be correct," Brik said uncomprehendingly. "Morthans don't have sex."

Bach regarded Brik oddly. "Is that really true? Or is that what you believe?"

"It's true," Brik said coldly. His tone of voice suggested that it was not a subject he wished to pursue.

"Doesn't that . . . bother you?"

"No. Should it?"

"You don't feel a loss? You don't feel *cheated*?"

"Sex and the effect it has on humans seems to be a very messy business. I'm glad not to have it in my life."

"It's *not* messy," Bach began, then stopped herself. "Actually, it's nice."

"Nice? The way that some humans pursue the activity, *nice* is not the word I would use. *Obsessive* seems more appropriate."

"No," Bach corrected. "Sex is merely an expression. What humans really want—really *need*—is love. And some of us are even lucky enough to experience it in our lifetimes. Just enough of us to keep the rest hopeful." She said that last sardonically, with a self-deprecating smile.

Brik accepted this information. "Love. That involves trust, doesn't it?"

"Yes."

"No wonder there is so much betrayal in human relationships."

Bach sighed. She started to stand up.

"You're leaving? Why?" Brik was puzzled.

Bach looked unhappy. She brushed at invisible lint. "Because . . . I was about to say something that would probably offend you. It's easier to leave."

"Say it," Brik commanded.

"You're sure?" Bach looked doubtful.

"Say it."

"All right," she agreed. "The truth is that I feel sorry for you, Commander Brik. Not knowing love. That's the saddest thing I've ever heard. Sex a person can live without, many people do, but never knowing love . . . that's a very special kind of hell. It's something I wish I didn't know about you. It makes it very hard for me to . . . I mean, you deserve love. Everybody does."

Brik accepted this judgment without apparent reaction. At last, he responded. His voice was stiff. "There's pity in your words. It implies superiority on your part. It suggests weakness and failure on mine." He stood up, towering over Bach. "The truth is, you don't understand. You're locked inside your own perceptions. You can't know what an honor and privilege it is to be a Morthan. You can *never* know that. And for that you're the one who deserves the pity. You're a human and you're enslaved to your hormones. I'm not. I'm the one who's free here."

"Have it your way," Bach said. "Believe it or not, this was productive. Because now I see how wide the gap is between us." She stopped at the door. "Thank you for your honesty." She didn't add anything else.

The door popped shut behind her. Brik stared at it for a moment, then sat down again. She hadn't said something. He didn't know what it was she should have said, but he sensed the absence of it. Some acknowledgment that she enjoyed their talk perhaps? Or perhaps some kind of invitation to talk again in the future? Despite the apparent pleasantness of their parting, he was certain that it had actually been an angry one somehow.

Humans.

He was going to have trouble sleeping again tonight.

Gamma

Quilla Gamma was a thin blue woman, as hard-looking as a man, and probably as strong. Armstrong wasn't willing to speculate anymore. He'd already made too many wrong guesses about Quillas. The two of them were loading the last few equipment cases into the *Houston*'s cargo boat; it was the last load. Armstrong had reached a grudging accommodation with himself and was now concentrating on the job and the joys of long-term celibacy.

Gamma was saying, *"LS-805* had an imp. She came home hinked so badly, her crew wore starsuits the whole way. We should be wearing starsuits too."

Armstrong grunted as he hefted a case of gallinium rods. He'd noticed that Gamma was suited, but hadn't said anything. In fact, all the Quillas were geared up. He'd thought about it, but hadn't wanted the extra encumbrance while he was working the cargo deck. Without robots—Korie had traded them away too—everything had to be loaded manually. The gallinium rods were heavy enough under the best of circumstances. Although the ship's gravity had been reduced to one-quarter gee in the cargo deck, the crates still had *mass*. Size and inertia had not been canceled, and the job remained just as difficult as if they were operating under normal gravity. "What happened to the *805*?" Armstrong asked, turning back for another trip.

"Well, the black box showed six hinks. Could have been twenty aboard. They were never sure."

"But how did they—"

"Plasma drivers fired immediately after docking," Gamma said bluntly. "Docking was the signal that set it off. One of the hinks they did take out was a bit that would have turned the singularity containment field off and then inverted the singularity. No Stardock left if that one had gotten through. What they missed was still pretty bad. The torches turned a corner of the station cherry-red and fried everyone on the spur. But better than eighty percent of Stardock L.R. survived. Almost half the personnel."

Armstrong considered that in uncomfortable silence.

The Quilla added softly, "The 'intimate contact' suffered by the *LS-805* consisted of a pair of Morthan infantry, captured and taken into custody after their transport craft was disabled. They escaped custody and fought a pitched seven-hour battle with the crew of the *LS-805*. Every trap they set was set during those seven hours before they died."

Armstrong looked around nervously. "And how many traps have we found now? Twenty-seven? How many more are there still undiscovered?"

Gamma rolled the last keg of Chief Leen's Southern Starshine into the cargo boat without comment. She met Armstrong's gaze directly. "The good news is that we're still alive."

"That's good news?"

She shrugged. "We had a Morthan assassin aboard for twelve hours. If he'd wanted to destroy us, we'd have been dead by now."

Armstrong shook his head. "He wanted the high-cycle fluctuators."

"That was plan A."

"He had a plan B in case of his own death?"

"Stardock," Gamma confirmed. "Everyone knows it."

"Whew," Armstrong exhaled in amazement. "I can't imagine thinking that way. No wonder Korie's so crazed about detoxing the ship. It doesn't make sense to me. How can we ever be sure we found everything. We'd be better off scrapping her."

Gamma smiled, an expression as mysterious as the Mona Lisa's.

"You know and you can't say, right?"

Gamma smiled again.

"Yeah, well I heard the same rumors you did," Armstrong said, trying to bluff the Quilla into talking. "They did try to scrap her, and Korie tried to resign, and the admiral's ulcer was acting up so bad, she left the whole thing in limbo. We were all supposed to be transferred out and Korie squelched it. That really pisses me off. Y'know, I applied for a transfer three times."

"Yes, we know," Gamma said quietly. "We also know how you got transferred *to* this ship."

"I didn't know she was underage," Armstrong protested. "She told me she was eighteen. And how was I to know her mother was a vice admiral?"

Gamma didn't respond to that directly. "Perhaps you should learn to think about something else once in a while?"

Armstrong snorted contemptuously.

"Besides," added Gamma, "Korie may have done us all a favor."

"Huh?"

"Keeping us away from Taalamar. The casualty rate will be high."

"Mpf," said Armstrong, almost thoughtfully.

The Bridge Crew

Korie entered the Bridge through the upper access, crossed to the starboard ladder, grasped the rails with both hands, and easily slid down the few steps to the Ops deck. Brik, Bach, Tor, Jonesy, Hodel, and Goldberg were waiting around the large elliptical table that held the holographic astrogation display.

"Good," said Korie, acknowledging their presence. "Thanks for being here." He glanced around the table, meeting each one's eyes. They were looking at him curiously. He was wearing his starsuit and carrying a foldable plastic helmet. "Um, just a readiness test," he said casually. "Nothing to worry about. Because of our recent experience with unauthorized EVAs, our security officer"—Korie nodded meaningfully to Brik—"has pointed out to me with justifiable concern that we are behind on our starsuit certifications. So I thought I'd wear mine for a few days to get it recertified, that's all. Please be seated." He sat. The others seated themselves too. One or two were frowning to themselves.

Korie continued without apparent notice. "Before we

begin, I want to acknowledge something. We know that there's an imp aboard. We know that we can't really keep anything secret from it. We're not going to try. Isolated as we are, there's nothing it can do to affect any other ship. And because we're effectively dead in the water now, there's little it can do to affect us. So, in that regard, we've pretty much neutralized it. For the moment anyway."

He turned his clipboard on and turned to the first page. "What we need to do now is consider the larger context in which we're operating. It'll give us a better sense of direction. I want to stress that this is an informal conversation. What we're going to discuss here is strictly for our own benefit. There are some things I've been thinking about, and I want the benefit of your input. This is not an Admiralty-authorized backgrounder, but even so let's keep this discussion to ourselves. There's already enough idle speculation about the war."

They nodded their agreement and Korie began. "Thank you. Harlie, are you with us?"

"Yes, Mr. Korie."

"Bring up the first display please." A graphic representation of the immediate neighborhood—a hundred light-years in each direction—shimmered into place. Korie pointed toward the upper part of the display where three red lines slanted down toward the center. "Those are the three fleets of the Morthan advance. We've code-named them Dragon for the center thrust, Worm for the one on the right, and Tiger for the one on the left. Dragon is commanded by Admiral Tanga. Worm was under the helm of Admiral Gellum, but intelligence says that he was killed in a duel and Worm is now apparently under the command of the ultra-militaristic Admiral Tofannor. Tiger is being led by someone named R'nida. No title given. We know nothing at all about R'nida, who he is, where he came from, nothing. The other two are ranking members of the Military High Command. R'nida is the joker in the deck. We have no background on him; we have no way of knowing what he might be thinking, or what are his theories of war. The War College currently believes that he may be someone else operating under a code name specifically to confuse us. But we really don't know for sure."

Korie held up a hand. "But that's not our concern right

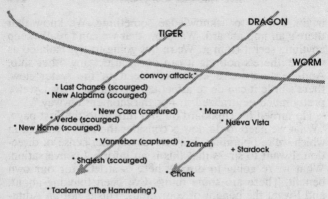

now. I just wanted you to know who the players in the game were. More important, I want you to look at this schematic of the Morthan advance." He pointed up at the representation again.

"First, there's the mauling at Marathon. The Silk Road Convoy gets hit by the *Dragon* in the center. Within days after that, Last Chance and New Alabama are scourged by *Tiger* on the left; *scourged,* despite the fact that neither has significant military value. Almost simultaneously, Worm, on the right, hits Marano. *Dragon* in the center doesn't spend much time mopping up at Marathon, but advances to capture Vannebar and . . ." This one was hard to say, but Korie forced himself to continue. ". . . and scourges Shaleen."

There was a moment of uncomfortable silence on the Bridge. The others *knew.*

Korie ignored it. "If you backtrack the fleet movements, you see that *Tiger* and *Worm* both had to be en route to their targets even before the mauling at Marathon. If *Dragon*'s attack had failed, the others would probably have turned back as well. Harlie says that an operation of this size must have taken at least ten years of preparation. The Silk Road was not a major trade route until just a few years ago, and it was never a military threat to the Morthans until last year, so clearly it was a target of opportunity in a much larger plan. All of this is fairly well known, I'm not revealing anything new here. But look, if you put the Marathon mauling into the context of the larger battle plan—"

He drew their attention back to the map, where the schematic of the attacks was playing itself out again and again and again. "It's obvious what the main thrust of the Morthan advance is. Direct to the center. The Admiralty believes that Taalamar is next. I should probably note here that we've got every significant target in a twenty-light-year crescent ahead of the Morthan fleet frantically evacuating as many of their citizens as they can.

"But . . . if Taalamar is next," Korie asked. "Why hasn't it been hit already? Look at the timeline. They could have hit Taalamar six weeks ago. If they were trying to drive as far into Allied space as possible, they *should* have hit Taalamar. Why didn't they? So, where are they now? And what are they doing?"

"They're preparing to hit Taalamar?" offered Jonesy. "That's what everyone says."

Korie sat back in his chair. "Yes, that's what everyone says, because that's the *logical* thing to believe." He looked to Jonesy. "And in fact, it's such a *likely* thing to believe that the best military strategists would move every available warship into the Taalamar theater to resist such an assault. If there's any place where we're going to stop the advance of the Morthan fleet, it's Taalamar. If we can cripple their advance, they'll have to regroup. The logistics of maintaining communications between three distinct fleets is staggering. It limits the speed of your forward advance, because you have to send ships sideways between the armadas. If they had to regroup, it would cost them months. So Taalamar represents a very real opportunity for us.

"So, now I have to ask, if they know that every day they delay their assault on Taalamar, that's one more day we have to prepare, why didn't they hit Taalamar as soon as they were able?" He looked around the table. "Anyone?"

"Resupply," offered Goldberg. Nominally a quiet man, he only spoke when he had something significant to add. "They've advanced so fast, they've outrun their own supply lines."

"Their ships are semi-autonomous. Like ours. They

don't need food or fuel," Korie responded. "So what supplies would they have run out of?"

"Missiles? Warheads?"

"Maybe. But the War College estimates they may have expended only one third of their total capacity to date. And they've got to have tenders traveling with them. So, if it's not weapons, what else could it be?"

Goldberg shook his head and sat back. "Sorry, sir."

"Don't be sorry. It was a good suggestion. Wars are won or lost not on the battlefield, but on the supply line. Anyone else? Come on, people, *think*. If you were a Morthan, what would you do?"

It was such an obvious line that everybody turned to look at Brik, which was exactly what Korie had intended. He wanted Brik's input here. The huge security officer had not been able to fold his three-meter body into a human-sized chair; instead, he perched uncomfortably on a stool. When he spoke, his voice rumbled in the lowest registers. "Well . . ." he began slowly. "If I were a human, I would start by assuming that whatever I was thinking about the Solidarity was *exactly* what the Solidarity *wanted* me to think."

Korie looked up sharply, as if Brik had just confirmed something for him. "Go on, Brik," he said quietly.

"Morthans never let anybody know anything about them. If you know anything about a Morthan, it's because that's what he wants you to know. That's true on an individual level. It's even truer in battle. You've asked the right question," Brik said. "If the Solidarity wanted Taalamar, they would have gone for Taalamar. Therefore, Taalamar is not the target. Look at the map."

They did.

"What happens if the fleets all suddenly turn and sweep right?" Brik asked. "Nothing. They head out along the edge of the rift. What if they head left. Same thing, opposite direction. The rift is a natural barrier a hundred light-years across. To send so many ships that far, they intend to stay. To do that, they have to secure a permanent beachhead. That means advancing as far across as they can and destroying all human installations that represent possible staging areas for counterattack. So, yes, it doesn't make sense for them to *not* advance on Taalamar immediately unless there's something *else* they want more." Brik met Korie's eyes. His expression was grim. Both already knew the answer to the unasked question.

"Stardock," whispered Tor, a shocked expression on her face. "They want Stardock."

"Precisely," said Korie. "That's how we figure it too. Thank you, Brik." He looked to the others. "They have to destroy Stardock. They have to do it before they can go on. They can't leave a major enemy stronghold functioning behind the wave front of their advance. They can't allow us to maintain such an access to their supply and communication lines. Stardock represents the last serious threat to their advance. That's why I believe the whole assault on Taalamar is a feint, to draw the fleet away from Stardock. The Solidarity is trying to 'lure the tiger out of the mountains.'"

"Huh?" asked Tor. The others looked puzzled too.

To Korie's surprise, it was Brik who explained the allusion. "Your executive officer is quoting one of the thirty-six stratagems of war, as postulated by the medieval Chinese military philosophers, premier among them the legendary Sun Tzu. The Chinese warlords were experts at the art of misdirection and the study of their history can be very useful." He met their startled expressions. "In this particular allusion, the tiger cannot be captured or killed when he hides in the mountains. That's his home territory. You must lure him down onto the plains where he is vulnerable. The Morthan Solidarity has succeeded in doing just that. They have put the Allies into a position where we must spread our resources all the way from here to Taalamar. Both Stardock *and* our fleet are now vulnerable."

Korie nodded his agreement. "Very good, Mr. Brik. I had no idea you were so well educated."

Brik gave Korie a foul look. "Then you've made a terrible mistake, Commander. You've underestimated a Morthan. So has the Admiralty."

"Yes," agreed Korie. "I see your point. Thanks for the object lesson."

"Wait a minute," said Tor. "The location of Stardock is so secret even *we* don't know where it is. Only Harlie does. If a ship's integrity is compromised, that's the first information that gets wiped. Doesn't secrecy count for something?"

"In this case, no," Korie said. "You see—"

"Hey, wait a minute—" Bach broke in abruptly. "Excuse me, sir, for interrupting, but if that's so, about Harlie forgetting the location, then *how* did we get back here? Once Cinnabar was aboard, Harlie should have forgotten that information."

"Harlie?" Korie prompted.

"Thank you," the intelligence engine replied. "Do you remember the emergency detoxification necessary after the death of Cinnabar? That was to ensure that there were no tracking or transmitting devices aboard that would betray our location to long-range listeners. Once we achieved a critical confidence level, I was able to reconstruct my memory. I can't be any more specific than that about the process of critical reconstruction without compromising security. Let me just say that once a piece of data is put into personal memory escrow, it is irretrievable unless certain confidence conditions are met."

"What Harlie isn't saying," Korie added, "is that had we not met that confidence level, he would have permanently forgotten the location and we would have had to proceed to a planetary base for recertification."

"Wait a minute," said Jonesy, visibly disturbed. He hadn't been following Harlie's part of the discussion because he had been worrying at another part of the problem. Now he looked across the table to Korie. "Let's get back to the other thing. Are you saying there are three armadas searching for Stardock right now?"

"That's my estimation of the situation, yes," said Korie. "Harlie agrees with me. Brik?"

The big Morthan nodded.

"Well, see here's the point," said Jonesy, looking from one to the other. "No disrespect intended, sirs, but if you and Brik and Harlie can figure it out, why can't the Admiralty?"

"Well, first of all," said Korie. "We have the advantage of being paranoid extremists." He grinned. "Brik does by birth. I do by training. Harlie dabbles in it as a matter of research into malevolent psychology."

Jonesy shook the joke away. "I mean it, sir. What's to say that you're right and the War College is wrong?"

"The War College isn't wrong," said Brik. "They're coming up with the very best answers they can, based on the information they have." And then he added, "Unfortunately, most of the information they have about the actions, motives, and location of the three Morthan armadas is being supplied by the Morthan Solidarity. We have no way of knowing which ship movements are feints and which are real until *after* the fact."

Jonesy looked worried. "But, Mr. Korie, are the brains at the War College even *aware* of the possibility that their information is wrong?"

"Of course they are," said Korie. "In fact, I'm sure that they're considering possibilities that even you and I would overlook. But as our security officer has pointed out, usually the only thing we know about a Morthan is what he wants us to know, and even when we factor that into the equation it still doesn't allow us to discredit the facts we already have. It only makes us crazier because we can't trust anything—which is also what the Solidarity intends. So we look and we observe and we study and we think and we extrapolate and we do our best to figure out what's really going on, all the time knowing that whatever false information the War College is getting, it is of such a consistent pattern that it will overwhelm the truth. So we try to prepare for the worst, all the time knowing that as long as we're still on the defensive, we're losing. Lieutenant Jones, have you ever had to do a report on Operation Overlord?"

"No, sir."

"I'll expect an oral presentation tomorrow at sixteen hundred hours. Harlie will give you the relevant information. Wear your starsuit. Here's the question I want you to answer. What lesson should we learn from Overlord?"

"Operation Overlord, yes, sir."

"But getting back to your point, I'm certain that there's a lot of War College intelligence being applied to this very problem. There are probably people sitting around a table just like this one, looking at a display just like this one, and coming up with the same disturbing conclusions we are. And they are probably reporting it to their superiors. And their superiors are weighing all the evidence as carefully as they can . . . and they are making decisions based on all the information they have. They are probably finding it very hard to leave Taalamar undefended on the strength of a hunch by a handful of trained paranoids, while all the tangible evidence suggests a very real danger for the people of the Taalamar system. Given the same evidence, what would *you* do? You and I don't have anything at stake in this conversation. We're indulging ourselves in a thought experiment. If we're wrong, no lives are lost. But if the War College chooses wrong . . . millions, perhaps billions, of people will suffer. So, given the same evidence, what *would* you do?"

"I see your point," said Jonesy. "I'm sorry for wasting everyone's time." He shrank into himself, chastened. He looked like a beaten puppy.

Korie realized too late that he had made a serious mistake; he saw his own past in Jonesy's face; he remembered the first time he had been burned by a superior officer in a discussion. He couldn't do that to a young officer as committed as Valentine M. Jones. "No, Mr. Jones," he said. "Don't do what you're doing now. Don't withdraw like that. You've made a very important contribution to this discussion. We're considering *all* the possibilities here. The fact that we dismiss a possibility doesn't mean it wasn't worth considering. This is part of your training. All consideration leads to wisdom."

"Yes, sir. Thank you, sir." Jonesy smiled tentatively.

Korie nodded an acknowledgment. "Good man."

"Wait a minute," said Tor, interrupting. "If the Admiralty is aware of the situation, then they're not going to leave Stardock undefended, are they?"

"Mm," said Korie. "That's the *other* part of the problem. You have to understand how badly the admirals want to take a bite out of the Morthan fleet. Every available ship is being put into the target sphere. Even Stardock is cannibalizing its resources. They've even stripped its hyperstate installations for the fleet. We're that desperate."

"Then they *are* leaving it undefended," Tor said.

Korie frowned; he didn't like admitting it. "Think about it. There's no real way to defend Stardock. She's a very large stationary target. Yes, she has guns, she has missiles, and she has ships patrolling around her, but it really doesn't matter how many guns, missiles, and ships we have; all the enemy needs is one more ship and one more missile than we can stop. Given that situation, and given the Solidarity's commitment to destroying her, maybe we have to sacrifice her to defend Taalamar. Maybe Taalamar will be where we make our stand. Maybe that's the Admiralty's plan all along. Maybe Stardock is *bait*. See, that's why I wanted to talk this over with all of you. There's something going on. If we can figure it out, we can *use* it. We can do something that makes a difference."

"Little us?" Hodel grinned. "And I thought *I* was the magician."

"Well, right now," said Korie, "we're operating without orders, so we have the freedom to go wherever we want and do whatever we think needs doing. Let's use that freedom."

Hodel smiled wryly. "You make it sound like we have a lot more freedom than we do. Without engines, we're just a big dead lump."

"So is Stardock," retorted Korie. "An even bigger deader lump."

"Wait. Wait a minute," said Tor. "I want to get back to the other thing about Stardock. Is she *really* being left undefended."

"Yes and no," said Korie. "Stardock's only real defense is secrecy. If no one knows where she is, no one can attack. So we make Stardock hard to find; she gets moved regularly; the timing of the move and the location are always selected at random, usually within a five-light-year radius. But if you're the enemy and you know that Stardock is likely to move every six weeks or so, then the most unlikely place to look is the place where it moved from. So—theoretically at least—Stardock is safest left where it is. For now, anyway."

"But that still doesn't resolve the real problem," Tor said. "The Solidarity is looking for an installation that is now essentially undefended. And with every ship that they detect, they get a little bit more information about where Stardock is likely to be."

"That's right," said Korie. "But it's even worse than that. If the point of this whole operation is to find Stardock, then they aren't searching casually; they've most likely spread their ships out across the entire sphere of probability, and each one has a specific sector of space to sweep. Last night, I asked Harlie to run some simulations. The amount of time it would take for three Morthan fleets to sweep the sphere of probability is just about the same length of time as has already passed since they should have attacked Taalamar. They're actually overdue here. Assume some logistical difficulties, the usual snafus, and we can assume that we have maybe a day, maybe a week." He looked around the table; all of the officers present were grim-faced.

Tor said it for all of them. "So the question is no longer *if,* is it? It's *when.* What happens *when* a Morthan scout finds Stardock? Then what? Are there any defenses at all?"

"There are patrols," said Korie calmly. "And we'll be joining them."

"We will?" Tor asked, surprised.

Korie nodded. "Remember, we have no orders. And I expect that state to continue for some time. The admiral is pretending we don't exist. So there's really nothing to keep us from lifting anchor and running our own operations. We'll call it a shakedown cruise."

"Okay," said Tor grimly, "let's game this out. Let's say we detect a scoutship and destroy it. Won't that tell the Morthan armada that something important is in the area of the missing scout?"

"Yes, it's definitely a lose-lose situation. You can't let the scout go and you can't destroy him. What do you do?"

Brik grunted for attention. They all looked to him. "The Morthan Solidarity knows how humans think. They do not expect humans to think like Morthans. Therefore, you have to do what a Morthan would do. Make him think what you want him to think."

Korie mulled that one over. "Good. Very good . . . in principle. But make him think what? And how? And with what resources?" He looked around the table. "That's the problem," said Korie.

Nobody replied. They were as stumped by the question as he. Korie stood up to leave. "Okay, that's it. We'll reconvene after dinner to consider possibilities. Please check your starsuits."

"Just tell me one thing," asked Tor abruptly. They all looked to her. "Was this meeting for our benefit? Or for the imp's?"

"Yes." Korie grinned. And then he left, leaving them frowning after him.

Sex

"Thank you for coming," said Brik.

Bach didn't answer. She glanced around Brik's cabin. There were two chairs in the room now, facing each other.

Brik gestured. "Would you like to sit?"

"Thank you," said Bach. She sat. The chair was not particularly comfortable. Brik had gotten it from the mess.

Brik sat opposite her. "May I offer you something? I have tea. Morthan tea."

"Yes, thank you."

Brik got up and busied himself for a bit, then returned with two ship's mugs, both steaming.

Bach took hers and held it in both hands. She brought it close to her face and inhaled deeply of its essence. "This is very good tea," she said.

"Thank you," said Brik. He sat down again, facing her. He sniffed his own tea, rolling the cup back and forth between his two huge hands.

Bach waited. Whatever Brik wanted, he would tell her in his own time.

"I think I owe you an apology," Brik said. "I said things that were thoughtless."

"No, you were honest. I should not have been offended by your honesty."

"Nevertheless, it was not my intention to offend."

"I know that."

"I don't know human mating rituals very well."

"No, you don't," she agreed.

"I've been reading in the ship's library."

Bach waited. She sniffed at her tea again.

"I still don't understand."

"I'm sorry," Bach said.

"I'm frustrated."

"I can imagine."

"No, I don't think you can. No, I'm sorry. I shouldn't say that. But even if you can understand, it doesn't change the frustration. There are all of these discussions of experiences that I have no referents for." His voice dropped to a whisper. "I don't like this," he admitted.

"You don't like what?"

"This. Everything."

"I still don't understand."

"I read the books. All of them. They made no sense to me. I don't like not knowing. I don't like knowing that there are things I cannot know." He fell silent.

Bach looked across the intervening light-years at the Morthan, her superior officer. Now, more than ever, she felt sorry for him. Sad and sorrowful. Such a mighty warrior, confessing weakness to an underling. What did he want from her?

Abruptly she stiffened. Her eyes narrowed. "Brik?" she asked.

He straightened.

"Is this a performance?"

He didn't answer.

"There's something you want from me, isn't there?"

Still, he said nothing.

"I thought we promised each other honesty."

"Yes," he admitted.

"What?"

"You said you found me attractive. I don't understand that, but I recognize that you meant it as a compliment."

He hesitated, then added, "I have become curious about . . . about sexuality."

"Why didn't you just say so?"

"The book said not to. The book said I should . . . *flirt.*"

Bach laughed abruptly, then caught herself and tried to suppress it, waving it away with one hand while hiding the rest of the giggles behind the other. "I'm not laughing at you, Brik. I'm laughing at the book. Trust me. Don't flirt. Morthans should not flirt. Is the word *grotesque* in your vocabulary? No, please, don't be hurt, let me explain."

She put her mug of tea down on the deck and crossed to him. She went down on her knees before him. She took his mug and placed it on the deck, then took his big hands in her two tiny ones. She looked up—and up—into his eyes. "Listen to me. You are about strength. Don't be afraid to be strong. That's what's attractive about you. Don't try to be anything else. I want you to be exactly who you are. All right?"

Brik stared down at her, not really comprehending. But he nodded anyway.

"Now, just tell me what you want."

Brik nodded slowly. He cleared his throat. He wet his lips. "I would like . . . I would like to know what it means to be *kissed.* Would you show me?"

Bach blinked. She nodded, both flattered and pleased. She stood up slowly, then took his hands as if to pull him to his feet. He rose—and rose. She looked up—and up. "Hmm," she said. She looked around. She went and pulled her chair over closer. As she stepped up onto it, Brik took her by the waist and lifted. She felt as if she were floating up onto the chair.

She turned to face him. She put her hands on his broad shoulders. She looked into his huge dark eyes. She studied his wide mouth. "Wet your lips," she said. "Pucker."

Brik did so.

"Close your eyes."

"Why?"

"It helps the experience. Now close your eyes."

Brik looked like he wanted to protest. Instead, he closed his eyes.

"Now don't do anything, just lean forward and press

your lips against mine. Ready?" She leaned forward, so did he. She opened her eyes. His were already open. The two of them stared at each other, both too close to really focus. She pulled back. "I told you to close your eyes."

"I wanted to see what you were doing."

"Stop being paranoid and trust me."

"I'm a Morthan."

"Do you want to be kissed?" She didn't wait for his answer. "Now close your eyes and see what happens when you put all of your attention on what your lips are doing."

"All right," said Brik. He closed his eyes again.

Bach leaned forward and pressed her lips to his. She allowed herself to relax and feel the strength of his being. She parted her lips slightly so that his upper lip was between hers. Then she moved her mouth downward and took his lower lip between hers. Then she moved her mouth upward again, opening it slightly to his—

He pulled back abruptly. "What are you doing?"

"Kissing. What are you doing?"

He didn't answer. "Can we try again?"

Bach nodded, a little weakly. Brik steadied her with his hands on her waist. "That's good," she said. "Just keep doing that." She leaned forward again, leaning herself against him. His arms folded delicately around her. His lips were suddenly very . . . *very.*

After a moment she pulled back and looked at him, her eyes wide and shining.

"Was that all right?" Brik asked. "I was practicing my focusing techniques. . . ."

Bach's face was flushed. "Oh, my," she said. "Oh, my, yes. That was—that was quite all right. Yes."

"Can we do that again?" Brik asked, frowning in puzzlement.

Bach swallowed and caught her breath and pushed her hair back. She put her arms around his shoulders again and leaned forward. . . .

Houston

"Commander?"

"What is it, Harlie?"

"Incoming message from the *Houston*. Captain La Paz. She sounds angry. Will you take it now?"

Korie took a breath. "Yes," he said slowly. "I'll take it." He took another breath, then sat down in the captain's chair. *Deliberately.* He swiveled to face the reception wall. "Go ahead," he said.

There was a brief blare of *Dixie*—Korie frowned in momentary annoyance; did Captain La Paz ever stop to think how irritating that noise was?—and then the wall cleared as if a curtain had been drawn aside. Juanita La Paz sat opposite him.

"Juanita. It's good to see you."

"Don't you hand me that bullshit, Mister. I know what you did."

Korie considered trying to bluff it out. It wasn't worth the energy. He shrugged. "You did what you had to. We did what we had to."

"You delayed delivery of those fibrillators, Jon. And

when you did deliver them, they were filthy—and deliberately misaligned. Very cute," La Paz said. "You kept us from Taalamar."

"Good," said Korie.

"Good?" La Paz's eyebrows climbed up her forehead. *Good?*

"Yes," said Korie. "We saved your lives. You're not battle ready, 'Nita. This has nothing to do with the *Star Wolf* anymore. And it's not about you and me either. It's about responsibility. Come on! I figured it out early that the *Wolf* wasn't going to get there. Once we started stripping her parts, we sent them where they would do the most good— to the ships we thought had the best chance. Look at your confidence rating. Would you really go into battle in that condition?"

"We don't have a choice, Jon. There's a war on—"

"We do have a choice, 'Nita. The war isn't going to be won today. We can choose our battles where we have a chance of making a difference."

"I thought we had a chance."

"I didn't."

"You overstepped your bounds, Jon. My ship is *my* responsibility."

"And my ship is mine," said Korie dispassionately. "And I can easily justify keeping those fibrillators. If we could have gotten the *Wolf* ready to fly, we'd have been in better shape than you for Taalamar."

"You don't have a command, Jon. *I do.*"

That one stung.

Korie took a breath. Control.

"Command or not, I still have a responsibility." He met her gaze.

For a moment, the two just studied each other. Neither broke the silence.

"You're a son of a bitch," she finally said. "You know that, don't you?"

Korie nodded. "I believe that's what qualifies me for this job."

A hint of a smile cracked La Paz's hard expression. "Yeah," she agreed. "That is the essential qualification."

Korie considered his next words carefully. "Have you

and your officers . . . had any thoughts about the strategic situation?"

"What do you mean?"

"I mean, what if Taalamar is *not* the target?"

"If it's not Taalamar, it's Stardock."

"That's our estimation too."

"It's not too hard to figure out."

"Well, that's my point."

La Paz considered it. "Yes, there is that. We might very well have a much larger responsibility to stay exactly where we are. But do you really think one ship can make a difference?"

"Two." Korie corrected her.

"One and a half," retorted La Paz, but she was smiling.

"One and a half sounds about right," said Korie. "Seventy-five percent for us. Seventy-five percent for you."

"Eighty-five, sixty-five," smiled La Paz.

Korie lifted a hand in surrender. "Yes," he said. "I really do think we can make a difference."

"Do you have a plan?"

"Nothing I can discuss."

"Your imp has compromised you that badly?"

Korie reacted sharply to that. He hadn't realized she knew about the imp. How many others knew? Having an imp aboard your ship was like having a sexually-transmitted disease. Something you didn't talk about. "That's just it. We don't know how badly we're compromised. We're assuming the worst."

"Well . . ." she admitted. "On those grounds alone, you can justify holding back the fibrillators as long as you did. Nevertheless, you owe me big time, mister. Big time."

"I know that. I didn't make the decision casually."

"I know that too."

"Thanks," Korie said.

She nodded. "Let's hope we're both wrong about Stardock. Otherwise you didn't do either of us any favors." She touched a button and her image winked out.

Followed by a quick phrase from *Dixie*.

Korie sagged in his chair unhappily.

Orgasm

"My, God!" exclaimed Molly Williger, rising from her desk. "What happened to her?"

Brik didn't answer. He carried the convulsing Bach directly to an examination table. Her body jerked and thrashed; she nearly threw herself out of his arms. She made choking noises in her throat. Brik strapped her to the table with difficulty and began attaching scanning devices to her body, until Dr. Williger slapped his hands away. "I'll do the doctoring. What happened?"

"She . . . appears to be injured."

"I can see that!" snapped Williger, loosening Bach's jacket. "Just tell me what happened."

Brik looked dazed. "We were . . . she was . . . I didn't realize. . . ."

Something in his tone. Williger looked up abruptly, narrowing her eyes. She came around the table and pushed Brik backward. "You. Over here. Lay down. Don't move." She pulled a scanning array down over him and switched it on. "Don't talk." She hurried back to Bach and pulled a similar scanning unit into position. "Hyperventilating." She noted. "Heart racing. Feverish. Eyes . . . dilated. Brain waves—what the hell?!! What were you two doing?" She pulled a buzzbox down and pressed the crown into place around Bach's forehead; she switched it on and waited. Bach's movements started to ease, but she still kept writhing on the table. Her grunts became animal moans, discordant and disturbing.

Williger came back to Brik and started shaking him. Hard. "What the hell did you do to her, you stupid sick bastard?!!"

Brik blinked. And blinked again. He looked drugged. He looked more alien than ever. He looked as if he'd been to the other side of the sky and only his body had come back. Williger looked from Brik to Bach and back again, confused, angry, upset. She studied the displays over each of their beds. Again, she could make no sense of it. "Harlie?" she demanded.

Harlie considered the situation for a moment. "Mr. Brik is in shock. Lieutenant Bach is . . . experiencing an intense flurry of nervous activity. She does not appear to be in pain. The spasms are orgasmic in nature, only far more intense."

"Orgasmic?"

"Yes," Harlie confirmed.

Williger turned and stared at Bach. Amazed. Then she turned and stared even harder at Brik. Horrified. She looked back to Bach. "Is she drugged?"

"I find no evidence of it."

Williger shook her head in disbelief. "All right, let's see if we can bring her down." She turned to the medical cabinet and pulled out a spray-syringe. She checked its settings and held it up against Bach's arm. There was a soft hiss. Williger studied the overhead displays and watched as the jiggling lines began to ease. "All right," she said at last. "That'll do it."

She turned to Brik. She rubbed her forehead and studied his charts. She turned to the medicine chest and surveyed its contents. No. Nothing useful there. Not for this. She turned back to Brik and thought for a moment. "Oh, the hell with it," she said. And slugged him in the solar plexus as hard as she could. Brik jerked in reaction, grunting softly, but that was his only reaction.

Molly Williger returned to her desk, sat down, and . . . started to giggle. "If I hadn't seen it, I wouldn't have believed it." She sighed. "I can't even write this up. Nobody'll believe it."

She got up from her desk, crossed to a medical supply cabinet, unlocked it, and took out a bottle. It was halfway filled with a honey-colored liquid. She took a small test tube and carefully measured 10cc of amber fluid into it. Still holding the test tube, she recapped the bottle and returned it to the cabinet, and relocked it. She turned around and faced both Brik and Bach on their respective medical tables; she raised the test tube in a toast to them, then downed its contents in a single startling swallow. Then she tossed the test tube into a sink, where it clattered unbroken.

She returned to her desk, sat down again, put her head in her hands, and watched Bach for a bit. The lieutenant's moans were finally easing. Her body movements were already more relaxed. Her face was flushed.

Molly Williger waited a bit more, then opened her bottom drawer and took out two knitting needles and a ball of yarn.

Half a sleeve later Brik sat up at his table. He looked around, almost as if he didn't know where he was.

Williger put her knitting aside. "How do you feel?"

"I don't know," said Brik. "I've never felt like this before."

"What were you two trying to do?"

"The lieutenant was showing me some . . . moves."

"They must have been some moves," Williger said.

Brik didn't acknowledge it. "Will she live?" he asked.

"Probably. But you and I have to have a talk. A very important talk. . . ."

CHESS II

By the end of the third day, the crew of the *Star Wolf* had installed over two hundred separate traps, chess sets, and cameras. Some of the camera buttons were in the open. Some were concealed. Some were real, some were dummies. With Korie's approval, Gatineau's eventual target was the installation of a thousand separate traps.

Some of the traps were so ridiculous they could have only been designed by Hodel. One was a stuffed bird with a salt shaker hanging over it. If a piece on the board was moved, the salt shaker dropped grains of salt on the bird's tail. Another was a box with a small hole, and a stainless steel nut just inside the hole. That one was Gatineau's. Other traps were more sophisticated; they were genuine attempts to capture the imp.

Most of the serious ones had been designed by Brik. One trap had the chessboard in the center of a high-gravity panel, triggered to generate a local field of twelve gees if any pieces on the chessboard were moved; the imp would be pinned to the floor by its own weight. Another trap was engineered to shoot anesthetic and transmitting darts into

the imp. A third would have sealed off the entire compartment. A fourth was set to deliver a paralyzing electrical
shock. A fifth . . . et cetera. There were others that were
identical to these, but not armed, and still more that *looked*
identical, but did nothing at all. One trap was a maze, with
the chessboard at the center. One trap was nothing more
than a lever to pull beside the chessboard and a net hanging overhead. The lever was not connected to the net. One
trap was a net with no lever. One trap was a lever with no
net.

By the end of the third day, the imp had initiated one
hundred thirty-three separate chess games. It had made
sixty-seven different obscene gestures or grotesque faces at
the cameras. It had dismantled seven traps. It had ignored
twenty-three traps. Of the twenty-three it ignored, sixteen
had rude graffiti about Morthans scrawled on them.

Harlie analyzed the progress of the separate games and
ventured an opinion that the imp's processing abilities
were being fully utilized. Increasing the number of traps
would put it into a condition of early stress.

Concurrent with the trapping effort, Korie had begun
sending security teams around the ship, sealing and searching one sector at a time. One team was working its way
aftward, securing each and every compartment in a specific
hull section before moving onto the next. A second team
followed in their wake, resecuring the same compartments.
A third team moved around the ship checking and sealing
compartments seemingly at random. Harlie generated
their assignments in realtime, so that not even the team
knew what compartment they were going to be securing
until they got there. Some compartments were secured six
times in a six-hour period. Others were never checked at
all.

Neither Korie nor Brik nor Leen expected the teams to
succeed against the imp, but they did expect that all the
activity would seriously curtail the imp's freedom to move
about the starship. It was Harlie's opinion that the increasing pressure of the pursuit was affecting the imp's stress
levels. On some of the videos, the imp was demonstrating
signs of agitation and impatience.

Korie shrugged when he saw. "I don't think we should
believe it. Not yet." He was leaning on the forward rail of

the Bridge, studying the main screen. Tor and Hodel were
on duty on the Ops deck. Brik and Leen had both come
forward for this conference. Straightening to face them,
Korie said, "I don't think the imp has forgotten why it's
here. Someone left a plate of feces on the table of the
officers' wardroom this morning. That's a pretty clear message, don't you think?"

Brik didn't comment. Tor made a face. Leen looked
sour.

"Can't blame it." Hodel grinned. "I've sometimes
thought the same thing myself."

Korie ignored the jibe. "Dr. Williger is analyzing the material. Let's find out what it's eating. Maybe we can slip
something into its food or water . . . ?"

"And maybe it'll slip something into ours," said Brik.
"Don't give it ideas. So far, it's been playing fair. If you
start playing dirty . . ."

"Point well taken." After a moment he asked, "Playing
fair?"

Brik nodded. "There are rules for combat."

Korie's eyebrows went up. "Morthan rules?"

"Yes. Morthan rules."

"Oh, really? What's the first rule of Morthan combat?"

" 'Win,' " said Brik.

"Yes, of course. Silly me. And what's rule number two?"

" 'See rule number one.' "

"Right. Why am I not surprised?" Korie shook his head
in amused disbelief. "All right, at least we're making progress. We've seized some initiative in the situation. How
many problems do we have to give it before it overloads
and makes a mistake? That's the real question." Korie
looked to Brik, to Leen. Both looked back at him blankly.
"Don't worry," he added. "It was only a rhetorical question. We'll get the answer empirically." He shook his head
in quiet exasperation, a reaction to the size of the task that
still lay ahead.

Harlie interrupted then. "Mr Korie?"

"Yes, Harlie?"

"We have received a signal."

"Yes?"

"We must return to Stardock immediately. For decontamination."

"They can't be serious!" Korie said.

"I'm sorry, sir. That's the message."

Brik snorted. His opinion was written on his face.

Leen scowled angrily. He turned away, leaned on a console for a moment, and muttered something as nasty as it was unintelligible. The work station's displays flickered in horror and then went out. He turned around abruptly. "It's a hoax. The imp is doing it."

Korie shook his head. "Harlies don't lie. They *can't.*" To Harlie he said, "What's your confidence rating?"

"Eighty-three and holding," Harlie replied.

Korie looked blandly to Leen, as if to say, "You see?"

Leen shook his head grimly. "We can't do it. We don't dare."

"He's right," said Brik.

"I know it. Harlie, send this signal." Korie selected his words carefully. "We can't do it. We have a . . . a security problem."

"They are aware of the problem, sir." Harlie phrased his answer just as precisely. "There may be a solution."

"They know we have an imp?"

"The message is quite clear."

"I'll look at it in my cabin."

"Yes, sir."

Korie and Leen and Brik exchanged worried glances. Tor and Hodel too.

"I believe," said Brik coldly, "that the issue is being forced."

"What are you going to do?" demanded Leen.

"I can't disobey the admiral, can I?" said Korie. He hoped he'd said it convincingly. There were still no insignia on his collar.

"But you can't risk letting that thing get to Stardock!" Tor insisted. "You *can't* do this. You simply can't!"

"What do you want me to do?" Korie snapped back angrily. "Exorcise it? Hodel—how much to exorcise a Morthan demon?"

"Uh—sorry, boss. I'm out of the exorcism business. For good. I saw what happened last time."

Korie turned back to Tor. "Do you have a *better* idea? If so, I want to hear it!"

Tor blanched at his anger. She swallowed hard and shook her head. "I just—I'm sorry."

"I know what's at stake, goddammit." And then he added, in a quieter tone, "I'm sorry I yelled at you, Tor. We're all under a lot of pressure here."

"Yes, sir," she said sullenly.

Korie turned to Brik. "Let's put the entire crew on red drill. Four hours on, four hours off. Everybody who isn't in an essential job is on a search team. Everybody puts out traps everywhere. See to it, Brik. You too, Chief. Tor?"

"Yes, Mr. Korie?"

"Set a course. Your very *best* course. A. Very. Careful. *Slow.* Course. Take all the time you need setting it up. Check your work carefully. Do you understand? And don't initiate anything until I see it."

"I understand." She nodded her assent.

Korie ran both hands through his hair, a sign of exhaustion. He rubbed his eyes wearily. He looked around at the others. "Well, we're in for it now."

Dwarf Point

Korie entered the Bridge of the *Star Wolf*. He was still wearing his starsuit; his collapsible helmet was hanging from his utility belt, but he was carrying a metal helmet as well. He hung the helmet on the captain's chair and stepped to the forward railing. He put his hands on the railing and then put his weight on his hands. He studied the forward screen without seeing it. It showed stars. Nothing else.

After a moment Korie straightened. Whatever thoughts had passed through his mind, they weren't apparent on his face. "Commander Tor?" he asked. "What's our position?"

"Holding at Dwarf Point One." Tor was wearing a starsuit too.

"Thank you." Korie spoke to the air, "Chief?"

The chief was in the engine room. His voice was approximately one meter to Korie's right. "CINTI," he said. "It's all CINTI."

Korie smiled. CINTI was an acronym. *Cleanliness Is Next To Impossible.*

"Thank you," said Korie, allowing himself the slightest

smile. It didn't matter anymore. Either they had succeeded. Or they had not. They would find out soon enough. He glanced down to the Ops deck. "Quilla Delta? Are you ready?"

A starsuited figure turned around. "Yes, Mr. Korie. We are."

"Then please come up here to the Bridge."

Quilla Delta came up the steps to the Bridge and took a position to the rear of Korie and Brik. She waited expectantly.

"All right," Korie said, his voice becoming somehow larger. *"Now hear this."* Harlie would relay his words to every crew member aboard the ship. "This is an order. We are about to initiate our final docking maneuver. All hands who are not yet wearing starsuits must put on starsuits immediately. There will be no exceptions." He glanced meaningfully across the Bridge to Brik, who stared dispassionately back. Brik's starsuit was stretched across his massive frame.

Both Korie and Brik picked up their helmets at the same time. Still watching each other, both individuals pulled their helmets down over their heads. They locked them into place. Korie turned around so Brik could check his seals. Brik did likewise. When he finished, Korie turned and surveyed the Bridge. Hodel, Jonesy, Tor, Goldberg—all were suited.

"Chief?" Korie asked.

"Just a moment. Waiting for Gatineau and Stolchak . . . got it. It's green. The entire crew is ready for vacuum."

"Thank you, Mr. Leen. How long did it take?"

"About fifteen seconds."

Korie allowed himself another smile. Yes, it can be done in fifteen seconds, if you make starsuits the uniform of the day. "Harlie."

"Yes, Mr. Korie?"

"I apologize in advance for any discomfort we are about to cause you."

"No apologies are necessary, Mr. Korie. I understand the need."

"I appreciate that." Korie nodded to Brik. Brik looked grim. He stepped down from the Bridge to the Ops deck, from there he ducked under the Bridge to the Ops bay, and from there—

"He's really going to do it?" asked Tor.

Korie nodded.

They waited silently. The screen continued to show stars. After a moment Brik returned. "It's done," he said.

"Harlie?" Korie asked.

There was no answer. The silence was *eerie*.

Korie reached into his starsuit equipment pocket and pulled out a set of memory clips. He handed them to Tor. "Here are the programs you'll need for docking . . . and any other eventuality. Harlie has been disconnected. Completely. You have total control of the vessel from your console. The Bridge has had six consecutive detox operations without turning up any bugs. This Bridge has never been unmanned. Your work station is the most secure place on the ship."

"Thank you," said Tor, taking the clips. She handed them to Jonesy who laid them out carefully across the rack on the top of the display. He sorted them by color.

"Now hear this," Korie spoke to the crew again. "I know it's been a difficult time. I know it's hard living and working in a starsuit round the clock. I know it's hard *sleeping* in a starsuit. I've been just as uncomfortable as all of you. I appreciate how well you've kept your spirits up. I'm very proud of you. We've made it to the final lap. This is the hardest part, so please don't let your guard down."

"We are now in our final approach for docking. We have secured every part of the vessel. We have set out more than seven hundred separate traps. Harlie has won more than four hundred chess games—four hundred and two, to be exact. We have been holding at condition yellow for three hours. The imp has not been seen by any camera for six and a half hours. I must tell you that of the three thousand camera buttons we set out, only four hundred and twelve remain operational and those are in noncritical locations. The imp is still somewhere onboard and it is still active and it is still taking down cameras. We must assume that it could be anywhere by now. We must assume that it has a plan that it will implement immediately upon docking.

"Each of you has been given sealed *handwritten* orders. You are authorized to open your orders now and read

them. You will immediately carry out your orders." Korie
hesitated, then . . . despite his own feelings . . . he
added, "May God be with us all."

He sat down in his chair and fastened his safety harness.
He waited while Tor and Jonesy opened their orders. They
too sat down and secured themselves in place. Korie
glanced over to Brik, questioningly. Brik scowled, then he
too secured himself.

First, the lights went out. Then the consoles went out.
Even the screens went dead.

The forward screen simply disappeared.

They hung for a moment in darkness and silence.

The first light came from the direction of Tor's console.
She had switched on her suitlight. She continued reading
her sealed orders. Others around the Bridge began illumi-
nating themselves too. Several finished their orders, pock-
eted them, and switched their lights off again.

Korie switched on his suit radio. "Section heads. Report?"

"Leen. Yellow."

"Tor. Blue."

"Hodel. Purple."

"Stolchak. Orange."

"Hall. Black."

"Brik. Brown."

"Williger. Magenta."

"Goldberg. White."

"Green. Green."

Korie grinned at that last. Communications Officer
Darian Green.

"All right," said Korie. "Code Sleepy. Repeat. Code
Sleepy. Go." He waited. He looked to Brik. "This had better work."

"And if it doesn't?"

"Well, then my successor will have to worry about it."

"If it doesn't work, you're not going to have a successor."

"There is that, yes." Korie switched on his helmet lamp
and pulled a thick envelope out of his equipment bag. He
opened the envelope and took out the first page. He held it
up before his faceplate so he could read it as he listened.

Chief Leen came back online first. "Gully Foyle is my name. . . ."

Korie checked the list of code phrases in front of him. *The engine room is offline. We're powered down and under manual control. All autonomic nervous functions are disconnected.*

Stolchak checked in next: "Call me Ishmael."

Again Korie referred to his list. *The farms are secured.*

Hall: "It was the best of times, the worst of times." *The cargo bays are secured.*

Williger: "Once upon a time, there was a Martian named Valentine Michael Smith." *Med bay.*

Goldberg: "Sredni Vashtar went forth. His thoughts were red thoughts, and his teeth were white." *All weapon systems controlled through the ship's autonomic nervous system have been physically disconnected. Certain independent manually operated weapon systems remain operable only to those who have the appropriate key.*

Hodel: "It was a bright cold day in April, and the clocks were striking thirteen." *All traps are armed.*

Green: "I have no mouth and I must scream." *All communications systems have been physically disconnected. Except the portable unit that Lieutenant Green wore strapped to his chest.*

Tor. "Alice was beginning to get very tired of sitting by her sister." *All navigation systems have been taken offline.*

Korie looked to Brik questioningly.

" 'Twas brillig, and the slithy toves did gyre and gimble in the wabe. . . ." *Internal security systems have been disconnected. They cannot be used against us.*

It was a onetime code, never to be used again. If the imp was listening in, it would have no way of knowing what was really being said.

"The imp has got to be getting a little anxious about now, don't you think?"

"Morthans don't get anxious," said Brik. "I doubt that the imp has been programmed for that particular emotional reaction."

"Right," said Korie. "Thanks for reminding me." He wondered what the imp used *instead* of anxiety. *"Now hear this,"* he said. "Code Sneezy. Code Sneezy."

He couldn't feel what was happening, but he could imag-

ine it. All over the ship, crew members were manually dog-
ging every hatch, then locking each one shut with a security
clamp. Every self-contained module aboard the ship was
now isolated from every other self-contained module.
Once again, he waited for crew members to report in.

Again, Leen was first. Korie studied the paper in front of
him, waiting for the appropriate code phrases.

"There was an old man from Nantucket, who kept all his
cash in a bucket. . . ."

"There was a young lady of Riga, who smiled as she rode
on a tiger. . . ."

"There was a young plumber of Leigh, who was plumb-
ing a maid by the sea. . . ."

"There was a young man of Bengal, who went to a mas-
querade ball. . . ."

"A marvelous bird is the pelican, whose beak can hold
more than his belican. . . ."

"There was a young man from Belgrave, who kept a
dead whore in a cave. . . ."

"There was a young lady named Bright, whose speed was
much faster than light. . . ."

The recital went on for several moments. Korie checked
off each code phrase. When he finished, he looked to Brik.

Brik looked very unhappy. "A lesbian who lived in Khar-
toum invited a queer to her room. . . ."

Korie gave Brik a nod of acknowledgment. Brik curled
his upper lip just enough to reveal his incisors.

"Now hear this. Code Bashful. Code Bashful."

This time the wait was longer. Korie looked to his right.
Brik had opened a floor panel and was manually operating
a set of valves and handles. Korie felt his starsuit slowly
hardening around him. . . .

Once more, the signals came in:

"Pawn to Queen Two."

"Knight to King's Bishop Three."

"Wizard to Rook Four."

"Hobbit to Volcano Six."

"Troll to Queen's Knight Three-Sub-Three."

"Dragon to Dragon Four Probability Fifty-five and
King's Bishop Two Probability Forty-five."

Korie looked to Brik.

Brik said, "Colonel Mustard to the Conservatory with the Candlestick."

The ship is now open to space. Unless the imp has a starsuit, it's immobile. From this moment on we're dealing only with preinstalled booby traps. I hope.

Korie looked to Brik. "Reassure me again. Can the imp breathe vacuum?"

"I believe it can endure prolonged periods of vacuum. I do not believe it can function in it."

Kore nodded.

"Now hear this. Code Grumpy. Code Grumpy."

"Grandpa Blue Jacket."

"Betty Pancake."

"Sweet Wilma Bumble."

"Martha Moose."

"Christmas Billy."

"Doorway Denny."

Korie looked to Brik.

Brik sighed inaudibly and said, "Bertha Six-Pack."

Korie grinned. He didn't even bother to refer to his code sheet. These codes were decoys. Phonies. They meant nothing at all. Throughout the ship, crew members were doing meaningless activities; opening and closing compartments, taking things out, rearranging them, putting them away in new compartments. There was absolutely no strategic value at all to any of the exercises. If the imp was listening and monitoring, it would have to be going crazy trying to figure out what was happening.

At least that was the theory.

Korie waited a moment, then said, "Code Happy. Code Happy."

Korie removed the transceiver module from his starsuit harness and handed it to Brik. The big Morthan moved quickly around the Ops deck collecting transceiver modules from the entire crew. He put them into a shielded lockbox, closed it, armed it, and pressed a red panel on its lid. The transceivers inside would shortly be junk.

Korie took a communications cable out of his equipment case and plugged one end of it into the communications jack of his starsuit; the other end he handed to Quilla Delta who plugged it into her starsuit. She accepted a similar plug from Brik and plugged that in too. As Korie watched, the rest of the crew on the Ops deck were similarly creating themselves as a local area network. All over the ship, the process would be repeated, with each cluster of crew members cabled directly or indirectly to one of the Quillas. The Quillas linked all the separate networks.

If they had succeeded, they now had a secure communications network. The optical cables were sending coded signals only. The codes were updating themselves a thousand times a second. Even if the imp could monitor the signals, it still wouldn't be able to decode them on the fly. And even if it could link into one network, it still wouldn't be able to tell what any other network was doing. The Quillas' communications channels were holographic and therefore unreadable by anyone not part of a Quilla cluster.

Korie turned to Quilla Delta. "Status?"

"We are Happy," the Quilla reported. "We are very Happy."

"Good." Korie nodded. "Very good. We are now the first manually operated ship in the history of the fleet."

"A singular honor, to be sure," Brik remarked.

"Whatever works," Korie replied grimly. To the Quilla he said, "Send this message. Code Doc. Code Doc."

"Message sent and acknowledged," said the Quilla.

Korie sat down in the captain's chair. Brik sat down in the chair beside him. The Quilla took the third seat behind the two of them. Korie secured his safety harness. The others did likewise. Across the Ops deck, the Bridge crew were also securing themselves. Jonesy was opening the overhead access of the Bridge and climbing up toward the observation bubble; he was trailing a long communications cable behind him. This was the *crucial* part of the operation. Hodel was standing on the hull at the aft of the vessel, there to provide the only guidance cues they would have for the docking maneuver. They needed to establish a secure communications link with him; it would be critical for manual docking.

Jonesy reported abruptly, "We can't make the optical connection through the observatory port. The glass has been frosted with some kind of . . . I don't know, but it's opaque."

Korie and Brik exchanged a glance. *The imp? Yes.*

"All right," said Korie. "Use the external emergency net." The external emergency network was installed on the hull of the ship for exactly this kind of situation. Self-powered, separate from the rest of the ship, it provided an auxiliary channel for operations.

"Sir?" Jonesy asked, concerned. "Are you sure?"

"We have no choice." He added, "Chief Leen has detoxed the network seven times since the imp was detected. The most recent decontam was seven hours ago. Let's trust it."

"Okay," said Jonesy uncertainly. He disappeared into the overhead again.

Korie looked to Brik and held up his hands with his fingers crossed. Brik gave him *that* look. Korie shrugged.

"We have completed Doc," said Delta abruptly. Jonesy came floating back down into the Ops deck.

"Thank you," said Korie. "Code Dopey. Code Dopey."

A moment more, and all gravity in the starship went off. It did not go off gradually, it simply disappeared. One moment Korie was sitting in his command chair. The next instant he was falling, and the moment after that he was relaxing into the familiar drift of zero-gee. *So far, so good.*

"All right," Korie said. "Hi-ho. Hi-ho. It's off to work we go." He waited until the command had been sent, and then said, "Commander Tor. She's all yours. Take us in."

Docking

Astrogator Cygnus Tor turned to her console. It was dead. She bent down to the floor and brought up a jury-rigged board, which she plugged directly into her starsuit. She studied its tiny display. There were only rudimentary read-outs connected; Hodel wore three positional scanners, no camera. If the scanners failed, he would talk the ship into the docking harness.

Tor's job was further complicated by the fact that the usual docking thrusters had been disconnected from the ship's control network, along with all of the other units of the drive system. She was working with handmade cold-firing rockets, installed by Chief Leen's machine shop crew. Her control of the vessel was nowhere near as accurate as she would have had with a more precise propulsion system.

Plus, she was working without an onboard intelligence engine. She had none of the usual instrumentation and automatic guidance circuitry. Her approach would be a process of correction and countercorrection all the way in. In other words, she was "parking by ear," aiming at the docking harness and listening for the crunch.

Korie watched her from the Bridge. Her small display showed a red dot inside a green circle. Her job was to keep it centered. She worked in a steady rhythm. First she checked the schematic display on her board, then the approach program on her clipboard. Then she either waited or made an adjustment. She kept her burns short and soft. Then she checked her displays again. She waited and watched. Occasionally, she would report, "Confidence is high," or, "In the channel."

Korie licked his lips. They were dry. His throat was dry. He took a sip of water and waited.

"One minute," reported Tor. A lifetime later she said, "Thirty seconds."

Somewhere they had crossed an invisible line. It was too late to abort. Whatever was going to happen when they docked was now inevitable. Korie had often brooded about this invisible "point of inevitability." It bothered him. After studying all of the lessons of the *zyne,* about possibility being the author of choice, and choice being necessary for freedom, the moment when choice actually disappeared from the situation unnerved him more than he could say. It was a loss of control. But all he could do now was ride it in and hope he hadn't missed anything—

"Fifteen seconds. . . . Ten . . . five . . ."

Something behind him went quietly *clunk.* He could feel it locking into place. They were *docked.*

"Hello, Dolly," Korie whispered to himself.

Nothing happened.

He waited.

They all waited.

He looked to Brik. Brik looked back. Expressionless.

Tor switched off her board. She replaced it on the deck. She swiveled around in her chair. She gave Korie a thumbs-up sign and a grin.

Korie wished he could rub his nose. He didn't like this. It was *too* quiet. He tapped the arm of his chair nervously. *How long do we have to wait?*

He shook his head. This wasn't good. Something—*any-thing*—should have happened.

He wasn't so arrogant as to believe they had so thoroughly confused the imp that it had been unable to sabotage the docking. No. The imp had known they were going to try docking manually. It had opaqued the observation port, forcing them to use the external emergency net. Therefore, the net was compromised. Therefore, something in that net was waiting for the docking confirmation. Therefore. . . . Therefore. Therefore. Korie's mind chased the thought around. What had he missed? What *else* was connected to the external emergency net? Had he made a fatal error here? Had they detoxed the external network *too well*?

And then, Hodel spoke. "All right, there it is. A coded signal. It's using the entire ship as a broadcast antenna. Wait a minute, I'm tracking it. Wait a minute. . . ." Hodel was on the hull of the ship with a hand-built systems-analysis board. On the first six detox operations, Leen's crew had routinely replaced the signal monitors at every node of the network. It was easier to replace them than to test them in place. On the last detox, the crew had replaced the signal monitors again . . . but these latest units were reporting directly to Hodel's board. Hodel was silent a moment more, then he said angrily, "Albert Flaming Einstein on Heisenberg's cross! I'll be skeltered!"

Korie grabbed his code list. Albert Einstein—the signal scrubbers! The signal was entering the network through the aft signal scrubbers! All over the ship now, individual detox crews would be leaping toward their assigned targets; but one crew knew that they were handling a live bomb. Candleman and Hatano. If everything was going to plan, some of the crews were even detaching themselves from their local area networks. The imp would have no way of knowing where they were now.

Korie studied his watch. There would have been no way to drill this operation. Still, they had projected less than five minutes of actual broadcast time before the transmitter was found and disabled. The seconds ticked voraciously into the past. Korie imagined an expanding sphere of radio noise. It didn't matter what the signal said. Its presence was beacon enough. How far would it travel before it was intercepted by a Morthan probe? Three light-days? Six? Twelve? How big was the time window? How long would it scream, *"Here! Over here! Stardock! Here it is!"*

Quilla Delta said quietly, *"Be vewy vewy quiet. We're hunting wabbit."*

Korie looked at his watch. Three minutes. "Double bonus for Candleman and Hatano," he said without thinking. He glanced at the code sheet. The transmitter had been located, a destruction button had been placed on the interconnect, and the crew was now backing out to a safe distance.

There was a faint thump transmitted through the keel of the ship. "It is now duck season," said the Quilla.

Korie grunted. The destruct button had been triggered. The connection to the net had been broken. The transmitter had then exploded violently. Exactly as they had expected it to.

"Hodel?" he asked.

"Signal is still going out," Hodel reported grimly. "It's singing like a flaming princess."

Flaming princess. Beta singularity harness. Damn. They were going to lose part of the singularity cage. Leen was prepared for it, but still—

Quilla Delta reported, "Ye Gods and little fishes."

Korie looked to his watch. Leen had trained his crew well.

Another thump. "Bouillabaise," said Quilla Delta.

"Hodel?"

"Loud and clear. This is not my idea of a good time!"

Good time. The starboat harness. Cappy and MacHeath would be up there by now. *Thump.*

"Are we having fun yet?" asked Quilla Delta.

"Hodel?"

"What are you guys doing?" he replied. "Singing along with it? *'We all live in a yellow submarine'* " Engine room. Singularity harness. Gamma. Dammit. *Thump.* Quilla Delta annotated, "She came in through the bathroom window." Korie wondered if Leen was already checking the Alpha harness.

The imp had never been spotted in the engine room. It couldn't have had access to the harnesses. Of course not, there was always a crew on watch around the singularity containment. The imp would have had to have had access to the replacement parts. Which was *exactly* what Korie had hoped. "Helter skelter," he said to the Quilla.

"We copy," she replied.

"Hodel?"

"I'm an old man, I'm gonna die soon, I have a right to be cranky."

Bingo! The engine room again! They were getting closer. The imp had been frustrated by their security measures. It had retreated to the main module of the ship and had concentrated all of its operations there. Exactly as they had guessed. *Thump.* Another transmitter explosion. He was afraid to think how bad the damage was going to be. Quilla Delta reported, "Isn't it amazing how time flies when you're having fun?"

Korie put his finger on the next phrase on the code sheet. Sure enough, Hodel reported, "Yngvi is a louse." And a little bit after that, "Ward, I'm worried about the Beaver." Korie was actually starting to feel pride in the speed of the Black Hole Gang when Hodel said, "I tawt I taw a putty-tat. . . ."

Thump. Thump. Thump.

And finally . . . Hodel reported with a sigh, "What we have here is a failure to communicate." And in the clear he added, "The system is silent!"

Korie was too pleased to be annoyed with the breach.

"It's over . . . ?" asked Tor.

"Not yet," said Brik.

"Stand by," said Korie in the clear. Waiting. "Helter Skelter?" he asked the Quilla. She shook her head. Nothing yet.

Korie realized his whole body had gone tense and rigid. He was cramped forward. He forced himself to straighten out, leaning back in his chair. He took a deep breath. They weren't half done yet. He had to pace himself.

"Mr. Korie?"

He opened his eyes. It was Jonesy.

"What do all these code phrases mean?"

"I don't know. I don't think they mean anything at all. Harlie generated over ten thousand onetime code pads. They're probably all just nonsense phrases."

"Oh," said Jonesy. He turned back to his work station.

And then, abruptly—Quilla Delta spoke. "Elvis has left the building."

That's when the rest of the traps went off.

Disaster

He couldn't hear it. He felt it.

He had his hand on the railing when he felt a sudden sharp vibration. He recognized it, but—filtered through the soundlessness of space, filtered through the hull of the ship —it took him a moment. Then he realized. *Oh, my God, the missiles—!!*

There came two more thumps, and then a fourth and final one. He was already pulling a new transceiver pack out of his gear belt. These had been specially coded. They didn't use any single channel, but bounced around random channels several thousand times a second.

Korie caught Quilla Delta's eye and held up the transceiver so she could see it, then clipped it into his suit harness. *"Status reports. Now!"* he shouted, not waiting to hear who was online. He waited impatiently. "Come on, you bloody bastards. Come on. Status reports. Now! Leen?"

"All right, it's like we figured. The damn missiles have launched themselves. The trigger was the docking confirmation—"

"Where are they now? Goldberg?"

"They're drifting. They launched, but didn't fire. No hyperstate plugs. We gave those to the *Houston* with the warheads. We've got good tracks on all the birds. They're drifting, they won't go far. We're sending out the retriever teams."

"What about the other four?"

"As near as we can tell, they're moribund. We're checking now."

"Well, be careful. No telling what else the imp has done. Hodel?"

"Sir?"

"How soon can we bring Harlie back online?"

"Six hours."

"No good. Okay, power up the autonomics, run the idiot code. Deflex, disrupt, skelter, and remix. Viricide everything. You know the drill."

Goldberg again. "Sir? We've got disruptor activity."

"I thought we pulled those out of the circuit."

"Yes, sir. We did. We're still getting power directly from the portside fuel cells to the aft disruptors."

"Unplug them."

"We have, sir. They're still charging."

"How long till full charge?"

"Four minutes."

"If you can't abort, blow them."

"Sir?"

"You heard me. Those things aren't going to go off politely. Discharge them or jettison them."

"Aye, sir."

"Leen?"

"Here."

"The hole?"

"Nothing in it that we didn't put there."

"You've lost your singularity control, Chief. How do you know the imp hasn't diddled your grapplers?"

"The grapplers have all been pulled out of their harnesses. Actually blasted out. They're on their way to the machine shop already."

"What about disruptor charges?"

"We're scanning now. I've got the hole in an isolation bottle. It can't be inverted."

"Is the bottle secure?"

"We didn't build it until after we opened the ship to space. We detoxed as we built. It's secure."

"You built a *passive* bottle?"

"I only look stupid, Commander—"

"Sorry, Chief. I just—"

"I know. You're feeling guilty because you sacrificed my engine room. Now you're trying to make up for it. Do me a favor, Mr. Korie?"

"Chief?"

"Trust my judgment?"

"Right. Sorry. Thanks. Out."

"You're welcome."

Korie stopped himself. He wanted to run his hands through his hair and rub his eyes. But the starsuit prevented that. Instead, he took a breath. And another. And a third deep breath. Finally, he reseated himself in his chair —he hadn't noticed when he'd come floating out—and secured the safety harness. He forced himself to shut up for a moment. He'd trained this crew. They knew what to do. It was time to stop jiggling their elbows.

He forced himself to sit back. He waited for the rest of the status reports to come in.

He looked around, Brik was already beside him; he hadn't even noticed when the big Morthan had returned. How long had he been waiting there?

"I don't suppose anyone has found the imp?"

Brik shook his head.

"All right. Secure the hatches. Forget about repressurizing. We can't risk it. Let's get the section heads up here. We need to scramble."

Brik nodded and began relaying orders.

Something *shuddered*. They felt the vibration through the skeleton of the ship. Korie looked to Brik—

A Hole in the World

Armstrong saw the flash before he felt the shock wave. In fact, he never felt the shock wave at all. Suddenly a stanchion leapt up and slammed him across the chest. He grunted involuntarily; the stanchion swam away. Everything was red. He couldn't hear. Armstrong grabbed instinctively for something. He was tumbling. He saw stars swirling past. He caught one arm—almost accidentally—on a twisted bar of metal. He hung on, blinking, still not certain what had happened or where he was or what he had been doing a moment before. Something had exploded—

His eyes focused. There was a hole in the world. There were stars on the other side of the hole. A starsuited figure was hung up on the jagged edge of the hole. His face was blue. *Lambda*. He was twisting and turning. In a moment he would work loose and plunge out the hole. Armstrong was sure of it.

Armstrong struggled forward; he pulled at Lambda's leg, pulled him away from the hole in the world. Lambda's suit was ripped. Armstrong swung him around. His mouthpiece was secure though—but the air bottles were punctured. Had the safety seals closed? Yes!

Armstrong unclipped his own air hose and shoved it into Lambda's emergency intake valve. He gasped for breath, more in sympathy than real need. He began pulling Lambda toward—he wasn't sure. Everything here below the portside disruptor feeds was blown away. Some of it was still sparking and flashing. There were places that were still glowing hot. He headed back the other way.

The door was clamped. He fumbled for the security card. It was missing from his belt. He pulled Lambda around and looked for his; his was missing too. He began banging on the door, hoping that someone on the other side could hear.

That didn't work. He was getting panicky now. He took his air hose back and sucked eagerly for a few seconds, then gave it back to Lambda. Lambda's eyes were open and dilated. He looked bluer than usual. Armstrong didn't know. He'd heard that Quillas were augmented somehow. Maybe Lambda was still alive. He couldn't take a chance.

Impatient, Armstrong towed the other back to the hole. He pulled himself out of the hole first and grabbed an external handhold, then pulled Lambda carefully out after him, trying not to catch his starsuit on the jagged metal.

Towing Lambda, he started pulling him steadily aftward toward the emergency evacuation locks. He had to stop frequently, to share the air from their common tank. The entire time he kept talking, "Stay with me, Lambda. Only a little bit more. Only a little bit. Okay, we're almost there, almost—"

And sure enough, they were. By the time they got to the stern of the ship, there were others in starsuits coming out to meet them. They separated Lambda from him, Armstrong didn't see where they went. They gave him fresh air and pulled him in through the revolving lock and from there to a pressurized bubble inflated in the cargo deck where Dr. Williger waited.

"Lambda? Is Lambda okay?" Armstrong kept asking. No one would answer until Quilla Gamma grabbed his arms and held him steady and looked directly into his eyes. "It's all right, Brian. We're all right. The Quilla Cluster is fine."

"But Lambda—where's Lambda?"

"We're sorry," said Gamma. "The Lambda body has died. Your efforts were noble, Brian, but Lambda was killed in the explosion."

"No, no—" Brian didn't want to hear it. "No, Lambda was the only one who understood—this isn't fair! Oh, God, no!" He started to scream his rage and then something hissed on his arm and he went over the top and out.

The Ops Deck

Korie took the news grimly.

"We missed one," he said. "All right, Brik, how many more have we missed?"

Brik grunted. "All the rest. This is how we find them."

Korie looked at him sharply. And realized something. The big Morthan bulked like an immovable wall. "You know something, Brik—" he said quietly. "There are times when I don't like you. And then there are times when I *really* don't like you. You're the best officer aboard this ship. And I don't like you."

"The feeling is mutual," Brik acknowledged.

"Good," said Korie. "Let's keep it that way." He pulled himself over the railing and down to the Ops deck where the section leaders were gathered. Brik followed. "The imp is still loose, so we're going to have to be careful," Korie said. "We can't afford any more casualties."

He glanced around the darkened Bridge. Leen, Tor, Hodel, Stolchak, Hall, Brik, Goldberg, and Green floated around him, hanging onto consoles, stanchions, railings, chairs. Their helmet lamps were muted, so no one would have a beam shining directly in their eyes; still the effect was like faces looking out of the open mouths of a school of pilot fish.

"I'd like to reactivate the Operations deck," Korie said. "I hate being blind. And scanners—we're going to need some kind of scanning. Chief, can we rig a passive lens right away? The imp had fifteen minutes of uninterrupted broadcasting. I figure we've got three days before that signal is picked up by a probe. Assuming the probe can generate a hyperstate pulse, we've got maybe at most five days before the first Morthan vessel shows up. Assuming it waits for reinforcements, we might have as much as a week. I need to know as soon as possible, how much can we rebuild in five days? Can we continue?"

"Excuse me?" said Tor. "But . . . we're docked. Aren't we? Don't we have the resources of Stardock?"

Korie smiled. "Someone want to tell her?"

Leen was closest. "Hello, Dolly," he said.

Tor shook her head. "I don't understand."

"Dolly is a docking platform, and a small life-support module. It's anchored to a singularity containment to give it roughly the same mass as Stardock. We just used it to trigger all the imp's traps. Well . . . as many as were set to go off when we docked.

"Dolly is a decoy?" Tor asked, incredulous.

"One of several," Leen confirmed. She makes the same kind of stress field impression as Stardock. If the *Star Wolf* is decommissioned, her singularity might be used in a dolly too. A Morthan probe doesn't scan for radio signals; transmitters are cheap; it scans for stress field impressions made by large masses."

She looked to Korie, upset. "You *lied* to me! Again!"

"It was a need-to-know basis, Commander Tor," Korie said. "You didn't really need to know, did you?"

Tor held back her words for a moment while she considered the answer to the question. Korie was right.

"We knew we'd never be able to stop the imp from sending a signal to the Morthan probes," Korie continued. "So we made sure the signal was sent from a place where there'd be no immediate danger to Stardock."

Tor looked confused. "But what about Harlie? How did

you fool him? If he knew about the dolly, then the imp might have known too."

"That's right," said Korie unhappily. "Didn't you think it was a little unusual for us to take Gatineau out for a starboat certification when we did? We dropped a transmitter at the flipover point. Later Harlie received a signal from it. He reported it. Everybody assumed it came from Stardock, yourself included. I never said differently."

"But the signal wouldn't have had Stardock's authentication code. Harlie would have known it was false."

"It had my signature," said Korie. "I was counting on him figuring it out for himself. He did. Did you notice the phrasing of his announcement? At no time did he say the orders came from Stardock. Neither did I. We just let you and everybody else assume it."

"You son of a bitch," Tor said. "I really hate when you do that."

Korie ignored it and continued: "Meanwhile, Harlie knew he couldn't discuss anything with anyone until the matter of the imp was resolved. He knew his own security was compromised. Brik didn't shut him down. He shut himself down. He had to. This wouldn't have worked any other way."

"I'll be damned," said Tor.

"Probably," agreed Korie. "But not today. Now let's get back to work. We've got a whole Morthan fleet headed our way. How soon can we get out of here? Chief?"

"That's the bad news," said Leen. "We can't. Not until I rebuild the containment. It's a week's work just to get the calibrators refocused."

"What about the torches?"

"We'll have to check their alignment too. We took some pretty heavy damage amidships. We're doing hull-integrity tests first; then we'll see if we can risk firing the plasma tubes. That's at least a week's work too. And don't forget we're living off our fuel cells until we can tap the singularity again. If you want to fire those torches, you'll be paying for it with life support."

"I figured that," said Korie. "All right, let's get those wayward torpedoes back in their tubes. We'll use the dolly." To all of them he added, "And let's be careful. Remember, the imp is still out there—"

And then suddenly they were gone and he was alone, for just a moment remembering the last time he'd floated alone in a darkened Bridge.

Captain Lowell—

Lowell

≫►▲◄≪

Captain Sam Lowell had found a useful niche in the service, certifying ships fresh off the assembly line and then handing them over to their new young captains. It was an easy duty, but a necessary one; plus, it gave him the opportunity to go to space again. It also gave him an authority that he would otherwise never know. His cards had been dealt and played; he would reach the rank of admiral, but only on retirement. And that was not too far away.

Lowell was not a bad officer; he just wasn't an extraordinary one. He had risen through the ranks by being dependable, by doing exactly what he was told, but he had never demonstrated the kind of initiative that set him apart from others, so his superiors rightfully regarded him as a man who was better at following orders than giving them. The navy depended on men and women like Lowell; it repaid them with comfortable responsibilities, not bold ones.

Despite the popular view of the star navy as a vast fighting force, the great majority of ships were never intended to see battle at all; instead, they were needed to ferry supplies and equipment, to serve convoy duty, to move troops, to carry pilgrims and colonists, to train new crews, to carry mail, to perform research and surveillance missions, to patrol and guard. Indeed, it was estimated that only ten percent of the ships on active duty would ever see combat at all; most of the rest would provide support and service—it had been only in the last three decades that the decision was made to increase the proportion of combat vessels to thirty-three percent. This was accomplished primarily by having the liberty ships designed and built as multipurpose vehicles. The intended result was a navy that was both powerful and adaptable.

A not unforeseen side effect of the increased production of FTL vessels was an increased access to FTL travel. Industrial and commercial interests began leasing more and more transportation services from Fleet Command. Some ships were also outfitted for the carrying of passengers, even tourists. Throughout the entire sphere of Terran authority, transport prices fell as access to transport increased. The more that new ships became available, the more demand there was for the services they provided. The economies of the Allied worlds flourished.

The bad news, however, was that the increasing size of the Allied star navies created significant unease among the worlds of the Morthan Solidarity. The Morthan world view was already invested with a high degree of self-absorption and paranoia. The highest councils could not help but observe the continuing long-term buildup as a military one— and they could not help but consider themselves the target of such a buildup. Indeed, they were incapable of considering themselves as anything *other* than a target for the aggression of others; it was the only way they could justify their own aggressive stance. That the Allied military buildup was primarily a defensive reaction to the Morthans' own increasingly belligerent military posture and growing weapons production was not considered part of the equation.

On the Morthan side of the rift, well away from the Morthan sphere of authority, lay a cluster of star systems known as Far Cathay. Although it was a six-week journey from there to the closest world of the Solidarity, the Morthans still regarded the human-occupied worlds of Far Cathay as potentially hostile. When the Silk Road Convoys began ferrying equipment for the creation of an industrial base, the Morthans' most paranoid fantasies came bubbling to the surface. They were certain that the Allied worlds intended to establish a military presence from which a flank attack could be mounted against the westernmost worlds of the Morthan Solidarity.

The Morthans were correct in their assessment that the Allies intended to establish a stronger military presence on Far Cathay. They were inaccurate in their assessment of its purpose. The actual goal was to provide a base from which to launch a flank attack on the Morthan supply lines, should the Morthan Solidarity attempt to advance into the Allied sphere.

Although the Allied authorities made it well known that the purpose of the Far Cathay expansion was entirely defensive, this was only believed on the Allied side of the rift.

Throughout this time, Commander J. T. Korie was well aware of the tactical situation; it validated his earlier extrapolations. War in space was a game of three-dimensional chess played in realtime, in the dark. As he and others had predicted, most of the war would be spent jockeying for position. Whoever ended up with the strongest position would win the war before the first shots were fired. The rest would be follow-through and cleanup.

In the meantime . . . Korie's first assignments as a captain had already been determined. He had been briefed by Vice Admiral O'Hara, and the first three years of his command career lay before him as clearly as if they had been mapped out on the holographic display of the astrogation console.

After a preliminary series of shakedown cruises, the *LS-1187*—still under the command of Sam Lowell—would join the Silk Road Convoy to ferry cargo and supplies across the rift. Upon the completion of this mission, Captain Lowell would turn the command of the starship over to Commander Korie who would then assume the rank of captain.

Captain Korie would then begin his career assigned to specific patrol and surveillance missions that would give Fleet Command an opportunity to gauge his initiative—to see if he would be a captain like Margaret Faslim-Arub or a captain like Sam Lowell.

That was the game plan. Unfortunately, that was not how events played out.

The Morthan Third Fleet *followed* the LS-1187 to the rendezvous point and attacked the Silk Road Convoy as it formed up near a small barren world named Marathon. Captain Lowell was killed, as were eighteen other members of the crew; the LS-1187 was crippled in the assault and left drifting in space like a derelict. Without power. Without gravity. Without a captain. With barely enough oxygen and food to survive long enough to repair the damage.

Under Jon Korie's direction, it took the LS-1187 six and a half months to limp home, and when they finally did return to Stardock, they found they were a Jonah. They were blamed for the war that was raging everywhere. Three Morthan fleets had swept violently across the rift and whole worlds had been destroyed.

Including Shaleen.

And Carol. And Timmy. And Robby.

Gone. All gone.

Korie did what he always did when his emotions were raging out of control. He immersed himself in his work and waited for the storm to pass.

It never did.

Incoming

For three days they worked desperately. The situation was eerily familiar. They had been here before. They had done this before.

The ship was adrift. It remained unpowered. No gravity, no lights, no air. No Harlie.

Reluctantly Chief Leen had repressurized part of the keel, the Ops bay, the Bridge, the officers' deck, the wardroom, and the messroom. He rigged an emergency airlock at each end, not much more than a series of valve locks to be pressed through. It provided quick access both in and out. Crew members came in to eat and take short naps anchored to a deck or a bulkhead. Some of them slept in their starsuits, tethered just outside. Most of them worked around the clock, pausing only to eat and sleep.

Three squads went through the ship doing emergency decontaminations everywhere they could. The imp remained unfound.

Another team took the starboat and went out to catch the drifting torpedoes. They brought back three of them and lashed them to the dolly. They lashed the starboat to the dolly too. They installed the missiles so that their hyperstate simulators were focused on the pinpoint black hole within the dolly's singularity containment shell. They tapped into the dolly's power supply and fed it to the starboat; they cabled the controls of the torpedoes together and connected them to a jury-rigged board in the flight deck of the starboat.

But they couldn't test their construction, not without causing a major stress-field ripple. They had no way of knowing if it would work.

Aboard the *Star Wolf,* the crew continued to labor. Their starsuits slowed them down. Zero-gee slowed them down. Their own exhaustion slowed them down. Everything took three times as long. Exhilaration kept them awake. Fear kept them glancing at the time. They raced the clock. They sat in the center of an expanding sphere of radio noise. The signal swept outward at lightspeed in all directions. How thoroughly had this sector been seeded with probes? Harlie had guessed they would have less than three days before the signal was detected by a probe. The probe would then generate a hyperstate bleep. And how long would it take for the warships to come sharking in then? Another day. Maybe two.

But Harlie was down, and so were all the sensors. They had no way of detecting the bleep, so they had no way of knowing *when* exactly they had been spotted. It might be three days, it might be thirteen. It might be never. They wouldn't know until their passive lens detected an incoming bogey.

They worked harder.

The last hour of the third day passed like a kidney stone. It took forever. The crew sweated.

And they still hadn't found the imp.

The fourth day began. The odds continued to shift against them. Morthan warships were coming.

Korie went out to the starboat and double-checked its controls. Everything came up green. He slipped a memory clip into a reader and copied the latest set of operating programs into the starboat's intelligence engine. He hadn't dared risk piping the files across; they still hadn't detoxed the network on the other side of the umbilicals; the starboat had to stay clean. He ran a virucide suite and scanned the displays. The files had copied green. The starboat was ready.

Korie's fingers twitched. He wanted to power up. He wanted to look across the hyperstate horizon. He wanted to go hunting. He held himself back. He didn't dare take the risk. He knew better. Every hour that passed was one more hour on their side.

But . . . he could run simulations.

These were simple exercises; he'd written them himself; Harlie could have done better, but they couldn't risk it, not until the imp was destroyed. And besides, they couldn't bring Harlie back online without additional detox first. It didn't matter. They didn't need sophisticated simulations. Not for this.

Korie awoke when his oxygen alarms went off. He was down to thirty minutes air supply. He'd been asleep for two and a half hours. "Oh, shit!" he said. He hadn't meant to allow himself such a long rest. He unstrapped himself from his seat and headed back to the *Star Wolf.*

He replaced his air tanks in the cargo bay and headed for the engine room. Chief Leen was supervising the reinstallation of the last singularity grappler. Korie floated up next to him.

"How bad?" he asked.

Leen shook his head. "If it works, I want a Heisenberg trophy."

"Are you certain?" asked Korie.

"Spare me the old jokes," said Leen sourly.

"Sorry," said Korie. "For what it's worth, I've already written you up for a serious recommendation."

"I'd rather have a good stiff drink."

"That can be arranged too. You've got two kegs of starshine behind the scrubbers. As soon as the ship is repressurized, you can open one." Leen looked at him, surprised that Korie had such accurate knowledge of his inventory. Korie ignored it. "It's been aging for two weeks, that should be enough, shouldn't it? Now tell me about the stardrive."

"Can't test it," Leen said gloomily. "I don't know that it'll work. This was all done by hand. We had to jack those grapplers into place and secure them with hand clamps. We lined them up with lasers. Maybe they'll hold. She passed the preliminaries. We're checking secondary calibrations now. I don't think she'll pass, if she does I'll be surprised. But we have no way of focusing any tighter, so you can forget about fine-tuning. We lost our last ventriculars when the traps went off. We didn't dare take them out, we'd have made the imp suspicious, or triggered a deadman trap, and you traded away our spares, so you've got no call to complain. The only calibrators we have left are junk. And we're working without alignment tubes anyway, so it's a moot point." He made a sound of disgust and disbelief. "*If* she works, we'll be running with a very loose focus. You'll have lousy control. She'll skid like an ice cube on a griddle."

"Good. That'll make us harder to hit. What kind of speed?"

"Your guess is as good as mine. Either we'll slide or we'll grind. There's no in between." The chief added, "I'm thinking of applying for a transfer."

"Oh?"

"I don't want to be on a ship where the C.O. treats his engines like this."

"Oh," said Korie. "You didn't tell me you wanted to live forever. I wish you had. I would have planned things differently."

"I'm *serious*," Leen said. "Give me one good reason why I should work my butt off for you, if this is what you do to my engines."

"One reason? Okay. You'll never find a C.O. who will challenge your engineering skills as completely and as thoroughly as I will. You'll never be on a ship again where you'll have to solve problems this impossible. You're not fooling me, Chief. You like playing superman. Any other ship, you'd die of boredom."

"Don't tempt me. I don't mind dying. I just don't want to do it today."

"You're welcome to get off here," said Korie. "But you'd better do it soon, because—"

His headphones chimed. "Mr. Korie?" It was Tor. "We have a bogey."

"I'm on my way," he replied. "Sound the alarm." To

Leen he said, "Heat those tubes. We're going to find out how they work the hard way. You can finish quitting tomorrow. I may go with you."

"If we live," muttered Leen, already pulling himself down to his work station.

Watching

Korie was last to arrive on the Bridge. He had the farthest to travel, and he had to go through the valve lock in the keel. He swam up through the Ops bay and up onto the Bridge, where he strapped himself into the captain's chair quickly. He began pulling off his helmet.

Work lights had been strung across the Bridge, and three of the consoles had been detoxed and reactivated. Brik was already in his chair, speaking to his headset. Korie unclipped his own from the side of his chair and listened to the chatter for a moment; then he called to Tor. "ETA?"

"Three minutes. We've got a bearing."

"How big is she?"

"Big. Very big."

"Can you be a little more precise than that?"

"That's as precise as I can give you. It's possibly a juggernaut."

"We never get the little ones, do we?" Korie said to himself.

"The starboat's ready," reported Goldberg.

"Sounds good." To his headset: "Chief?"

"We're ready. We've got forty percent and rising."

"That's better than I hoped for. Thank you. Prepare to initiate warp."

"Aye, sir."

Korie was already leaning forward, ready to give the next order, when Tor spoke quietly. "We've got a second bogey."

"Where?" said Korie.

Tor held up her board for him to see. A small white dot was arrowing inward from a high starboard angle.

"What the hell—?" he started to say, then caught himself. "My God, it's the *Houston.*"

"She got her stardrive working!" said Tor.

"With our fibrillators, dammit! We should never have given her those things! She's making an attack run—"

"She's going to get creamed—" said Hodel.

"Belay that," said Korie.

They watched in silence as the small white dot converged on the larger pink one. Suddenly the pink blip disappeared. A second later the white one too.

"They're dropping missiles," Korie said.

"They don't have a chance," said Brik. To Korie's sharp look he explained, "They don't have the range. The Morthan missiles have three times the running distance. They can't get in close enough."

"There they are," said Tor. "The *Houston*'s back in hyperstate."

"Can they outrun the Morthan birds?" asked Jonesy.

"No," said Brik, with finality. "They can't."

"They're going into evasive patterns—" Tor reported.

"It won't work," said Brik. "It will only delay the inevitable."

"You're a lot of help," said Tor, annoyed.

"Can you pick up the missiles at all?" Korie asked her.

"Not at this distance. Not with a passive lens. Maybe if we could open a hyperstate window . . . ?"

"No, I won't take that risk."

"I didn't think so," said Tor.

"There's the Morthan," said Hodel. "What's he doing?"

Korie peered over Tor's shoulder at the display. The Morthan ship was moving rapidly to overtake and pass the

Houston. "He's power-loading his bubble. He can do that for about thirty seconds. It's very dangerous."

The Morthan ship pulled ahead of the *Houston,* went a little farther, and then dropped off the screen again.

"They're doomed," reported Brik. "He's dropping another spread. He's got her bracketed."

"Shit," said Korie. They watched helplessly. The white dot continued to skitter back and forth within an ever-narrowing circle of probability. For a moment it looked as if it were going to escape. It raced suddenly upward—

—and then abruptly vanished.

"They're gone," said Jonesy, unnecessarily.

After a heartbeat Brik spoke. "On the plus side," he said, "the Morthan juggernaut may now believe that was us he destroyed."

To the others' uncomprehending looks he explained, "They knew there was a ship here. That's what they were looking for. They found a ship and destroyed it. That gives us a small strategic advantage."

"You know . . . ?" Korie said abruptly to Brik. "Remember when I said that there were times that I don't like you and times that I *really* don't like you? This is one of those times when I *really* don't like you."

"Thank you for sharing that," Brik said dryly.

"Let's hope *they* believe it," said Hodel, pointing at the display, trying desperately to get the subject back on purpose.

"Would you?" asked Brik.

Tor interrupted. She pointed at her screen. "There they go. The Morthan is back in hyperstate. He's heading in again. ETA is now two minutes."

"Well, there's your answer," Korie said. "He doesn't believe there's only one ship out here either. So much for our small strategic advantage." He turned forward again and gave an order. "Jettison the dolly."

Good-bye Dolly

"Roger that," said Goldberg. He unclipped a plastic cover on his board and flipped the red switch beneath it. Something went *thump* at the aft end of the vessel. "The dolly is free," he reported.

Korie looked to Brik. "Tell me that we fooled the imp. Tell me that it went through the docking harness and trapped itself in the dolly."

Brik stared impassively back at Korie.

"I didn't think so," Korie said ruefully. He turned forward again. "Wake the boat, Mr. Goldberg. Send the signal."

"Roger that," Goldberg said, and flipped the next switch over. "The starboat is now tracking."

"Distance?"

"Three kilometers and widening."

"Too close. We're cutting it too close," Korie said. "We should have jettisoned her earlier."

"You wanted to upgrade her programs one more time," said Brik.

"So call me a perfectionist." To Tor: "Where's the bogey?"

"She's coming in almost straight toward us—wait a minute. She's dropped out of hyperstate."

"Too far away!" Korie almost came out of his chair. "What the hell is she doing?"

"Not giving us room to shoot back," said Brik. "She's dropped a spread of hunting torpedoes. She'll be gone in a minute."

"If she doesn't see something blow up, she'll come back—"

"Then we'd better blow something up. She thinks she's found Stardock."

"Goldberg?"

"Starboat is seven kilometers away."

"We're going to get fringe effects," warned Brik.

"Unavoidable. *Now hear this.* Secure yourselves. We're going to get brushed by a hyperstate fringe." Korie wished he could wait just ten seconds more, but he didn't dare. *He didn't dare.* "Trigger the boat."

"Done," said Goldberg, simultaneously throwing the third switch on his board. He tossed it aside. "The boat is now triggered."

"Nothing's happening," said Tor.

"It was always chancy," agreed Korie. To his headset: "Chief, stand by to run like hell."

"Wait a minute," said Tor—and then reality flickered for a moment as—

—*Carol was with him and Timmy and Robby and they were*—*"Oh, Jon, I'm so scared!" He reached for her and*—

. . . came back to consciousness quickly, it wasn't as bad as the last time, the first time. It wasn't a big field, it hadn't been too close, and besides they hadn't been enveloped themselves, so there were no internally reflected effects and so this wasn't as bad, it wasn't as bad, if only it had lasted just a moment longer—

The lights were flickering back on.

"Starboat away," gasped Brik.

"And?"

"Just a fmcking minute," mmfled Tor. She picked up her jury-rigged board and banged it once on the console, then looked at it again. "I've got the boat." Then she added, "The bogey is still down."

"They've got to have seen the boat by now." To Tor: "What does the boat look like?"

"It looks like . . . nothing I've ever seen before. It's got the weirdest signature."

"That's the torpedoes. They're not designed to work with so much power."

"They're going to burn out," said Goldberg.

"The boat is closing . . . closing. . . . The boat is down," reported Tor. "The signature just went out."

"How close did she get to the bogey?"

Tor shook her head. "Halfway. Maybe."

There was silence on the Bridge. Korie rubbed his nose, his forehead. He ran his hand through his hair. They waited. The moment stretched out.

"Anything?" asked Korie.

"Nada."

"They had to have seen the boat," he repeated to himself. "What are they doing?"

"They're probably trying to figure out what it was," said Tor. "Its signature was bizarre."

Korie rubbed his ear. "Maybe," he admitted. He tried to imagine the situation from the Morthan side.

Here's a bleep from a probe. A suspected location for Stardock. Fast attack in. Drop out of hyperstate, drop a spread of hunting missiles, and—*something* makes a run at you, then disappears from your screens. What do you do? Hide? Or fight?

He looked to Brik.

Brik shook his head. No comment.

Tor was looking back to them both, a questioning expression on her face.

"We wait," said Korie.

"How long?"

"As long as it takes."

"Those hunting torpedoes are coming this way," she reminded.

"Yep," agreed Korie. "Mr. Goldberg, drop the package."

Goldberg pulled a second board onto his lap. He unclipped a plastic cover and flipped an arming switch, and then pressed a launch button. Again, they felt a *thump* through the metal of the ship, through their chairs. This one wasn't as large as the last one.

"ETA for the hunting torpedoes?" Korie asked.

"Seven to ten minutes. If they have a fix. Twenty to thirty if not."

"That's what they're waiting for," Brik said. "For something to go boom. They need confirmation of the kill."

"Something will go boom real soon now," Korie agreed. "Goldberg? As soon as the package is three kilometers away, arm it. *Now hear this.* Stand by to power-down. Total power-down in fifteen seconds." To his headset: "Chief, this means you too." To Tor he ordered: "Keep your lens open, shut down everything else." Korie leaned back in his chair, readjusted his safety harness. He glanced at the time. Six minutes. Maybe less. Maybe more. . . .

Waiting

"Is it getting cold in here?" asked Tor.

"It's your imagination," said Korie. "It takes a lot longer than this to lose heat."

"We've been powered down for an hour and a half."

"Are you uncomfortable?"

"I'm working on it."

"Good. Just remember, as uncomfortable as you are, it's worse for the imp."

"You think so."

"I *hope* so."

"Those torpedoes are overdue."

"They'll get here. Goldberg?"

"Sir?"

"How's the package?"

The package was eight hyperstate warheads in a bundle. They had been pulled from their own torpedoes, and kept under twenty-four-hour guard, suspended in the center of the cargo bay and surrounded by motion detectors. They were detoxed daily. They were presumed clean. They gave off signals resembling an attempt to shield Stardock-like activities. Homing torpedoes wouldn't search for mass but noise, so the *Star Wolf* had to be as inert an object as they could make it. They needed the torpedoes to aim for the package.

"Package is still alive," said Goldberg. "Nothing yet."

Korie turned to Brik. "Tell me you found the imp."

Brik looked impassively back.

"It knows," Korie said impatiently. "I swear to Ghu, it knows. All of our plans, everything, no matter how careful we've been—handwriting all our orders, using onetime code pads, detoxing, securing, isolating, spacing—it still knows. I'm sure of it. Somehow, it found out."

"That is a possibility," said Brik. "And even if it isn't a possibility, that's still what it wants you to think."

Korie shook his head in exhaustion. "There's a limit to just how deep a head game I can play, Brik. My brain hurts." He shuddered, partly from the cold, partly from the strain. "I think it's waiting till we get back to the real Stardock. What if all the traps it set off are decoys?"

"There isn't much left it can do," Brik said. "We're dead."

"The package just armed itself," said Goldberg quietly. He was listening to his headset. The package had given off a distinctive bleep.

The Bridge went silent.

"Torpedoes approaching. Three torpedoes. ETA in ten seconds . . . five . . . three . . . one . . ." He put his headset down. "The package is gone."

"It went off!" said Tor. "We saw it on the lens! Multiple spikes!"

Korie exhaled softly. "Okay, okay . . . something went boom. Maybe, they'll believe it was the Stardock."

"They'll come looking," said Tor.

"They don't dare," said Korie. "Where's the boat?" To his headset: "Chief, the package went off. Prepare to power up."

"The boat is coming back online!" Tor reported. "The program worked!"

"Of course it worked. I wrote it," said Korie. "What's it doing? Dammit, can we get the main display restored?!!"

"It's charging the last known position of the bogey. Its signature is larger than ever. It looks like some kind of super-juggernaut. Closing . . . closing . . . closing . . . it's down again."

"Mm-hm. Good." Korie explained, "You can only run those torpedoes so long and then they burn out. We run them for fifteen seconds and stop, it looks like a monster warship making an attack run. The other side doesn't know what it's doing when it drops out of hyperstate. They have to assume it's doing the same thing they just did—dropping a spread of hunting torpedoes. Watch your board, Tor. Fifteen . . . ten . . . five . . .' '

"There they are! They're running!"

"Gotcha, ya sons of bitches!" Korie exulted.

"The boat is back in hyperstate! It's chasing!"

The main display came back on then, so did the astrogation table. Two blips racing across hyperstate. One was large, the other was larger; its signature was spiked and blurry. Korie pulled himself over the railing and down onto the Ops deck. "Watch," he said. "They're going to drop out of hyperstate for ten seconds, just long enough to launch a torpedo of their own—there they go." One of the blips on the screen disappeared. Korie counted out loud. "Ten . . . nine . . . eight . . . seven . . . six . . ." The blip reappeared.

"They launch fast," said Brik.

"They're very good," Tor agreed. "I wish we could match that."

"I promise you, one day we will," Korie said.

"We can't see the torpedoes," said Tor. "We don't have the resolution."

"Wait . . . there you go. The starboat's evading and . . ." The larger blip, the weird one, disappeared from the screen. "They got it. *Yes!*" They watched for a moment as the Morthan bogey retreated across the hyperstate horizon. Its signature slowly faded and became more and more indistinct, until at last it vanished in the distance of light-years.

"They're running home with a confirmed kill on a nonexistent Stardock and a juggernaut-class vessel that we don't know how to build yet. And we're home free!" Korie exulted.

"Except for the imp," Tor reminded him.

"No," said Brik. He was listening to something on his headset. "We found it."

The Imp

"Gravity?" asked Tor. "Power?"

"Not yet," said Korie. "Who knows what was armed when power went off. Everybody hold present position."

"This way," said Brik, already pushing himself out of his chair. Korie followed. The two swam aftward, down the upper corridor, out through the engine room, down to the machine shop below the containment, and then out through the access to the inner hull—the farm was devastated. He'd expected it. He'd mourn the loss later. There were pieces of dead greenery floating everywhere; it was like swimming through a glimmery yellow snowstorm.

Their helmet lamps made everything flash and sparkle. They could barely see their way. They swam slowly aft, finding their way around the curve of the inner bottle until they came to a place behind the signal scrubbers, behind the place where Chief Leen had stashed his illicit kegs of starshine, where six crew members floated in a silent circle. They parted as the chief of security and strategic operations and the acting captain swam up.

There it was. Illuminated by a single work light. Attached to a strut. In a transparent plastic sac. The imp. Huddled in a fetal position. Dead. Its skin had already gone blue. It looked like a baby. A baby in a tank. Waiting to be born. Korie remembered . . . his own son. It looked so fragile, so delicate.

He started to approach for a closer look, but Brik pulled him back. "No. Don't get near it." Brik touched helmets to the nearest crew member and ordered them all away. Reluctantly they began to move back. They disappeared into the gloom of the inner hull.

Brik pulled himself around to look at the thing from as many different sides as he could see it.

"It looks so innocent," said Korie.

Brik snorted.

"Well, it's dead now."

Brik hesitated.

Korie caught it. "What?" he asked sharply.

Brik didn't answer.

"You're too suspicious," Korie said. "Did it ever occur to you there's such a thing as being *too* paranoid?"

"No," said Brik innocently. "Should it?"

Before Korie could answer, his communicator beeped. "Yes?"

It was Cappy. "We found the imp, sir. Forward."

"Excuse me? Say again?"

"We found the imp. Starboard bow. Section two, fifteen degrees. In an Okuda tube. It's dead. It was caught without protection."

"I'll be there shortly. Korie out." Korie looked to Brik sharply. "There were *two*?"

"At least."

"At *least*?"

The big Morthan floated back down to Korie and faced him directly. "When I went out on the hull—I didn't tell you this—part of the reason was to see how much I could carry inside my harness. I could have carried one live imp, or two eggs in an incubator. I needed to know *everything* that Cinnabar was capable of. Now I know. He had at least two eggs for the *Burke*. Maybe more. But he didn't need to use them, so he never warmed them up. When he came across to the *Star Wolf*, he brought the eggs with him. I don't think he intended to warm them up here either. I said before, these things are supposed to be pretty good eating. I think he stashed them somewhere, intending to come back later. He didn't come back. The eggs warmed up by themselves. A fail-deadly."

Korie thought about that. "An imp is born knowing how to sabotage a starship?"

"When we find the eggshells, we'll also find an incubation frame, which programs the imp while it's still in its shell. And we *have* to find that frame; it's probably booby-trapped too, but it'll tell us how many there were. I was hoping we'd find it with one or the other of the imps, but . . . we didn't."

Korie took a breath. "How many *more* imps are we looking for, Brik? One? Two? A dozen?"

"Not that many," Brik said calmly. "Not a dozen. I estimate that Cinnabar could have carried as many as six eggs, if he'd had the packing; but I don't think he would have wanted to take the risk. Imps are monosexual. And they mate ferociously. I expect that if we scan the two dead imps we'll find they're both carrying eggs. I doubt that any eggs have been laid yet, though. If there are other imps still alive, however, we have only a few more days before they start hiding their eggs all over the ship. And the offspring won't be programmed, they'll be feral. You don't want to know what trouble feral imps can be. That's why even Morthans handle imps carefully."

A new thought clawed its way to the surface of his consciousness, and it wasn't one he liked thinking about. "Why didn't you tell me this before?"

Brik shook his head. "You still believe it *is* possible to be *too* paranoid. Besides, I thought we had a chance against one imp. Against more than one . . . I wasn't sure."

"You lied to me!"

"No I didn't. You never asked."

"You misled me then."

"All right. Yes."

"I don't like that, Mr. Brik." Korie felt the anger rushing to his face. At the same time, he couldn't help but feel a certain sense of irony at the situation.

"I didn't think you would."

"But you'd do it again if you thought it would make a difference, wouldn't you?"

"Yes."

"And even if I order you not to do it again . . ."

"I would prefer that you not give that order."

"So you wouldn't have to disobey it, right?"

Brik didn't answer.

"I see," Korie said. "You realize we're on very dangerous ground here."

"Yes, Mr. Korie. It is the same ground you are standing on with the vice admiral."

Korie opened his mouth to speak. Then shut it again. He took a breath. Then another. Then a third. Brik was right.

"We'll have to stay depressurized for a few days more," Brik said. "I'll use nanos to search for eggs and imps. If it will reassure you any, I believe that our various detox procedures kept the imps seriously off balance. I expect that the only imps we find are going to be dead, and that we are unlikely to find any egg clusters. This imp still looks immature and the others are probably equally so. But we will need a robot to remove the bodies."

"We haven't got one."

"Homer-Nine," said Brik.

"We traded it."

Brik grunted. "No, we didn't. It went into failure mode. The *Houston* wouldn't take it."

"Oh, yes. Now I remember." Korie thought for a bit. "Would you know anything about that failure, Mr. Brik?"

"I can only put it to human error."

"I see. You thought we might need a robot, did you?"

"There is a certain ironic convenience to the situation," Brik admitted.

Korie exhaled in exasperation. "You deceived me again, didn't you?"

Brik didn't answer.

"Right. I didn't ask. Okay, okay. Let's do it. Let's take a look at the other one, and then I want you to get these things out of here." He headed forward.

The Stars

Three days later Brik came to Korie on the Bridge. "Homer-Nine is at the forward airlock."

"Display forward," Korie ordered.

Brik touched a control on the work station in front of him. The image came up showing a six-armed robot, holding on to handholds with two of its arms. The other four were carrying containments with imps inside.

Korie looked to Brik. "You sure about this? I really hate to lose the robot."

Brik said, "I'm sure."

"Go ahead."

Brik gave an order. Still carrying its deadly cargo, the robot pushed itself away from the starship. They watched as it tumbled slowly in the glare of the ship's spotlights. It dwindled into the distance.

"Okay," said Korie.

Brik gave another order.

In the middle of the screen something flashed soundlessly.

"Tell me that's the last of it," Korie said.

"That's the last of it," Brik replied.

Korie glanced over at him. "An actual declarative sentence. My goodness."

"Sarcasm is wasted on me," said Brik.

"At least you recognize sarcasm," Korie started to say, then stopped himself. "Sorry. I'm in a very bad mood. All right—to the cargo deck. Everybody."

This ceremony was much more somber.

A single draped body lay on a gurney. Crewman Armstrong and all of the surviving Quillas stood by dispassionately. Korie wondered what the Quillas were feeling. How did a massmind feel when it lost part of itself? He wondered what kind of recovery therapy would be needed for the cluster. He made a mental note to talk it over with Williger.

Korie had never presided at a funeral before. He'd been to enough of them. He'd never been the ranking officer. He didn't look forward to this. He opened the book and began reading. There were words here about God. He didn't trust God. Not anymore. Not since God had taken his family away.

He read the words and he felt like a hypocrite as he read. What he really wanted to say was, *God doesn't keep her word. God gives with one hand and takes with the other. God doesn't deserve our faith.* But he didn't.

Because he knew that the others still believed. Some of them anyway. And he wasn't going to take that away from them. They'd find out soon enough. Or not at all. It didn't matter.

They worked hard, they fought hard, they survived, that was victory enough.

But acknowledgment? Reward?

Not in this lifetime. Not the way things were headed.

Korie finished reading. He knew his performance had been mechanical. He felt regret about that. The crew deserved the best he could give them. Maybe God wouldn't give them her best, but he would. The hell with God. He closed the book and looked up at the others. They were grim-faced, stony. He had no idea what they were feeling. Perhaps they were expecting him to say more . . . ?

He took a breath.

"We've lost too many friends since this war started," he

said. "And we're going to lose too many more before it's over. It's very likely that . . . most of us here will end up as names on a wall somewhere. I know that I should offer you all some solace, some hope, some words of healing. I'm sorry, but I can't do that. Not today. The best I can offer you today is my anger.

"But the good news is that our anger has brought us this far. We've survived to fight another day. So let's see how much farther our anger will take us. Let's see how much we can hurt them for every death they've given us. It isn't enough to make up for our losses, but it's something useful we can do with the pain they've given us. We can give it back."

He nodded to Chief Leen.

Lambda's body rolled into the airlock. The airlock hatch popped shut behind it. A moment later the music began. A fanfare, something Hodel had picked out. He'd have to ask him later what the name of it was.

Good Friends

Brik found Bach in the gym, an area of the inner hull just forward of the orchards. Bach was running vigorously on the treadmill when Brik came in. She saw him and nodded. Brik waited patiently. After a moment Bach slowed her pace, first to a trot, then to a walk; a moment later she stepped off the treadmill, grabbed a towel, and wiped the sweat from her forehead. She looked up—and up—at Brik. Her eyes shone, her face was flushed, but Brik couldn't tell if it was the exercise or anything else.

"How are you feeling?" he asked.

"Better," she said.

Brik considered his next words for a long moment. "I regret that you were hurt."

"I wasn't hurt," she said. "Well, that's not quite true. I was . . ." She shrugged and smiled, both at the same time, a wistful gesture. "I was exhausted."

"Yes," Brik agreed.

"It was a good exhaustion," she acknowledged.

"Dr. Williger said there was considerable strain on your heart."

"She also said there was no permanent damage. I just needed a few days rest and exercise to work out the stiffness, that's all." She began toweling her hair. She added, "I'm not sorry we did it."

"Nor am I," said Brik.

"Did you, um . . . find out what you wanted to find out?"

"I think so," the big Morthan admitted.

"And?"

"And . . . I think I understand why this is such a difficult subject for humans. It is hard even for me to discuss."

"Yes. Me too."

"Yes, you're a human."

"Yes, I am."

Brik took a breath. "I don't think we should try this again."

Bach did not react. Or perhaps she had been expecting him to say something like this. She continued to meet his steely gaze. "Why not?" There was only curiosity in her question, no anger.

"I don't think it would be a good idea, that's all. I don't want to cause you any further hurt."

"I wasn't hurt."

"I don't want to cause you any further embarrassment."

"I wasn't embarrassed," she said.

"And . . ." added Brik, "I am concerned that my integrity as a Morthan officer could be compromised."

"Ah," said Bach. "Yes. There is that. Your integrity. As a Morthan officer. Yes." She nodded to herself. "Yes, of course."

"It's not that I didn't like the feeling," Brik admitted quietly, "but it has had an unpleasant effect on the rest of my mental processes."

"Yes," said Bach. "I understand. I understand *completely.*"

"Good," said Brik, still not getting it. "Then we can continue on as . . . just friends."

"No," said Bach. "No, we cannot. *We cannot be just good friends!*" She whirled on him, poking him ferociously in the chest. "And I'll tell you why, you flaming Morthan idiot— because you just said to me that I'm second best. That I'm not good enough. That your stupid Morthan stability is

more important to you. That sex with me makes you so
uncomfortable that you'd rather pretend it didn't happen.
And that's not what I felt at all. What I felt was exhilarating and wonderful and joyous and passionate and exquisite.
And what you're doing now is telling me it can be dismissed, discarded, put away like an exercise box. And if
you don't understand what a devastating insult that is, then
fuck you and the horse you rode in on. I'm applying for a
transfer. And maybe sexual rechanneling as well. Stolchak
was right. I should have been a lesbian! Men! Morthans!
You're all alike! Assholes!" She flung the towel at him and
headed for the showers. "Good friends! I don't want any
more friends! I want a lover! You can kiss my big black ass
good-bye, because that's all the kissing you're ever going to
get!"

Brik thought about going after her. He even took two
steps in her direction.

But then he stopped himself.

He'd thought this decision out very carefully. Very, very
carefully. He'd been very logical about the whole thing.
This was the only way.

Bach was the one who was acting illogically. Later when
she calmed down, when she thought about it logically too,
she'd see the logic of it. She'd see that he was right. He was
only being logical.

He tossed the towel in a bin and left the gymnasium.

Vice Admiral
O'Hara

"All right, Jon," said Admiral O'Hara. "Sit down." She pointed. Korie sat.

She leaned back in her chair, regarding him with a renewed respect. She nodded grudgingly. "You made your point."

She opened her desk drawer, hesitated for a moment, then withdrew Korie's bars. She slid them across the dark gray surface of her desk. "Here," she said.

Korie made no move to pick them up. They still weren't the stars he'd earned. He looked to the admiral questioningly.

She returned his gaze dispassionately. "Go ahead, Jon. Put them on."

"They aren't the stars I've earned."

"No, they aren't."

"May I ask why I'm not being promoted? I think I'm entitled to an explanation."

Vice Admiral O'Hara nodded. "Actually, no. The decision-making process of the Admiralty is confidential."

"I see," said Korie. He began to rise—

"But I will tell you, it's not for the reasons you think. Sit down, Jon."

He lowered himself back into the chair. And waited.

"You proved your point," the admiral repeated. "It was a proud thing to do. Admirable. Heroic."

"Thank you," he said.

"*But* . . . to do that, you had to disobey the orders of this office. And that," the admiral said, "is intolerable. I can't have captains in the fleet who don't follow instructions. Fleet Command needs to know that it can depend upon its captains. We cannot depend on you the same way we can depend on our other shipmasters. We can depend on you only to have a strong stubborn will of your own. So far, you've been lucky."

Korie sat forward in his chair. The admiral saw the change in his posture and raised her eyebrows expectantly. Korie was preparing to argue. She was right.

"Ma'am, with all due respect, the fleet also wants captains who are capable of independent thought. A captain has to take the initiative when he has no higher authority to rely on. I've demonstrated my ability to handle that responsibility. Three times over. If you're not going to promote me now, then it's obvious that I have no future in the navy. You'll have to accept my resignation."

"I'm prepared to do that," the admiral said. "But if you resign, I will also have to decommission the *Star Wolf.*"

"I beg your pardon? I thought you said I proved my point."

"Yes, you did. Perhaps too well. You've demonstrated that your crew are dedicated and capable people. We have other ships in the fleet that need their skills. Your people have an extraordinary loyalty to you; but without your presence, they're not the same crew, are they? There's no glue holding them together."

"They've earned their ship."

"Yes, they have. And they've also earned officers who are loyal to them. If you resign, I'll put them onto ships with officers who follow orders and don't act like *prima donnas.*"

Korie hesitated, torn by conflicting emotions. "This is blackmail!" he blurted.

"Tut tut—that's not a word you want to use casually,

Commander Korie." Then she added, "But if it is black-mail, then it's appropriate, isn't it? You earned it. The kar-mic chicken always comes home to roost. Not too long ago, in this very office, you tried the same thing on me. You threatened me. Remember? So, you established the prece-dent that blackmail is an appropriate way to get what you want—or punish someone else if you don't."

"You're punishing me, then?"

"You can view it that way, yes. Or . . . you can look at it this way. I'm hoping to teach you a lesson. We're bring-ing twelve new ships online every month. We're going to need captains. We're going to need crews. You have experi-ence; someday you *might* be a good captain. I certainly hope so. You're at your best when your anger is targeted appropriately. Now do your crew a favor and put your bars back on."

Korie started to shake his head—but it wasn't a rejection of the vice admiral's instructions; it was simply an ironic acknowledgment of disbelief and acceptance. A sad, wry expression spread across his face. "You got me," he admit-ted. "You got me good."

"I told you before," Vice Admiral O'Hara said. "Rule number one: Youth and enthusiasm will *never* be a match for age and experience."

Korie nodded his agreement. Slowly he reached out and picked up his insignia from the admiral's desk.

"Be patient, Jon," she said gently. "Trust me. We do have plans for you. Important plans. Just be patient a while longer."

Captain Hardesty

"Are you still alive?" Hardesty's voice rasped from the speaker.

"Are you still dead?" Korie shot right back. Hardesty's body was motionless on the bed. The maze of tubes and wires around him had grown more elaborate.

"Only clinically." The voice faded out for a moment, then came back stronger. "What do you want this time?"

Korie grinned. "I came to say thank you."

"For what?"

"For what you said last time I came to visit."

"And what was that?"

"You don't remember? You told me I wasn't fit for command."

"Mm," said the voice. "I must have been in a good mood."

"I walked out of here saying, 'I'll show you, you son of a bitch.' And I was angry enough to do it. Well, it worked. And I wanted to thank you for it. I learned something."

The voice remained silent for a moment longer. Finally: "You're assuming that I told you that because I wanted to produce a result. That's a very big assumption, Commander."

"I'm assuming that as a certified star captain, you would not be nasty to anyone, and certainly not your executive officer, without a very good reason. You don't waste."

"Very good, Commander. But you're still assuming. That's a dangerous practice. Remember, I'm dead. Dead men don't care."

"Yes, sir. I'll remember that. In the meantime, whether you intended it or not, the anger you gave me saved the ship . . . and very possibly the Stardock."

"Mm." The sound was an acknowledgment, nothing more. "Anger is useful," Hardesty finally replied. "But anger is still a reactive emotion. You can't depend on it to carry you the distance, Commander. There will come a day when you run out of anger. That's when you're going to have to find out what your *real* source of energy is."

Korie's eyes widened, both at the length of Hardesty's speech and at the content of it as well.

"I didn't know you'd studied the *zyne,* sir."

"There's a lot you don't know. It's called the arrogance of youth. The real adventure is the wisdom that comes with experience. You're on your way."

"Y'know something, Captain. I've always respected you, but I think I'm actually beginning to like you."

"This news will not make my heart beat any faster. If it were beating at all."

"Nevertheless, Captain Hardesty, I appreciate the service you performed for our ship." Korie took a step back so Hardesty's electronic eye could see him clearly, straightened to attention, and snapped a perfect salute.

Hardesty did not return it.

Commander Korie

He returned to the *Star Wolf* feeling better than he'd expected to. As he stepped through the boarding tube, he felt a sense of familiarity and pride. He was coming *home*. His ship was safe.

The crew in the cargo deck noted his jaunty mood, and Chief Petty Officer Toad Hall quickly reported that the weather was moderate and sunny with only a few high clouds. Then he noticed there were still no stars on Korie's collar and passed that word too. "The *Star Wolf* still has no captain." A few groans of disappointment ricocheted around the Bridge and the wardroom and everywhere else the news was heard.

Hall watched as Korie climbed the ladder to the forward catwalk. Abruptly he made a decision that he would never be able to explain. "Never mind. Operation Flag is still go!" he said quickly. "He's coming up the starboard passage."

Korie hadn't been listening to the all-talk channel. He missed Hall's weather report. And he was so involved in his own thoughts that he didn't notice immediately that the corridor ahead of him was filling up with more people than usual. Some of them were heading aft, others were just standing and waiting.

What did startle him out of his thoughts was the fact that each and every one of them he passed *saluted*. Goldberg. Reynolds. Cappy. MacHeath. Even the Black Hole Gang. And Leen—yes, Leen! The chief engineer scowled, but he still saluted.

They knew. How could they *not* know? Korie was suddenly struck by the *humanity* of this crew. The corridor was so full now, he almost had to push his way through. Williger. Ikama. Green. The Quillas. He hadn't realized there were so many of them. Alpha, Beta, Gamma, Delta, Epsilon, Zeta, Eta, Theta. . . .

He felt an ember of pride glowing in his chest. He nodded his acknowledgment of each and every salute as he passed. Stolchak. Bach. Brik—Brik saluting? Korie did a double take. Armstrong. Saffari. Hodel. Jonesy. Even the new kid, Gatineau. Eakins. Freeman. Hernandez. All of them. Every single member of the crew, he realized.

The surges of emotion he felt were almost overwhelming. He had to blink quickly to keep his eyes from tearing up as he realized; it wasn't the ship that was *home*.

It was the crew that made it so. They were his family now.

Somehow he made it to his cabin without breaking. The final few meters were the hardest walk of his life. He had always known how to withstand abuse. He did not know how to accept appreciation and acknowledgment; and the intensity of the feelings was staggering.

Tor was waiting beside his cabin door. She snapped the last salute. Korie hesitated for an instant, totally at a loss for words. He met her eyes and *knew*. This had been her idea. "Thank you," he said. He glanced down the filled corridor at all the proud faces and added quietly, "Thank you all."

Then he stepped quickly into his cabin before they could see how moved he was. He crossed to his desk and sat down quickly, the tears welling up in his eyes and flowing freely down his cheeks. He wiped his nose, then his eyes. He couldn't believe how overwhelmed he was. He couldn't remember the last time he had felt like this about the crew of a starship.

He wished . . . he wished he could put the thought aside that he had let them down. But he couldn't. Wistfully, he took a tiny box out of his jacket pocket. He opened it and looked inside at the two bright captain's stars. Carol had given him these stars, the last night they'd been together. He'd been carrying them ever since.

Sadly, he closed the box again and put it back on the shelf next to the only other award he cherished, a small black plaque bearing a golden moebius wrench with his name, Jonathan Thomas Korie, inscribed below the handle. The sight of it gave him a poignant mix of sad and happy memories all mixed together. It made him remember again how much he cared. And how much caring *hurt*.

While he was standing there, Harlie chimed for his attention.

"Yes, Harlie?"

"I have some information for you."

"Is it important?"

"I believe so."

"Go ahead."

"There was an evacuation off of Shaleen before it was scourged. Over three hundred ships participated. Perhaps half a million refugees got off-planet. The records are confused, possibly inaccurate—"

"Tell me!"

"A child matching the description of one of your sons may have been aboard the *Wandering Cow,* a cargo vessel. The identification is uncertain, but it is possible that Timothy Korie is still alive. I have requested all the records."

"Where? Where did they go?" demanded Korie.

"Taalamar," Harlie answered. "The *Wandering Cow* went to Taalamar."

"Oh, my God. . . ."

"I'm making additional inquiries now. I'll inform you as soon as I have word."

"Is that it? Is that all you have?"

"I'm sorry, sir. That's all there is at the moment."

Korie sank into his chair, tears of joy and fear streaming down his cheeks. He buried his face in his hands and began to weep.

Fanfare

There was one more thing to do.

It was six weeks before they could do it, and even then half of the refits had not been completed; but a series of shakedown runs had been called for, and Korie decided to take advantage of the opportunity.

At eighteen hundred hours, the ship arrived on station. Korie stepped onto the Bridge wearing his whites. He glanced around and took note of the fact that every other crew member present was also wearing his or her dress uniform. Even Brik. On the big Morthan the uniform looked somehow . . . bizarre; but if Brik felt ill at ease, he did not display it.

"Is this the point?" Korie asked his senior astrogator.

Tor nodded. "As close as we could figure it."

"Good," said Korie. He stepped down to the Ops deck and looked up at the big display. An empty starfield beckoned.

"Mr. Jones? Is the package ready?"

Jonesy nodded and stood up. Around the Bridge, the

other officers were standing up now too. Tor. Green. Goldberg. Hodel.

"Go ahead, Mr. Jones."

At his work station, Jones leaned forward and pressed a single button. There came a soft *thump* through the floor of the ship. After a moment something became visible on the forward screen. It was a wreath. A large green wreath, glowing in the illumination of the *Star Wolf*'s intense spotlights.

Hodel tapped a button on his board. The music began softly, slowly. He'd written a new arrangement, especially for this ceremony. The steady beat of a military drum came snapping up first, followed by the near-plaintive wail of a golden horn; it sounded faint and faraway—then the rest of the band came swelling up. Korie could almost hear the words. *"Oh, I wish I were in the land of cotton. Old times there am not forgotten. Look away, look away, Dixieland. . . ."*

Slowly Korie raised one hand in salute. Around him the other officers did likewise. Throughout the ship, at their stations, in the corridors, in the cargo bay, in the engine room, in the messroom, in the bright channels of the farm, wherever brave men and women remembered their own, the rest of the crew stood tall and proud as well. They all wore their whites, and they all stood at attention. And each and every one held a salute to their fallen comrades. On more than a few faces, tears rolled slowly down their cheeks.

And then, finally, it was over. Korie lowered his hand slowly and turned away from the screen. His throat was painfully tight. He wondered if someday, someone would be dropping a wreath for the *Star Wolf*. He wondered if they would be as proud of their duty.

And he wondered what music would be played.

"Mr. Hodel," the acting captain asked, "did you find an appropriate piece of music to represent this vessel?"

"Yes, sir, I did. Aaron Copland's Third Symphony, Fourth Movement."

Korie raised an eyebrow at his helmsman. "I'm afraid I don't know that one—"

"Yes, you do," said Hodel. He tapped another button, and as the ship started to ease forward again, a softer sound was heard across the Bridge and throughout the ship.

First the distant twinkling notes, then the horns, coming up in a dramatic fanfare, and Korie recognized the same bold statement he had heard at Lambda's funeral. He recognized not only the music, but the meaning behind it as well.

The music had been written long ago and far away, and yet across all that vast gulf of time, it still spoke eloquently. It had not been written by a starman, nor had it been written with star travelers in mind, and yet . . . and yet . . . it was still about the experience of challenging the darkness.

The same theme had been adapted for the composer's *other* piece, the more famous one: *The Fanfare for the Common Man.* But this symphonic arrangement was even grander. This was a work that honored life itself. The music swelled and filled the Command Deck.

Korie looked to Hodel, surprised and honored and pleased. He had not realized that his helmsman had the soul of a poet. It was a gratifying discovery. "You did good," Korie said, quietly patting Hodel on the shoulder. "Commander Tor. Log this music as our official calling card."

"Aye aye, Cap—Commander."

"Not yet. Not yet. But thank you. Now, take us home please. Take us home."

ABOUT THE AUTHOR

DAVID GERROLD made his television writing debut with the now classic "The Trouble with Tribbles" episode of the original *Star Trek*® series. Since 1967 he has story-edited three TV series, edited five anthologies, and written two non-fiction books about television production (both of which have been used as textbooks) and over a dozen novels, three of which have been nominated for the prestigious Hugo awards.

His television credits include multiple episodes of *Star Trek, Tales From the Darkside, Twilight Zone, The Real Ghostbusters, Logan's Run,* and *Land of the Lost, Superboy,* and *Babylon 5.*

His novels include *When H.A.R.L.I.E. Was One Release 2.0, The Man who Folded Himself, Star Hunt, Voyage of the Star Wolf,* as well as his popular *War Against the Chtorr* books—*A Matter for Men, A Day for Damnation, A Rage for Revenge,* and *A Season for Slaughter.* His short stories have appeared in most of the major science fiction magazines, including *Galaxy, If, Amazing, Twilight Zone,* and *The Magazine of Fantasy & Science Fiction.*

Gerrold has also published columns and articles in *Starlog, Profiles, Infoworld, Creative Computing, Galileo, A-Plus, PC-Magazine, PC-Techniques,* and other science fiction and computing periodicals. He averages over two dozen lecture appearances a year and also teaches screenwriting at Pepperdine University.

Turn the page for a special preview
of
STARHUNT
by David Gerrold

The adventures of the *Star Wolf* continue in a very unusual novel which has a history as long as David Gerrold's distinguished career. Here is a special preview of the opening scene of *Starhunt*, a new Bantam release that also includes a fascinating essay by the author detailing the novel's history. **Don't miss STARHUNT, available now in paperback wherever Bantam Books are sold.**

If anything can go wrong, it will.

MURPHY

The operations of a destroyer-class starship consist of more than seven hundred thousand separate and distinct functions. All of them can be monitored from its Command and Control Seat.

The seat is a harsh throne on a raised dais. It is the center of the bridge and the man in it controls the ship. Right now, Jonathan Korie is that man. Thin, pale, and motionless, he is the first officer of the United Systems Starship *Roger Burlingame*.

The ship has been on battle alert for twelve days, and for ten of those days, Jon Korie has been the highest ranking officer on the bridge. Ten days ago the captain retired to his cabin, and he has not been seen since. So Korie sits in the Command and Control Seat and is bored.

Lean and angular, he sprawls loose across it; his colorless eyes gaze disinterestedly at the giant rectangle of red dominating the front of the bridge. On it is a single shimmer of white, the stress-field projection of the enemy ship. Superimposed below that is a number, 170; the enemy's speed is 170 times the speed of light. The speed of the *Burlingame* is 174 lights.

They are gaining, but only slowly. It will take at least twelve more days to close the remaining gap—and even then, when they do catch up to the enemy, they may not be able to destroy him. As long as the quarry stays in warp, he has the advantage; he is easy to pursue, but difficult to catch. Either he must be outmaneuvered or he must be hounded until his power is exhausted. Both procedures are difficult and wearying.

Korie stares without seeing. The huge screen bathes the room with a blood-colored glow; the image burns into the retina. His nose no longer notices the familiar odors of old plastic and stale sweat. His ears no longer hear the muted whisper of activity, the ever-present, almost silent humming of the computers.

A speaker in his headrest beeps. He touches a button on the chair arm. "Korie here. Go ahead."

A laconic voice. "Mr. Korie, this is the engine room. We're picking up some kind of wobbly on the number three generator."

"What's wrong with it?"

"I don't know, sir. The damn thing's been throwing off sparks for a week."

Korie grunts. And swivels his chair sixty degrees to the left. Above the warp control console is a medium large screen, one of many that line the upper walls of the bridge. On it, the power consumption levels of the ship's six warp generators are shown. The red bar of number three is hazy at its tip with a shallow but extremely rapid oscillation.

"It looks mild enough," Korie says to the waiting communicator. "Could one of the secondaries be out of phase?"

"Negative. If it were, we wouldn't be able to hold a course. It was one of the first things we checked."

"Well, how bad is it? Can you manage?"

"Oh, sure. Just thought you ought to know. That's all."

"Right. See what you can do about it. Let me know if it gets worse."

"Yes, sir." The communicator bleeps out.

Forgetting the wobbly, Korie swivels forward again. He pushes his hair—light, almost colorless—

back off his forehead. Stretching out his long legs, he shifts to a less uncomfortable position.

Idly, he smooths out a wrinkle in his dark tights, scratches vainly at a spot on his grey and blue tunic. He wets a pale forefinger against his tongue and rubs at the persistent stain until it fades. Satisfied, he reclines again in the chair.

A chime sounds, a bell-like tone. Korie's gaze strays automatically to the clock—abruptly he checks himself. (It isn't my relief that's coming.) The thought echoes rudely in his mind.

The bridge of the starcruiser is a bowl-shaped room. The wide door at the rear of it slides open to admit four low-voiced crewmen. They cut off their talk, move quickly into the room, and separate.

Two rows of gray-blue consoles circle the bridge, the outer row surrounding the room on a wide raised ledge, the other just inside and below. Despite the spaciousness of the room's original measurements, the additional consoles and equipment that have since been added force a cramped feeling within.

Brushing past their shipmates, two of the men move around to the front of the ledge, called the horseshoe. They tap two others and step into their places at the controls. The other relief crewmen step down into the circle of consoles in the center, a low-ered area called the pit. They too tap two men. Drop-ping easily into the quickly vacated couches, the new men settle into the routine with a familiarity bred of experience.

The men going off watch exit just as quickly, and once more the bridge is still. The crew are sullen figures in the darkened room, sometimes silhouetted against the glare of a screen.

One man—a small man on the left side of the horseshoe—is not still at his post. He glances around the bridge nervously, looks to the Command and Control Seat just above the rear of the pit.

Working up his courage, the man steps forward. "Sir?"

Korie peers into the darkness. "Yes?"

"Uh, sir . . . my relief—he hasn't shown up yet."

"Who's your relief, Harris?"

"Wolfe, sir."

"Wolfe?" Korie frowns. He rubs absentmindedly at his nose.

Harris nods. "Yes, sir."

Korie sighs to himself, a sound of quiet exasperation, directed as much at Harris as at the absent Wolfe. "Well . . . stay at your post until he gets here."

"Yes, sir." Resignedly, Harris turns back to his waiting board.

At the same time, the door at the rear of the bridge slides open with a *whoosh*. Red-faced and panting heavily, a short, straw-colored crewman rushes in, still buttoning the flap of his tunic.

Korie swivels to face him. "Wolfe?" he demands. He touches the chair arm, throwing a splash of light at the man.

Wolfe hesitates, caught in the sudden glare. "Yes, sir . . . ? Oh, I'm sorry I'm late coming on watch, sir."

"You're sorry . . . ?"

"Yes, sir."

"Oh." The first officer pauses. "Well, then I guess that makes everything all right."

Wolfe smiles nervously, but the sweat is beaded on his forehead. He starts to move to his post.

"Did you hear that, Harris?" Korie calls abruptly. "Wolfe said he was sorry. . . ."

Again Wolfe hesitates. He looked nervously from one to the other.

"Harris?" Korie calls again. "Did you hear that?"

"Uh, yes, sir." The answer is mumbled; the man is hidden in shadow.

"And that makes everything all right, doesn't it, Harris?" Korie's eyes remain fixed on Wolfe.

"Uh, yes, sir," Harris answers, "I guess it does—if you say so—"

The first officer smiles thinly. "I guess it does then." His voice goes suddenly hard. "In fact, Mr. Harris, Mr. Wolfe is so sorry that he says he's going to take over your next five watches for you. In addition to his own. Isn't that good of him?"

'Sir!"

"Shut up, Wolfe!"

"Uh, sir—" insists Harris. "You don't have to do that—"

"You're right, Harris. I don't have to—*Wolfe* does."

"Sir!" Wolfe protests again.

"I don't want to hear it."

"But, sir, I—"

"Wolfe . . . !" says Korie warningly. "You are now ten minutes late in getting to your post. Are you trying for twenty?" He cuts off the spotlight, darkening the bridge back to Condition Red, and swivels forward.

Wolfe stares at the first officer's back for a moment, then mutters a nearly inaudible, "Yes, *sir* . . . !" He steps across the horseshoe and ritually taps Harris's shoulder.

In the Command and Control Seat, Korie exhales angrily through even white teeth. Ignoring the sound of Harris's quick exit, he forces himself to gaze forward at the screen. (There, that's the only thing to be concerned with—the enemy.) That pale shimmer of white remains tauntingly near, maddeningly far.

Somewhere a computer hums as it measures the gap between the two ships. Murmuring to itself, it notes the ever-narrowing distance, notes by how much it has narrowed since the last measurement, and records the difference. The gain is imperceptible to all but the most sophisticated of electronic eyes. On the screen, the image remains frustratingly unchanged.

Eyes narrowed, Korie stares—seeing and yet not seeing. He ticks nervously at the chair arm.

"Mr. Korie?"

He glances up. A crewman on the right side of the horseshoe, near the front, waits expectantly. In the dim light, Korie can barely make out his face. Thin and lanky, barely postadolescent, the man is Rogers, crewman third class and assigned to duty on the gravity control board.

"Yes?" Korie grunts. "What is it?"

"Ship's gravity is down to 0.94 again—and still slipping."

Korie nods. "You might try checking your available power. That's what it was last time."

"Oh—yes, sir." The youngster turns back to his console and Korie turns back to his thoughts. The problem of the fluctuating gravity is relegated to the same dark corner of his mind as the persistent wobbly of the number three generator.

Idly, he swivels his chair to the right. On that side is Barak, the astrogator. A big, raw-boned black man, he is hunched over his console at the edge of the pit. Jonesy, the assistant astrogator—small, wiry and curly haired—is standing next to him.

"There," says Barak, tapping at a monitor.

"There's the error—0.00012 degrees." He drops back into his couch. "We'll just have to watch it for now. It's too small to correct. Give it a couple of days to grow."

Jonesy nods. "I wonder where it came from."

"Engine room, probably," Barak murmurs. "One of the generators must be picking up a bit of heat." He touches a button and the projection on the monitor dissolves.

"It figures," Jonesy snorts. "Can't those field jockeys do anything without screwing up?"

"That's funny." Barak's broad face splits into a grin. "They were just asking the same thing about you."

Jonesy snorts again, pulls his headset back down over his ears, and turns back to his board.

Watching, Korie is troubled. He doesn't like errors. Even the slightest one could add days to the chase. But Barak knows his business; this one won't have a chance.

A sound from the horseshoe attracts his attention. Rogers is standing at his gravity control board crying into a microphone, "Now it's down to 0.89 and still falling. Who's taking all my power?"

A laconic voice answers from the speaker, "The engine room. They've picked up a wobbly, so they're overcompensating—"

"Yeah, but I need power too! I'm supposed to keep the gravity within 2 per cent Earth normal, and I can't do it if I don't have power."

"Power . . ." sighs the speaker. "Everybody wants power. . . . All right, let me know when it hits critical and I'll cut in the auxiliaries."

Korie frowns. That damned wobbly is making its presence known all over the bridge. He swivels left to look at the warp control console.

There, an engineer is yammering into a mike, "Listen, there's nothing wrong on this end! All of *our* settings are correct. Are you sure your fields are—"

A tinny voice from the communicator cuts him off. "We just finished checking them for the third time. It's definitely a reflex phase wobbly."

The engineer pauses, scratches his chest. "I'm not so sure. The curve doesn't feel right."

"I don't care what your curve feels like. I know what it feels like down here, and we've got static up the *wazoo*!"

Korie's gaze flickers to the screen. The number three generator is shimmering dangerously, a red piston vibrating faster than the eye can follow. A wide hazy area indicates the depth of the wobbly.

He stabs a button. "Engine room! This is Korie. You're wobbling too much. Can you correct?"

The answer is immediate. "Sir, we've got our hands full just trying to stay on top of it. It won't respond."

"What's causing it?"

"We don't know yet. Mr. Leen is down in the well now."

Korie grunts. "Well, damn it—try to hold it within limits. I'm not going to lose that bogie!"

"Yes, sir." The communicator winks out.

Korie shifts his attention forward to the pilot console. "What's our warp velocity?" he demands.

One of the officers straightens in his couch, leaning forward to read his monitor. "Uh . . . holding a 174, plus a fraction; but it's not firm . . ." Questioningly, he looks back at Korie, his face a dim blur in the dark.

Korie frowns. "Damn. If it starts to drop, let me know immediately."

"Yes, sir." The other turns forward again.

Korie glances back to the left, to the warp control console. Angrily, he glares at the flickering red bar on the screen—*that damn number three generator!* Able to do nothing but watch, he beats intensely at the chair arm with a clenched right fist.

"Fix it already . . ." he mutters, "I don't want to lose that kill . . . !"

The screen flickers redly. Somewhere a warning bell starts to chime. Eyes flicker toward the screen as the oscillation increases, widening past the danger levels.

Sudden red flashes on all the boards—the insistent chiming becomes a strident alarm, its shrill clanging shatters across the bridge. Crewmen turn hurriedly to their controls.

A voice: "We're losing speed! One hundred and sixty and still falling!"

Simultaneously a communicator bleeps. The first officer hits it with the butt of his fist. "Yes?"

"Engine room, sir." In the background another shrill alarm can be heard. "Mr. Leen requests permission to shut down."

"Can't do it," Korie snaps. "Is it absolutely necessary?"

"Uh—just a moment. . . ." There is a bit of off-mike mumbling, then the voice returns. "Mr. Leen says no, it isn't *absolutely* necessary, but, uh, if he had another set of engines, he'd junk these."

Korie taps indecisively at the chair arm. He stares ahead with pale eyes. The bogie shimmers and flickers across the screen; the wobbly is affecting the sensors too. Agonized, he hesitates—

"Sir?" asks the speaker.

"Just a moment." He takes his hand off the button, snaps at the officer ahead of him. "What's our speed now?"

"One hundred and forty-three and dropping steadily. It's—"

"Never mind." He stabs at a button on the chair arm. "Radec!"

"Yes, sir?" A new voice on the intercom.

"That bogie—you still have him." It is as much a statement as a question.

"Yes, sir, of course—but he's flickering pretty badly—"

"If I have to shut down, can you pick him up again?"

"After we unwarp, sure, I should be able to."

"How long will you be able to keep him on your screens?"

"Uh—five, maybe six hours . . . We can't scan more than a hundred light days, no matter how big his warp is. After that—well, the whole thing gets pretty fuzzy."

Korie sucks in his lower lip, bites it hard. *Damn!* "Do you have anything else on your screens? Anything suspicious? I don't want to be caught by surprise."

"Uh—no, sir. Nothing. No major field disturbances at all—and nothing faster than light."

"All right." Korie disconnects him. Hardly seeing it, he stares at the empty red screen ahead. The enemy shimmer coruscates wildly and uncontrollably across the crimson grid.

"One hundred twelve and still dropping," calls a dark voice.

Damn!

Every eye in the bridge is on him, but he sees only the screen.

"Ninety-six lights."

The first officer is torn with pain—that flickering blur—

"Eighty-seven lights—sir . . . !"

"I heard you."

"Sir! The engines are overheating—"

"I know it!"

Suddenly, Barak is standing beside him. "Damn it, Korie! Admit it! We've lost him! Now let go! Shut down those engines before they burn out—"

Korie looks at him, his pale eyes suddenly hard. "We'll shut down when *I* say we'll shut down!"

"Yes, sir!" Barak spits out the words. "But you'd better do it while you *still have* engines to shut down."

Korie stares at the other. They lock eyes for a clanging moment—

—And then the moment is over. Korie reaches for the button. "Engine room."

The answer is immediate; the crewman has been waiting at the mike. "Sir."

"Stand by to shut down."

"Yes, sir."

Korie disconnects. There is nothing more to say. He looks at Barak, but the astrogator is silent.

Korie turns away then, calls to the warp control console, "Prepare to collapse warp. Neutralize the secondaries."

The routine takes hold. Crewmen move to obey and orders rattle down through the ranks.

"Remove the interlocks. Stand by to neutralize."

"Interlocks removed. Standing by."

"Cycle set at zero. Begin phasing."

"Cycle set at zero. Beginning phasing."

Around the horseshoe, crewmen exchange wary glances. The smell of defeat hangs heavy across the bridge. The chase has been abandoned.

Korie sinks lower into his seat; he stares grimly ahead.

(So near . . . so near and yet so goddamned far!)

Confirming lights begin to appear on the boards. Red warning lights blink out, are replaced by yellow standbys. The strident clanging of the alarm dies away, leaving only a slow fading echo and a hollow ringing in the ears.

(So this is how it ends . . . with a whimper. With just a futile petering out of momentum. . . .)

The ringing fades into a persistent beeping, a sound that has been continuous for some time. Korie looks at the chair arm. A yellow communicator light flashes insistently.

He flicks it. "Bridge. Korie here."

"This is Brandt." The captain's thick voice comes filtered through the speaker.

"Yes, sir."

"What's the trouble? What was the alarm?"

"We've lost it, sir. We've lost the bogie."

There is a muffled curse, then a pause. "I'll be right up." The lighted panel winks out.

Korie stares at it. (Damn it all anyway!) He bites angrily at his lip, a nervous habit. (Damn! It all happened too fast!)

"Sir." It's one of the warp engineers. "The secondary fields are neutralized."

"Good," Korie says dourly. It is not good. "Go ahead. Collapse the warp."

The man turns back to his console. On the screen over his head the third red bar drops to zero. Numbers one and five follow suit; a second later, the rest.

Imperceptibly—on a submolecular level—the ship shudders throughout its length. Its protective cocoon of warped space unfolds, dissolves; the ship mutters back into normal unstressed space. The bright flickering screens that circle the upper walls of the bridge go dark. They become sudden windows of hollow blackness. Space, deep and vast, repeated a dozen empty times, stares hungrily into the bridge.

Simultaneously, the crew reels under the sudden surge of added weight as the excess power flows back into the gravitors. One of the men stumbles in front of Korie while crossing the pit.

"Watch your step," Korie mutters automatically, hardly noticing.

The man catches himself, cursing softly. He looks up to the horseshoe. "Damn it, Rogers! Pay attention to what you're supposed to be doing."

The object of his wrath turns to apologize, embarrassed. He stammers something to the bridge in general.

"Forget it," the man growls in annoyance, swinging himself up onto the horseshoe. "Answer your board."

Rogers turns back to his console, flicks glumly at a blinking light. "Gravity control here. Go ahead."

"This is the galley . . ." says a gruff, sarcastic voice. "I don't suppose you would be so kind as to warn me the next time you're planning to up the G's like that, would you?"

"I'm sorry, Cookie," he says. "It was an accident. I didn't mean to—"

"Well, 'sorry' isn't going to bring back a dozen cakes that you ruined. Just watch it, dammit!"

Rogers stammers, "I'll try—" But the light winks out abruptly, cutting him off. The other crewmen on the horseshoe snort contemptuously at his discomfort.

"Hey, Rogers," growls one of them, "don't give Cookie any complaints, huh? You got it rough enough as it is."

Rogers ignores him, stares glumly at his control board. Thin and round-shouldered, he toys with one of his safety switches, pretends to adjust it.

The man steps in closer and lowers his voice. "For your own good, huh? Nobody likes having his meals ruined just because some wobblehead isn't watching his board, so pay attention, huh?" He scowls heavily. "Otherwise, you're going to be eating your meals alone, boy—"

A sudden motion at the back of the bridge—a panel in the rear wall slides open. The men on the horseshoe turn quickly back to their boards.

Haloed by the orange light of the corridor behind, Captain Georj Brandt of the United Systems Command strides heavily into the room.

BANTAM SPECTRA

CELEBRATES ITS TENTH ANNIVERSARY IN 1995!

With more Hugo and Nebula Award winners
than any other science fiction and fantasy publisher

With more classic and cutting-edge fiction
coming every month

Bantam Spectra is proud to be the leading publisher
in fantasy and science fiction.

KEVIN ANDERSON • ISAAC ASIMOV • IAIN M. BANKS • GREGORY BENFORD • BEN BOVA • RAY BRADBURY • MARION ZIMMER BRADLEY • DAVID BRIN • ARTHUR C. CLARKE • THOMAS DEHAVEN • STEPHEN R. DONALDSON • RAYMOND FEIST • JOHN FORD • MAGGIE FUREY • DAVID GERROLD • WILLIAM GIBSON • STEPHAN GRUNDY • ELIZABETH HAND • HARRY HARRISON • ROBIN HOBB • JAMES HOGAN • KATHARINE KERR • GENTRY LEE • URSULA K. LE GUIN • VONDA N. MCINTYRE • LISA MASON • ANNE MCCAFFREY • IAN MCDONALD • DENNIS MCKIERNAN • WALTER M. MILLER, JR. • DAN MORAN • LINDA NAGATA • KIM STANLEY ROBINSON • ROBERT SILVERBERG • DAN SIMMONS • MICHAEL STACKPOLE • NEAL STEPHENSON • SHERI S. TEPPER • PAULA VOLSKY • MARGARET WEIS AND TRACY HICKMAN • ELISABETH VONARBURG • ANGUS WELLS • CONNIE WILLIS • DAVE WOLVERTON • TIMOTHY ZAHN • ROGER ZELAZNY AND ROBERT SHECKLEY

Bantam Spectra publishes more Hugo and Nebula Award-winning novels than any other science fiction and fantasy imprint. Celebrate the Tenth Anniversary of Spectra—read them all!

HUGO WINNERS

A CANTICLE FOR LEIBOWITZ, Walter M. Miller, Jr.	_____27381-7	$5.99/$6.99
THE GODS THEMSELVES, Isaac Asimov	_____28810-5	$5.99/$6.99
RENDEZVOUS WITH RAMA, Arthur C. Clarke	_____28789-3	$5.99/$6.99
DREAMSNAKE, Vonda N. McIntyre	_____29659-0	$5.99/$7.50
THE FOUNTAINS OF PARADISE, Arthur C. Clarke	_____28819-9	$5.99/$6.99
FOUNDATION'S EDGE, Isaac Asimov	_____29338-9	$5.99/$6.99
STARTIDE RISING, David Brin	_____27418-X	$5.99/$6.99
THE UPLIFT WAR, David Brin	_____27971-8	$5.99/$6.99
HYPERION, Dan Simmons	_____28368-5	$5.99/$6.99
DOOMSDAY BOOK, Connie Willis	_____56273-8	$5.99/$6.99
GREEN MARS, Kim Stanley Robinson	_____37335-8	$12.95/$16.95

NEBULA WINNERS

THE GODS THEMSELVES, Isaac Asimov	_____28810-5	$5.99/$6.99
RENDEZVOUS WITH RAMA, Arthur C. Clarke	_____28789-3	$5.99/$6.99
DREAMSNAKE, Vonda N. McIntyre	_____29659-0	$5.99/$7.50
THE FOUNTAINS OF PARADISE, Arthur C. Clarke	_____28819-9	$5.99/$6.99
TIMESCAPE, Gregory Benford	_____27709-0	$5.99/$6.99
STARTIDE RISING, David Brin	_____27418-X	$5.99/$6.99
TEHANU, Ursula K. Le Guin	_____28873-3	$5.50/$6.99
DOOMSDAY BOOK, Connie Willis	_____56273-8	$5.99/$6.99
RED MARS, Kim Stanley Robinson	_____56073-5	$5.99/$7.50

Ask for these books at your local bookstore or use this page to order.

Please send me the books I have checked above. I am enclosing $_____ (add $2.50 to cover postage and handling). Send check or money order, no cash or C.O.D.'s, please.

Name _____

Address _____

City/State/Zip _____

Send order to: Bantam Books, Dept. AA 2, 2451 S. Wolf Rd., Des Plaines, IL 60018
Allow four to six weeks for delivery.
Prices and availability subject to change without notice.   AA 2 2/95